Praise for *Coconut Cowboy*

"Inimitable.... The Serge books are often hilarious, but there's always something serious underpinning the antics." —*Tampa Bay Times*

"It's all fun in the Sunshine State.... Nobody does wacky Florida like Dorsey." —Shelf Awareness

"Heartily recommended for readers who like their mayhem served up with belly laughs." —*Booklist*

"Always over the top, Dorsey has peaked with *Coconut Cowboy*, creating a tough act to follow for No. 20." —*Florida Times-Union*

"Dorsey keeps the body count low but the energy high as he proves again that enough is enough, but too much is plenty." —*Kirkus*

"Fast-paced.... If you have not read any of Dorsey's novels, join the fun." —*St. Augustine Record*

"Exquisite, zany, and yet sincere." —*Florida Weekly*

"Pure Dorsey.... Weird and funny and silly." —*South Florida-Sun Sentinel*

"The side-splittingest entry in the Serge A. Storms library." —FloridaBookReview.net

Praise for Tim Dorsey

"Tim Dorsey has become quite adept at leading readers on a madcap romp through Florida's finest and foibles, mostly its foibles."
—*Chicago Tribune*

"Dorsey is compulsively irreverent and shockingly funny."
—*Boston Globe*

"Dorsey can indeed spin a truly warped yarn."
—*Charleston Post and Courier*

"[Dorsey is] wildly funny, maniacally disrespectful, and genuinely out of control."
—*Dallas Morning News*

"Tim Dorsey is the Three Stooges of mystery fiction."
—*Fort Lauderdale Sun-Sentinel*

COCONUT
COWBOY

TIM DORSEY

COCONUT COWBOY

WM
WILLIAM MORROW
An Imprint of HarperCollins*Publishers*

COCONUT COWBOY. Copyright © 2016 by Tim Dorsey. All rights reserved. Printed in the United States of America. No part of this book may be used or reproduced in any manner whatsoever without written permission except in the case of brief quotations embodied in critical articles and reviews. For information, address HarperCollins Publishers, 195 Broadway, New York, NY 10007.

First William Morrow premium printing: January 2017
First William Morrow hardcover printing: January 2016

ISBN 978-0-06265631-5

William Morrow and HarperCollins are registered trademarks of HarperCollins Publishers in the United States of America and other countries.

16 17 18 19 20   QGM   10 9 8 7 6 5 4 3 2 1

For Fred "Catfish" Dorsey

A sane person to an
insane society must appear insane.
KURT VONNEGUT

COCONUT
COWBOY

Prologue

Motorists watched helplessly as the man in a panda suit was beaten stupid in front of the strip mall.

His bulbous black-and-white head had been twisted around so the eyeholes were over his left ear, blinding him to vicious rib-stomps. A second, smaller panda had escaped with the aid of a skateboard and a stun gun.

As they say in the Sunshine State: If you don't like the weather, wait a few seconds. Same thing with boredom.

Moments earlier it was normal. A red light turned green. Drivers accelerated and resumed driving duties: painting nails, playing invisible drums, making out, scratching lottery tickets, taking selfies, rehearsing arguments for upcoming pricks, eating pasta.

The traffic wove around motorized wheelchairs and women pushing baby strollers full of scrap metal and attic insulation. Others wheeled luggage far from any transportation hub. In the highway's median, people sat in lawn chairs selling bags of shrimp in the sun. A prostitute who couldn't get anyone's attention took a seat at a bus stop and filled out an application for the Border Patrol.

Inside a nearby building, a man in a baseball cap and dark sunglasses approached a window and handed a robbery note to the teller, who looked up. "Sir, this is where you pay your water bill." The man sighed again in a long, imprecise life footnoted entirely by sighs. He went out and took a seat next to the hooker. They both sagged in the humidity and gazed across the road at a cardboard arrow:

Chinese Buffet

The red-and-yellow arrow was twirled by a dancing panda with earphones inside his costume head. The panda was required to learn new choreography to increase his pay, but the mobility of the panda arms was holding him back. The headphones played an audiobook about improving relationships by talking less.

Next to him was his partner, a smaller panda who wore a kamikaze bandanna and waved his own sign indicating Sino-Japanese détente:

Sushi

The tiny panda flung his sign in the air and caught it behind his back, worth an extra seventy-five cents an hour and a growing source of tension with the larger panda.

Traffic lights continued changing, a hooker licked a postage-paid envelope with penalty for private use. Shrimp went bad. Such is the milieu of modern inertia.

Then the Florida un-boredom switch was thrown.

A Toyota screeched to the curb. Out poured more costumes: pirate, Statue of Liberty, gorilla, and a large foam pizza with a pepperoni-colored face in the middle. *"There they are!"* *"Get 'em!"*

The beat-down had begun. The gorilla wrenched the bigger panda's head sideways and thrust a knee to the groin. Then they all piled on, clubbing him with his own cardboard arrow. The pirate went for the smaller bear. *"Ahhh! He zapped me! . . ."*

Out in the street, a thunderous roar as a massive vintage motorcycle idled up to a red light. High handlebars, low-slung seat, gleaming chrome forks. The rider wore amber-tinted hippie sunglasses as he stared at the Statue of Liberty peeing on an advertising arrow.

Suddenly, yelling from the other three corners of the intersection. *"Hey! Leave them alone!"* The new people all dropped their own arrows and dashed through traffic.

The gorilla finished dumping a garbage can on the bear. *"We better get out of here!"* The attackers crammed back into the Toyota and sped off as other sign-spinners arrived and helped the panda into a sitting position. *"Bill, are you okay?"*

The motorcyclist calmly removed his sunglasses

and wiped them with a lint-free cloth. He watched as they pulled off the panda head and opened a first-aid kit. "Another turf war," said Serge, replacing the sunglasses and nodding to himself. "The economy is bouncing back."

The light turned green, and he cranked up the stereo in his helmet.

"Born to be wild! . . ."

The chopper roared away.

Chapter ONE

ONE MONTH EARLIER

The index finger had a nail that was painted pink with a dollar sign. It pressed buttons on a keypad to enter the secret code.

A tiny compartment opened behind the keypad, and an actual metal key was removed. The hand inserted it into a knob and opened a door.

"Come on in!" said a bubbly Realtor named Maxine, wearing an aggressively bright orange blazer that suggested self-empowerment seminars. "You're going to love this house."

A demure couple from upstate New York tentatively entered, as if they were intruding. Peter and Mary Pugliese, to be specific. They'd lived their whole lives in the Empire State and had loved it the way you love not stubbing your toe. Then Peter had received a job offer in an exploding new field in Florida that doubled his pay. Can't turn that down. Mary was a traveling expert trial witness and could live anywhere. It was a job that required specialization, and hers was shoes. She had been the chief tri-state purchasing agent for a chain of mall footwear boutiques and could now testify to a 95 percent certainty that a plaster footprint mold pointed to the killer. They had a son. Feet were paying for an Ivy League tuition.

The Realtor's orange blazer was optional. While showing homes the day before, Maxine had sported culottes and a yellow T-shirt that indicated she had once run five kilometers to raise awareness. Her energetic pace had opened a distance from the couple. There was an empty can of sugar-free Red Bull in her car. "I see you're admiring the original hardwood floors. Solid oak. All the wiring's been updated. Call me Max."

The Puglieses exchanged glances. They felt they had been playing catch-up ever since driving onto the property. It was a modest Victorian clapboard estate built in 1909 that would have been on the historic register, but the town was so small it didn't have one. It was painted periwinkle blue, with the white gingerbread trim found on many of the older southern country homes in the central part of the state.

"Check out the kitchen! Look at all the space in these antique cabinets . . ."—which she opened—". . . and extra-large windows . . ."—which she also opened—". . . for exquisite cross breezes. You can almost see an apple pie cooling. And you're on a hill! You don't get many of those around here. The view! Where are you from?"

"Saratoga Springs."

"Where's that?"

"The Adirondack Mountains."

"So I guess this is kind of flat."

"It's fine."

She was already running upstairs. "Come see the master bath!"

They arrived in the doorway.

"It's got an old cast-iron tub," said Max. "And it's on claw feet. I don't know what kind they are."

If they were in shoes, Mary would be able to tell her.

"You'll never beat the price of this place because it's a divorce sale." Max opened more roomy cabinets. "State law says I'm not supposed to tell you that, so I didn't."

Peter turned around. "Where'd she go?"

Mary pointed. "Down the stairs."

They regrouped in the living room.

"Most people who move to Florida want the beach," said Max. "But there's much more value in these small inland towns."

"We like small towns," said Peter.

"The smaller the better," said Mary. "I see enough cities in my work."

"Me, too," said Peter.

"What do you do?" asked the agent.

"I'm a geologist."

"What do you do for that?"

"It basically means I'm one of those white-collar guys who wears a hard hat."

"That's super," said Max. "Have you seen enough?"

"Think so," said Mary. "But we need to—"

"No problem. I'll let you talk it over in private." Max went into the next room and hid against the wall to listen.

"What do you think?" Peter asked his wife.

"We've already looked at eleven others and nothing's even close. I love how the second story also has a wrap-around porch."

"And she's right that we can't beat the price," said her husband. "But you know the old saying: Never buy property in a small town you don't know about."

The agent barged into the room. "Oh, I thought you were finished. I just wanted to tell you it's a great small town. Lived here my whole— . . . last three years. The charm, the churches, the schools, the annual fair where the farmers—"

"What about neighbors?" asked Mary.

"What about them?"

She looked down the hill into wooded lots. "Well, the houses on each side look a little . . . Are they trailers?"

"In this town, even the bad houses have great people. Salt of the earth, give you the shirts off their backs. Plus you know how they say that fences make for good neighbors? But even better than fences are acres, and you've got over five. You'll probably barely ever see them."

Mary nodded at her husband.

"We'll take it," said Peter.

"Great." Max reached in her purse and pulled out a contract with sticky yellow arrows next to blank spots for signatures. She handed them a pen.

"It's already got our names and everything typed in?" asked Mary.

"I just had a feeling about you two."

"But it also has the price," said Peter. "And we haven't negotiated yet."

"My advice?" said Max. "It's a steal. Can't tell you how many times other buyers have scooped up a place while someone was indecisive."

Mary looked at her husband. "Remember when that happened to us?"

"Okay," said Peter. "Where do I sign?"

"Arrows."

They finished up the paperwork and Max told them to keep the pen.

"When will we know?" asked Mary.

"It's a done deal." The Realtor hoisted the purse over her shoulder. "If you offer the full listing price, they have to sell or else pay the full real estate agent's commission. It's state law."

"Who got a law like that passed?"

"Us agents. Welcome to town!"

MEANWHILE . . .

A '72 Mercury Comet sped west across the part of the Florida Panhandle in the gravitational orbit of Alabama. Vegetable stands, Dollar General, John 3:16, TIRE REPAIRS written on a half-buried tire in a front lawn.

"It's all about small towns," said Serge. "That's where I'll find my answer."

"What was the question?" asked Coleman.

"Haven't you been listening this whole time?"

Coleman picked at a dried stain on his shirt, then tasted it. "What?"

"The American Dream! That's my new mission in life: to find out where it went." Serge grabbed a travel mug of coffee. "When I was growing up in a small town in the sixties, the American Dream was all around. Back then, if you worked hard and followed the rules under the Declaration of Independence, you got to pursue happiness on the weekend with a Barcalounger and a hibachi. The mood of the middle class came down to one word. Relaxed."

"And today?"

"You do everything right and you're rewarded with a weekend of dread: Will I get a pay cut? Will I get laid off? What if I get sick? Are we all destined to work part-time? How will my kids do better than me? Which other Americans did that radio host say I should hate about this?"

"But what do small towns have to do with it?"

"They still play lawn darts in small towns."

"Darts?"

Serge nodded. "The sixties were a looser time. Parents remained relaxed enough under the American Dream to give their kids lawn darts to fling around the backyard. What could possibly go wrong?"

"I remember getting stuck in the foot."

"Everyone does," said Serge. "And nobody thought of shutting down the whole program just because we were all limping."

"I had to get stitches."

"It's a kid's job to get stitches," said Serge, cranking up the radio. "Since then, cities have evolved with franchised ferociousness, but small towns still preserve the old ways."

"... *Pulled into Nazareth* ..."

"It's like an archaeological dig," said Serge. "Drive into any tiny hamlet and you can still see what we used to stand for. You can still see *hope*. Like when I was the lawn dart champion."

"I didn't know they had champions."

"They weren't exactly passing out bushels of trophies for everything like they are now," said Serge. "Which I blame for the decline of the current generation. Every little kid has a bedroom full of gold hardware. 'What did you get this one for?' 'Showing up.' 'And this one?' 'So my feelings wouldn't get hurt.' But when I was their age, I competed for the love of the sport, which I revolutionized. None of the other children could see the possibilities until I said, 'Hey everyone, we're limiting ourselves by throwing darts for accuracy when these babies were built for distance. Give me some elbow room!'"

"What happened?"

"I set the record, but it was unfairly nullified just because I hit the side of an aboveground pool two houses down. It might have gone better if just the tip poked a tiny hole, but my ballistic arc built up such force that the whole dart went through the pool, fins and all, bursting a seam and spilling water in the house so fast it shorted out a bunch of electricity. And shoddy engineering is *my* fault?" Serge pulled up to a red light. "I tried to explain that the civil defense siren made me jump at the moment of release."

"I remember those sirens, too."

"Every Saturday at noon, the Riviera Beach Fire Department would blast a siren that could be heard for miles. And once again the other kids wouldn't cooperate. We all knew it was a test, but by definition tests are meant to be taken. The rest of the first graders continued playing in the sprinklers, ignoring my commands: 'We're under atomic attack! Gather the lawn darts and follow me!'"

"What did you do?"

"Mustered at the rallying point to take cover," said Serge. "There was this storm-water drainage canal on the next street, and since it was the dry season, I could walk right in the big concrete spillway and get myself deep beneath the city. In the event of hydrogen bombs, you need several feet of earth to stop fallout radiation. But the adults instead told children to get under furniture, which I saw as a ploy to thin the herd because food would be scarce in a nuclear winter. During the sixties, it really was us against them."

"What did your folks say when you got home?" asked Coleman.

"Deaf ears again," said Serge. "I waited until nightfall just in case the Russians heard about our siren and planned their attack at noon to throw us off. I walked in the house after dark, and my parents are like 'Where on earth have you been all day!' I say, 'Obviously under the city.' My mom says, 'What were you doing there?' I say, 'Fallout buffer.

Nobody else is doing the tests right.' Then she holds something in her hand. 'Is this your lawn dart?' I said, 'You're obsessing. Where were *you* during the test?' That's the thing about parents: If the kid is right, he gets spanked twice as hard."

They rolled up to another intersection. "Something's going on at the corner," said Coleman.

"Looks like that old man is having problems with his electric wheelchair," said Serge. "The battery's dead or wires have come loose. He's rocking back and forth trying to get it to budge."

"And he's got to be a long way from his house because there are just stores around."

"Probably his only mode of transportation to get food and medicine," said Serge. "He's in a serious jam, stranded out here in the sweltering concrete badlands with a bum wheelchair, no better than if he was floating alone in the ocean."

"Why'd you hit your blinker?" asked Coleman.

"Because we're coming to his rescue," said Serge. "Remember in the sixties when there used to be 'shut-ins'? You never hear about them anymore. I guess they're now shut-*outs*. Is that progress?"

"Serge, look at those two thugs," said Coleman. "They're going after the guy!"

"Just when I thought we'd scraped bottom." Serge reached under his seat for an automatic pistol. "What's next? Hospice invasions?"

"Both of them are reaching down behind his chair," said Coleman. "They're going to dump him in the gutter!"

"No doubt to pawn the scooter." The traffic light

turned green. Serge put on his hazard lights. "And I was hoping to cut back on my office hours . . ."

"Hold on," said Coleman. "They're not dumping him."

"No, they're twisting wires together." Serge stowed his gun. "They're doing repairs like good citizens. I love small towns!"

"They got it fixed," said Coleman. "The old man is rolling away and waving at them."

"I'm overcome with emotion." Serge wiped away tears. "My work in this state might finally be coming to an end—"

Bump, ba-bump, bump, ba-bump . . .

"What the heck is that sound?" said Coleman.

"I don't know," said Serge, "but it's getting closer."

Bump, ba-bump, bump, ba-bump . . .

Coleman bent around in his seat. "I still can't locate it."

"Because it's so loud it's echoing off buildings from all directions," said Serge. "And it just knocked my rearview mirror out of my favorite position."

Bump, ba-bump, bump, ba-bump . . .

The growing reverberations splashed Coleman's drink in his lap. "What on earth can it be?"

"Oh no, not again," said Serge.

"What is it?"

"Take a gander." Serge pointed at the pickup truck in the next lane. "Another hip-hop redneck with a tricked-out audio system. How many have I had to deal with now? Five, six? And I was hanging my hopes on self-extinction."

"What do you mean?"

"Haven't you heard the joke: 'What were the redneck's last words?'"

"No."

"Hold my beer and watch this."

"Serge, I think he made some kind of mistake," said Coleman. "His stereo speakers are pointing the wrong way."

"I'm afraid that's no mistake. I think I've spotted the biggest voluntary dunce cap in my life," said Serge. "He flush-mounted gigantic speakers on the *exterior* of the pickup's cab, so they're pointed out at other motorists. I never would have believed it if I wasn't staring at it right now."

"But that doesn't make any sense."

"To him it does," said Serge. "First we had jerks who played music too loud. But that wasn't sufficiently broadcasting their superior taste in tunes, so they started keeping their windows down. And now we have this visionary who thought: Wait, I've got a way to let the maximum amount of people know my IQ."

"My eyeballs are starting to hurt."

"Roll your window down," said Serge. *"Hey! Buddy!"*

"He can't hear you," said Coleman. "The music's too loud."

Serge leaned on his horn.

"Still can't hear you," said Coleman. "His windows are up."

"Probably doesn't like to be bothered by loud music in traffic . . . Throw some of your M&M's."

"But I'm eating them."

"Take one for the team."

Coleman began pinging them off the pickup's glass. The driver finally looked around and noticed Serge leaning across Coleman, giving him the signal to roll down his window.

"Yeah?" snapped the driver.

"What do you think you're doing?" asked Serge.

"What do you mean?"

"Your speakers are facing the wrong way."

"That's how I want them."

"I hate to be presumptuous," said Serge, "but I believe I'm on solid ground when I say that's how everyone else in the community *doesn't* want them."

"Go fuck yourself." The driver rolled up his window and increased the volume.

The light turned green. The vehicles rolled side by side a few more blocks and stopped at another light. Serge stared down in his lap.

"What are you going to do?" asked Coleman.

"Nothing."

"I'm stunned." Another beer cracked. "You've never let somebody like that slide. Remember what you did to the last guy with a pounding car stereo? It ruled!"

"And ate up an entire day of my preciously short life," said Serge. "I must accept that jerks will always be around unless we can get them to live together in special colonies in the salt caverns."

Coleman shrugged and drank beer. The light turned green. Up ahead, an SUV pulled out of a shopping center with plenty of time and eased to a stop at the next red light.

The pickup was right on its bumper, horn blaring. *Bump, ba-bump, bump, ba-bump . . .*

"Just ignore him," Serge said under his breath.

"He jumped out of the truck," said Coleman. "He's running up to that other car."

"And it's got a mother with her small children in the backseat."

The man stuck his face in the SUV's open window. *"Get out of the car, bitch!"*

Chapter TWO

CENTRAL FLORIDA

Two cartoon felines were carrying a grand piano. The scene was painted on the side of a truck. The van for MOVING CATS drove away.

Peter and Mary Pugliese unpacked china and picture frames.

"I'm so glad we found this place." Peter set a family portrait on the mantel.

Mary scattered packing peanuts removing a Tiffany lamp. "She was right about the breezes."

Knock, knock, knock.

"What's that?"

Peter began walking. "Someone's at the door."

"But who?"

"I know a way to find out."

Peter opened the door to find an old man in bib overalls. "Can I help you?"

The man removed a baseball cap with a faded

slogan: You Say Potato, I Say Tater Tot. He wiped his brow and distractedly glanced at his watch. "I'm here about the water bill."

"But we just moved in," said Peter.

"You did?" The visitor looked left and right. "Then payment's due up front."

"It is?"

"Afraid so."

Peter always liked to please when he was the new guy somewhere. "Okay."

"Okay."

They stared at each other.

"Well?" said Peter.

"What?"

"Where's the water bill?"

"We don't use those," said the visitor. "It's a small town."

Peter took a deep breath. "How much?"

"Two hundred."

His eyed widened. "Water's that much around here?"

"How does a hundred sound?"

Peter stared again. "Who *are* you?"

"The mayor."

"Pleasure to meet you," said Peter. "And don't take this the wrong way, but could I see some identification?"

"I'm Vernon."

"Okay."

"Everyone knows me."

"We just moved in."

Vernon shrugged and opened a billfold.

"That's a badge."

"I'm also the police chief."

"Let me get my checkbook."

"We kind of like cash around here."

"Can I get a receipt?"

"No."

"But I have a home office, and my tax returns—"

"How about this: I can go fifty for a campaign contribution, and get you for water at the end of the month?"

Peter was off balance. "Is this for real?"

"You're not from around here, are you?"

"We just moved in."

"We got a nice little town," said Vernon. "We don't like trouble."

"No, I didn't mean . . ." Peter got out his own wallet. "Here's fifty."

Vernon pocketed it and started walking away. "Probably be seeing you around Lead Belly's."

"What's that?"

"Everyone knows Lead Belly's."

"We just moved—"

Mary tapped him on the shoulder. "Who was that?"

"The mayor."

"What did he want?"

"I'm still trying to process it."

"There's only a couple of sparkling waters in the fridge," said Mary. "Let's see where they eat in this town, and you can tell me over dinner."

Motorists watched in shock at the unfolding road rage.

"*Get out of the car, bitch?*" Serge repeated to himself. "Are you kidding me? It's a mother grocery-shopping with her kids."

"He's reaching through the window," said Coleman. "She's trying to pull away from him and get the window rolled up at the same time."

"He's running alongside the car still trying to grab her," said Serge. "Now his arm's stuck in the window."

"She's dragging him through the intersection," said Coleman. "I've heard of people doing this at street brawls."

"Except she's not trying on purpose," said Serge. "That maniac has her terrified out of her mind for her children's safety."

"The window busted out of the car. He's tumbling in the street." Coleman winced. "He's going to need some Bactine."

"Another sixties favorite," said Serge, "but no time to cherish that nugget."

"Why not?"

"He's running back to his truck and tearing off through the intersection after her."

"Doesn't he have somewhere better to be?" asked Coleman.

"Of course," said Serge. "But the latest wave of road-ragers has an impressive work ethic. They just follow and follow."

"I think there's going to be a chase," said Coleman.

Serge smiled and threw his car in gear. "I *know* there's going to be a chase."

It was indeed a chase, technically, so to speak. Not quite as slow as the O.J. thing in the Bronco. The mom was splitting the difference between eluding the tormentor and not endangering her children. Plus there was a lot of traffic and red lights. The pickup's driver used those opportunities to pull alongside and scream profanities, but the woman couldn't hear them because his stereo was too loud.

Serge followed the pair of vehicles as they turned into a neighborhood. "That mom's making the classic mistake. She should look for a police station or remain in some other public place with a lot of people. But in her panic for the offspring, she's reflexively seeking the safety of her home. Even if she has time to unlock the door and get everyone inside—which she won't—she's leading this cretin right to their address."

"She just passed that fire station," said Coleman.

"Which reminds me of Vietnam."

"Go for it."

"Remember my hometown fire station with the civil defense siren? I vividly recall them blasting the thing at the official end of the Vietnam War. Where can youth get that today? And now, whenever I hear a siren of any kind, I think about cartoons."

"Because of Vietnam?"

"No, the firehouse siren would wail on Saturdays right after I finished watching the Warner Brothers classics. Kids today need more Foghorn Leghorn."

"I'm a chicken hawk." Coleman giggled.

"I say that boy needs a talkin' to," said Serge.

"Remember Pepe Le Pew?" asked Coleman.

"A sexual harassment lawsuit in every episode," said Serge. "And Daffy Duck."

"'It's fiddler crab season,'" said Coleman. "Bang!"

"But my favorite was the Road Runner," said Serge. "I was enthralled by the coyote's irrepressible interest in experiments, which inspired me to conceive my own projects. It also taught me to separate reality from fiction because, no matter how great an idea it may seem at the time, nothing good ever came from igniting model rocket engines on my roller skates."

"I liked how the coyote could get whatever he wanted from the Acme company," said Coleman.

"That was the best part," said Serge. "Anvils, foot springs, hot-air balloons, giant magnets . . ."

The Mercury Comet turned onto a sleepy street where an SUV had just raced up a driveway, followed closely by a pickup truck.

". . . *Please don't hurt my children!* . . ."

The duo parked at the bottom of the driveway and began walking toward the source of the shouting on the front doorstep.

". . . Bat wings, TNT detonator plungers, iron birdseed, tornado pills, earthquake pills. And all his shit would arrive right away," said Serge. "Nobody besides me has made the connection, but that's where Amazon got their business model: wide selection, prompt delivery."

The woman's trembling hands fumbled with her

keys as she rushed to get the door open. The pickup driver snatched them away and seized her by the arm. Three little tykes hid behind her legs.

". . . *You miserable cunt . . .*"

"Now, now," said Serge. "Let us all come together at the banquet table of humanity."

The pickup driver spun around. "Who the hell— . . . Oh, *you* again!"

"That's right. I'm the producer of a famous regional reality show," said Serge. "I'm sure you've heard of it."

"What's it called?"

"*Florida's Got Dicks, Season Twelve.*"

"What's that got to do with me?"

"You've heard the saying 'Too bad stupidity isn't painful'?" Serge grinned. "I bring tidings of great joy."

Zzzzzzap!

The man fell hard to the ground, twitching and moaning from a Taser.

"Ma'am, everything's okay now." Serge retrieved the woman's house keys from the assailant and handed them back. "Please be safe and lock your doors."

"Are you a police officer?"

"No, but I am with the state."

"I can't thank you enough." She stuck a key in the knob.

"Come on, Coleman . . ."

They dragged their quarry to the rear of the car.

The woman turned around before closing the door. "You're putting him in your trunk?"

Serge grabbed a pair of ankles. "We don't have one of those police cars with the cage separating the backseat, but I've been doing this for years. Have a nice evening." The trunk lid slammed shut. "Everything's back to normal."

Chapter THREE

DINNER

Peter and Mary Pugliese walked arm in arm along Main Street. It was a shaded street. A single traffic light blinked. A striped barber pole rotated. Potter's Drugs still had Old Man Potter counting pills. There were portable drills in the window of the hardware store, along with a sign saying the local post office counter was in back by the penny nails, but everyone already knew that. A crimson caboose stood in the courtyard of the Railroad Hotel.

Mary stopped to stare in a window. "They have antique shops. There's a gumball machine." She squeezed her husband's arm. "I already love this town."

Across the street, sandwiched between a paint store and a locksmith, was an old red wooden building with a steep roof. VOLUNTEER FIRE DEPARTMENT, EST. 1901.

"Check out the vintage engine," said Peter. "All that's missing is a spotted dog."

"They still use something that old?" asked Mary.

"No, it must be a museum now, to go with the antique stores for the tourists," said her husband. "Doubt that thing even runs."

Suddenly there was a siren and flashing red lights. A locksmith and a paint salesman flew out their doors. Someone else with shaving cream on his face ran from the barbershop. The men piled in the quaint engine. The siren seemed to be laboring for volume, because it was the original model that worked on a hand crank. A dalmatian jumped aboard. They took off into the countryside.

"That answers that," said Mary.

They continued to the corner and Shorty's Garage. A "Closed" sign in the window, next to a display of fan belts and wiper blades for all occasions. The building sat amid a sea of non-running vehicles that Shorty had promised he would "get to."

"Look." Peter gestured up the block.

"Where?"

"That dirty old neon sign sticking out from the building."

"The black one with flickering orange tubes?" said Mary. "*Lead Belly's?*"

"So it's a barbecue joint."

"You've heard of it?"

"I'll tell you over dinner." Peter picked up the pace. "I haven't had good barbecue in like forever!"

The front of the ramshackle restaurant featured

weathered wooden shingles, with narrow horizontal slits for windows. The couple entered to the loud gong of a brass bell over the door. "Did we do that?"

"I can't see anything." Peter stopped to prevent tripping as his eyes adjusted. "It's so dark."

"The only light is more orange neon," said Mary. "There's a fiddle player somewhere."

"*Peter!*"

"Is someone calling you?"

"We just moved here."

His name was shouted again.

"I think someone is," said Mary.

Her husband squinted through kitchen smoke at a table in back by the restrooms. Actually it was three tables pushed together, each a sturdy maple square with a half inch of slick lacquer to fight the wear and tear for which the barbecue community is known. There were two pitchers of sweetened iced tea, a basket of biscuits, hand wipes, and racks of giant ribs surrounded by eight men of uncannily similar appearance.

Peter noticed a familiar person in overalls at the head of the table, waving. "Peter!"

"I know him," he told his wife.

"Where from?" asked Mary.

"He was the man at our door."

Vernon Log stood and shook Peter's hand. "Guys, this is our new neighbor, Peter Pugliese."

"*Hi, Peter.*" "*Pleasure.*" "*Nice to meet,*" etc.

Peter smiled back, thinking about his now rib-sauce-sticky hand he was holding away from his chinos.

"Who's that behind you?"

"Oh." Peter stepped aside, and all the men at the table quickly stood. "This is Mary, my wife."

"Pleasure." "You're a lucky man." So on.

"Told you we'd meet again at Lead Belly's," said Vernon. "Join us."

"I wouldn't want to intrude—"

"Nonsense." Vernon swung a hand to dispel the concept. "Guys, pull up that other table."

Peter paused. "But a family is about to sit down at it."

"They'll find another."

Soon they were all gathered together. A young woman in an apron arrived with a notepad and pen. She blew a bubble with her gum. "What'll ya have?"

"Get the ribs," said Vernon, gnawing a bone.

All the men at the table wore plastic bibs. Each bib had a large lobster.

"They serve seafood?" asked Peter.

Vernon looked down at the crustacean on his chest. "No, these were just cheaper."

Peter handed the waitress their menus. "Two orders of ribs."

"Comes with three sides. Coleslaw, hush puppies, mac and cheese, black beans, black-eyed peas, okra, corn on the cob, off the cob, sweet potatoes, regular potatoes, crinkle-cut potatoes—"

"Dixie," said Vernon. "These are our new neighbors. Bring 'em a little of everything."

Gum smacked, and she left.

A loud wail from a hand-cranked siren went by outside the restaurant.

"Another fire?" asked Peter.

"No," said Vernon. "They went the wrong way again . . . You want a beer?"

"Sure." Peter turned to look for the waitress.

Vernon shook his head. "They don't sell any. No license." He reached down into a cooler next to his chair and pulled out a dripping-cold longneck Budweiser. "Here ya go."

"Thanks," said Peter. "Customers are allowed to do this?"

"*We* are," said Vernon, and a wave of laughter ran round the table.

Peter laughed, too, nudging his wife, who forced a chuckle.

"Let me introduce the gang," said Vernon. "This is my cousin Bo, the fire chief, and my brother Floyd, the tax collector, and my other brother Jabow, who we call Bo unless the other Bo is around. It's caused problems. He's a city councilman, along with everyone else, and so is my nephew Clem, and my son-in-law Otis, and the twins, Harlan and Haywood . . ." Each of the men nodded in turn at the couple.

Peter smiled back. "Sounds like you got most of the government here."

"The *whole* government," corrected Vernon. "We're actually having a commission meeting right now."

Peter looked over his shoulder. "What about the city hall up the street in the town square?"

"No good," said Jabow.

"Tried that before," said Clem.

"People showed up," said Harlan.

"Asked questions," said Haywood.

"We got us a nice little town here," said Otis.

"Take care of our own," said Vernon. "And at that table next to us are the three young bucks, Elroy, Slow and Slower, the town's next generation. Still wet behind the ears, but we'll bring 'em around. They're not allowed to sit at the main table yet."

"What kind of names are Slow and Slower?" asked Peter.

"Nicknames, because they're slow in the head, one a bit more so," said Vernon. "We're straight talkers around these parts." He used a desiccated rib to point across the rest of the diner at children and grandparents and more overalls. "Couldn't ask for a better bunch of neighbors . . ." Then he cupped hands around his mouth, calling out to a man in a crisp plaid shirt sitting alone in back. "Steve! Will you stop with the utensils already?"

The man smiled back and waved a piece of cutlery.

Vernon shook his head benevolently. "Still eats ribs with a knife and fork. But we'll learn him."

"Another newcomer like you," said Jabow. "Bought Old Man Maynard's farm last year."

"He's a farmer?" asked Peter.

"No, just a city boy who don't like the city no more. Has some kind of wholesale brokerage job he can do at home with a computer, so he moved here." Vernon refilled his iced tea and squeezed lemon, hitting Harlan in the eye. "More and more city folk are discovering what we got here, but we don't want it *too* discovered, if you know what I mean."

The front door opened, and a disheveled man stumbled over to the table and whispered in Vernon's ear. The mayor nodded and handed him a Budweiser from the cooler.

"You know I'm good for it," said the man.

"Forget about it, Grady."

He staggered out the door.

Vernon saw the question in Peter's eyes. "The town drunk. Every small place needs one. Practically an official position . . ."

The door opened again. Peter expected Grady's return, but this time he saw the opposite. A trim man in his fifties, hundred-dollar haircut, khakis and a button-down oxford shirt. He stood beside the table with extra-white teeth. "Gentlemen."

"Ryan, grab a chair," said Vernon.

"No time. I just wanted to check on that thing—" He stopped when he noticed they weren't alone.

"Ryan," said Vernon, "these are our guests, Peter and Mary Pugliese . . . Peter and Mary, meet our state senator, Ryan Pratchett."

He shook their hands with another large smile. "Visiting this fine community we've got here?"

"No," Vernon interjected. "Just bought a place out in the pines, our newest neighbors."

"Even better," said Ryan. "Two more votes!"

More chuckles around the table.

"Vern, I'll talk to you later about that other thing," said the senator. "Guys . . ."

"Take care, Ryan."

The front door of the restaurant closed again. The Puglieses were getting dizzy.

"So what do you think?" asked Vernon.

"About what?" said Peter.

Vernon spread his arms. "Everything."

"It certainly is a lot different from the big city."

"And we mean to keep it that way." Vernon yanked off his bib and stood. "I have to take a squirt. Welcome to Wobbly, Florida."

Chapter FOUR

BORN ON THE BAYOU

The oncoming pickup truck approached the motorcycle on a lonely country road.

A shotgun poked out the window.

Bang.

The cyclist crashed, and the red-white-and-blue teardrop gas tank exploded in a fireball.

Serge watched the flames rise on his laptop screen. He turned off the device and dabbed misty eyes.

Coleman exhaled smoke from a bong he'd fashioned out of a toy airplane. "Why are you so upset?"

"The last scene in *Easy Rider* always chokes me up." He aimed a camera out the window. "Two free-thinkers exploring the limitless road of our great nation, and they're wasted by a pair of mental dead ends."

Coleman exhaled again as pot smoke filled a tiny

cockpit. "I remember that movie now. It was about those cats doing weed all the time. What a great plot!"

"Coleman, that wasn't the plot—"

"It most definitely *was* the plot." Coleman nodded emphatically as he packed another bowl in the luggage compartment. "I mean morning, noon and night, coast to coast, blazing fat ones with everyone they met, listening to righteous music, munching out, then torching up again before driving to meet new people with their own weed, passing more doobies until they all finally fell asleep. Then they'd wake up and do the same thing again, day after day. Why don't they still make movies with great plots like that?"

"Coleman, *Easy Rider* was about the American Dream."

"Like I just said."

"No, not like . . . Never mind."

Conversation took a break as the powder-blue 1972 Mercury Comet sat quietly on a deserted shoulder off Highway 105.

Serge and Coleman. An unforeseen permutation of the odd couple. Theirs was a long-standing alliance of mutual tolerance with a perpetual sound track of camera clicks and bong bubbles.

Coleman raised his hand.

Serge pointed at him in recognition. "Yes, the transfer student from Cannabis County."

"Why are we in Louisiana?"

Serge twisted the camera's telephoto lens. "Because it happened right there . . ." *Click, click, click.* ". . . the shooting location of the final scene from *Easy Rider*, a few miles north of Krotz Springs."

"How'd you find it?"

"Exhaustive, frame-by-frame analysis of the closing aerial shots fading back from the burning motorcycle." *Click, click, click.* "That modest bayou out there was the last clue. I studied Internet satellite photos until I located it alongside the Atchafalaya River." He lowered the camera as a dragonfly flew in the open window. "Except they used a little geographical liberty to choose this filming site because the story line had them heading east out of New Orleans, not northwest."

Coleman's eyes rolled in their sockets as they followed the insect buzzing along the inside of the windshield looking for an exit. "Dragonfly, dragonfly, dragon . . . fly, dra-gonnnnn-fly, dragonflyyyyyyy, dragon-fffffly, dragon! fly! . . . fly! dragon! . . . dra-fly-gon! . . ."

"Coleman, whatever the fuck it is you're doing, can you please stop?"

"Hey, Serge, you know how if you keep repeating the same thing over and over, it just becomes meaningless gibberish?"

"I do now."

"That's seriously messed up. It's all I'm saying."

"Keep those bulletins flowing."

"You got it." He leaned back over his airplane.

"But here's the part that really hacks me off." *Click, click, click.* "Peter Fonda and Dennis Hopper were heading to Florida. That was their ultimate goal. And after they trip on acid in that cemetery and hit the road, I'm rubbing my palms in anticipation: 'Okay, here comes the best part of all! My home state!' And then suddenly it's over. I bought the DVD to scour the bonus material for an alternate ending, but no luck there, either."

Serge started up the car.

"Where now?" asked Coleman.

"The key to my quest for the American Dream. Those two cyclists were always hitting small towns on their quest for the Sunshine State." Serge pulled back onto the road. "So we're going to pick up the baton that Fonda and Hopper dropped right here and head south to create our own alternate ending."

An hour later, the Comet rolled east out of Slidell on Route 190.

"Man, you must really love that movie," said Coleman. "I remember you swearing you'd never leave Florida again, after that last time."

Serge studied the side of the road with intention. "Technically we're still in Florida."

"What are you talking about?" asked Coleman. "We're not even back to Mississippi."

"The sign we passed a while ago said we crossed the Saint Tammany Parish line."

"Parish? You mean like nuns and shit?" Coleman rubbed phantom pain from his knuckles.

"The other forty-nine states have counties, but because of Napoleonic law and influence, Louisiana has parishes," said Serge. "The French are a curious tribe."

"But what's that got to do with Florida?"

"When you say Louisiana, people think, sure, Louisiana Purchase, 1803, I was paying attention that day in school."

"I was home with the mumps."

"But the purchase was mainly west of the Mississippi River. So where did Louisiana get the rest of the land that makes up the eastern bottom of its L shape?"

"I'd like to buy a vowel."

"Florida!" said Serge. "Back then our Panhandle stretched all the way to the Mississippi in a region controlled by Spain. But settlers of British descent didn't dig it, and in 1810 they successfully stormed the garrison at Baton Rouge and proclaimed independence. It blows the mind! Few realize it today, but in the early nineteenth century, there was actually a separate country within the United States. They drew up a constitution—which officially referred to the new nation as the 'State of Florida'—established branches of government, elected a legislature and designed a flag of a lone white star on a blue field. The president was named Fulwar Skipwith."

"You're making that up."

"History has an imagination greater than any writer," said Serge. "Sadly, the new nation only lasted ninety days. The U.S. government looked south and said, 'Nice work with the Spanish, boys. Now we'll take that land, please.' Then they annexed it to what became the state of Louisiana, but to this day the land is still referred to as the Florida Parishes. There are eight of them, including Saint Tammany. Discovering that kind of insane Florida trivia is so intense that I become temporarily incontinent." Serge glanced around the empty stretch of road and pulled the car over. "This is as good a place as any."

"For what?"

Serge grabbed a long pole from the backseat. "Just stay alert."

The pair headed up a grassy embankment. Serge climbed over a barbed-wire fence, and Coleman crawled under it. "Ow, ooo, ow . . ."

Serge reached the top of a small hill and jammed his pole in the ground, unfurling a blue flag with a white star. Then he scanned the horizon. "I don't see any opposition."

"What's that noise?" asked Coleman.

"Sounds like a tractor."

They turned around. A furious farmer dismounted and stomped up the back side of the mound. "Just what in the hell do you think you're doing on my property?"

"We're from Florida." Serge raised the front of his tropical shirt to reveal a Colt .45 in his waistband. "You're welcome to continue plowing this land if you shift your allegiance to my state."

The farmer began backing away slowly, then turned and ran.

"Make that ninety-one days and counting. And without a shot fired. I always wanted to be president." Serge handed his camera to Coleman. "Take my picture next to the flag."

He grabbed the pole and stared off proudly.

Click.

Coleman handed the camera back. "What just happened?"

"We formed our own country."

Coleman froze. "Wait, what? . . . I can't believe it! This is so incredible! I don't know what to say! It's the best idea you've ever had! I'll never forget this day as long as I live!"

"Uh, thank you Coleman." Serge rubbed his chin. "I always thought my history stuff kind of bored you."

"Shit, no! I've never been so excited!"

"This is an astonishing development," said Serge. "There still may be hope for you—"

"Hold on! Hold on!" Coleman turned to light a mondo joint against the wind. "Pot's legal here, right? This is going to be so fantastic! I'll be the drug czar, but like in the cool way. I'll, you know, sit on a royal throne and point at people: 'Yes, you may get stoned. Let it be written.' This is so freaking great!"

"Settle down, Beavis."

"When do we plant the crops? I know these dudes who can help. Man, they'll all flip!"

"Coleman, there are much more serious issues when you become sovereign." He gestured back at the flapping blue flag. "You think we're just playing fort here?"

"Sorry. What do we need to do?"

"First, get recognition from another power as a bulwark against annexation. Maybe I'll back-channel to establish diplomatic ties with the Conch Republic." Serge smiled at the notion. "They'll understand our struggle."

"Who's the Conch Republic?"

"In 1982, the federal government roadblocked the Florida Keys, searching for drugs and illegal immigrants. This pissed off the chamber of commerce because it choked tourism, so they seceded from the United States, and in short order declared war, surrendered and applied for foreign aid. The publicity stunt worked and the roadblocks were removed."

"That's pretty weird."

Serge nodded and headed back to the car. "The second weirdest surrender in Key West history."

"What's the first?"

"In 2003, four armed Cuban soldiers docked their Coast Guard boat at the Hyatt and marched in uniform past the T-shirt shops on Duval Street looking for a police officer so they could defect."

Serge reached the barbed-wire fence by the road. "What's that racket?"

Coleman pointed toward the Comet. "Banging from inside your trunk."

Serge slapped himself on the forehead. "Damn, I completely forgot about him."

TWO HUNDRED MILES SOUTH

An empty chair sat in the noon sun.

It was the standard folding metal variety found in school auditoriums. Everyone's seen them a million times.

This one stood in the middle of the Florida Turnpike.

Cars swerved around it at the last second because paying attention out the windshield was considered madness. But the long-haul truckers knew better. They sat high up in semi cabs, keeping their eyes on the horizon for swerving cars, which indicated either debris in the road or someone preventing another driver from passing.

Highways in other states were mainly strewn with strips of shredded tires, but Florida had imagination, and the truckers had seen it all. Sofas, washing machines, outboard motors, giant stuffed bears from carnival midways, fondue equipment, and statues of underrated saints. So, next to a holy concrete sculpture of Ulrich of Augsburg, patron saint of fainting conditions and rodent control (true), a simple chair barely drew a second thought, except maybe how it had come to be upright.

The next truck was one of those double-decker automobile carriers that dealerships use. But the chair was still a ways off. Before the truck got there, a Datsun pulled over and the driver threw the piece of furniture in his trunk, then drove away slightly happier.

The car carrier continued south past the exit for Hobe Sound. Many such trailers are loaded with shiny, virgin vehicles fresh from the factory. Then there are flatbed trucks stacked with wrecked vehicles that have been crushed like beer cans. This particular carrier was somewhere in the middle. The paint on the cars did not sparkle anymore, and all the odometers were into six digits. These were the dubious trade-in vehicles that dealers immediately wanted off the property before they became eyesores. The somewhat-running cars were then dumped at bottom-feeding auctions to bidders who looked exactly like people at a dog track.

Each car had a story, some more fascinating than others. But at one time they were all the source of great joy, just driven off the lot with that new smell and a new owner buoyed by the notion that this was a move up.

Take the third car on the bottom deck of the southbound carrier: an '02 Altima put together at the Nissan factory in Smyrna, Tennessee, where a woman named Noreen had spot-welded the muffler before attending a baby shower that received mixed reviews. From there, the car was shipped to a dealership in Jacksonville and sold to a bilingual call-center manager named Keagan, who held a correspondence degree and a lifelong fascination with the Gabor sisters. After replacing the manifold, the title was transferred to a lactose-intolerant data entry clerk, then to her nephew-in-law, who street-raced it in Titusville before entering the vehicle's on-and-off period of being towed with a rope by another car before ending up on blocks in the front yard until code enforcement stepped in.

A private buyer who earned a modest income scouring the classified ads had offered to purchase the disabled car for the cost of removal, and with a little work on the piston rings, it was running again and auctioned to A-OK Auto Brokers, who leased space on the vehicle carrier that was just about to exit the turnpike in Opa-locka.

A few miles away stood one of those derelict used car lots with chain-link and a dancing sign spinner that made passing motorists think, *There but for the grace of God.* A man in Bermuda shorts followed the salesman down a row of Camaros and Jettas and Hyundais. "These are all cream puffs despite the high mileage."

"The higher the better," said the customer. "It's for my son. He's not going to take care of it."

"Kids love the Coopers. We just got this baby—"

"Is that a coat hanger holding the trunk lid down?"

"For you, a special price."

The customer removed his panama hat and looked around. "I don't know. I've heard good things about Nissans."

"Sold our last one Wednesday, but we have a Saturn right out of the body shop. *Very* minor accident. Not really even an accident. In fact that was another car entirely."

"I was kind of hoping for a Nissan."

A deep horn blared from the street.

"Excuse me a second," said the salesman. "Don't go anywhere." He ran across the lot and swung open an especially wide gate for the transport truck. The driver handed a manifest to the salesman, who ran back to his customer. "This is your lucky day!"

An hour later, the just-sold Nissan pulled up the driveway of a ranch house in Hialeah overlooking the Miami Canal. The garage darkened as the door rolled down. A naked lightbulb came on. Three muscular men in wifebeater shirts were waiting. They opened the driver's door and slashed the headrest with box cutters, removing two kilos of high-purity Bolivian chunk heroin. Without speaking, they tossed the driver a brown envelope of cash as if they were mad at him, then left quickly through the backyard.

A-OK Auto Brokers was the perfect front. Because nobody at the company knew what was going on. Not the buyers who attended the auctions, or bookkeepers or secretaries; not the drivers of the transport trucks, nor even the salesmen at the bargain car lots in Miami who received delivery. The only ones in the loop were a mechanic who performed repairs in his shop where the kilos got inserted, and the final customers, who were always coincidentally shopping at the car lots when the trucks arrived.

That way, if authorities ever intercepted a shipment, everything was insulated by a wall of clueless, innocent people. And the smuggling car itself had changed hands so many times that who could account for all those lives? Even if the guilty customer was stopped leaving the used car lot: "Hey, I just bought the thing ten minutes ago."

Why not? With all the drugs and cash flowing through the state, some was always getting loose. Law enforcement constantly received calls from concerned citizens who'd discovered packs of white powder stuffed inside secondhand office equipment and bamboo patio furniture.

The brokerage's owner rarely went near the business, preferring to enjoy his penthouse condo, where he now stood overlooking the ocean and reading a text message from a man in Bermuda shorts from Hialeah.

HOME.

The owner was an extremely tall man with extremely fine black hair. He had one of those nebulous foreign looks where his South American descent was often mistaken for European, even in Europe. Fingers pressed buttons again on his prepaid, untraceable phone, sending a text to a different number.

GREEN.

A mechanic drove another junk car to an isolated farm in Central Florida and, just after dark, Christmas lights came on in July. The lights were strewn across a flat pasture, marking the ad hoc runway for a low-flying Cessna that touched down, handed the goods out the window, and took off.

The mechanic pulled out his cell.

SAFE.

The resident of the Fort Lauderdale penthouse read the text, broke his phone apart and rejoined two women in his bedroom.

Chapter FIVE

THE GULF COAST

A muscle car raced through Pascagoula, Mississippi, home of Peavy guitar amplifiers.

"The sixties also brought us Space Food Sticks, which went perfect with Tang," said Serge. "But kids today never get to experience the pageantry. Just like Shake-A Pudd'n."

"I remember that." Coleman packed a bong made from something discarded in a Dumpster. "You'd shake powder and water together in a special container until it thickened, and all the children got room-temperature dessert. Wonder why they don't make it anymore."

"And Jiffy pop!" said Serge. "I loved those TV ads: parents sliding a tiny disposable pan on an oven burner and suddenly the foil expands to the size of your head."

"That used to rip my mind." Coleman took a hit, filling the car with a loud tone in C sharp.

"Another engineering feat?" asked Serge.

A pot cloud exhaled. "Someone threw out a broken clarinet."

"Getting high and performing a concerto," said Serge. "You're an overachiever."

Toot! Toot! . . .

"But here's the moment in Jiffy pop history that I wish I could have seen," said Serge. "The day at the factory when they installed the first microwave oven in the employee break room. 'It does fucking *what?*'"

Thud, thud, thud.

Coleman pointed the wind instrument toward the trunk. "That dude's awake again." *Toot!*

"Could have sworn I conked him harder than that."

"I still can't believe the guy followed that mom all the way home."

"Less amazing than you'd think," said Serge. "Crime now has delivery service. Most people aren't aware because they don't read the tiny newspaper stories on page seventeen, but there's a growing epidemic of people being attacked in their own driveways—unilateral road rage where the jerk won't let it go until he's at your mailbox. That's why my radar was up for that jerk. It's a sad commentary, but particularly true in Florida: If you're coming home at night, start checking the rearview three turns away. If someone else makes the same turns behind you, keep driving past your home. It's down to that."

Thud, thud, thud.

"Luckily I have delivery service, too."

The Comet continued into an industrial section of town and parked along a dark alley.

Coleman leaned out the window. "Medical supply?"

"Medical supply houses are the coyote's new Acme company: all kinds of great stuff you can't get elsewhere." Serge slipped out of the car and quietly closed the door. "The best part is lax security. While it may be a candy store to me, nobody else wants this stuff or even knows it exists."

"But I thought medical places had outrageous security," said Coleman.

"You're thinking of the ones with drugs."

"I am." *Toot!*

"No drugs, no security," said Serge. "Like that transom window that's ajar. We just need to get over this fence."

Serge walked to the motel bed where their captive was tied down spread-eagle. "You're finally awake! That's great, because I've been meaning to talk to you. What was it you said to that mom with her children in the backseat? Something ending with *bitch*? By definition bullies are cowards, but that's just embarrassing. Not to mention your external speakers. To be fair, I understand it's your mating call, and you need to locate the big-boobied airheads. But could you be a touch more courteous to the rest of the gene pool and maybe instead wear a T-shirt that says 'I'm with Stupid,' except with the arrow pointing straight up?"

"*Mmmmmm! Mmmmmm!*"

"Where are my manners?" said Serge. "Here you are my guest, and I'm nitpicking your faults . . . The real reason I wanted you to wake up is that I got you a gift." He opened a large molded case on the side of the bed. "Recently picked this up but realized it's way too big for me to keep lugging around. Since you're obviously into high-end audio equipment, I knew you'd appreciate it far more than anyone else I could think of. And audio doesn't get any more high-end than this. Want to see how it works? I'll show you!"

Two hours later, a muscle car thumped through the dark streets.

"Serge, you never play your music this loud," said Coleman. "You always say it's not polite."

"Except this time manners require me to be a polite host."

"*. . . Ooo-ooo, that smell! . . .*"

Serge glanced in the backseat at a wide-eyed passenger who no longer needed to be restrained. "And every polite host needs to stay sharp and pick up on each of his guests' special preferences. I doubt he's into finger bowls and hot towels."

The car eased into a parallel parking slot beside a self-service car wash. The music stopped. Serge turned all the way around in his seat and rested his arms casually atop the headrest. "I explained the bonus round earlier in detail, so you're up to speed there. All you need now is directions to the nearest emergency room. And you're in luck! It's six blocks straight ahead." He grinned.

Big eyes stared back.

"What are you waiting for?" said Serge. "Get going!"

"That's it?"

"Unless you want to hang out and be buddies."

The back door flew open; the pickup driver jumped onto the sidewalk. He took three running steps, then swayed and stuck his arms out for balance.

"The whole key is to find your comfort zone," Serge called out the window. "Go on, now, get comfy!"

The released prisoner headed off.

"He fell down," said Coleman.

"Practice makes perfect," said Serge, cranking up the stereo again.

A quarter mile ahead, an ambulance driver strolled out of the emergency room for a non-emergency smoke break. He leaned against a light post after spending the last hour with another shower-fall victim. Why were the fat ones the most slippery? And why did so many people not use rubber mats or stickers? He subconsciously thought of those retro flower shapes from *The Dating Game*. Then his mind drifted to bathrooms in general: toothbrush holders, brass towel rings, joke books designed to be read a minute at a time, the last hotel he was in that had a single shower knob to control both water volume *and* temperature that he could never figure out. He realized he hadn't used soap-on-a-rope in a long time.

He stopped. What was that sound?

Bump, ba-bump, bump, ba-bump . . .

His eyes strained down the street, but no vehicle in sight.

Bump, ba-bump, bump, ba-bump . . .

"Wait," said the ambulance man. "I know that song."

". . . The smell of death's around you! . . ."

The night suddenly became quiet. Movement way down the dark street. The EMT rubbed his eyes until he was sure the silhouette was actually there.

It slowly came into focus. Definitely a man, a big one who could take care of himself. As the image grew closer, the ambulance guy thought he was looking at some drunk. The figure wasn't weaving so much as shuffling extra slow, like he knew he was hammered and trying to deal with it.

Then he just tipped over like a gale-force wind had hit him. Except there wasn't even a breeze. He got up and shuffled even slower, walking a tight-rope. A quiet whimper: "Somebody help me."

The man's right knee buckled, and he went down again with a scream. He tried to pull himself up against a fence using his left leg. That knee gave way.

The paramedic took off running. "Stay down!"

The mystery man wasn't a good listener. He tried pushing himself up with his hands. Wrists and elbows couldn't hold the load. He nose-dived into the sidewalk just as the first responder responded. "Don't move! You're going to be okay!"

A second paramedic ran up with a cervical collar. "Roll him over so I can get this on his neck. Ready?"

Snap, snap.

"Aaaaahhhhhhhhhhhhhhh!"

"What did you do to him?"

"Nothing."

"A couple of his ribs just broke."

"I heard it, too," said the second EMT. "I barely applied any pressure."

Other guys arrived with a stretcher.

"Be careful," said the original paramedic. "Something weird's going on."

"Weird?"

The EMTs grabbed him under the legs. "He seems to be falling apart right in front of us. Be gentle getting him on that thing."

The quartet of paramedics raised him as gingerly as possible. But still:

Snap, snap, snap.

"Aaaahhhhhhhhhhhhhhh!!!"

The stretcher flew through the hospital's automatic doors and straight into operating room three. An oxygen mask was already on the patient's face. The surgeon arrived with his own paper mask, slipping sanitized hands into thin gloves. "Who was the first to find him?"

"Me," said a paramedic. "Never seen anything like it."

"I still don't know *what* I'm seeing," said the surgeon. "Why is he in here?"

"I don't know," said the paramedic.

The doctor turned and arched an eyebrow. "You're now just wheeling perfectly healthy people into my operating room?"

The EMT shook his head. "There's definitely something wrong. He's so delicate that every time we touch him, something bad happens. It's like a ninety-year-old guy walking through his kitchen, and out of the blue his hip breaks. You expect that because of advanced age, but this guy's so young."

The doctor walked around the patient. "Wounds?"

"Nothing."

"Internal injuries?"

"No bruises or redness. Just a few scrapes from falling down, but not enough to cause anything. Otherwise, he looks perfectly fine."

A nurse looked at a beeping machine. "Blood pressure dropping."

"Get an IV going." The physician spread the patient's eyelids to inspect pupils. "What was the first thing you noticed?"

"I saw him walking down the street and then it was just broad-spectrum skeletal failure—"

A buzzing alarm went off. "Code!" yelled a nurse. A green line tracked straight across a screen.

They grabbed the electric paddles. "Clear!"

Boom . . .

"Nothing."

Boom . . .

"Chest compression."

Snap.

"What was that?"

"Sternum . . ."

An hour later, police detectives huddled with a surgeon in the lobby.

"So you think we have a homicide?" asked a suit with a notebook.

"Don't know," said the doctor.

"Cause of death?"

"Don't know that, either."

"Foul play?"

He shrugged.

The detective stopped writing. "With all due respect, why did you call us down here if there's no sign of a crime?"

"That's the whole point," said the doctor. "There's no sign of anything at all. He just fell apart. One of the paramedics put it best: It's as if someone had loosened the bolts on all the wheels of a car and sent it out on the freeway. That's why we need a full autopsy."

Chapter SIX

A map lay open in a lap. "I've never been to Daytona Beach before."

"You can drive on the sand," said Peter Pugliese. "Or so I've heard."

"Why would you want to?" asked his wife.

"People do it."

Mary looked up from the route she had marked in pencil. "Let's never take an interstate again. You see so much more out here."

"The homemade signs alone are worth it."

"There's another person selling hay," said Mary. "Someone with discount landscaping rocks. Horse-riding lessons. Teaching ceramics in their garage by appointment. Someone else hates the president . . . Why are you slowing down?"

"All those flashing lights up ahead," said Peter. "Must be some kind of big accident."

More colorful lights, this time from behind.

Mary turned around. "Peter, how fast are you going?"

"Why?" He checked the rearview and speedometer. "We're good."

The police officer pulled them over behind the other blinking patrol cars on the shoulder. The couple sat quietly. The cop took forever to get out. It was that universal period of needless panic where motorists mentally audition a catalog of stilted dialogue to win the officer over.

The cop arrived at Peter's window, and so began an epoch of bad acting. A crooked smile. "Good morning, Officer. Is there a problem? Was I doing something wrong? I sure hope not, because I would never want to. Taillights? That must be it. Because I was really watching my speed—"

Mirror sunglasses. "License, registration and proof of insurance."

"Sure thing. Here's my license and insurance card . . . Where's that registration? Mary, can you check the glove compartment? Or maybe it's in this console . . ."

"Sir, you do have registration, don't you?"

"Oh, definitely, it's right around here somewhere . . ." Fishing in seat pockets. "Do you mind if I ask why you pulled us over?"

"Registration, please."

Peter continued the hunt. "I had the car on cruise control. I'm sure I was only doing fifty-three. I like to keep it a couple miles under the limit, you know, to do the right thing."

"I clocked you at fifty-three."

"There you go," said Peter.

"In a thirty zone."

Peter stiffened. "But the sign back there said fifty-five."

"And the sign up there says thirty."

"*Up* there?" Peter pointed ahead toward six other pulled-over motorists. "You mean where I haven't driven yet?"

"The sign was in view, under state statute."

"Is this some kind of speed trap?"

"Sir, please step out of the car."

"But I was under the limit," Peter protested.

"Sir, I'm not going to ask you again."

Mary clutched his arm. "Please do what he says."

The cop stuck his ticket book in his back pocket. "I'd follow the lady's advice."

Peter gave his wife a last something's-rotten glance and slowly climbed out the driver's side.

The officer immediately spun him around and slammed him against the side of the car. Arms twisted behind his back. Handcuffs snapped closed.

Mary leaned across the seat. "What on earth are you doing to my husband?"

"Ma'am, please stay in the vehicle and remain quiet."

Peter craned his neck in a vain attempt to see behind. "Officer, if I'm in handcuffs, that means I'm technically under arrest, and then you're required to tell me what for. I watch TV."

"Anything over twenty miles in excess of the limit can be considered reckless driving, plus you weren't cooperating, which might add a felony depending on how the judge sees it."

"But I was under the limit!"

"Come with me." The officer escorted him by the arm to his patrol car.

"I'm going to have to appear before a judge?"

The officer didn't answer. He walked Peter around to the passenger side, where someone in a black robe rolled down the window.

"Judge," said the officer. "Caught him going twenty-three over the limit without registration."

"Peter?" asked the man in the patrol car.

"Vernon?" said Peter.

Vernon nodded at the officer. "It's okay, Boyd, I know Peter. He's good people. You can uncuff him."

"Yes, sir." A tiny key twisted in the locks.

Peter rubbed his wrists. "You're a judge, too?"

"You wouldn't believe how people fly through here. You got your spring-breakers heading to Daytona that way, and everyone else going to Orlando theme parks the other. They think because this ain't the interstate and just a country road, nobody's watching," said Vernon. "We got a nice little town and mean to keep it that way."

"But this isn't your town." Peter jerked a thumb over his shoulder. "It's at least five miles over there."

"That's right." Vernon pulled a longneck Bud from the cooler between his legs. "So we annexed a five-mile-long, hundred-yard-wide corridor of land, and now a little piece of the town stops just over the edge of this highway. Want a beer?"

"I'm driving."

"You're good people."

Peter leaned against the edge of the police car. "But why are *you* out here?"

"Case backlog. Try to settle as many of these on the spot . . ." He gestured in the backseat at a cash box and credit-card swiper.

"This is an outrage!"

They both looked ahead at a cuffed man in a tennis shirt being pushed down into the back of a squad car.

"We still get a lot of hard cases," said Vernon. "But a night in county lockup tends to crack the shell. You're lucky I was here or that's where you'd be heading."

Peter turned forward again and examined all the other law enforcement vehicles that had stopped motorists. One looked like the patrol car he was standing next to, but all the rest were beat-up sedans and pickups with revolving red lights on the dash. "So you're also using unmarked cars?"

"Not on purpose." Vernon stuck a hand inside his robe to grab a pint of Southern Comfort. "Too many speeders and not enough officers, so we had to deputize. Up there's Bo, Clem, Otis and I think Haywood."

"That's most of the city council," said Peter.

"Ha! We got a quorum!" Vernon grinned that he was finally able to work *quorum* into conversation.

"Well, Mary's probably getting worried," said Peter. "Probably should be heading back to the car."

"Just watch your speed along here." Vernon reached between his legs again. "Take this."

"What is it?"

"My campaign bumper sticker." He took a swig from his bottle. "Stick it on your car, and there won't be any more misunderstandings if you're pulled over again."

"Okay, then, I'll keep my speed down."

"Hell, drive as fast you want. Give my best to the missus."

Peter got back in his car with a dazed look.

"That cop had me scared crazy," said Mary. "What the heck happened?"

"I got a bumper sticker."

He put the car in gear and drove off, just as a convertible BMW pulled up.

A fit man in an oxford shirt walked to the patrol car. "Vern, how's business?"

"Where's this recession everyone's talkin' about?"

"Got some good news on that other thing," said Ryan. "Don't worry another second about the investigation. It's officially closed."

"But I thought we were getting subpoenaed."

The senator shook his head. "Did a little horse-trading in Tallahassee on the budget committee and threw the investigators a bone. Hampton."

"Hampton? That inbred town up north?" said Vernon. "They couldn't find their own asses if they had ten arms."

"Blue-ribbon panels are so predictable," said Ryan. "Don't care who they skin for corruption, just as long as they get a pelt once in a while to hold up for the cameras."

"Speaking of pelts . . ." Vernon opened the glove

compartment and tossed a brown paper lunch sack out the window. "Need to count it?"

"I know where to find you," said Ryan.

"Oh, and Peter just left. Got pulled over."

"So now he has a bumper sticker," said Ryan.

"How'd their background checks go?" asked Vernon.

"Both look clean," said the senator. "From Saratoga Springs just like they said. Don't think they'll be any trouble. Did you hear what he does for a living?"

"Something about geography."

"*Geology*," said Ryan. "And you know what that means?"

"Not really."

"He might be very useful to us. As long as he doesn't decide to become the hero type."

Chapter SEVEN

Mississippi detectives pushed open steel doors just as the medical examiner finished scrubbing down.

"Got anything yet?"

The coroner dried his hands. "Just preliminary until I check my findings with some experts, but this most definitely was a homicide."

"What experts?" asked a detective. "Thought you were the final word around here when it came to cause of death."

"Different field of medicine entirely," said the examiner. "Couldn't find much on the X-rays, so I ran several MRIs. The results were most troubling."

"You're just going to leave us hanging?"

"Little pieces were missing throughout his body."

"Pieces? Of what?"

"Bone, cartilage, you name it," said the doctor.

"All very small, all highly scattered; knee, elbow. That's why the X-rays didn't pick it up."

"That killed him?"

"The strategic positioning of the damage left him like a structurally unsound building. Then the damaged bones in his inner ear knocked out equilibrium and sent the whole thing teetering. Did you know they're the smallest bones in the human body? Three of 'em called the hammer, anvil and stirrup."

"What are you talking about?"

"The inner ear," said the examiner.

"The murder!" said the detective.

"Oh, sorry . . . Anyway, had me stumped. Even after the MRI discoveries, I still didn't have any answers. There were no injuries or other underlying pathologies to explain any of it. Stuff was just *gone*."

"This is starting to sound like *The X-Files*."

"And it would still seem like that except I went over the films again and found one of the tiniest missing pieces still lodged in his urinary tract. That's when it all clicked," said the examiner. "He must have peed out the rest of the missing stuff before we found him."

"Pee?" said a detective. "I'm still no closer to grasping this."

The examiner grabbed a large molded-plastic case from a shelf. "I had the hospital send one of these down."

The lid opened and the detectives leaned. "What is that thing?"

"Your murder weapon," said the coroner. "A lithotriptor. This is one of the smaller mobile models. You wouldn't be able to move the table-mounted jobs."

"Never heard of it."

"Most people haven't." He closed the lid. "But many know what it does. If you have kidney or gallstones and don't want surgery, this thing stays outside the body and uses a focal point of high-impact sonic waves to smash them."

"Sonic?"

"In the wrong hands, this device is the world's deadliest boom box."

"So our killer's a doctor?"

"Not necessarily," said the coroner. "Normally it would take rigorous medical training to focus the sound beams accurately. That's to cure a patient. But if you were going for this . . ." He gestured at the deceased on the cold table. ". . . Not so much."

WOBBLY

The sound and smell of frying bacon filled the kitchen.

Peter rushed into the room, tying a Windsor knot on his way to the skillet.

"Already poured your orange juice," said Mary, sitting at the table with her laptop.

"Thanks." Peter plopped down and buttered toast. "What are you doing?"

"Googling 'Florida speed traps.' Triple-A has

a bunch listed. Some places named Lawtey and Waldo."

"I know where those towns are," said Peter. "Up north on 301, probably trying to catch college students on the way down from Jacksonville to the University of Florida. I shouldn't eat bacon."

"A little won't be bad," said Mary. "Here's a place called Hampton. Wow, less than five hundred people live there, yet they issued almost thirteen thousand tickets in two years. The city's under investigation."

"For all the tickets?"

"And some of the money's missing. They said the records got lost in a swamp."

"Are you making that up?"

"It's so Florida." She continued reading. "The town leaders annexed a thin strip of land to reach the highway so they'd have jurisdiction to pull people over."

"Sounds familiar." Peter jammed toast crust in his mouth and chased it with juice as he got up.

"Where are you off to today?"

"Longwood. New mall."

"Who's paying?"

"Everyone. Florida's combination of sediment, limestone and aquifers are the perfect storm."

Mary reached across the table. "Don't forget your hard hat."

A ten-thousand-acre lot sat on the north side of Orlando in the inexorable path of suburban sprawl.

Twenty men wearing silk ties stood in the field.

"We haven't even started building the mall yet," said one of the executives. "Why do we have to wear hard hats?"

"Insurance," said an insurance man.

They all observed workers packing up an exotic scientific contraption that vaguely reminded them of a moon rover. Then they turned to Peter. "Well?"

He scribbled on a clipboard. "Ground-penetrating radar checks out."

"So we're good?"

"Almost," said Peter. "You paid for the full treatment."

The workers began inserting a series of evenly spaced metal rods in a straight line across the property, attaching wires and instruments.

"What's that?" asked a leading expert in the field of food courts.

"Electric resistivity test," said Peter. "We're going to pump a bunch of current into the ground."

"Stand back," said the insurance guy.

"What's that do?" asked the anchor-store tenant manager.

Peter gave a high sign for his subordinates to hit the power. "Measures discrete intervals of conductivity, which are then processed through inversion software to create a cross section of substrata."

"Huh?"

Peter flipped a page on his clipboard. "Tells us whether this land will hold your buildings."

"It never used to be this involved," said the guy who made the architectural scale model that included tiny customers on escalators that he got from train-set kits.

"It's getting more so . . ." said Peter.

". . . Ever since that sinkhole swallowed the Corvette Museum in Bowling Green, Kentucky," said the insurance man.

"What's a sinkhole doing in Kentucky?"

"What's a Corvette museum doing in Kentucky?"

"Just about finished." Peter received a data sheet from one of his colleagues. "Still have to bounce this off our baseline models at the home office, but I'd sleep well tonight."

"So you're saying we won't have any sinkholes?"

"I'd never say never," replied Peter. "But if it was my money, I wouldn't hesitate to build here."

A cell phone rang. Everyone checked pockets. "That's mine," said Peter, turning around for privacy. "Pugliese here . . . You have another job for me? . . . Of course I know where Wobbly is. I live there . . . What? They asked for me by name?"

U.S. HIGHWAY 31

Nothing but cows and fields and webs of vines covering power poles. Keg-chested men in camouflage proudly emerged from a forest with assault rifles and trophy squirrels. The sky was so blue. A '72 Mercury Comet sped through southern Alabama.

"Here comes the state penitentiary in Atmore," said Serge. "Home of their death chamber."

Coleman held his joint down as they passed the guard towers. "Have I seen this place before?"

"Probably recognize it from the Prison Channel."

"Prison Channel?"

"That's what I call MSNBC," said Serge. "A lot of people hate that channel because of its politics, but my main beef is an abject neglect of journalism. Here's this twenty-four-hour news outlet with the unlimited resources of the NBC mother ship, faced with a million news stories exploding in our shrinking world, so I'll turn it on in the middle of the night to update my global perspective, and immediately smack myself: 'Dear God in heaven! Not another six-hour binge-athon of *Lockup Raw*!'"

"They use dental floss like fishing lines to pass notes between cells."

"Possibly interesting the first time," said Serge. "But it's like a freakin' bass tournament, and my brain's hard drive has exceeded capacity on things to make a shank out of."

"Toothbrush, melted comb, mop handle, glued Bible pages," said Coleman. "They also have an impressive number of uses for their turds."

"Plus I now know far more about prison romance than I'd ever want. It pisses me off."

"Because you're prejudiced?"

"No, envious," said Serge. "If I live to be three hundred, I'll never figure out my own relationships, but jailhouse love is so straightforward. A nice couple is out in the exercise yard, then one wrong look and they're hosing blood off the barbells. No room for nuance. But in the real world, it's prolonged periods of the silent treatment and slamming doors, and me with that dazed look on my face: 'I still have no idea what I did wrong.'"

Coleman stubbed out a roach. "Like your ex-wife?"

"Molly said the key to bringing us closer was honesty, but that was a lie. 'Serge, which of my friends do you think is the most attractive?'"

"I was there when she asked that," said Coleman. "I told her you thought Jill was super hot, remember?"

"What the hell were you thinking?" said Serge. "It's not like in prison. You can't call the guards, can't lock yourself in your cell, and definitely can't let her even *find* a shank. No, when you're married, you need a diplomatic advance team to vet a menu of highly polished responses."

"So what was the right answer to her sexiest friend?"

"'It's about to rain and I left my windows down!'"

"What if it's not going to rain?"

"'Don't move! A spider!'" said Serge. "Making the effort to prepare multiple diversionary tactics shows you're committed to the marriage."

The Comet turned south and approached the Florida state line.

Bang, bang, bang.

"Serge, you're firing a gun out the window."

"It's the state line." He stuck the pistol back in the glove compartment. "Road trips are all about tradition."

Coleman punched holes in an empty beer can to

make it a pipe. "When did you first get interested in road trips?"

"I was three," said Serge. "It was the weirdest thing, but for some reason I spent my entire preschool life in utter dread after becoming aware of a simple, existence-consuming truth: 'If all the adults suddenly disappear, I'm totally fucked.'"

"Goes without saying," said Coleman.

"Years of sheer panic. Parents usually keep a close eye on their kids, but with me it was the opposite, staying glued to them in department stores in case they tried to ditch me. Meanwhile, I continued work on my exit strategy. If they ever *did* vanish, the only hope was to make a marathon road trip to the secret land where all the survivors had set up shop. First, I already had a tricycle, so I could check transpo off the list. Then before the next Christmas, I told my parents—and I was extremely emphatic about this—'All I want is a Frosty Sno-Cone Machine and a Matchbox Car collecting briefcase.' And my folks said, 'That's it?' And I said, 'Believe me, it'll be enough.' And I kept grabbing them tight by the collar each time I reminded them. 'You absolutely must get these items for me!' And they're like, 'Okay, okay, Serge. Jeez! Why do you want this stuff so bad?' Obviously I couldn't tell them that it was in case they died or were part of a conspiracy, so I just said I had my reasons and it was personal."

"Did you get the stuff?"

"It got hairy leading up to Christmas. Most kids are filled with the ecstasy of anticipation, but for me it was the jitters of self-preservation. That morning I ran from my bedroom in a freak-out until I saw those two gifts under the tree, and I exhaled in relief: 'Now I can live.' Before my parents were even up, I cut the cardboard dividers for the little cars out of the Matchbox briefcase—'Now I have luggage'— and the snow-cone machine meant I could provide my own sustenance. So I packed the Matchbox container with pajamas and underwear, then went in the kitchen to give Frosty a dry run, and my heart sank. 'It's just shaved ice; these little flavor packets won't carry the day . . . All right, think, think! What's abundant in Florida that you can always get your hands on to nurture the body? Coconuts!' I ran outside before it was light, found one under a palm tree and tried bashing it open in the driveway, then grabbed it by the husk, repeatedly slamming it against the side of the house, but nothing worked. I wouldn't be strong enough for years, so now it's terror-time again and I run back inside. Meanwhile, my parents woke up from all the thumping against the wall under their window. 'What on earth is all that banging?' And they walked in the living room to find me facedown on the carpet, kicking and crying, next to a cut-up Matchbox suitcase with my clothes spilling out, and a coconut crammed in the ice hole of a destroyed Frosty machine. That's how I got into road-tripping."

"Yeah, but what happened to your survival plan?" asked Coleman. "You could have died."

"I kind of got distracted when I realized I'd also received some G.I. Joes that Christmas, and my parents came back in the living room later that morning: 'What the hell is going on with the Nativity scene?' I said King Herod had gotten wind of the Messiah and was killing all the firstborns, so I deployed my G.I. Joes to the manger and set up a perimeter with a sniper on the roof. Then I rearranged the other Nativity figures so the Three Wise Men were standing in line at a checkpoint. 'Can I see some ID?'"

"You think of everything."

"My folks still made me withdraw the troops." Serge pointed out the windshield. "There it is."

"The Korner Kwik convenience store?"

"No, the town of Century, located in the most extreme northwest tip of the Florida Panhandle." Serge clicked pictures out the window. "It's where Walkin' Lawton Chiles began his one-thousand-and-three-mile foot-trek down the state to Key West in his successful U.S. Senate campaign. And he did it while *Easy Rider* was still in first run at the theaters."

"That's some heavy shit."

"It was a special time. I reached my sixth birthday, and opportunities were wide open, especially since I'd completed my survival plan through a regimen of strenuous exercise until I could breach coconut shells. My mom would come out: 'Lunch is ready.' But I'd just stay sitting in the driveway, drinking coconut milk through the hole I'd bashed. 'Mom, you've done more than enough; I'm on my own now. You don't have to worry about me anymore.' Except they did just the reverse."

Coleman gazed out the window at the rusty tin

roof on a hundred-year-old cracker house, then a roadside stand with boiled peanuts and a hand-painted sign for free pet rabbits. "Could this town be any smaller?"

"That's the theme of our journey: Shun highways and modernism to discover the real Florida through its back roads, flea markets and finger-lickin' county fairs. Small towns are the heartbeat of this country, and if anyone knows what's happened to the American Dream, it'll be the genuine folks who still live there. So our route will take us on an odyssey through a bygone time, exactly like Lawton Chiles saw, except with meth labs."

"I see big buildings up there," said Coleman.

"That's why we're turning."

The Comet swung east above Pensacola, beginning a long run on a low-slung bridge over the marshes and deltas of Escambia Bay. Serge gazed south across the water at the more massive, contemporary bridge for Interstate 10, running parallel a few miles south. A wry smile as he nodded to himself. "They never saw this coming."

A few minutes later, the Mercury approached the twin cities of Milton and Bagdad. Old church steeples and unmowed cemeteries and onion rings at a drive-in. They parked in front of a corrugated aluminum building with a gravel lot and a plywood sign: ED'Z DEAD SLEDZ.

A bearded man emerged from the open garage door wearing an untucked blue shirt with oil stains. The beard was red. He would eat a pickled egg later that afternoon but didn't know it yet.

"You must be Ed," said Serge.

"Ed's dead." The man wiped greasy palms on crusty jeans. "Name's Bear Claw."

"You're named after a pastry?"

"Hell no! The pegs."

"Pegs?"

"Where you put your feet on the motorcycle," said Bear Claw. "You *do* ride, don't you?"

"Oh, we ride all right," said Serge. "We even ride in our sleep."

"And we sleep when we ride," said Coleman.

Chapter EIGHT

WOBBLY

The afternoon sun twinkled through the oaks on Main Street.

As of that morning, each block had a banner draped high across the road that would remain for the next two weeks.

FOUNDERS' DAY CELEBRATION.

Smaller banners with the same idea hung from each of the street's antique lamp posts. A fireworks tent was pitched in the parking lot of the Primitive Baptist Church. Against the last post in front of Lead Belly's barbecue stood a ladder. There was a man at the top and another at the bottom.

"Get that damn thing straight," shouted Vernon. "We got people coming."

"Yes, sir."

Footsteps. Vernon turned. "Oh, Peter and Mary. Pleasant afternoon."

Peter gazed up at the long row of fluttering flags

with the town's official seal of a pioneer in a coon-skin cap gallantly pointing at something just off the edge of the seal. "Looks like you got a big event planned here."

"Founders' Day is the biggest!" said Vernon. "Means the world to this community."

"I respect that," said Peter. "Fewer and fewer people seem to know how important it is to preserve heritage."

"Heritage?" said Vernon. "This is rivalry!"

"Rivalry?"

Vernon nodded extra hard. "Our section of Florida has a growing number of quaint old boutique towns fighting for visitors' dollars. You got Deland, Deltona, Debary, Casselberry, Cassadaga, Lake Mary, Lake Helen, Mount Dora. *Mount!* Give me a break!"

An unseen buzzing sound grew louder in the distance.

Peter looked around like he was trying to follow a moth. "Where's that coming from?"

"Crash," said Vernon.

"An accident?"

"No, Crash Boggs." He pointed straight up.

A small but nimble acrobatic plane appeared above the tree tops. Red, white and blue. If Evel Knievel had a plane, this would be it. The craft climbed skyward, glinting in the sun as it performed a series of barrel rolls.

"Your Founders' Day has an air show?"

"Forced to. These other small towns aren't fooling around." He looked back up the ladder. "The goddamn thing still isn't straight! Don't make me come up there and kick your ass!" Then toward Peter and Mary again: "There's a fiercely aggressive competition to prove who's the most laid-back."

"Any way we can help?" asked Peter.

"Bring your checkbook inside and join us."

He opened the door to the rib joint, which was hosting some kind of low-grade organizational party. Schoolchildren made decorations, a bluegrass band rehearsed, volunteers signed various sign-up sheets: work the ticket booths, run the concession stands, judge prize pumpkins, and prevent mishaps at the pig races like last year. One table held rows of identical tote bags.

Someone ripped a check from a checkbook, and Jabow stuck it in his pocket. "Hundred dollars makes you a platinum circle patron. Here's your tote bag."

Vernon patted the man on the back. "Really appreciate it, Steve. Always nice when newcomers take an active interest in our community."

"Just want to do what I can."

"Then stop eating ribs with a knife and fork."

They both chuckled at the semi-joke. Steve left, and the mayor stopped to sign for delivery of the rental dunk tank.

The Puglieses stood respectfully.

Vernon handed a pen back to a delivery guy in brown shorts and turned to the couple. "So can I talk you into becoming patrons?"

"Uh, honey," said Peter.

"Sure." Mary dug in her purse for the checkbook. "What's the usual?"

"Well, twenty-five is silver level, fifty for gold, but I saw you had your eye on a tote bag."

"I think that's a hundred," said Peter.

Mary handed Vernon the check and stared at the Founders' Day button pinned to his shirt pocket: SLOW DOWN IN WOBBLY.

"Here's your bag," said Vernon. "Two buttons are in there. Why don't you have a seat? Iced tea?"

"Sure."

Mary pulled a string of ten complimentary coupons from the bag.

"Those are good for everything," said Vern. "Kissing booth, fried elephant ears. I'll get that tea."

Peter opened the official program with an event schedule that was subject to change. Ten a.m., pie-eating contest; eleven, turkey calling; noon, line dancing; one o'clock, pig races, with an asterisk about stronger fences this year.

"Here's your tea." Vernon set two dripping mason jars on the table.

Peter looked up puzzled from a certain item in the program. "Two o'clock, cornholing?"

"Kids throw bean bags through a hole in plywood, not the other." He leaned to read Peter's program upside down. "But it should just say corn*hole*. Shit, there's an *i-n-g* at the end." Vernon shouted over his shoulder. "Louise, get a Magic Marker. I need you to go through the rest of the tote bags . . ."

Peter flipped to a page with the pictorial history of Wobbly, Florida, founded 1854 by Thaddeus "Wobbly" Horsepence (1802–1856), who became destitute trying to market unpopular uses for the area's abundant persimmon trees. Black-and-white drawings illustrated a colorful town history. The great fire, the crop failure, cattle rustlers, Indian massacres, mining collapse, the night the levee broke.

Peter looked up. "Did all this really happen?"

"Not exactly," said Vernon. "But we did have a crop failure, except it didn't totally fail. Actually it was pretty good. But nobody checks. All the other towns are doing it."

Peter glanced at his program again. "Doesn't say how the founder got his nickname."

Vernon touched the side of his head. "Some kind of bad-balance sickness."

"He got his nickname for falling down a lot?"

"Just once, broke his neck. Died. They found his barn full of persimmon molasses."

"They nicknamed him posthumously?"

"Looking back, probably not the most sensitive thing for his kin."

Peter reached the last page of the program. "This says Wobbly was founded in 1854, but you didn't incorporate until 2012?"

"Folks around here don't like to be rushed," said Vernon. "But Senator Pratchett told us it was required if we wanted to annex the highway."

"That reminds me," said Peter. "There's something I wanted to ask you . . ."

The mayor suddenly felt a silent presence behind him and spun. Elroy, Slow and Slower. "Jesus, will you not *do* that anymore?"

"Sorry," said Elroy. "We just wanted to let you know about the . . . errand."

"What errand?"

"You know." The youth tilted his head in the general direction of Jabow's house.

"No, I don't know!" Vernon said with growing impatience. "Speak English. Where was this errand?"

Slow rubbed his fingers together, indicating cash. "The hiding place."

Elroy elbowed him. "Shut up!"

Vernon shot a quick, forced grin at Peter and Mary. "Apologize, but I'm going to have to take this in private. Family, you understand." He gathered the trio in the back of the room. "Don't you ever bring that up in here! What's wrong with you guys? The last two I know the answer, but I expect more from you, Elroy . . ." The mayor turned again to smile at the couple. "Just be a minute. We're really talking about Founders' Day."

The couple exchanged awkward glances.

Vernon finally came back. "There, then, where were we? You wanted to ask something?"

"My company called and said I had a job coming up in Wobbly. You requested me personally?"

"That's right," said Vernon. "When we heard what you did for a living, it was a perfect fit. We always like to throw business to locals. It's only neighborly."

"So what is this job?"

He waved a hand in the air once again. "I don't know all that fancy book-learnin' stuff. I got common sense. But I hear it's real easy work, and the pay is more than great. Since it's government money, we spend it like it's someone else's."

"It is someone else's," said Peter.

"I told everyone you were sharp," said Vernon. "Need to go check on those banners. They won't get straight by themselves."

"I don't know how to repay you," said Peter.

"You will."

The high-pitched whine of a stunt plane passed over the restaurant's roof.

THE PANHANDLE

Serge held up a finger for the mechanic to wait while he finished draining a jumbo travel mug of coffee.

Bear Claw covertly rolled his eyes. "So what can I do you fellas for?"

Serge decisively placed his hands on his hips and assessed the property. "I aim to buy some mean machines. Money up front. Where do we pay?"

"You seem to know what you want."

"Absolutely," said Serge. "We're on a journey. Small towns, Lawton Chiles, Coleman's the drug czar."

Coleman pointed at him. "You may be stoned."

Bear Claw squinted, then shrugged and began

walking ahead of them. "You probably want a hog. You *better* want a hog, 'cause I don't carry no rice-burnin' crotch-rockets." He spat on the ground.

Serge spit, too. "Hogs put the *American* in American Dream. Plant us on Harleys!"

"Here's a nice one. A sharknose with low miles. And we got a Super Glide . . ."

"No, no," said Serge. "Keep going."

"A couple of Road Kings, a Sportster, a Street Bob . . ."

"No, no, no."

The man tugged on his beard. "That's pretty much the range. I thought you really wanted one."

Serge's neck jerked around. "Where's the Holy Grail?"

"Why don't you just tell me straight out what you're looking for?"

Serge's arms shot up over his head as he gripped the sky. "A bitchin' chopper with those super-high handlebars."

"You mean a hardtail with ape-hangers?"

"Ape-hangers, right!" Serge's arms stayed up. "*Ooo! Ooo! Ooo!* Those were chimpanzee sounds. It doesn't come up often in conversation, so I like to go with it. Ape-hangers."

Bear Claw leaned casually against a metal drum. "Don't mind me asking, but what kind of riding are you fellas planning on doing?"

"The big trip, all the way through Florida!"

"Then you definitely don't want ape-hangers. That's insane," said Bear Claw. "Your arms will fall off."

Serge shook his head vigorously. "I possess a rare physical constitution that demands I ignore advice."

"No, really. They're just for short runs. A lot of idiots bought those bikes after *Easy Rider* came out and tried to take them cross-country."

"I can't believe you said that!" Serge hopped with glee. "*Easy Rider* is the whole reason we're here! We've completely rededicated our lives—"

"Dear God, no!"

"What?" said Serge. "You didn't like the movie?"

"I *used* to love the movie." Bear Claw put a hand over his eyes. "I thought you guys had stopped coming in here a long time ago."

Serge looked behind himself. "What guys?"

"Never mind." Bear Claw exhaled with frustration. "Follow me. I got a chopper around back. It's pretty dirty from sitting, but it'll clean up well."

Serge sprinted past him and disappeared behind the building. His voice echoed back. "It's exactly what I'm looking for! I'll take it!"

"You don't even know the price."

"Price, shmice!" Serge returned into view. "Now for Coleman. Got anything like Dennis Hopper rode?"

"Well, over there's an old police bike with pan-heads."

Serge ran up behind Coleman and shoved him hard in the back. "Go see how you like it!"

"Hey!"

Serge turned back to Bear Claw and pointed at some orange and black blow-by streaks on the side of the garage. "Looks like you do some paintwork."

Another frustrated breath: "I'm guessing you want the red-white-and-blue teardrop gas tank."

Serge pulled out a wallet so crammed with bills that he could hardly fold it.

"Dear Lord!" Bear Claw was a new man. "Anything you want."

"I do want a new paint job on the gas tank, but—"

From behind: *Crash. "A little help over here."*

They came running. "Coleman, what are you doing under that motorcycle?"

"There's something wrong with the kickstand."

They pulled the bike off him, and Bear Claw reached down to jerk the metal rod. "Kickstand's fine."

Coleman got up and rubbed something that would turn into a bruise. "I don't like that bike."

"Okay, so find one you do," said Serge.

Coleman moseyed off.

"You were talking about a paint job?" asked Bear Claw.

"Yeah, the gas tank," said Serge. "Except I don't want an American flag. What I really need is an exquisite—"

Crash. "Bad kickstand again . . ."

A half hour later, Bear Claw handed Coleman a bag of ice. "You tried eight bikes that all fell over on you. Every kickstand can't be defective."

"You're right," said Serge. "I believe we've isolated the malfunctioning variable."

"What?" said Coleman, picking at the butterfly

bandage on his eyebrow. "Why are you looking at me like that?"

Now it was Serge's turn to heave in frustration. He glanced at Bear Claw. "Think I'm going to need more work on that chopper than just a paint job . . ."

Chapter NINE

TV satellite trucks sat on the edge of a road.

"*This is Jody Choice with* Eyewitness Six, *coming to you live from eastern Calusa County . . .*"

Behind the news crew was an ornate brick entranceway with slate lettering. SAGE CREEK BLUFF GLEN ESTATES. And behind that lay a grid of modest neighborhood roads stretching to the horizon. Lots of street lights and fire hydrants and surveyors' stakes marking property lines. No homes yet.

With one exception.

In the middle of the platted subdivision stood a single building, sort of.

A group of men in hard hats gathered in a front yard where a banner read MODEL HOME.

"What do you think, Peter?"

"Doesn't look good."

It was one of those four-bedroom mini-McMansions constructed from the lowest-bid materials and quickest methods. Two-car garage, screened-in pool, vaulted-arch portico made from stucco on wooden forms.

"How do we fix it?"

"Bulldoze it," said Peter.

"But it's the model home."

"Guys," said Peter. "The middle of the roof is practically at ground level, and probably lower by nightfall. You got a serious sinkhole. What test method did you use?"

The other hard hats stared at their shoes.

"Who did your testing?" asked Peter.

Still looking down.

"You didn't *test*?" said the insurance man. "We're pulling out!"

A black Lincoln Town Car rolled through the brick entrance and parked near the commotion. A man in a button-down oxford emerged from the backseat. "Gus, what's your hurry? Where are you going?"

"Those clowns never tested the substrata," said the insurance man. "That voids our underwriting!"

"Let's just slow down," said Senator Pratchett. "You and I go way back. Come with me so I can talk to the others and see if something reasonable can be worked out."

"Won't change anything."

"Fair enough. Just a moment of your time."

The pair returned to the rest of the group.

"Peter," said the senator. "It is Peter, right? I didn't know you were on this project."

"The mayor in Wobbly personally requested me,"

said Peter. "They phoned my company just after the place fell in."

"What a coincidence," said Pratchett. "Glad to have you on board!"

The insurance man pointed. "We're not paying for that."

"Gus," said Senator Pratchett. "Fuck the model home. We're not even going to file a claim . . . Now, everyone, listen up. My people gave me the short version, and apparently there was some kind of testing issue."

"That's an understatement."

"Gus, just try to keep an open mind. That's all I'm asking." The senator turned back to the rest of the group. "Here's what's going to happen. We'll be performing a thorough re-testing." He placed a genial arm around Peter's reluctant shoulders. "And we have the best man in the business to do it. So let's just get out of his way and allow him to go to work. And whatever he finds out, for good or ill, we'll let the chips fall where they may . . . Gus, how's that sound? *Gus!*"

"*All* right."

"Peter?"

"I can't promise you'll like what I find."

"We're not asking you to promise anything. Just do what you do and give us the honest truth."

"Okay, I can have the equipment here in a couple hours."

"That's the spirit. Here's a card with my private numbers. Feel free to personally call me anytime, day or night. Leave a message." A squeeze of the shoulders. "Now let's all get out of here. Those TV people are making me nervous."

SOMEWHERE BETWEEN MILTON AND BAGDAD

A '72 Comet rolled into the lot of Ed'z Dead Sleds.

Serge jumped out and tossed a just-chugged 7-Eleven coffee cup in the trash. "Still love those little amaretto creamers. I use five, same as sugar. Now I'm ready to rock! Are we out of the car yet? Yes, good, onward . . ."

Bear Claw was already waiting with a big smile. "You're going to love it—completely finished and ready to ride."

"You work fast," said Serge. "Just like me. It's the only way. Can't tell you how insane I get when some human snail slows me down and there's nothing I can do about it, like at a tollbooth when a driver hasn't even started looking for change yet and begins searching seat cracks or digging through a purse the size of a beach bag, then leans their elbow out the window and becomes chatty with the toll collector about directions and good places to eat nearby. When I said before there's nothing I can do about it, there's *always* something I can do. But my rule is to leave a cushion of courtesy because it's only right to help the backward kids in the class keep up with the pack, like Coleman . . ."

Coleman grinned and raised his hand.

". . . I politely wait until the toll collector points in the third different direction, and if the driver is still yapping, I gently ease up to their bumper and give it the gas for their own good. Of course their foot is on the brake, so I have to spin my tires, generating a ridiculous amount of smoke—"Off you go!"—and they shoot through the tollbooth like a Matchbox car in a Super-Charger. Hoo-wee, the look on their faces in the rearview mirror, stunned that someone would care enough to turbo-boost their lives. Remember those classic Super-Chargers? But I opted for the Matchbox suitcase instead. Long story. G.I. Joe parachuted into the manger. How much time you got?"

"Thought you were in a rush," said Bear Claw.

"Was I chatting?" Serge clapped his hands and glanced around. "Where's my baby?"

Bear Claw waved an arm. "This way."

They turned the corner of the building. Serge froze with a hand over his heart.

Bear Claw stood like a proud father. "Told you it would clean up nice. The chrome actually sparkles now. And I got the leather jacket you custom-ordered."

Serge tiptoed over and caressed his new steed. "It's the most beautiful thing I've ever seen."

"And I found someone to take your Comet in trade," said Bear Claw. "They haggled down a little on price, but—"

Serge held up a hand. "It's all good." His other hand pulled out his wallet. "Just remember to give the inside of the trunk a good scrubbing. You watch *Forensic Files*? They have microscopes."

"What?"

"We'll also need some of those radio headsets you have inside so we can talk to each other on our journey and play rebellious theme music."

Bear Claw chuckled. "Sorry for being annoyed the other day. You're a little on the eccentric side but the enthusiasm is, well, contagious. I watched the movie again last night and it's even better than I'd remembered."

"I made Coleman watch it again last night, too," said Serge. "It's a perfect film, like *Citizen Kane*."

"Actually, there's a big blooper at the beginning," said Coleman.

"You're talkin' crazy," said Serge.

"No, really. When they sell all that cocaine to the rich guy by the airport, they didn't keep any for themselves."

"Phil Spector, for those playing along. And that's not a blooper!"

"It most definitely is. Anyone knows that coke gets stepped on at every stage. The buyer expects it and is almost insulted if you don't. Those cats could easily have scraped off a few grams, tossed in some baby powder—"

"Shut up!" yelled Serge. "I'm not listening to this blasphemy!"

Coleman stared down and kicked dirt with the toe of a sneaker. "Destroyed the realism for me."

Serge scooped currency from his wallet. "Been a pleasure doing business."

Bear Claw tucked the cash in his jeans. "I'll run inside and get the rest of your stuff."

Coleman looked over at the chopper and scratched his tummy. "The motorcycle didn't look like this in the movie."

"Necessary adjustment for the local market."

Bear Claw returned with an armload. "Here are your helmets, the radio headsets, and make sure this jacket fits."

Serge slipped it on. "Like a glove."

"You've inspired me," said Bear Claw. "Soon as I get a few days, I'm hitting the road. Where you guys off to now?"

"Several answers," said Serge, handing a helmet to Coleman. "Geographically, we're tooling east across the Panhandle on Route Ninety, small towns all the way to Live Oak. Philosophically, the *Easy Rider* ethos. We're hippies now."

"But you have short hair."

"That makes us more radical." Serge donned his helmet. "Society now mocks hippies as obsolete self-caricatures, like all those people in the eighties who wore Michael Jackson *Thriller* jackets. But there's something to be said for a naive optimism that you can change the world with positive energy and lawn darts."

Bear Claw nodded. "Then you get older, have kids and bills to pay."

"Which leads to the third and most important

reason for our pilgrimage." Serge threw his right leg over the low-slung seat and grabbed the handlebars. "Politically, we're on a search for what in God's name happened to the American Dream. The gap between the rich and the rest of us is now the Grand Canyon, and our pursuit of happiness has been swapped for a white-knuckled struggle not to celebrate our seventieth birthday on the side of the road spinning a cardboard sign."

"Tell me about it," said Bear Claw.

Serge turned on the engine and gunned the throttle. "I'm so jazzed! This is like the beginning of the movie!"

Bear Claw smiled. "Aren't you forgetting something?"

"That's right!" Serge held up his left hand. "After Fonda climbs on his new chopper to head out for the first time, he symbolically discards a symbol of the plastic society, abandoning time and choosing to live in the moment."

As in the film, Serge removed his wristwatch and threw it on the ground. He grabbed the handlebars again. He looked back at the ground. He leaped off the bike, retrieved his watch and got back on.

"What about the symbolism?"

"My symbols can't be late for appointments," said Serge. "Plus I found a new symbol for what divides all of us from the top one percent. It's something everyone else enjoys like crazy, but you'll never, ever see a billionaire do."

"What's that?"

"Eat a Dorito taco." Serge raised a knowing eye of brotherhood. "Think about it. And no flavored potato chips either, because the rich are allergic to anything with a taste supplied by chemical dust that sticks to your fingers in the way the rest of us have grown to know and love . . . Come on, Coleman. Let's get tacos!"

Bear Claw waved as they roared off down the highway.

Chapter TEN

WOBBLY

The sturdiest building in town was the bank, built in 1919 across the street from city hall. It had a clock tower. Tiny spikes on the roof fixed the pigeon situation.

As with many such small-town banks from that era, it became something else. An art gallery in 1987, then an antiquarian bookstore, a showroom for Persian rugs, and a restaurant with private dining in the vault. Now it was a bank again. It had just opened for the morning.

A collection of wooden chairs sat in the lobby. A table with magazines. The chairs were filled with unhurried men reading newspapers, drinking coffee and chewing toothpicks. Overalls and grungy caps advertising tractors.

Big-city banks tend to frown on loitering, but here it was more like getting a haircut or a slice of pie: a community gathering spot for gossip and politics. Most of the gang was present: Vernon, Jabow, Clem, Otis, Harlan. Their job of running the city involved a frantic schedule of racing from one location to another and looking laid-back for the tourists: the bank, the diner, the rib joint, sitting in a row in front of Shorty's Garage. It was amazing how many visitors stopped to take their photos at the garage, because they deliberately framed themselves in perfect optical composition under the window with the fan belts. A consultant got a hooker for that.

The conversation this morning touched on all the day's high points.

"Yup."

"Mmm-hmm."

"Hoo-wee."

Pfffffft. "Ahhhhhhhh."

"Did you just fart?"

Actually there had been a rare piece of real city business earlier in the morning that found the group gathered on the side of the highway, staring skyward in disbelief.

"Triple-A put up a billboard saying we're a speed trap?"

"When did this happen?"

"Probably over the weekend."

"They can't do that!"

"Apparently they have."

"No problem," said Jabow. "I'll get the boys to come out tonight with a can of gasoline."

Vernon shook his head. "Already suggested that

to Pratchett over the phone. He pointed out some problems. More like shouted them."

"So we do nothing?"

Vernon's head shook again. "Ryan said we can always put up our own sign."

"But theirs will still be up," said Otis. "It'll hurt business."

They looked down the road at flashing red-and-blue lights, where a half-dozen motorists who had just passed the billboard were pulled over.

"Maybe not," said Vernon. "Let's get back to our rounds."

And now they all sat in a spacious marble lobby.

A page of a newspaper turned. A lone teller sat behind the counter filing her nails.

The heavy bronze door of the bank opened. The gang looked up. A man in jeans and a plaid shirt. Red stains on his chest and stomach.

"Steve," said Vernon. "Barbecue sauce?"

"Tried it your way. Now back to utensils."

Jabow slapped an empty chair. "Join us."

"All right."

One of their newest neighbors took a seat and set down a knapsack of deceptive weight.

"Slide it over," said Vernon.

Clem grabbed a strap. "Cripes, you got rocks in here?"

Vernon hoisted it into his lap and removed a zippered deposit bag filled with checks. Then he gazed into the sack bulging with countless packs of American currency. "How much this time?"

"One-sixty and change."

"This I gotta see," said Otis, leaning over the bag. He whistled. "There's really that much in auto brokering?"

"More than people think," said Steve.

"How does it work again?" asked Clem.

"All those fancy new car dealerships will take *anything* in trade. Then they dazzle the customer: 'Give you two grand.' And the customer thinks, 'For that clunker? Hell, yeah!' But it's all built into the inflated price of the new car, and the dealer dumps the old one to an auction house. That's where I come in."

"Sort of like a livestock auction?"

"Precisely like that," said Steve. "Except scummier. You should see some of the other guys. And then I ship the junks to a bunch of dubious used car lots in Miami that sell to people with no credit."

"No credit?" Jabow crunched his eyebrows. "Those are the people most likely to lapse on payments. Doesn't sound like good business."

"It's *great* business," said Steve. "The dealers charge down payments that are more than what they gave me, so they're already ahead. And every payment the customer makes afterward is pure gravy. At that point it's almost better if they *do* lapse, because the dealership will repossess and sell it again. Either way, the customers are fleeced."

"How is that possible?" asked Clem.

"The simple math of trickle-down economics," said Steve. "It's expensive to be poor."

A round of country chuckles.

Otis glanced at the bag again. "And that's from you going to these auctions?"

"No," said Steve. "The rule in running your own business is to multiply yourself, whether it's opening more franchises or, in my case, contracting a bunch of guys to hit other auctions and go through the classifieds in small-town papers. That's where the biggest margins are. Especially when the cars aren't running and we can lowball, then make cheap repairs." He turned to Vernon. "By the way, thanks for the good word with Shorty and jumping me to the head of the line."

"That's why nobody else around here can get their cars fixed."

More mirth.

"But why so much in cash?"

"I'm guessing some of these Miami buyers are dealing under the table."

"But aren't you worried carrying all that around?" asked Clem. "I'd use an armored car."

"Extra cost," said Steve. "And creates a big target. This way . . ." He swept a hand down the front of his low-key attire. ". . . You're invisible with a dingy backpack."

"Speaking of backpack." Vernon stood. "Let's get this put away safe in the vault . . . Glenda?"

The woman looked up from her nails. She opened an unseen drawer and removed a fancy electronic machine.

"A currency counter?" asked Steve. "You didn't have it last time."

"Got one just for you," said Vernon, heaving the

bag up onto the ledge in front of the teller. "Always nice to see newcomers invest in the community."

They all sat again to chat. Steve stretched and yawned.

Clem noticed a green cross on the back of his wrist. "Didn't make you for the tattoo type."

"Youthful indiscretion."

"I got an anchor from the navy," said Otis. "But now it's all wrinkly and purple. Who knew?"

Glenda came out from behind the counter to hand Steve a receipt.

He thanked everyone and headed for the door. "Pleasure talkin' with you."

"Until next time."

The door closed.

"Interesting guy," said Jabow. "You know how we get new city types in town, and we act all friendly to their faces?"

"But we secretly hate their guts?" said Clem.

"I kind of like Steve," said Otis.

"He's a sharp one."

"Yup."

"Mmm-hmm."

Pfffft.

The back door of the bank opened. Elroy, Slow and Slower loaded the just-deposited cash into a pickup truck and headed out into the countryside.

U.S. HIGHWAY 90

The chopper raced through the towns of Chipley and Marianna. Serge adjusted the microphone on the inside of his helmet. "Coleman, sound check. One, two . . ."

"Loud and clear," said Coleman, fidgeting his butt.

Serge looked over to his right. "How does that sidecar feel?"

"A little on the tight side."

"It's either that or master the kickstand."

"It's not that tight." Coleman glanced back at his buddy. "How do you like your paint job?"

Serge stared down at a teardrop gas tank that now looked like a coconut, which matched the embroidered design on the back of his new black leather jacket. "Time for the opening tunes."

"Coming right up." Coleman pressed a button on an iPod, and harsh guitar chords filled their helmets.

"Get your motor runnin' . . ."

"Steppenwolf rules," Coleman shouted into his microphone. "I love 'Born to be Wild'! . . . One question, over."

"Roger," said Serge. "How may I feed your mind?"

"Why is the coconut on the back of your jacket wearing a cowboy hat?"

"Because *Easy Rider* was actually a Western."

"Please explain, over."

"They begin their journey with magnificent panning shots crossing the American West, while Hopper often refers to Fonda as Wyatt. And they eat lots of grub sitting around campfires. But perhaps the most emblematic moment of the horse-cum-motorcycle theme is when they stop at that rancher's hacienda to work on their bikes, and as Fonda reattaches the rear tire in the open barn, the foreground juxtaposes the rancher hammering a horseshoe on one of his mares."

Serge and Coleman crossed a bridge into the eastern time zone in a rhapsodic panning shot of western Florida: the flow of the Apalachicola, goldenrod sunlight flickering through Spanish moss, heron taking flight.

"Are we really hippies? Over."

"The late sixties were my wonder years," said Serge. "I saw the whole counter-culture evolve, but I was too young to understand. Like every Saturday my mom would take me shopping at the West Palm Beach mall, and her favorite department store was Jordan Marsh. I still thought she was trying to ditch me . . ."

"Snow-cone machine."

". . . Then one weekend everything changed. We went inside and they're playing rock music really loud against a total redecoration with posters of the Beatles and Woodstock. And throughout the store—in a surreal twist from corporate America's concept of commercializing youth trends—all these *Clockwork Orange* cubes of varying height with live go-go dancers on top. A bunch of teenagers in the store were cackling their heads off while I wandered away from my mom and stared hypnotized up at something on the wall. Turns out my mom wasn't trying to ditch me after all because she ran over and hustled me out of the store in a panic. At first I thought she freaked because I'd briefly gone missing, but she was actually terrified by the growing drug fringe saturating the news, and found me in the men's-wear department mesmerized by a black-and-white movie poster of two longhairs on motorcycles. Ever since, I've always felt I was born too late and missed out . . . So now we're heading to a special Florida place where the sixties still thrive."

"I can dig it." Coleman's helmet bobbed to the music. "We're going to stand in another field where something cool happened years ago. Or a place where old hippies who are now bums share Ripple."

"Ah, but you're wrong," said Serge. "This is a bona fide, living-and-breathing tear in the universe—unlikely located in one of the most redneck swaths of North Florida—where a new generation of flower children are vigilantly tending the eternal flame of the sixties."

"Where's that?"

"We're heading to it right now."

Serge twisted the throttle wide open, and the chopper thundered over the crest of a hill in the waning sky.

Chapter ELEVEN

LATER THAT EVENING

Another small town.

This one had a modest dusting of snow on the ground.

Nassau Street was a long road, but the buildings only went a few blocks. Barely any traffic except up at the Wawa convenience store because it was the only place to buy smokes after eleven.

A few young people strolled the sidewalk in orange down vests with cold hands buried deep in pockets, their breath visible under the moonlight. They turned into a warm doorway beneath a sign: THE TIGER TAP. Its hardwood colonial facade made it look more like a Boston tavern than something you'd find in New Jersey. A lighted marquee next to the road said they allowed karaoke on Wednesdays.

Inside, memorabilia on the walls. A poster of Russell Crowe because *A Beautiful Mind* was filmed in the town. A framed photo of movie legend

Jimmy Stewart, class of '32, and another of Brooke Shields, a more recent graduate. Variations on the tiger theme: stuffed animals, safari paintings, fake striped rug. And a felt pennant. PRINCETON.

From the stage, an off-key sound. *"You've lost that loving feeling! . . ."*

The young man concluded his performance amid a smattering of sarcastic applause. He returned to a table where two pitchers of Sam Adams were under way. More down vests hung over the backs of chairs. Jeans, polos, L.L.Bean.

"You might have just mangled that song worse than *Top Gun*," said one of the gang.

Matt didn't care. He grabbed a pen. The other five around the table had textbooks next to their beers, because Princeton didn't sleep. All working on theses. The more narrow the topic the better.

Clockwise from the end chair: "Insurance Algorithm for Self-Driving Cars," "Study of Sexual Differences in Stegosaurus Fossils," "Long-Range Entanglement of Electron Spin Ensembles," "The Use of Asymmetrical Tail-Hedging Strategies to Accumulate Wealth," and something titled "Sympathy for the Lehman Brothers."

There are plenty of reasons not to like college kids. Arrogant and entitled, clinging and wormy, the ones who drive nicer cars than their professors. But these guys were cool. Not the classic cool, like big men on campus. The easy-on-your-nerves cool. It was that Goldilocks just-right mixture of deference, confidence and long hours in the library. Matt in particular was the average of averages. Healthy weight, five-nine, short black hair, the ultimate everyman face. Matt was just athletic enough to play intramurals, but not more. Just handsome enough to have gone to his prom, but not more. Just likable enough to be likable. The only distinguishing feature was his smile. Not because it would land a toothpaste ad—just an infectious, happy-go-lucky expression that was devoid of guile. He wasn't old enough yet for life to have steam-rolled over him. But Matt's most endearing trait of all: He was constantly eager to learn from his elders.

Someone finished jotting notes and looked up from his laptop. "Still stuck on your thesis?"

"Not anymore." Matt smiled and set a plane ticket on the table.

"What?" A laugh. "You're going to take a vacation in Florida instead of writing a paper?"

"Florida *is* my thesis," said Matt.

"I thought it was the American Dream. Or rather its decline."

"That's right," said Matt. "Remember how you all told me it was too broad a topic?"

"It is fairly encompassing."

"I got the idea watching CNN last night." Matt turned his tablet's screen to face the others.

"Is that an elephant in the ocean?"

"And notice how all the people on that busy beach are strolling along like nothing's out of place," said Matt. "Some woman rented the animal for her kid's birthday party. The elephant needed cool-down breaks in the water."

"What's that got to do with your thesis?"

"Haven't you guys noticed the avalanche of weird news coming out of that state?" asked Matt.

"Sure." "All the time." "They shoot each other over texting in theaters."

"And someone else pistol-whipped a Dunkin' Donuts clerk for getting his coffee order wrong." Matt called up another item on his tablet. "The legislature also had to pass a law against using food stamps in strip clubs."

"Very amusing," said the student delving into fossil sex. "But again, the thesis?"

"There's no arguing with all the empirical data that proves the American Dream of our grandparents is a memory," said Matt. "Changing corporate cultures, merging conglomerates, corrupt campaign finance laws, and tilted tax codes have all opened a chasm between the classes. Fifty years ago, everyone was the product of post–World War Two teamwork, and companies honored the unwritten contract of mutual loyalty. If citizens worked hard and respected their employers, that respect would be returned in kind. But today, shareholders reign supreme, and too many companies are increasingly viewing workers at best as adversaries, and at worst as prey. A wholesale shaving of compensation, benefits and job security to please Wall Street. That kind of trend can't continue, so where are we heading?"

The other five shook their heads.

"Florida," said Matt. "It's already the nation's pace car of dysfunction. People laugh and think it's just chaos, but my thesis will postulate that all this bizarre behavior is the spear tip of coming effects from the national sea change. You wouldn't believe all the news stories I turned up about people throwing feces down there."

"But that's just crazy people acting crazy," said the Lehman Brothers advocate. "They're not holding signs demanding better pay or tax reform."

"Who's to say that the coming crash will look rational?" said Matt. "I believe Florida has become the classic canary in a coal mine. It just might be showing us the first signs of a new dissociative syndrome."

"Have to admit you've sufficiently narrowed the topic," said the self-driving car expert. "Excrement trajectories of the disintegrating social contract."

"I'm leaving tomorrow." Matt grabbed the plane ticket.

"And go where?"

Matt turned his iPad around again. "Found this great website."

They leaned closer. "Looks like some kind of kooky travel tour."

"I think it's supposed to look that way," said Matt. "But once you really unpack the site, it's crammed full of academic data and cultural treatises that most tenured professors would envy. I believe he's deliberately appearing wacky in order to make dry history lessons more entertaining and digestible, like a movie where Robin Williams plays an unconventional teacher at odds with the administration but who connects with his students through madcap antics and clown noses."

"Do we need to cut you off from the beer?"

"No, really," said Matt. "This guy must be one of the leading experts on Florida because only a bone-deep knowledge could have produced this website."

"Or he could be just another nut job down there. You have no proof he's a real professor."

"Has to be," said Matt, pulling up a photo on his tablet. "Here he is with an automatic pistol, planting a flag in Louisiana to reclaim the Republic of West Florida."

"Nothing weird there."

"It's his teaching technique to champion heritage studies," said Matt. "Otherwise it *would* be unhinged behavior. If anyone can help me with my thesis, it's him."

"So you've gotten in touch and set up an interview?"

Matt shook his head. "No e-mail or any other contact info on the site."

"Then you're just going to roam around the third biggest state in the country and hope to randomly bump into him?"

Matt tapped some more on his tablet. "I think I'm getting into the rhythm of the lessons. His current academic project is a road trip through small towns to quantify the American Dream—which is how I first found him in the search engines. I'll just have to pick up his trail and anticipate the next stop."

MIDNIGHT

The proverbial sidewalks had been rolled up. Founders' Day banners fluttered lazily in the dark.

A light breeze through the trees. Eerily quiet. The only traffic signal blinked yellow.

A lone pair of headlights rounded the corner and rolled slowly up Main Street. It parked against a curb at an expired meter. A "Closed" sign hung in a nearby window.

Knock, knock, knock.

The door to Lead Belly's opened.

"Peter! Thanks for coming by!" Vernon changed his expression. "You look a little upset."

"I'm beyond upset! And what's with all the cloak and dagger, meeting here in the middle of the night?"

Another voice: "Peter, why don't you come over and take a seat?"

Peter squinted toward the back of the empty restaurant and a dark silhouette. "Senator?"

Vernon led the way and pulled out a pair of chairs. A bottle of Johnnie Walker Black sat on the table. Pratchett poured a generous glass and slid it across the wood. "Have a drink."

"I don't want a drink."

"It's not about want. You *need* a drink," said Pratchett. "You were practically hysterical when you called."

"How would you expect me to react?"

"I don't know," said the senator. "I'm not sure what's going on."

"Because you cut me off and said we had to meet in person."

"The conversation seemed to be drifting into terrain that we don't discuss over the phone."

"This is too shady for me."

"Nothing's shady," said Pratchett. "It's just that if you're in politics long enough, you become a cautious person." He glanced down at the table. "Now, your drink."

Vernon raised his own glass. "Go ahead, it'll do you good."

Peter took a tentative sip and made a face.

The other men laughed and knocked back their own liquor in a single pull.

"Finish it," said Pratchett. "All at once. It'll go down easier that way."

Peter paused with the glass in front of his mouth.

"Everything's going to be fine." Vernon patted him on the back. "We're neighbors now. We take care of our own around here."

"You're among friends," said Pratchett.

Peter took a deep breath and upended his glass, then began coughing his brains out.

"Much better," said the senator. "Now, why don't you back up and tell me what this is all about?"

Peter rubbed watering eyes. "I turned in my geology report as usual, and went back out to the construction site today because we left some equipment. And when I arrived, it was so odd. There were all these workers and flatbed trucks full of concrete blocks and roof trusses."

"Right, we're building homes," said Pratchett. "It would be odd if they weren't there."

"But my report recommended *against* building."

"What?" Pratchett said in surprise.

"The substrata is totally inappropriate."

"That's not what was in your report."

"And that's what I was trying to tell you on the phone," said Peter. "That wasn't my report."

"But they faxed me a copy," said the senator. "I have it right here. You signed the bottom."

"I know that's my signature. I got a copy, too. It's a totally different report."

"I'm confused," said Vernon. "Are you trying to tell us that someone altered your findings?"

"Yes!"

The senator leaned back in his chair. "Now I understand why you're so upset. This is extremely disturbing news. I'm going to get to the bottom of this."

"I'm outraged," said Vernon. "And you did the right thing by coming to us with it."

"You haven't told anyone else, have you?" asked Pratchett.

Peter shook his head. "You're the first. I was too rattled to call my company. I could lose my job."

"Nobody's losing any job," the senator said calmly. "But you need to do exactly as I say. Don't speak a word of this to anyone until my people can discreetly look into it."

"But what about the subdivision?" asked Peter.

"What about it?"

"They have to stop building."

"Now hold on," said Vernon. "We still don't

know what we have here, and a stoppage would cost thousands a day. A lot of the investors are neighbors like you and me."

"He's right," said the senator. "What if you're wrong?"

"I'm not wrong!" said Peter. "The limestone has a high-risk coefficient."

"But the project's already a go."

"Based on a falsified report," said Peter. "You saw what happened to the model home."

"Let me phrase this a different way." The senator held out his palms. "Can you guarantee there will be problems with the homes we're building?"

"Nobody can guarantee that, but—"

"Well, there you go," said Vernon. "Why worry about what might never happen?"

"But—"

"And if something does happen," said Pratchett, "we'll simply make good. I hear your company has special repair techniques: pumping stuff in the ground, compression, piers, but you know all that technical stuff much better than us."

"You don't build and plan on remediation," said Peter. "You just don't build."

"Now we're going backwards," said Vernon. "Believe what we're telling you and relax."

"But—"

"But what?"

"They used that report to get the insurers to underwrite," said Peter. "It could end my career. I've even heard of guys going to prison for fraud . . ."

Pratchett moved his foot and felt something strange. He glanced down and thought: *Shit*.

A HALF HOUR EARLIER

Knock, knock, knock.

The door to Lead Belly's opened.

"Gus, come on in!"

"We've got serious problems," said the insurance man. "Someone screwed us but good."

"Wait, what are you talking about?"

"The geology report was switched," said Gus. "I underwrote a piece of shit, but you're in even worse shape, exposed to a bunch of lawsuits. Must be one of the investors who did it."

"You're hitting us with a lot at once," said Pratchett. "Why don't you have a seat and go over this slowly?"

"I prefer to stand," said Gus. "I won't be here long. I'm going to the authorities."

"Then I hope you don't mind if *I* sit."

"Just wanted to come by and give you a heads-up," said Gus. "Because this could hurt you politically. We're talking fraud."

"Are you sure?"

He pulled folded pages from his back pocket. "Got copies of both reports from a friend I have on the inside. We need to get out ahead of this. If we can prove who did it, we might be able to walk away unscathed."

"You're right," said Pratchett. "This *is* bad. And it definitely would hurt me at the polls. You did the right thing coming to us."

"Did you tell anyone else?" asked Vernon.

"Not yet," said Gus, turning toward the door. "Like I mentioned, fair warning."

"Wait!" said the senator. "Okay, I always hate to appear weak, but this could do more than a little political harm. I could lose my seat."

"What are you saying?"

"That I need a big favor."

"I'm not holding back on this," said Gus. "I got a family."

"All I'm asking is a few days until I can look into this and prepare a public relations defense."

Gus shook his head. "Since I already know, that would add obstruction of justice to my pile of crap."

"Then let's balance the scales," said Pratchett.

"What's that supposed to mean?"

"A lot of money is in the lurch," said Vernon.

"There's plenty to go around," said Pratchett.

Gus paused and looked at each of them. "Are you offering me a bribe?"

"Oh, no, no, no! A consulting fee."

"I don't think we should talk anymore without lawyers present." He began leaving again.

"Gus!" shouted the senator. "Cards on the table. Two hundred thousand."

The insurance man turned. "Two hundred?"

"I'm desperate," said Pratchett. "Please?"

Gus just stared.

The senator searched his eyes. "Is that a yes or no?"

Gus slowly began backing up. He raised a shaking arm and pointed. "You!"

"Me?"

"How could I have been so naive?" said Gus. "Of course! It was you all along! And to think I came here worried about *your* career!"

"That's absurd," said Pratchett. "You need to calm down before you do something you'll regret."

"Hell with this town! I'm out of here!" He ran toward the door.

Vernon lunged and tackled the underwriter. They rolled across the floor. Gus soon got the upper hand, and Vernon felt his left arm twisted behind his back. "I could use a little assistance down here."

Pratchett stared stupefied. "How on earth did this get so fucked up?"

"Any time now," said Vernon.

Pratchett ran over and pulled Gus off the mayor, wrapping his arms around the insurance man from behind. Gus furiously pedaled backward and slammed the senator into the bar. "Ow, mother—"

Vernon raced forward to punch him in the stomach, but Gus kicked him in the crotch first. The mayor doubled over. Wrestling continued. The senator and underwriter ended up on top of the bar, then crashed behind it. "Vernon! He's stronger than he looks! Get over here!"

"One second." The mayor ran through the restaurant's swinging doors to the kitchen. He urgently looked one way and the other—"Ah-ha!"—bolting over to a thick wooden table where the ribs were prepared.

"Vernon, where'd you go?"

"Be right there!"

He dashed out of the kitchen and dove behind the bar. "You son of a bitch!" Swinging down hard, again and again.

Pratchett squirmed out from under the insurance man. "Finally!"

"Here," said Vernon. "I brought one for you, too."

"That's mighty neighborly." Pratchett began swinging. "Take that, cocksucker!"

The swinging continued until both were exhausted.

"Think he's dead?" asked Vernon.

"Most definitely."

"Let's make sure."

"No harm, no foul."

Chop, chop, chop, chop . . .

Knock, knock, knock.

The two men jumped up from behind the bar and froze with big eyes, holding bloody meat cleavers in silence.

Knock, knock, knock.

"Who can that be?"

"Damn," said Pratchett. "I forgot we told Peter to meet us."

"You got some blood on your shirt."

"We'll kill most of the lights and sit in the corner."

Knock, knock, knock.

"Coming . . ."

BACK TO THE PRESENT

Pratchett looked up from the floor and the spreading pool of blood seeping beneath the bar. A countdown clock had begun to tick. "I'm sorry, Peter. You were saying?"

"That I could go to prison." He crossed his hands over a queasy stomach. "Maybe I should just go to the authorities. Then it's all on the record in real time, and they can't come after me."

Vernon and the senator exchanged glances. The blood crept closer to Peter's chair.

The geologist leaned toward the senator. "What's on your shirt?"

"Barbecue sauce. They ran out of lobster bibs."

Vernon grabbed Peter's arm.

"What are you doing? That hurts."

Pratchett shook his head vigorously.

Vernon released his grip. "Sorry, just trying to be reassuring."

The blood reached the near leg of Peter's chair. The countdown clock entered James Bond warhead-disarming territory.

"Peter," said Pratchett. "When we mentioned earlier that you were among friends, you're among something even better now: *powerful* friends. There's a whole world operating on a level you've never seen. We won't ever let anything happen to you."

"Trust us." Vernon checked his watch. "And get some sleep."

The liquor was now working. "Thanks. You've made me feel a lot better." Peter stood and stretched. He began taking a step into the bloody slick.

Vernon yanked him from behind. "This way."

"What?"

"It's shorter."

"No, it's not."

"I misjudged," said Vernon. "But since you're already going this direction . . ."

They escorted him out the door and closed it.

"Jesus!" said Vernon, fastening locks. "I thought he'd never leave."

"Let's get that body out of here."

The pair walked behind the bar and stared down, gauging weight and volume.

"Your thoughts?" asked Pratchett.

Ten minutes later, the pair strolled down a quiet sidewalk under a row of silk flags. A traffic light blinked yellow as they crossed the street.

"I don't know about Peter," said Vernon. "Seems shaky."

"Just keep tabs on him."

They reached the other side of the road and headed down into the woods, each holding a handle of a large wheelbarrow.

"What a night."

Chapter TWELVE

A gleaming chopper with a coconut gas tank rode loud and proud over the hills of North Florida.

"Radio check," said Serge.

"Coleman here, over."

"Another thing that pisses me off about the Internet," said Serge. "I'll see something a stupid criminal did in Fort Lauderdale, so I click to read the article, and instead I have to watch a video. And I can't even watch the video because first I have to watch a commercial for cold cream."

"I don't even know what cold cream is."

"Neither do I," said Serge. "But it's out there and people are doing it. And apparently it's now even more refreshing, so I also have to investigate that, and then I finally get to the story."

"What was it about?"

"This burglar broke into a house and thought he was disabling the alarm system, but instead he disabled the thermostat, so not only did he get arrested but he was sweaty."

"Why are we stopping?"

"Another small town," said Serge. "Small towns are the best! Barefoot kids bringing home a string of catfish, an old theater on Main Street that plays *one* movie on *one* big screen, Esso and Enco gas signs, water tower that wants you to know about the high school Fighting Argonauts, handwritten notes in store windows for free kittens, faith circles and fill dirt."

"I'm still amazed you're so into small towns."

"This one's called Monticello, twenty miles east of Tallahassee." Serge grabbed his camera. "Its showpiece is the Perkins Opera House, built in 1890. Who would imagine that in this little speck of population surrounded by vast ruralness is one of the oldest, most famous—and still operating— opera houses in all the Southeast? Outside life is too fast; in order to notice such gems, you need to get in cadence with the beat of these little communities and slow way, *way* down."

Serge took a rapid burst of photos and screeched away.

"Radio check," said Coleman. "I thought we were going inside that old building."

"Negative," said Serge. "I love opera houses, yet I hate opera. The key in my climb for the top is to keep everyone guessing."

They continued eastbound over another hill on Highway 90 and the road opened up.

Serge's helmet rotated left to right. "This is the

part of the journey that really unwinds my head. The first few times you see *Easy Rider*, you're watching it for the story. But after enough viewings you start to *look* at the movie, and you realize the cinematography is one long love letter to America. Sweeping panoramas of western mountains, mesas, prairies and old-style truss bridges over canyons."

"Then it got better when they pulled over and smoked weed."

"This is *our* panorama." Serge's eyes scanned back the other way. "There are lots of fantastic scenic drives along the ocean, but this is a part of the state where you have to stop and remember to dig it: Florida's big-sky country, rolling hills and farms and sprawling beds of those lavender and harvest-yellow wildflowers in an intoxicating oil-painting palette like a Monet come to life. When I was a kid, bumblebees whizzed around those flowers, and one of my uncles said you could catch a bee in your cupped hands, and as long as you kept shaking them, the bee would rattle around and couldn't sting you."

"Did you try it?" asked Coleman.

"Stung me right away and hurt like a bastard," said Serge. "The sixties were all about the lies."

The pair rumbled on down the endless ribbon of tar. Coleman bent over in the sidecar with his lighter. They approached a county line.

Serge pushed his helmet microphone toward his mouth. "Better lower that joint. See what's ahead on the side of the road?"

Coleman looked up at a big blue traffic sign with an illustration of handcuffs: ZERO DRUG TOLERANCE. He leaned back down. "What a joke."

"Get serious," said Serge. "A lot of the highway patrol cars in these parts are canine units. You think they're just dog lovers?"

"I'm not disagreeing about that." Coleman took a hard drag on a one-hitter. "It's just that they're unknowingly tipping off stoners that drugs are actually readily available."

Serge glanced over at the sidecar. "What are you talking about?"

"The kinds of rural counties with anti-drug signs are the same places where you're most likely to find country gas stations selling bath salts in Scooby-Doo packets."

"Bath salts?"

"Synthetic designer drugs that act like coke and uppers." Coleman pocketed his tiny pipe. "The white crystals look like bath salts, and they're labeled 'not for human consumption' to avoid arrest. Those salts will mess you up! The kids love 'em."

"That's terrible!" said Serge. "But obviously law enforcement's hands are tied or they'd do something."

"Wrong again," said Coleman. "They don't even need to be concerned about the contents of the packets or drug laws. They can seize everything and make arrests for counterfeit goods and trademark infringement because of the licensed cartoon characters on the labels to attract kids. It's just like if a cop sees cheap handbags on a corner in New York that say Gucci: Into the back of the squad car you go!"

Serge scratched his forehead under his helmet visor. "How come you can suddenly sound so smart when— . . . Forget it. I already know the answer."

Twenty minutes later, Serge and Coleman rumbled alongside the tracks of the Seaboard Coast Line Railroad. The speed limit dropped again as they entered a town of 837 souls.

"Where are we?" asked Coleman.

"Greenville." Serge swung the chopper south off the highway and cranked up the music in their helmets.

". . . Hit the road, Jack! . . ."

Thin tires crossed train tracks and rolled through the kind of quiet, tree-shaded residential area that didn't have sidewalks.

Greenville was definitely green. Lots of lush trees and lawns and decorative shrubs showcasing sun-parched old wooden homes with rusty tin roofs. Bright clothes drying on lines, bicycles against utility poles. A fifty-five-gallon barrel on concrete blocks burned trash. A beach umbrella stood over another charred metal barrel, where more smoke rose from lunch being grilled for the whole block. Then an abandoned pickup truck sinking into the earth, its decay toward ugliness having bottomed out, and, now that nature was reclaiming it with grass and vines, becoming kind of pretty, if you're into that sort of thing.

"Radio check," said Coleman. "I haven't seen a place like this before."

"Greenville is a historic African-American town," said Serge. "As southern and rural as they come. The economy definitely isn't here, but they more than make up for it with pride and beautification. You can't help but feel the bonds of community."

He pulled the motorcycle off the side of the road to check a map.

A junky El Dorado came the other way and stopped in the street. The driver leaned out the open window. "Can I help you guys find anything?"

"As a matter of fact you can." Serge held out his map and told him.

The old man pointed backward. "Keep going that way until you come to the stop sign. If you think you've gone too far—don't. There's only one stop sign, way, way down. Then take a right and follow it to the bend. But don't take the bend. There's a road on the other side and you'll see it."

"Appreciate the courtesy." Serge stowed his map and took off.

More old houses and freshly cut grass. In the middle of the homes was another small building with another tin roof, this one concrete and lime green. Bare four-by-fours held up a weathered porch roof below a sign: H&R GROCERS. There was an air pump and a row of three retired guys sitting against the front of the building and liking it.

The old man's directions were spot-on. After the second right turn, Serge rolled a short distance to a stop at street address number 443. Just off the shoulder stood a compact four-room wooden house with a chimney and simple open deck with rocking chairs.

Serge removed his helmet. "You're in for a real treat."

"Whose house is this?"

"Glad you asked! From 1930 to 1935, it was the childhood home of the legendary Ray Charles, before his sight failed and he was sent to the Florida School for the Deaf and Blind in Saint Augustine."

"Ray Charles?" said Coleman. "I thought he was from Georgia."

Serge grimaced and pounded a fist on the coconut gas tank. "It's like Allman Brothers déjà vu all over again! Duane and Gregg were from Daytona, and Ray was from Greenville!"

"Easy now," said Coleman. "You're in a small town."

A camera clicked at a street sign: RAY CHARLES AVENUE. The motorcycle sped off.

They crossed the train tracks again and took Grand Avenue through downtown Greenville, which was a block long: connecting brick buildings with some of the windows bricked up.

Hardware store, closed pharmacy with mortar and pestle over the door, antiques place selling an ancient rust-streaked sign for TALLAHASSEE MOTOR HOTEL. PHONES, POOL, TV.

They turned the corner at Ike's Bait and Tackle, which had branched into the deli business and featured a drawing of a rattlesnake, the mascot of the traditionally black Florida A&M University. Then another small building whose entire front was a roll-down metal door below block letters that said FIRE DEPT and appeared to be out of business. The VFW hall advertised free breakfast for veterans. Serge stopped across the street.

"Where are we now?" asked Coleman.

"Hayes Park, the town center, a magnificent open space surrounding that tranquil lake. Playground, picnic area, and something few others have. A great place to slow down." Serge took off running.

Coleman caught up as his buddy aimed a camera at a bronze statue of a man in sunglasses playing the keyboard near the children's slides. "I must touch Ray. You touch him, too . . . Our work here is done." He took off back to the motorcycle. Coleman was barely able to jump in the sidecar before Serge screeched off and cranked up the stereo.

". . . *C.C. Rider!* . . ."

More hills and clouds went by.

"Radio check," said Coleman. "Can we take a break? All this slowing down is making me tired."

"We're about to take a very long break up ahead."

"Another small town?"

"Live Oak, established 1858 at the junction of two major rail lines." The chopper approached a bridge and passed a sign containing musical notes.

"What river are we crossing?"

"The Suwannee."

"Like in the song?"

"The same."

"Aren't you saying it wrong?" asked Coleman.

"No, I'm pronouncing it right. Su-wann-ee." Serge gazed over the side of the bridge at a winding, tea-colored tributary. "It's three syllables. But in 1851, Stephen Foster needed a two-syllable name of a river for his song, so he looked at a map and just lopped off part of the historic name like we're North Korea."

"Fuck that shit," said Coleman.

"My sentiments exactly," said Serge. "And then of all things it became our state song."

"Not good?"

"Have you ever heard the original words? It's titled 'Old Folks at Home' and was a minstrel song sung by a slave yearning for the plantation life. But aside from the controversy, there are so many better artists to choose from."

"Led Zeppelin!"

"Let's try to stay focused," said Serge. "Yes, the heavy-metal lads from Britain did play the long-since-closed Pirate's World amusement park in Dania in 1969—which I still can't get my head around—but the orgasm section of 'Whole Lotta Love' might be a hard sell to the legislature. We need someone more palatable."

"Like who?"

"Ray Charles," said Serge. "'Georgia on My Mind' was good enough for that state's leaders. Can you imagine the Florida Senate swaying to 'Unchain My Heart'?"

"That would rule!"

"One can only hope."

"Serge, my tummy's making those sounds again."

"And I need coffee. Here's a convenience store."

They pulled past gas pumps that still had mechanical numbers. Signs in the window advertised tomatoes, a charity car wash and Newports. Serge went straight for a round glass pot with a burnt aroma. He stared down inside. "Still good." Coleman loaded up on Snickers and Baby Ruths.

The door opened. A neatly pressed khaki uniform came inside.

Serge glanced furtively, then whispered the other way: "Coleman, be cool. It's a sheriff's deputy . . . *Coleman!*" Serge snatched a Scooby-Doo packet from his hands. "No bath salts for you!"

"Crap."

THAT NIGHT

A power outage in Calusa County left most of the alarm clocks blinking 12:00, but it was really closer to three. The moon lit up a piece of decorative latticework that lay on the ground next to the crawl space where it had been pried loose.

"*Shhhhh!*"

"*You shhhh!*"

"*Don't shhhh'sh me!*"

"Will you assholes be quiet? It's hard enough crawling under here as it is."

"Who cares? It's Jabow's house."

"And he doesn't like to be woken!"

"Then why not come out here during the day?"

"Duh! Because people might see what we're doing. You want to work your way up in this town or not?"

The trio continued slithering under the home and dragging a duffel bag as a tiny flashlight led the way. Elroy, Slow and Slower.

"Why can't I ever get the flashlight?"

"Because you're slow!"

"How much farther?"

"Three more floor joists, maybe four," said Elroy.

"I never noticed this before."

"What?"

"So these pipes are how they do plumbing?" said Slower. "I always wondered what happened after it went through the floor."

Elroy blinked hard. "Please stop talking."

They crawled in silence. Slower reached up to touch a toilet line, but decided not to comment.

"There's the spot."

"Where?"

"That beam I marked," said Elroy. "How many times have you been here?"

"Ten or five."

"Just start digging."

Three small camping shovels went to work.

"Are there snakes?"

"What about scorpions?"

"I'd be more worried about Jabow," said Elroy. "You know his temper."

"Why doesn't he just let us hide it *in* his house?"

"Because of something called a search warrant, you idiot."

"Why doesn't he bury it himself?"

"You two suddenly have a thirst for knowledge?"

"I'm just saying we're always the ones getting dirty."

"Because he and Vernon are at the top. And once you're there, it's easy lifting and sleeping in clean sheets. You assign all the filthy jobs to the young guys at the bottom who—and I may only be speaking for myself here—want to make their bones and reach the top themselves. Wouldn't you like to sit at the big table in Lead Belly's someday?"

"Heck, yeah."

"Then shut up and keep digging!"

A few more minutes and then, "I think I hit something." The shovels were cast aside and bare hands swept soil off the top of the discovery. "Yeah, it's where we buried the last shipment."

"Start unloading."

They reached into the duffel bag from the bank, grabbing large, waterproof bricks of tightly wrapped hundred-dollar bills. The new packs were piled on top of all the previously buried ones, which went down into the ground who knew how far.

Chapter THIRTEEN

THE NEXT DAY

The coconut chopper rolled into a time-frozen town and down another main street of brick storefronts and bygone lamp posts. It slowed near the junction with another highway. Serge planted his feet on the ground at a traffic light and aimed his camera up at the verdigris dome of a clock tower. *Click, click, click.* "The Suwannee County courthouse, built 1904, which means this is our turn."

The light became green. Serge hung a lazy left and gunned the throttle north on Highway 129.

"Radio check," said Coleman. "What's our next stop?"

"A big one." The chopper raced under an interstate overpass. "Remember I mentioned a spot where the sixties were still alive and kicking in Florida?"

"Nope."

"And in the most unlikely place," said Serge. "We're up here near the Georgia line, out in the sticks, the deepest part of the Bible Belt. As far as the eye can wander in every direction: red state and rednecks."

"Not that there's anything wrong with that."

"Absolutely not," said Serge. "They're free to play for their team, and I respect that."

"It's just a lifestyle choice, after all."

"Actually they were born that way, so you can't be prejudiced," said Serge. "In fact I've come to accept that I'm part redneck."

"Which part?"

"The genetic marker that likes to see things blow up. I'm just illustrating what an extreme anomaly of geographical culture this upcoming place is," said Serge. "Like finding Santana playing the Alamo."

"A bunch of cars are slowing down."

"That's our destination." Serge hit his blinker.

The chopper eased off the highway and through a wooded entrance with a sign:

Spirit of the Suwannee.

The surrounding fields were crammed with every kind of parked vehicle, from late-model Jeeps to VW microbuses. Trickles of people dripped from various origins and formed a single human river. The narrowness of the chopper allowed Serge to pass through. People waved cheerfully and flashed peace signs.

"This is unreal," said Coleman. "Look at all these young people. And they're all cool!"

"It's like that footage from the Woodstock movie of massive throngs coming up the road." Serge chugged the caffeine dregs from his travel mug. "I'm getting goose bumps looking around. Hundreds of kids in tie-dyed shirts, American-flag pants, Jamaican knitted caps, and flowers everywhere: in their hair, hanging from their necks, painted on their cheeks."

Coleman pointed. "I dig that one babe with a wreath on her head, wearing a bikini top, cutoff jeans and boots, doing the hula hoop."

"It's a magical place."

"But what *is* this place?" asked Coleman.

"A giant campground in the middle of nowhere that holds dozens of weekend-long music fests each year. It's so remote, the kids are free to be themselves." They parked the motorcycle and grabbed knapsacks of luggage hanging from the back. "This weekend's jamboree is called the Purple Hatters Ball."

"What's that?"

"In memory of Rachel Morningstar Hoffman, this fun-loving, footloose hippie chick who was a student at Florida State University, the kind of daughter any parent would love to have. She inspired an act of the legislature called Rachel's Law."

"Explain?"

"She smoked some pot and got busted."

"But it was college."

"Exactly." Serge led Coleman to the back of a long line. "Now, you know what a huge supporter of law enforcement I am. But every once in a while a few of them will go a bit cowboy. So in a plea deal completely out of whack with her transgression, they said they'd drop the charges if she made an undercover buy, and sent her out with thirteen thousand dollars to score a bunch of cocaine and a gun from these really bad dudes. Did not end well."

"That's awful."

"But out here her spirit lives on." Serge shuffled forward toward the ticket booth. "Rachel was known for her irrepressible smile and fondness for big floppy purple hats. Every year they host this festival."

Serge crouched down in a starting position like a track star.

"What are you doing?" asked Coleman.

"Only one more person ahead of us in line."

"And he's leaving."

Serge lunged at the counter with an open wallet. "Two tickets to the sixties, please. I need my wonder years. Only three channels and no remote control, sitting in a box with Tang till two a.m., national anthem, prayer, fade to static. Today, YouTube has shifted the collective consciousness from moon landings to elevator beat-downs. But the sixties ruled in every way except musicians choking on their own vomit. The squares always bring that up, but the fifties had separate drinking fountains, which more than outweighs spit-up." He checked his wristwatch. "What time is the Age of Aquarius? I can't wait! I've never actually seen love steer the stars!"

"Uh, do you want tickets?"

"Yes! That's what I've been talking about this whole time." Serge forked over cash. "I've rededicated my entire life to being a hippie."

"But you have short hair."

"That makes me more radical." Serge snatched the stubs, then noticed a stack of souvenirs behind the counter. "*Ooo! Ooo!*" He opened his wallet again . . .

The pair hoisted knapsacks and joined the sea of latter-day flower children heading into the park. Leather-fringed vests, bandannas, bell-bottoms, maxi dresses. Some held up tall sticks, literally flying freak flags.

"Serge," said Coleman. "You look funny in that floppy purple hat."

"You do, too," said Serge. "That's the beauty of all this. The youthful joy of being foolish."

They arrived at a row of cabins.

"I thought we were going to camp."

"Right, indoors. Never let others define your camping," said Serge. "I made a reservation online and there should be a key under the mat. Drop your gear inside, then meet me back at the golf cart."

"Golf cart?"

"Comes with the cabin. The noise of the chopper would shatter this tranquillity."

Moments later, they zipped off with silent electric power.

"Man, I can't believe what I'm seeing," said Coleman. "This is heaven. What are those kids doing in that field?"

"Yoga circle. That's the *Karate Kid* position."

The cart headed up the incline of a hiking path. On both sides of the trail, psychedelic-colored dome tents sprouted like mushrooms throughout the woods. Young people lounged in canvas chairs drinking Mountain Dew and munching granola bars.

"I thought this was all gone," said Coleman.

"Me, too." The cart struggled over a rocky crest. "People are always pooh-poohing today's youth, but this is the *anti*–spring break. No beer funnels, destroyed motel rooms or guys demanding to see tits like it's a birthright."

They passed another campsite with a giant flag of the African continent that said: COME CHILL. The path ended at a high embankment, and Serge climbed out onto an overlook, surveying a mighty river.

"Is this the Mississippi?" asked Coleman.

"The Suwannee, you knucklehead."

"That would make more sense."

"Let's go to the cabin and prep our staging area for tonight's concert."

"Now you're talking!"

The golf cart headed back down, much faster this time, hopping rocks and potholes. They swung by the country store to load up on provisions. More kids shot peace signs and toted bouquets of balloons. When the cart approached the cabin, a young man was out front by the road, sitting on a backpack.

The duo smiled as they passed him and headed up the driveway.

From behind: "*Serge?*"

Serge hit the brake pedal and turned curiously. "Do I know you?"

"No."

"Then how'd you know my name?"

"Tracked you down." He walked over and extended a hand. "Just came all the way from New Jersey. Name's Matt."

Chapter FOURTEEN

Towering glass-and-chrome condos had just surpassed business high-rises for dominance of the city skyline. They were clustered downtown, and south in Brickell, and north along Bayshore overlooking Biscayne.

The sun was setting as track lighting illuminated the forty-eighth floor of one such tower, which was the top. Almost everything in the penthouse purposely white: leather sofas, bar stools, cabinets, area rugs. The rest of the space remained minimal. Some artwork: impressionism, watercolors, signed lithographs. A shelf of rare first editions. Saltwater aquarium that included an octopus.

In the middle of the room sat a long, low coral table, where a pair of aspiring actresses cut lines of white powder. The two other people in the room, men with strong arms and semiautomatic pistols in shoulder slings, sat in chairs on each side of the suite's entrance.

The owner, a tall black-haired man about thirty-five, strolled barefoot in a white silk bathrobe. He was considered severely handsome in most cultures, particularly those that found wealth attractive. His hand held a remote control that dimmed the lights, turned on the oven and piped in jazz from hidden speakers. Miles Davis. He approached the aquarium and spoke in soothing cadence as he coaxed the octopus to the surface with a piece of lobster.

The two armed men remained in their seats by the door without opinion, where they had been for hours, because they were required to. The women could sit anywhere they wanted.

The owner moved toward floor-to-ceiling windows overlooking the bay's swank islands, which had begun to twinkle. He placed palms against the glass as his eyes followed tiny cars crossing the water on the Venetian Causeway. One of the women approached from behind and pressed herself against his back. She slid both hands around his waist and down between his legs.

"Not now."

She retreated, also without opinion, and rejoined her friend at the table. There was a squawking noise from the wall. One of the guards answered the intercom.

"Sir, it's Martin."

"Send him up."

Moments later, the doors of the penthouse—a

private elevator—opened, and a slightly shorter version of the owner emerged.

The owner didn't turn around. "What happened?"

"They tried to rip us off."

"And?"

"So we ripped *them* off. They could have been enjoying the fruits of a good deal. Instead, we still have our stuff *and* their money . . . The guys are waiting."

The owner pulled a cell phone from a pocket in his bathrobe and sent a text: *!*

He continued facing the window. "Binoculars." No need to raise his voice. One of the women ran to a closet and raced back with two pairs, regular and night vision. He grabbed the thermal model and aimed it southeast at a darkened part of the bay just outside a keyhole inlet.

A pleasure yacht provided pleasure. The boat slowed, and one of the deckhands released the anchor. The boat continued on because the anchor's chain wasn't attached to the yacht. Two sets of ankles were yanked off the stern's swim platform.

Splash, splash. Show's over. The condo's owner tossed the binoculars at the couch.

A woman: "Ow."

He approached the visitor named Martin, who simply handed him a briefcase.

Their similarity of appearance was no accident. Cousins. The owner was meticulously procedural and cautious. Only blood relatives were trusted for hand-to-hand transactions.

He gave the briefcase to one of the women, who knew that meant the floor safe. The other knew to get the Rémy Martin.

The cousins headed for the promptly evacuated sofa as cognac arrived with equal timeliness. The owner accepted the drink in a hand that had a green cross on the back. "Everything else?"

"Couldn't be smoother," said Martin, taking his first sip. "It's odd since you've been spending so much time away."

"Problems?"

"No, just different." He swirled the glass under his nose. "Glad it's you and not me."

"Why do you say that?"

"Stephan . . ."—he pronounced it *Stefawn*— ". . . my head would explode if I had to spend so much time around those people."

"It's about establishing patterns. And start calling me Steve."

"What for?"

"You'll understand once you meet these people."

"But you're down there, what? Four or five days a week? With a bunch of shit-kickers?"

"It's the perfect setup," said Steve. "Miami's far too big for us to have any influence, too *disorganized*. But up there in that small pond, I've bought off the whole town, mayor to beat cop, even a state senator. And they're laundering our money at the town bank. Couldn't be sweeter."

"I've never known you to trust strangers like this."

"Here's what I trust: their *dis*trust."

"You're confusing me."

"They've been wedged in that town for generations and almost everyone's related. If there's one thing they hate, it's outsiders poking around." Steve took his own sip. "Here in Miami, there's no honor anymore. Everyone offers to snitch before the police even have the cuffs on. But up there, if anyone starts snooping into my business with them, they know how to keep their mouths shut."

"Sounds like you respect them."

"Respect isn't the precise word." He thought and drank. "You know how in this city's business circles, we're required to rub elbows at all those cocktail parties and be charming?"

"But secretly we hate their guts?"

Steve nodded. "I actually think I'm growing fond of these guys."

"Bullshit." Martin idly sniffed a foreign smell in the air. "There's something else going on."

"Well, they got these young guys running errands for me. For *free*. They're making their bones. And making my life so much easier."

"I get it," said Martin. "You like the disciplined structure of this outback clan." An ironic laugh. "Like if *Duck Dynasty* went over to the dark side."

"Can't tell you how relaxing it is up there, because the whole security issue isn't an issue." Steve savored another sip and let the expensive burn roll out his nostrils. "Any outsider comes under the entire town's collective glare. Unless you're like me and arrive spreading the green. Then you're the golden goose that they protect behind the incestuous walls of the kingdom. It's a standing army waiting for hire."

"But I'm guessing I know another reason." The cousin glanced out the window in the direction of a yacht leaving Virginia Key. "If things go south with them, they have no idea the type of people they're dealing with."

"Well, there's that, too."

"We better start getting ready since it's a long drive tonight . . ." Martin stopped and sniffed the air. "Is something cooking?"

"Oh, forgot I turned that on." Steve checked the remote control's liquid blue display. "It's ready."

Martin followed his cousin into the kitchen. "What's ready?"

Steve opened the oven. "I never knew I loved barbecue."

SPIRIT OF THE SUWANNEE

Serge skeptically shook a young man's hand. "Excuse me, but what exactly do you mean that you tracked me down?"

"It was easy," said Matt. "I followed your current research project on your website, charted your future probability track like a hurricane, made a few educated guesses and here I am."

Serge stared at a knot in a tree. "I must be losing my edge. If you can find me . . ."

"Why?" asked Matt. "Do you have a lot of trouble with fans bothering you? If I'm intruding, please tell me."

Serge and Coleman exchanged nervous glances. "Does anyone else know . . . I'm . . . here?"

"Nobody." Matt stood and hoisted his backpack with a grin. "Can't tell you how much I've been looking forward to finding you. But I'm sure you hear that all the time."

"Thankfully, not enough," said Serge.

"I was waiting by the park's main gate and saw your chopper drive through. I tried to keep up, but by the time the cabin was in sight, you were already tooling away in the golf cart. So I just waited here."

"Forgive me for being direct, but what are you doing tracking me down in the first place?"

"I go to Princeton. Working on my thesis."

"And you took a break to enjoy the weather?"

Matt shook his head. "*You* are my thesis."

"Come again?" said Serge. "I had an ear malfunction."

"It concerns the decay of the American Dream, and Florida as the bellwether of collapse."

"Let's go up on the porch so you don't have to keep standing there with that sack," said Serge. "And I can get these bags of ice in the freezer."

They reclined in outdoor furniture, and Serge uncapped a bottle of domestic water. "Where were we?"

"I needed a hook for my thesis and noticed that

Florida is so weird and unraveling much faster than the rest of the country. It's the perfect symbol for the larger picture. Then I researched on the Internet—professors hate that, but I did it anyway—and stumbled across your blog. You've been discussing the same themes, except in the voice of psychotic rants. It's a howl! Where did you ever learn to write expository speeches like that? Anyway, I finally realized an in-person interview was absolutely essential for my paper."

"You really are on the level? You're not . . . working for someone else?"

"Here are my notes." Matt unzipped his backpack and handed over a spiral-bound book.

Serge flipped pages. "This is impressive. Okay, I'm sold. But how *exactly* did you find me?"

"The first time I noticed your website, you had just posted a picture planting that flag in Louisiana to start your own country. I nearly fell out of my chair laughing. And in the photo, you were able to fake such seriousness and authentic enthusiasm that I said to myself, 'This dude's completely wired in. He's got life all figured out: synthesizing 1920s surrealism and Swiftian satire while slipping in an essential disquisition to embrace our heritage, yet self-deprecating at the same time. Because otherwise it would have been completely ridiculous.'"

"Obviously," said Serge.

"I kept following your posts: picking up the *Easy Rider* chopper, the courthouse, Ray Charles's childhood home, and teasing about your next stop at a little-known Shangri-la where the sixties thrived in a most unlikely location. Then it was just a few minutes on a search engine, and when I found this music park way out in the woods in one of the most remote swaths of Florida, I figured this must be it. So I hopped a flight down here."

"That's it? That's all it took to find me?" Serge took a deep breath and stared up at the porch's ceiling fan. "I'm going to have to be more careful."

"That's why I asked if I was intruding," said Matt. "I'm sure you have lots of followers trying to locate you."

"That's one way to put it," said Serge.

A small stream of young people migrated past the cabin in purple hats, earth-friendly sandals and the oxymoronic long shorts. Throwing Frisbees, playing bamboo flutes, juggling bowling pins.

Serge flipped through the spiral notebook. "Casey Anthony trial, Zimmerman trial, exploding corpse damages neighbor's condo, topless woman destroys inside of McDonald's before sucking ice cream from spigot, man sprinkles fiancée's ashes in LensCrafters prompting hazmat evacuation, man in giant hamster ball fails to cross ocean to Bermuda, gubernatorial debate delayed by debate over electric fan . . . You've really done your homework."

"And that's just the low-hanging fruit," said Matt. "What's up with your state? It's like a Twilight Zone of insane phenomena."

Serge continued reading. ". . . Nike missile battery ruins in Key Largo, Apollo solid rocket booster ruins in Everglades, Jonestown massacre Kool-Aid jug in Captain Tony's Saloon . . . Where'd you get all this stuff?"

"From you," said Matt. "I went back and read years of your blogs. Such obscure tidbits they could only come from someone with Florida deep in his blood. That's when I knew you were crucial for my thesis . . ."

More youth walked by with butterfly kites and Dr. Seuss leggings, the stream steadily becoming thicker as night fell.

"I think the concert's starting," said Coleman.

Serge stood and stretched. "Matt, let's pick this back up over at the shows. I need to tap into what these kids are all about."

They locked up the cabin and joined the mellow march over hill and dale. Distant music grew louder through the trees. The path opened into a large clearing anchored on opposite ends by a pair of stages a couple hundred yards apart. It was a carefully planned arrangement, a band playing on one stage while roadies set up at the other, then the venues switched, and the crowd simply turned around, then switched back again, on and on through the night, a dozen bands in fluid performance.

The trio stood in the middle of the audience. Purple and pink spotlights swept the stage. More luminescence out in the crowd: glow sticks and glow hoops and hats with glowing insect antennas.

"I'm impressed." Serge nodded to himself. "I expected it to be good, but not like this."

"What do you mean?" asked Matt.

"Just look." Serge's right arm panned over the crowd. "They're so well behaved. Just enjoying friendship and good music. No marijuana smoke or other drug use, nobody falling down . . ." He looked at the ground where Coleman was trying to get up. ". . . No *kids* falling down."

Coleman stood and opened a flask. "What were you guys talking about?"

"Serge was marveling that nobody is doing drugs," said Matt.

Coleman involuntarily snickered.

"What's your problem?" said Serge.

"Nothing." Still giggling. "Didn't mean to laugh at you."

"Yet you are."

"It's just that you said nobody is doing drugs."

"That's right."

"Ever heard of Molly?"

"My estranged wife?"

"Not her," said Coleman. "It's short for Molecule, specifically MDMA, the latest craze with a more purified strain of ecstasy. Up till now, it's been too adulterated to attain the common spiritual unification that is now being widely reported. In one of her recent concerts, Madonna asked if anyone had run into Molly tonight, and the crowd went wild. All the kids know about it."

Serge looked back at the blissful, swaying crowd. "No way! I don't believe you!"

"Serge, the glow sticks are the big tip-off. You really don't know anything about the drug culture, do you?"

"That's a bad thing?"

"Not good or bad. But if you won't listen to Madonna . . ."

Serge looked the other way. "Matt?"

He put up his hands. "I'm just here to observe."

"Then I'm standing by my initial findings," said Serge. "These are some of the most decent kids I've met in a long time, so don't you go saying they're all on drugs."

"Suit yourself."

"And glow sticks!" Serge scoffed. "That's your evidence? I got one at the circus when I was a little kid. Look at how pretty and childlike they are, leaving tracers in the starry sky. And that excellent light show onstage, with a tight band playing hypnotic rock-techno-funk-jazz-dance fusion. It's the most excellent show I've ever experienced. In fact, this entire scene fills me with hope for our nation's future. I must discuss this at length with the kids . . ." He stepped forward into the crowd.

Matt glanced sideways. "Is he always like this?"

"You get used to it." They followed him.

Serge faced a group that had hitchhiked down from Valdosta, then shouted over the music: "Thanks for everything you're doing!"

"It's all good, man."

"You couldn't be more right. It *is* all good." Serge waved his arms to the side. "Give me some space." Then he made a shrill whistle with two fingers in his mouth. "May I have your attention, please! I am here to bring you the Big Message. Your anti–spring break is a complete triumph, and the impending national collapse has been averted. No amount of gratitude is too much! I feel a special bond with all your souls, like I've known each and every one of you since we were part of the prebirth universal self . . ." He began pointing individually. ". . . I love you, and you, and you, you, you, you, especially you . . . I—I think I'm going to cry . . ." Inconsolable sobbing.

Coleman whispered out the side of his mouth. "Matt, how much Molly did you slip in his water?"

"Just a little pinch. You said it would be all right."

"Thought it would take the edge off all the coffee."

"It's done that."

Serge wiped away tears and clawed toward one of the youths. "How much do you want for that awesome glow stick? I'll pay anything! I must have it or I'll die!"

"Jesus, take it, man."

"This is the best glow stick ever!" Serge spontaneously hugged the youth. "I love you so much my heart aches!"

"It's cool, let go of my neck."

He grabbed the next person. "You're my brother!"

"Dude, maybe you need to sit down a minute."

Coleman broke through the crowd. "I got this."

"Coleman? Is that you?" Serge spotted him and ran over for another big embrace. "Coleman, you complete me. I never told you that before. There's so much I've kept inside! Do you realize we're star pilots standing on the surface of a big round spaceship?"

"I want you to tell me all about it back at the cabin," said Coleman. "Matt, give me a hand with his other arm."

"Yes, the cabin," Serge said as they led him away. "After we stop for more glow sticks."

The kids from Valdosta watched standoffishly as the trio departed.

"What the hell was that about?"

"It's such a drag when old hippies bring drugs to these things."

"But he has short hair."

"That makes him more radical."

Twenty yards away, Coleman tugged Serge's shoulder. "No, the cabin is this direction."

"There's something I forgot to do! It's the most important mission ever! . . ."

"Matt, grab him!"

"He's too fast and slippery."

Serge disappeared into the crowd. The other two charged in after him. Matt was taller and got on his tiptoes.

"See him?" asked Coleman.

"Nothing."

Coleman shrugged and got out his flask again. "He'll turn up."

"But you said he doesn't do drugs, and I've never seen anyone have such a severe reaction," said Matt. "You sure he's going to be okay?"

"What's the worst that can happen?"

Behind them, a familiar voice boomed from the giant speakers up onstage: *"May I have your attention, please?"* Serge tapped the microphone. *"Is this thing on? . . ."*

"Oh no . . ."

Chapter FIFTEEN

SOMEWHERE IN NORTH FLORIDA

Shortly after midnight, a red beacon blinked atop a hill. The cell-phone tower silently relayed sweet talk, arguments and recipes. Down on the road, a vulture picked at what used to be an alligator. Headlights hit the bird and it took flight.

The black Mercedes continued speeding through the woods until it approached a "Reduce Speed" sign. The driver dutifully set cruise control on the exact number.

Another blinking light, this one yellow. It flashed over a remote intersection in the forest. Three corners of the crossroads were thick with pine trees. The fourth held a white clapboard convenience store with a sagging roof. Burglar bars, completely dark. Signs indicated that when it opened in the morning, they would sell chopped firewood, fishing bait, fried chicken and "fresh produce Wednesday to Saturday." It didn't elaborate whether there wasn't produce the rest of the week, or just not the best time to buy.

The Mercedes reached the light and hung a left. The driver checked his GPS. "Half mile to the turn." The passenger got out his phone, set it to clock mode and hit the stopwatch function. The sedan swung onto a dirt road and the passenger pressed the start button. *One second, two, three . . .*

They arrived at a farm, and the pair unloaded the trunk, wearing functional sneakers and black Under Armour gym outfits. They jogged briskly across the field behind the barn, in the same direction but thirty yards apart. *One minute forty, forty-one, forty-two . . .*

The men simultaneously completed setting up identical rows of battery-powered fluorescent camping lanterns at exact intervals. Just as the last light was in place, a motorized drone came from the darkness at the end of the field. A twin-engine Beechcraft King Air cleared the trees and touched down on the grass. The lanterns were urgently collected as the plane rolled to a stop near the edge of the pasture. *Four minutes ten, eleven, twelve . . .*

The pilot of the still-running craft opened his door and handed down a weighty suitcase. Then turned around and taxied back across the field for takeoff. Just as the men returned to the Mercedes, another car arrived. A Chrysler Valiant with a stuck odometer. Choreography continued. The driver got out and popped the trunk with no discussion. The suitcase went in. *Seven minutes twenty-three, twenty-four, twenty-five . . .*

A passenger in the older car switched to the Mercedes. Both vehicles departed down the dirt road.

They reached the pavement. The Valiant went one way and the Mercedes the other. The man keeping time with his phone pressed stop.

The driver glanced in the backseat. "How'd we do?"

"Nine-thirty-eight-point-one."

"Under ten minutes for the first time. Not bad."

The car's new occupant sat up front on the passenger side. "So what did you want to talk about?"

"The next drop. Monday."

"That soon?" He took a heavy breath in thought. "Might not be enough time. I know you guys don't like to use the same place twice, and I'm not sure I can secure another strip."

"We'd be willing to expand our range. Ideas?"

"I know this one guy with a spread toward the coast, but it's near a civilian airport with good radar . . ."

The man in the backseat opened a briefcase. Usually it would be filled with packs of hundred-dollar bills or bricks of white powder. This time, it held a polished metal box that didn't reveal its purpose. The only control was a single toggle switch. The man flipped it, and a green power light came on.

A short distance away in the government surveillance van, a man with headphones grabbed his ears in pain.

"What is it?" asked the agent in charge.

"They're using a jammer."

"And the homing device?"

"Gone, too."

"Our guy's been made." The agent slapped the

driver on the shoulder. "Speed up! Don't lose them, and don't worry about being spotted." Then, into the radio, "All units respond! Cover's blown! Take 'em!"

The driver of the Mercedes cut the lights and skidded onto the narrowest dirt road yet. The woods became dense. The front passenger watched branches scrape his window. "Where are we going?"

"You haven't ridden with us before," said the driver. "We also never take the same *route* twice."

"No routine, nothing to piece together," added the backseat voice. "We're not fond of risk."

"No kidding . . . Why are we stopping?"

Back on the paved road, a surveillance van pulled over: "Why are we stopping?"

"We lost them . . ."

A half hour later, ten unmarked government vehicles rolled slowly down every back road and turn-off they could find. Search beams swept the forest, illuminating shafts of fog and illegally dumped garbage.

The radio. "Anyone got anything yet?"

No news was bad news.

At the end of an abandoned logging road, a pair of men in black gym clothes leaned against the hood of a Mercedes.

"We need to rethink this."

"But it's the perfect plan. We've got our timing down."

"Any plan is only as good as its weakest link, and ours is the human element. In this business, everyone you deal with is potentially facing forever in prison and can be flipped." Steve stomped his foot down redundantly on an already smashed mini-microphone and transmitter lying in the dirt. "Informants are becoming too big a part of the equation."

Ahead in a small clearing, muted attempts to scream.

Martin glanced beside the car at a forty-eight-gallon cooler that would need a thorough hosing out. Then at another item rarely seen in Florida. "I was wondering what you were going to do with that snow shovel."

"You know, maybe varying the routine is the wrong approach." Steve stared up at the stars. "Maybe we need to tackle this from the opposite direction. Establish the foundation of a completely predictable routine."

"Why would you want to do that?"

"To hide in plain sight."

"What about the human element?"

"Use people not in the business."

"You aren't actually thinking of your new neighbors in that hick town," said Martin. "The landings are a precision operation."

"Why not?" said Steve. "They've handled everything else just fine. And they know far more about the backcountry than we could ever hope to learn. It's in ten generations of their family tree."

The muffled shrieks of desperation grew louder.

"How'd you know a snow shovel was the best way to collect roadkill?"

"Just seemed logical."

"At first I thought you had overplanned, but it

turned out we needed every bit of that shovel for that last armadillo."

"They get surprisingly big. Couldn't even close the cooler lid."

The pair gazed ahead at the filleted remains from their scavenger hunt, draped liberally over the gagged informant, who was staked down to the forest floor.

"Vultures get big, too," said Martin.

"They possess a philosophy not unlike ours."

"How's that?"

"Let others do all the real work. We just want to get paid."

"But they're not very accurate in collecting accounts due. They're just in a pecking frenzy."

"Possum, informant, what do they care?"

"That biggest bird on the left." Martin pointed. "What's it pulling out of him? That's not— . . . *ewwwww.*"

"I think they have it from here. Let's get going."

They headed back out on the logging road.

"I'm still shaky about these new people you want to use," said Martin. "Letting those hayseeds move money through their bank is one thing, but turning the landings over to them? I mean it's such a tight window. That's why you said you didn't trust the drops to anyone but ourselves."

"I don't need more close brushes like tonight," said Steve. "It's time to step back and allow someone else to insulate us."

"But these morons?"

"Don't let looks deceive you," said Steve. "Ever known people who have lived in the boondocks their whole lives? They develop almost paranormal instincts for the terrain. I wouldn't be surprised if their management of the drops is so precise that it makes *us* look like the morons."

MEANWHILE . . .

Coleman and Matt guided Serge up a wooded path until their cabin came into view.

Serge began to sway. "*Love shack baby . . .*"

"Make sure he doesn't trip on these steps," said Coleman.

They got him onto the screened porch and into a hammock.

"Look how fast he conked out," said Matt. "That usually doesn't happen."

"Got any more of that stuff?" asked Coleman.

"Sure, here."

Serge surprised them by jumping up in alarm. "I can't sleep. I'm too hot." He ran inside and cranked the cabin's air conditioner all the way up.

"Could have sworn he was crashed," said Matt.

Coleman claimed the vacated hammock. "Sometimes he keeps closing and opening his eyes and jumping out of bed twenty times or more before he finally nods off. Can last hours."

"Why?"

"To check on his wallet and car keys and make sure he hasn't left anything burning, then look up stuff on the Internet, check wallet and keys again, floss teeth, wallet, make sure the door's locked, keys . . ."

Matt looked inside through the sliding glass door. "What's he doing now?"

"Taking off all his clothes," said Coleman.

"I can see that," said Matt. "He's wiping his neck with a wet towel."

"Sometimes he gets hung up on temperature."

"Must really be hot," said Matt. "Molly does that to some people."

Serge stuck his face against the air conditioner vents.

Matt pulled out a notebook. "Mind if I ask a few questions? I'd like to interview you, too, for my thesis."

"You want to interview *me*?"

Matt clicked his pen. "Serge is doing some groundbreaking studies, and since you're his research assistant . . ."

Coleman sat up and tried to look important. "Why yes, I am his research assistant."

"What do you think of Serge's methods?"

"He claims he's misunderstood," said Coleman. "Doesn't like how some of the newspapers have described him."

"So his work is well covered by the media down here?"

"There have been a few articles."

Matt glanced inside the cabin, where a naked Serge was shivering with chattering teeth. "Seems pretty intense. Has his passion for Florida ever taken him too far?"

"Many times," said Coleman. "But he's always the first one to admit it."

Serge turned off the A/C, then set the heater on full blast. He began putting on layer after layer of clothes.

"Back at Princeton, there's tremendous competition and jealousy among the faculty," said Matt. "Does Serge have any rivals?"

"Most of them aren't around anymore," said Coleman. "I could tell you some bizarre stories."

"So Florida got too strange for them?"

"In the end, definitely."

The sliding glass door flew open. Serge ran onto the porch, inflated to almost twice his regular girth—"I'm burning up!"—frantically peeling off apparel until he was nude again. He ran back inside and jacked up the A/C.

Matt stared a moment before returning to his notebook. "Serge's website seems extremely engaging. Any insight about how he keeps people's attention when teaching a lesson in person?"

"Let me think." Coleman got out of the hammock and took a seat on the ground. "Oh! During most of his lessons, Serge likes to give a bonus round."

"Sounds like fun."

"For Serge it is."

Inside the cabin: *"Freezing again!"*

"Give me an example of a bonus round."

"Well, this one time he was really determined to kill these people—" Coleman cut himself off. "Uh, hope I didn't just say anything wrong. Serge wants me to be quiet about certain things."

"Don't worry about humility," said Matt. "At Princeton we're always getting great academic speakers who absolutely slay the audience."

"The whole audience?" said Coleman. "Jesus!"

Serge ran outside. *"I'm roasting . . ."*

The night eventually wound down, and the trio found their sleeping spots as other kids slowly drifted back to their dome tents in the forest.

Just after daybreak, Serge awoke and slung his legs over the side of a hammock. "Ooo, my head. I feel so weird. What happened last night?"

"Uh, we might have, you know . . ." said Matt.

". . . Put just a little something in your water," said Coleman.

"You drugged me?"

"And I also might have given you a little bad information yesterday," said Coleman. "It now appears that you were the only person at the entire concert doing Molly."

Serge covered his eyes. "This is so embarrassing. How did I behave? Did I do anything inappropriate?"

"Oh, no, no, no!" said Coleman.

"You were perfectly fine," said Matt.

Another youth migration, this one morning-style. Flip-flops slapped the dirt trail. Packs of kids in swimwear headed down to the river with inner tubes and rafts. As each group passed the cabin, they all pointed at the porch.

"Why are they laughing?" asked Serge.

"Guess they're just having a good time," said Coleman.

"Yeah, that must be it," said Matt.

Another bunch of kids came by. They raised Bic lighters toward the porch. "*Encore!*"

"Now I know you're holding back," said Serge.

Matt and Coleman glanced at each other.

"Okay, spill," said Serge.

Coleman cracked another dawn beer. "Might as well go ahead and play the video."

"What video?" asked Serge.

"I took this on my cell phone," said Matt. "*Everyone* was recording on their cell phones."

"Let me see that." Serge snatched it and held the tiny screen to his face. "How did I get up onstage?"

"Here's the volume button," said Matt. "You'll want to hear this . . ."

The musicians backed away as Serge paced with a microphone.

"First I'd like to make a few announcements. You *are* stardust. You *are* golden. Peace *will* guide the planets. Next, I'd like to thank the band for not choking on throw-up. Now, for my State of the Union. I'm staring out from this stage into the core of what makes America great. You're all rock stars at the Pursuit of Happiness, which is at war with the Pursuit of Blame because media personalities make a fortune inciting angry audiences: 'You know how your life is a runaway burning garbage truck of a disaster? But it's not because you did no planning whatsoever, and used such poor personal judgment every step of the way that you had to invent new wrong decisions, like when you wanted to be an Internet celebrity: "Hey, I got it! Let's get the dirt bike on the roof!" No, your failure is the fault of that other group of Americans!' . . . And that's cool. I don't want everyone to agree. I don't want everyone to be the same. I love all of you out there and agree with almost everything you believe, but take an honest look at yourselves. If you populated the entire country, things would go right in the shitter in a serious hurry. Nothing personal. I just dig the American mosh pit. Right-wing extremists, left-wing socialists, religious fanatics, godless pinkos, pro-choice, pro-life, gun nuts, gun-control freaks, tree huggers, oil drillers, intellectual elitists, the Golden Corral chocolate fountain. And everyone says, 'Good Lord, we're so polarized!' But I look at our fantastically wide spectrum of quarreling factions, and my heart bursts with joy! The same country allows both Sarah Palin and Barbra Streisand to roam freely. Now that's *strength*! In America, you can be whatever you want! Most important of all, you can be *wrong*! So when I see some asshole, I say, 'Don't let hospital bills crush your dirt-bike dreams, otherwise the terrorists win.' Which brings up Eskimos. What's their fucking problem? Hiding out under the borealis like nobody will notice. 'Yo! Put down the scrimshaw and get with the program!' And if they don't, someone new to blame. It's a win-win . . . Repeat after me! More Eskimos! More Eskimos! . . . Why are you all looking at me like that? Okay, you're not into mindless audience repetition, which is good because that's how Hitler got started . . . Hand me that guitar!"

One of the musicians hurriedly surrendered his instrument, then retreated to the rear of the stage.

"I'd now like to play 'The Ballad of the Easy Rider.'" Serge strummed. "I don't know 'The Ballad of the Easy Rider' . . . Any requests?"

"What the hell are you on?"

"I don't know that one either." Serge strummed again. "Wait, I've got it. Ever see the Woodstock movie? Sizzling climax with Hendrix playing 'The Star-Spangled Banner.' Here we go! From the top! . . ." *Strum.* ". . . I just remembered I don't know how to play the guitar, either, so I'll just jump to Jimi's hallucinogenic solo with rockets and bombs bursting in air."

Rrrrrrogggoshhh . . . Waawaaawoosh . . . Yayyaya-hoooowackackack . . .

Serge raised the guitar over his head and smashed it on the stage until only the neck was left in his hands. "I just remembered it's not my guitar." He reached in his pocket and pulled out a wad of cash— "This should cover it"—then grabbed the microphone one last time. "Thank you *for lettin' me be myself*! *Again!* Good night!"

The crowd stood silent. The video ended. Serge hung his head and handed the phone back. "Could it have gotten any worse?"

No answer.

Serge looked up. "What?"

"But on the bright side, nobody caught it on video," said Matt. "Not many."

"There's more?"

"Well," said Coleman. "As we were hustling you off the stage, you sort of said . . ."

"Actually more of a yell," clarified Matt. "Don't worry. Everyone took it with the best of intentions."

Serge gritted his teeth. "What . . . did . . . I . . . say?"

Coleman spoke rapidly. "That you had learned to love your enemies and promised not to murder them anymore. Hey! What about some breakfast!"

"How can you eat at a time like this?"

Coleman poked his belly button. "My tummy tells me."

"Now I'm definitely against drugs," said Serge. "I obviously don't want to kill anyone else, but *promise*? That's just crazy talk."

"Serge," Matt said with pause. "What you said last night, and again just now. You know, the murder thing? You're just staying in character with your over-the-top blog, right?"

"In character. Of course."

"That's a big relief." Matt held up his phone. "Because more good news. You're starting to go viral."

"What does that mean?"

"People sharing and posting their videos. Over half a million people have now seen them." He looked up from his phone with a grin. "Congratulations. You're officially a sensation."

"That many people know I'm here?" Serge sprang off the hammock and ran in the cabin.

Matt followed him inside. "Where are you going?"

Frantically cramming stuff in his knapsack. "Getting away from here!"

"But you're still going to continue your weird Florida tour, right?"

Serge yanked the final zipper closed. "I never had a choice."

Matt stared off the porch at empty space. "Boy, I sure wish I was coming with you guys."

Serge hoisted his backpack. "Got a helmet?"

"Oh, I have a helmet all right." Matt opened the top of his own pack. "It's a real beauty."

Chapter SIXTEEN

The snack menu board had been supplied by the Pepsi-Cola Corporation. It was one of those boards where you push in plastic letters. They'd run out of *L*'s and instead flipped over the number seven.

A young man in swim trunks stood at the counter with money. "A hot dog and a Coke."

"We only have Pepsi."

"Fine."

Someone started a microwave.

Next to the snack window was a door under a red flag with a diagonal white stripe. WOBBLY SPRINGS DIVE CENTER. It was technically still on Main Street, but a couple of country miles away on the outskirts of town near the water plant. Inside were rental snorkels, a compressor to fill tanks, disposable cameras and admission tickets.

An employee appeared from the business side of

the snack window with a checkered cardboard container. "Here are your nachos."

"I ordered a hot dog."

"Oh." She turned. "Darlene, press start on the microwave again."

"Forget it. I'll take the nachos."

The man grabbed a seat at a picnic table. Others came out of the dive shop with flippers and masks, hiking a short distance through the woods to a circular rock formation. A wooden staircase led down twenty feet to a pontoon swim platform surrounded by happy, splashing visitors.

Well, almost everyone was happy. A pair of scuba divers broke the surface and spit out regulators. "This is a farce!" They climbed back up the stairs and stomped away past the picnic tables, where Vernon sat with his mini-cooler of beer and a microwaved pretzel.

Someone took the seat across from him. "What's this you were jabbering on the phone about Peter?"

A pretzel dipped in mustard. "He was out at the construction site again."

"But I thought we'd convinced him to let us handle that falsified report," said Senator Pratchett. "What was he doing?"

"Walking around with a clipboard and taking digital photos."

"That doesn't sound good."

"Told you he was shaky." Vern chewed with his mouth open. "That's why I phoned and asked him to meet us at the springs."

"Why here?"

Vernon pointed at workers on ladders with another crooked Founders' Day banner. "Have to watch 'em like a hawk."

The senator turned back around. "Okay, let's hear him out before we worry needlessly."

"There he is now."

Ryan hopped to his feet with the broadest smile. "Peter! Great to see you! How's the wife?"

"Testifying."

The mayor hopped to his feet. "What!"

"Topeka. Double murder. Narrowed it down to Air Jordans."

"Oh, shoe-print specialist," said Pratchett. "You told us."

"Peter, what's going on?" asked Vernon. "Why were you back at the construction site—"

The senator held up a hand. "Peter, you know we really like you. There are all kinds of opportunities in this town. I mean, we still have that understanding with the tiny bit of confusion over the geology reports, right?"

"Absolutely," said Peter. "I got to thinking about it, and I'm sure you know what you're doing. You'll bring up the mistaken report in due course through proper channels. There must be all kinds of bureaucratic red tape you face every day that I'm unaware of."

"You have no idea," said Pratchett. "It drives me nuts."

"And besides," said Peter, "I promptly brought

it to your attention, and you're the authorities, so I've met my legal obligation. I'll just drop the whole business and leave it in your court."

"Now, that's what we like to hear," said Vernon. "Neighbors helping neighbors."

"You're a model citizen," said Ryan.

"But what *were* you doing today at the site?" asked Vernon.

"Well . . ." Peter removed a rubber band from a file folder and spread glossy photos on the picnic table. "It's been bugging me like crazy."

"What am I looking at?" asked Pratchett. "They're like the sonograms when Julie was expecting."

"Good analogy," said Peter. "These are the ground radar shots. They've got density issues that resulted in my negative recommendation. But given the passable resistivity tests, I couldn't pinpoint exactly why that model home collapsed. It was keeping me up nights, so I decided to take a closer look, purely off the books at no cost, to help you guys out."

"Help is good," said Pratchett.

"What did you find?" asked Vernon.

"First, a little overview." Peter pulled out some cross-sectional drawings. "For millions of years, Florida was underwater and reefs began forming from countless microorganisms that began leaving calcite particles during the Tertiary Eocene epoch . . ."

Two scuba divers with still-full tanks marched by. *"This sucks."*

". . . Then the sea level fell, our peninsula emerged and these reefs became a limestone substratum covered by an overburden including clay migrating down from the Appalachians and fine quartz, or sand. When rain percolates through the surface cover, it reacts with carbon dioxide, making it acidic, and, over time, dissolving the porous limestone . . ."

Vernon made a quick spinning motion with an index finger. "Short version."

"The result is that much of Florida's foundation is honeycombed with underground lakes and rivers, and sometimes they reach the surface, creating the many natural springs for which the state is well known." Peter pointed at the nearby rock formation as more enraged divers emerged at the top of the staircase. "The fact that you have a spring here indicates such conditions."

The divers passed the table. *"I want a refund."*

"But what's all that mean?" asked Pratchett.

"Fissures and instability in limestone usually aren't a problem, because the upward pressure of the subterranean aquifer acts as a counterbalance." Peter tapped the photos on the table. "But these light areas are low-density weak spots. I've only seen this sort of thing before from sinkhole investigations on the Gulf Coast."

"Still not following."

"This is what you'd see if someone was over-pumping groundwater," said Peter. "There are governing bodies that set limits, except some people do it anyway."

"But we draw all our drinking water from the spring." Vernon gestured through the trees. "The plant's right over there. We don't touch the aquifer."

"I know," said Peter. "The spring should be more than enough. That's why it doesn't make any sense." He gathered up his evidence. "Anyway, just thought I'd pass it along."

"You're good people," said Vernon.

"We like your kind in our town," said Pratchett.

"Motherfucker," said another diver.

"Excuse me," Peter called out. "Why are all you divers so mad?"

"There ain't no goddamn spring!"

"Watch your language!" Vernon pulled out his police chief's badge. "We got a nice little town here and aim to keep it that way."

Peter stood with his file. "What was that about?"

Vernon threw the rest of a pretzel in the trash. "Outside agitators."

Peter shook hands with the senator and mayor. "Call me if you have any questions."

The remaining pair at the picnic table watched until the geologist was out of earshot, then Pratchett leaned and lowered his voice. "How much pumping are we doing?"

"Just the usual."

It was the truth. Except "the usual" was now up 2,000 percent from ten years ago. That's when one of the workers from the nearby water plant had gone on lunch break and snuck a joint in the woods.

He didn't come back. Two weeks later, some bird watchers found him at the bottom of a recently opened sinkhole caused by the adjacent pumping station. They named the cafeteria in his memory.

Meanwhile, the sinkhole—in a nice cavity of limestone near the surface—quickly filled with rainwater. So as they often do out in the country, they made lemonade.

The town's movers and shakers had long groused: Other rival small towns were far crappier, yet attracted tourists in much bigger droves. Because they had one thing Wobbly didn't. A natural spring. It wasn't fair. How could they get one?

So after fishing the body out of the sinkhole, the city council put up signs and picnic tables and a snack booth, and built a staircase down into the ground. Open for business.

It exceeded all expectations. The town had tapped into a surprisingly deep reservoir of devotees to the state's finest springs—families, naturalists, cave divers—who made the rounds of some of Florida's finest natural features: Rainbow Springs, Silver Springs, Ginnie Springs, Fanning Springs, Wakulla Springs, Crystal River, Alachua Sink, Devil's Den.

And now Wobbly Springs.

Then it unexpectedly got better. Leaders from surrounding communities casually began dropping by. "So, I hear you, uh, might have a spring?"

"As a matter of fact we do."

"We seem to be paying an awful lot to those big-city management districts on the coast for our drinking water. You don't suppose you could spare a few gallons?"

Wobbly said, "Anything for a neighbor."

Word got around. The town was undercutting everyone's prices.

The only problem was what the scuba divers soon learned: "It's really only a sinkhole that doesn't connect to anything. There's no freakin' spring."

No problem. They just sucked the water out of the ground with as many wells as they could dig. Of course, as Peter mentioned, there were state policies and restrictions in place to prevent the inevitable. But who was going to tell them? Wobbly's water-pumping station became the small-town version of a homeowner who remodels without permits and just tapes newspapers over the windows.

"Cut back," said Pratchett.

Vernon opened his beer cooler. "On what?"

"The pumping!"

"That's good money."

"It's nothing compared to what we stand to lose if we have any more fiascos at the construction site," said the senator. "I trust Peter on this one."

"But—"

"Just do it."

DOWN INTO THE PENINSULA

A chopped motorcycle with a coconut gas tank roared through the horse-riding country of River Rise Preserve State Park. The rolling route south from the Suwannee music park had been town after small town. Lake City, Mason, Ellisville, High Springs. Peanut stands, tomato stands, baskets of peaches, sweet corn, decorative gourds, Moose

Lodge, Kiwanis, Optimists, someone's front yard selling birdhouses that looked like small red barns, another selling carved wooden flamingos with wings that turned like propellers, a sheriff's car hiding behind a billboard to TAKE BACK AMERICA, a diner called the Cracker Kitchen bragging about shrimp and grits, something that appeared to be a cemetery but was a tombstone outlet.

"... *Little pink houses for you and me* ..."

They followed Highway 441 under the interstate until wisps of another country town began to appear, this one growing a bit larger than the others.

"Radio check," said Coleman. "Where are we?"

"Gainesville, home of the University of Florida," said Serge. "I'm tracking one of our state's favorite sons whose wonder years paralleled mine."

"A student?"

"No, someone who used to work at the university."

They were still clearly on the outskirts when Serge made a right turn onto Northwest Forty-Fifth Avenue and almost immediately pulled off the road into a newly paved parking area. Everyone dismounted and stretched.

"Matt, what kind of helmet is that anyway?"

"I played a little lacrosse."

Coleman took off his own helmet. "What's that falling-down barn over there on the back of this field? Surprised to find it in a public park."

"It's the whole reason we stopped." Serge grabbed his camera. "The old Mudcrutch Farm."

"Mudcrutch?"

"The name of Tom Petty's formative band that evolved into the Heartbreakers."

"But Petty's music is from the seventies."

"That's correct." Serge began hiking across the grass. "But his wonder years began in the sixties when his uncle brought him to see Elvis filming a movie in nearby Citrus County, which inspired little Tom to pick up the guitar. This barn is where they used to practice endlessly, making the quantum leap from wannabes to a polished group . . . Right over there is where Petty and company would drag their equipment outside on weekends and play for whoever showed up. Today, so many people claim they were at those concerts that they would have been bigger than Woodstock."

Serge reached the porch steps and grabbed the broken handle of a screen door.

"There's a warning sign against trespassers," said Coleman.

"That's just for people who aren't running down a dream." *Click, click, click . . .*

Ten minutes later and just around the corner on Thirteenth Street, the chopper sat on the side of the road next to a mailbox with the number 4562. *Click, click, click . . .*

"Now, what's *this* place?" asked Coleman. "Looks like a boarded-up lounge."

"Second of three stops on the Petty tour. Used to be a nightclub called Dub's." *Click, click, click.* "Mudcrutch played six nights a week."

"You said he used to work for the school?" asked Matt.

"It will all be revealed at the final location. Back to the chopper!"

They cruised down into campus.

"Matt," Serge said into his microphone. "How do you like the radio headset we got for your lacrosse helmet?"

"The tunes are so crisp. Is this the Heartbreakers?"

"Good call," said Serge. "Plus, if you're with us, you're *with* us. You need to be in the loop of our tour-guide chatter."

"*. . . I need to know! I need to know! . . .*"

After a brief stop, the chopper pulled away from a convenience store with a back-to-school special for suitcases of Bud and Bud Light. An extra-large coffee sat in the motorcycle's drink holder, iced down for consumption velocity.

"Radio check." Coleman looked up as they rode past a massive edifice. "What's that place?"

"Ben Hill Griffin Stadium, home of the University of Florida Gators football team," said Serge. "Also known as the Swamp, because when you walk into the place from street level, you enter at one of the top rows of seats, and the rest of the stadium is below ground. Ain't that the shit? I never drank coffee on a motorcycle before. Little streams are dribbling past my ears. I don't like that. We need relevant tunes."

He cranked the stereo in their helmets.

"*. . . I'm free . . . free-falllllllling! . . .*"

The chopper drove a few blocks south and made a left on Museum Road. They pulled around the side of a modest single-story brick building with a pointed entrance arch that made it look like a church. The kickstand clicked into position.

"... *I won't ... back ... down ...*"

Serge removed his helmet. "There it is! The Phelps Laboratory!"

Coleman exited his sidecar like a deep-sea diver going backward over the side of a boat. He got up and brushed off dirt. "The Phelps what?"

"Lab. They do wetlands research."

"I thought you said we were going to a Tom Petty place."

"We are." Serge drained the rest of his coffee.

"Tom Petty had something to do with this lab?" asked Matt.

"Not remotely." Serge boldly led them up the walkway to the front door. "But I'm one of the few people who knows how to properly conduct a pilgrimage. You don't just rush in and grab the chalice off the altar. You have to sit in the pews first and let a damn-the-torpedoes excitement properly build steam."

"So what's inside this place?" asked Coleman.

"I have no idea." Serge tried the doorknob and found it unlocked. "But we're about to find out!"

At first there was no one in sight. The others followed Serge as he poked around until arriving at an open office door. A man in a white dress shirt looked up from behind his desk. "Can I help you?"

"Maybe," said Serge. "Are you a professor?"

"Yes."

"Then you can definitely help!" Serge clapped his hands a single time. "You look too young to be a professor. I was hoping for something bald with a pipe."

"You have a big brown stain on your shirt."

"I drank coffee on a motorcycle."

"Uh, are you a student here?"

"Without question," said Serge. "But that's my gripe with universities. They want you to apply and be accepted and attend class after class. All that just slows down my learning curve. I prefer to self-construct an individual, at-large curriculum of intellectual curiosity and live by my own spiritual definition of enrollment." He raised his eyebrows. "I understand that sort of thing goes over big in the philosophy department."

The professor paused to appraise one of the others in the trio.

"Coleman!" snapped Serge. "The flask! We're on campus!"

"What? Oh, sorry." He screwed the cap back on and stuck it in his pocket.

Serge turned back around and grinned. "There are also rules against drinking in the football stadium, but we all know how that goes."

"Excuse me," said the professor. "Did you guys just walk in here off the street?"

"Of course," said Serge. "That's how it works. We don't have *Star Trek* transporter machines yet."

The teacher's eyes measured the distance to his desk phone and how long it would take to call university police.

"You don't have to call university police," said Serge. "This is a friendly visit, not like some of my others. The whole reason I'm here is to express my total support for everything you're doing." He spread his arms. "This is the Center for Wetlands Studies. What a coincidence! I'm all about wetlands *and* studying! I love to research so much that I research things I don't even want to research. Just jump on the computer and start wandering the Net. You wouldn't believe some of the fetishes. Do you think we could grab a few chairs and sit here to watch you work? We'll be real quiet. Except I usually have a lot of questions. I'm sure that's encouraged around here."

"It's probably not a good idea."

"Even if I raise my hand?"

"Don't think so."

"Say no more." Serge gave a thumbs-up. "The politics of academia. Everybody acts so charming at the galas, but it's dog eat dog. Publish or perish. I'm sure you're working on a major wetlands breakthrough and can't risk a leak to the backstabbers." He placed a secretive hand beside his mouth and lowered his voice. "Between you and me, we were just up near Baton Rouge—don't even get me started on Louisiana!—and I got the vibe that the folks at LSU are on the verge of something big."

"I don't know what you're talking about."

Serge stood back up and winked. "Of course you don't."

The professor's eyes drifted to the phone again.

"That won't be necessary." Serge pointed out the office window. "We were leaving anyway to go see the Tom Petty tree."

"Oh." The professor relaxed in his chair with relief. "So that's what this is all about. Yeah, we get a few . . . uh, visitors from time to time asking about Petty."

"You were going to say weirdos," said Serge. "That's okay. It's a common mistake. I'm on a quest to discover what went wrong with the American Dream by tracing my snow-cone machine wonder years with a sixties road trip through small-town Florida that's a sequel to *Easy Rider*. Once you understand all that, there's nothing to be suspicious about."

The professor blinked.

Coleman hit his flask again. "Serge, what's the Tom Petty tree?"

"Tom was never a student here, but he worked on the grounds crew." Serge reached in his pocket and uncrumpled a treasure map. "Legend has it that as part of his job, he once planted an ogeechee lime tree."

"Far out," said Coleman.

"I heard that was a myth," said Matt.

"Because of an interview Tom did," said Serge. "Petty claimed he never remembered planting any lime tree. Then he joked that what he *did* plant wasn't at the university."

"Weed!" said Coleman.

"Down, boy," said Serge. "Anyway, there's so much data he did plant the tree—the specific species and exact location—that it can't be dismissed just because Petty says he doesn't recall forty years later."

"Why not?" asked Coleman.

"When you're working a crappy minimum-wage job, your mind is always elsewhere," said Serge. "On the rare occasions you were employed, what do you remember?"

"Watching the clock until I could smoke weed."

"Anything else?"

"It's just a big blank."

"Excuse me," said the professor, trying to wind things up. "I understand he's a very popular musician, but—"

"More than that. A genuine sun-kissed Florida product, now with more pulp!" Serge squinted down at his map, and the professor saw an exit strategy.

"You won't need that." The teacher went over to the window. "Just walk down the east side of this building to that Dumpster and those bicycle racks, then walk ten yards out in the common area. Can't miss it."

Serge looked up with large eyes, then abruptly ran out of the building.

The professor returned to the window and spread blinds with his fingers. Serge sprinted down the hill, punctuating his run with cartwheels and somersaults. He dashed the final distance and hugged the tree. Then he placed an arm around it like a buddy's shoulders, pulled out a cell phone and took a selfie.

Matt caught up first, followed distantly by Coleman.

"I'll take your pictures!" said Serge. "One on each side! I feel like singing! . . . *Don't do me like that . . .*"

Matt posed next to the tree. "Have to admit I was secretly skeptical after your references to violence yesterday. But all we've been doing is a lot of delightfully wacky trivia research. Nothing remotely dangerous."

"Fun and games all the time," said Serge, covertly checking something on his cell and growling. Then he looked up with a smile and raised his camera. *Click, click, click.*

The professor watched from the window until the three drove off on their chopper. Then he returned to his desk and opened the file on his latest wetlands project. "Louisiana bastards. I *knew* it."

Chapter SEVENTEEN

A rusty orange pickup truck drove through the countryside just before sunset. It had a sticker on the left end of its bumper. REDNECK SEX MACHINE. On the right was another sticker. SQUIRRELS: NATURE'S SPEED BUMPS.

It was one of those Ford F-Series jobs from the mid-1950s, with room for only two people in the cab. Sitting up front were Elroy, Slow, Slower.

"Move over, you're squishing me!"

"There's no room, shithead!"

"Blow me!"

"Can I have some of your Big Gulp?"

"Okay."

"Will you two shut up?" said Elroy. "I can't hear myself think!"

"What are you thinking about?"

"What we're supposed to be focusing on tonight, remember?"

The pickup continued on, passing a billboard where the American Automobile Association warned of an upcoming speed trap. Then a newer billboard: Welcome to Wobbly. Don't Believe What They Say.

Slower turned on the AM radio and found an all-night preacher reading straight through the Book of Leviticus. *"Do not have sexual relations with your sister . . . Do not have sexual relations with your father's sister . . . Do not . . ."*

"Can we at least get some music in here?" asked Elroy.

"Wait, this is stuff I need to know."

". . . Do not have sexual relations with your brother's wife . . ."

Slow elbowed Slower in the stomach.

"Ow."

"I told you it was in the Bible!"

"You idiots." Elroy turned the dial to Clapton.

"After midnight, we're gonna let it all hang out . . ."

GAINESVILLE

The chopper cruised west on Museum Road and pulled over again just after the bend at Lake Alice. Serge led them to a wooden fence.

"I need a nap," said Coleman.

"See those two buildings across that field?"

"Yeah," said Matt. "They look like a pair of houses, except it's just the attics on tall poles. The bottoms of the houses are gone."

"Check this out!" said Serge, holding up his cell

phone. The others peered over his shoulder as he navigated to a website with a streaming video. "This is from a live cam inside one of the attics."

"What am I looking at?" asked Matt. "It's just an amorphous giant vibrating mass."

"These are the bat towers," said Serge. "The early one down in the Keys never worked out because the bats didn't dig it, but the university got it right and you're now looking at the world's largest human-engineered bat colony, with more than three hundred thousand flying mammals living in those two structures."

A couple of people joined them at the fence, then a few more, and another handful. Coleman looked around at others beginning to pour in from all directions.

"What's going on?"

"It's the local evening tradition where people flock to this fence and wait for sunset."

"Why?" asked Coleman.

"The bats emerge en masse at dusk to feast on the plentiful insects at the lake across the street," said Serge. "It's practically apocalyptic in scale. The sun just went down."

"Cool." Coleman headed for the woods. "Be right back. I'm gonna need a joint for this."

Matt got out his notebook. "And Tom Petty helped build the bat towers?"

"That would be Floridaphile overkill," said Serge. "I have a big enough stiffy as it is. I should probably stand closer to the fence."

"Then what does this have to do with the Tom Petty tour?"

"Nothing." Serge set his camera on low-light mode. "And that's the mark of an excellent tour. This is so conveniently close to the Tom Petty tree that I'd be remiss not to post it on my website, sort of like when a bunch of podiatrists come to town for the big convention, and the chamber of commerce puts out brochures of Other Things to Do: 'After the riveting bunion symposium, the perfect evening starts with our flying rodents.'"

Matt scribbled quickly. "There's an undercurrent of tangential logic."

"But in the bigger picture, it has *everything* to do with the overall tour, because beneath it all, Gainesville is essentially a small town. Sure, there's the frenetic hive of a university, but it's one of those schools stuck out in the empty countryside, like Tuscaloosa, where everything around it is pastoral. Nothing screams 'small town' more than ritual sundown gatherings at the bat towers, except maybe a roadside attraction about a really big ball of yarn."

"It's already dusk," said Matt.

"And here they come!"

The crowd oohed and aahed as Serge raised his camera toward the flapping, swirling dark cloud that swooped over their heads toward the lake.

Coleman returned from across the street and stared straight up, rotating in place. "Serge, you should see this stoned. Whoa, it's out of sight!"

Matt tugged Serge's sleeve. "Why do a bunch of the other people have umbrellas?"

Coleman looked down at his arms. "What's hitting me?"

Serge continued clicking away. "I forgot to mention one thing. Tonight's forecast calls for intermittent urine and bat guano. But it's all part of nature, a small price for witnessing such an awesome phenomenon."

Coleman held out his arms and whimpered. "But I'm high."

WOBBLY

The orange pickup passed a row of rural mailboxes and turned onto a dirt road. Headlights lit up spooky eyes of critters that dashed into the underbrush. The landscape opened into a sprawling field, and a farmhouse came into view. The truck drove around back and parked by the barn, where someone else was already waiting in the shadows, leaning against a high-mileage Chevy.

Elroy jumped down from the cab. "Shorty, is that you?"

"Hope so." He stepped away from the car and into the moonlight. Shorty actually was short, because he'd grown up in a town of straight-talkers.

"So, a Malibu this time?"

"Just finished the camshaft this afternoon," said Shorty.

Elroy turned around. "Why are you still standing there? You know what to do!"

The brothers jogged toward the barn and opened the door.

Elroy faced Shorty again and shook his head. "My cross to bear."

From the barn: *"Stop it!" "You stop it!"*

"Think of the extra pay," said Shorty.

"That eases the burden. Slightly."

The brothers emerged with large spools over their shoulders and headed out separately across the darkness of the adjacent field, letting out line as they went.

The remaining pair sat on the pickup's tailgate and popped bottles of Miller High Life.

"Ready for Founders' Day?" asked Elroy.

"Ready for it to be *over*," said Shorty. "Could you believe what happened at the pig races last year?"

"That was the most insane shit I've ever seen in my life," said Elroy. "I suggested we race gerbils this year. But 'No, no, no, the people want pigs.'"

"What are you gonna do?"

"Yup."

"Mmm-hmm . . ."

After a third round of beers, they watched the brothers trotting back from the field.

"All done?" asked Elroy.

"Just like you told us," said Slow.

They headed toward the barn again.

"What are you doing?" asked Elroy.

"Going to turn it on."

"No!" said Elroy. "Not yet! Don't you remember? That's the most crucial part of the plan. We have to wait until the last possible second to minimize the chance of detection . . . What's that behind you?"

The brothers turned. "Huh?"

"Why is the barn on fire?"

Elroy and the brothers raced over and got to work with garden hoses. They quickly sprayed down a bale of hay.

"That should do it."

They hung the hoses back on the outside wall and returned to the pickup. Elroy glared at the pair. "I don't know what's so difficult to grasp about avoiding attention—"

"Shhh!" said Shorty. "Listen . . . I think it's him."

They all stopped and perked up as the familiar sound grew louder.

"You're right," said Elroy. He called over his shoulder: "Guys, turn it on. No fires this time."

The brothers went into the barn and hit the switches.

The field dramatically changed. Elroy and Shorty stood with open jaws.

The sound became even louder.

The brothers returned quite pleased with themselves. "What do you think?"

"What the hell is that supposed to be?"

"We strung out all those Christmas lights, just like you told us."

Elroy stared another moment in disbelief. "It was supposed to be two parallel lines marking the clandestine runway for the pilot." He extended a palm. "I have no idea what *this* is."

"I think there's an X," said Shorty. "With a large S and maybe the number four."

"It's hard walking straight in the dark," said Slow.

"We can fix it," said Slower.

"Too late," said Elroy. "He's about to land."

The form of a small aircraft cleared the trees at the end of the field and then seemed to veer with indecision.

"He's going the wrong way!" yelled Elroy.

The plane touched down at a weird angle on the far side of the field and struggled to stop.

"He doesn't have enough room," said Shorty.

The plane disappeared into a ravine.

"Come on!"

Elroy and Shorty jumped into the pickup's cab, and the brothers hopped in the bed. The truck raced across the field, ripping up Christmas lights. They approached the edge of the pasture, fearing the worst.

To their astonishment, the bruised pilot came crawling up the embankment. Luckily the ravine didn't have any hardwood, just reeds and more brush.

"Boggs!" shouted Elroy. "You're okay!"

"No thanks to you guys." He stood and dusted himself off. "What the hell kind of landing strip was that?"

"Long story—" Elroy spun. "Headlights! Get down!"

They all flattened themselves on the grass.

A Mercedes arrived. "You realize I can see all of you. The Christmas lights led me right to where they're tangled up in the wheels of your truck."

"Oh, it's you." Elroy got to his feet. "Everyone, this is Martin, Steve's cousin."

The new guest at the party looked left and right. "Where's the plane?"

The pilot stared in the direction of his prized possession. "The ravine."

"What's it doing— ... Why are all these lights still on? ... Do I smell smoke?"

"The barn!"

They all ran for the vehicles.

Suddenly:

Bang, bang, bang, bang, bang ... bang, bang, bang ... bang, bang, bang ...

Everyone hit the ground again.

Elroy looked up from the dirt. "Someone's shooting!"

"No," said Slow. "Those are just our firecrackers."

"Your what?"

"Yeah," added Slower. "We went to the Founders' Day fireworks tent and they had this great sale on black cats."

"You bought firecrackers?"

"And just a few Roman candles ..."

... Bang, bang, bang ... followed by a series of loud, shrill whistling sounds.

They watched through the open barn doors as dozens of flaming balls ricocheted around inside.

"What's all that doing in the barn?"

"We stashed them in there yesterday," said Slow. "To be safe."

The roof began to burn.

"But that's it, right?" Elroy said sarcastically. "Just firecrackers and Roman candles. Nothing crazy?"

"They were also selling these excellent air bursts!

I think the law changed or they're not enforcing it, but you can now buy these outrageous things like they use in real fireworks shows!"

A large hole had now burned through the roof, leaving an escape route for a screaming meteor that shot high into the sky before exploding in a shower of red, white, and blue streamers. Then another, and another . . .

The barn was now fully engulfed. Then a few last blasts toward the heavens, and the entire property soon turned to day, bathed by several points of incendiary phosphorus light that slowly drifted across the sky.

Slower pointed up. "And we spent the rest of our money on some military parachute flares."

A half hour later, there was a needed intermission where nobody talked. They gazed solemnly at the smoldering embers where the barn had been.

Martin took a heavy breath. "I don't know, I could be wrong. I'm not from around here. Maybe, just maybe, when your kinfolk decide to smuggle a load of contraband that can land you twenty years in the federal pen and stealth is the top priority, that actually means go crazy with Christmas lights, burn things to the ground, and fill the sky with bright explosions."

Elroy cleared his throat. "We're awfully sorry—"

In the distance, a stream of headlights came around the bend at the bottom of the hill.

Martin ceased leaning against his car. "Now, who the heck are all *these* people?"

A siren.

"Police cars!"

Martin stood rod straight. "Okay, everyone shut up and let me do the talking . . . and get that suitcase out of sight."

The cars skidded to a stop in front of the former barn. An older man in overalls leaped from the passenger seat.

"Dancing Christ!" yelled Vernon. "What the hell is going on out here? We've been getting calls from everywhere! People are reporting UFOs!"

An antique truck from the volunteer fire department arrived.

"Jerome!" shouted Vernon. "Will you stop with the hand-crank siren? We're trying to keep a low profile."

The noise ceased and the hoses came on, sending up ash and white smoke as the water hit the burnt debris.

Vernon bore down on the group with a look that said: *Start explaining.*

"Uh, there were a few glitches," said Elroy.

"Glitches?" Vernon stabbed a thumb over his shoulder. "We set up a blockade to stop the news trucks . . . Where's the plane?"

"In the ravine," said Martin. "Just follow the Christmas lights."

"What?" Something suddenly clipped Vernon in the back of his legs, knocking him to the ground. "Where did that fucking pig come from?"

"Apparently some have been living in the woods since last Founders' Day."

The mayor covered his face with both hands.

"Okay, we'll sort out this stupidness tomorrow. But right now, where's the shipment? Please tell me it survived whatever it was that happened out here."

"Got it," said the pilot, raising a hard-shell Samsonite.

"Hand it over," said Martin, laying it on the hood of his Mercedes and flipping latches. The lid opened to reveal sixteen undisturbed packs of powder.

Vernon closed the case and gave it to Shorty. "Stick this in the Chevy and get it locked up at your shop as fast as possible. Don't stop for anything. We'll give you a police escort."

From another direction. "What about my airplane?"

"Shorty," said Vernon. "Come back with the tow truck for Boggs . . . Everyone else, clear out of here and keep your mouths shut until this blows over."

"Mayor . . ." said Slower.

"What!"

He pointed toward a large, oncoming wave illuminated by Christmas lights. "Pigs."

"Run!"

Chapter EIGHTEEN

HIGH UP ON THE GULF COAST

The chopper left Route 19 behind at Crystal River and wound through the spongy lowlands of Florida's nature coast. Oak trees and cabbage palms intermingled in odd alliance for street shade. Pontoon boats were in favor among the locals, who docked them in canals when not navigating the shallow-drafting maze of tributaries that snaked through the marsh before emptying into the Gulf of Mexico's oyster and scallop spawning grounds.

Serge parked his two-wheel machine next to another, significantly older machine that also had wheels. Except the wheels were much bigger and the machine didn't run anymore. Rust-frozen gears were surrounded by the kind of ancient stone walls that evoked Spanish forts.

"Another great small town!" announced Serge. "Homosassa, founded by David Levy Yulee in 1851, and here"—he slapped the rock partition behind him—"are the ruins of the historic Yulee Sugar Mill."

"It's just a bunch of broken-down old stuff," said Coleman.

"Bite your tongue," said Serge. "Florida is so young that it has very few ruins. Actually half the state is in ruins, but I'm talking the traditional type, like Aztec pyramids."

"Aztecs were cool," said Coleman. "They pulled out beating hearts and shit."

"This is even more excellent."

"Really?" Coleman became semi-alert.

Serge nodded and waved an excited arm at the woods. "Once upon a time, all this overgrown emptiness used to be a bustling, five-thousand-acre sugar plantation with hundreds of workers. Unfortunately they were slaves, so I'm glad it's ruins." He spat on the ground. "Those big gears used to grind the cane with steam power. There's the chimney, and these massive metal bowls in the ground were the settling vats."

Coleman scrunched his face. "I thought this was better than beating hearts."

"They also produced a ton of molasses to make rum."

"It's getting better," said Coleman.

Serge surveyed the fallen-down stone masonry now overwhelmed with moss and vibrant green vegetation thriving on the wetlands' moisture. "I love to meditate in some quiet place when Mother Earth has taken back the site of once-furious activity. And if you clear your head and activate your imagination engine—luckily mine is nuclear powered—your genetic memory can conjure a spiritual connection with the souls who toiled here."

Coleman whispered to Matt, "He stands in a lot of empty fields."

"I heard that!"

"But it's boring."

"This is just the precursor," said Serge. "From the other-things-to-do drop-down menu of this tour stop."

"But there's nothing else out here," said Coleman. "Only a bunch of old rotting logs."

"Trust me. Back to the chopper!"

They cruised down Yulee Drive.

"Radio check. I see a building," said Coleman, straining for a better view. "It's the Old Mill Tavern. I knew you'd come through! . . . Serge, slow down. You're passing the bar."

"We're not stopping there."

"But it's a righteous place." Coleman faced backward in his sidecar. "The phone number on the sign is 628-BOOZ. That's a good omen."

"I have something better in mind."

Less than a minute later, the motorcycle rolled to a stop in front of what looked like a small house. Its front was a jigsaw-piece rock wall. Over the door stood a giant photo of a man in sunglasses and an *Alice in Wonderland* top hat, playing the bass guitar. Lighted words on each side of the picture announced the name of the place.

Coleman tried to scratch his head but forgot he was still wearing his helmet. "Neon Leon's?"

"Actually Neon Leon's Zydeco Steakhouse." Serge climbed off the bike. "Another theme running through *Easy Rider* is that they were always breaking bread: at that family's Western ranch where they repaired the bikes, the hippie commune, campfires, and the southern diner where they were run off. Except for that last place, the meals were always ceremonies of peace and camaraderie with new friends."

Matt removed his lacrosse helmet. "But why did you choose this restaurant in particular?"

"I needed to locate a Florida place with New Orleans cuisine to represent Fonda and Hopper's last supper in the French Quarter. And I found it!" A big grin as he led the march to the door. "What seals the marriage between the Big Easy and my home state is that the restaurant's namesake is none other than Jacksonville's own Leon Wilkeson of Lynyrd Skynyrd fame. His relatives now run the place."

They went inside and grabbed a booth under an autographed guitar on the wall.

"Is that a real gold record?" asked Coleman.

"The genuine article," said Serge. "From their debut album with 'Tuesday's Gone' and 'Freebird.' And in that other frame is an original front page from the October 21, 1977, edition of the McComb, Mississippi, *Enterprise-Journal* covering the plane crash that claimed six, including three members of the band." He pointed another direction. "That glass case holds one of Leon's trademark, concert-worn hats."

Matt scanned his menu. "What's good?"

"Everything," said Serge. "Gumbo, crawfish, jambalaya, crab cakes, Cajun Seafood Medley, Mighty Rad Creole."

The waitress arrived. "Had enough time?"

"One more second," said Serge. "What would Leon have?"

"I don't know."

"Probably the oyster po'boy . . . You guys?"

"Sounds good to me," said Matt.

"Beer," said Coleman.

Serge handed his menu back to the waitress. "Make it three. Plus coffee, and keep the refills coming."

She departed and Serge hopped up. "I must take contingency photos." He roamed as the restaurant became filled with camera flashes.

"Sure does like to take pictures," said Matt.

"I barely notice anymore."

The coffee was waiting when Serge returned. He scorched his tongue as he chugged, then hunched over the table. "Here's the critical part, since we're about to break bread: bonding through conversation . . . Matt, you're the newest friend at this ceremony, why don't you kick it off?"

"Okay, where are we going next on the tour?"

"Wrong!" said Serge. "In movies they're always staying on point and talking about the plot, but the dialogue in real life is about everything else. That's where *Easy Rider* shattered the mold. They chatted about a mother retrieving a football helmet from the trash, and aliens mating with us in an advisory capacity. You have to think free form. I'll get us started by picking the *Jeopardy!* category . . . Alex, I'd like pharmaceutical TV ads for a hundred."

"Oh, yeah," said Matt. "Those commercials are off the hook. Acid reflux, testosterone replacement, trouble sleeping, the purple pill . . ."

"Don't forget the crazy warning list of possible side effects," said Serge. "Dry mouth, constipation, dizziness upon standing, blurred vision, slurred speech, numbness, tingling, episodes of eating or driving with no memory of the event, breasts developing in men."

Coleman raised his hand. "Are you talking about me?"

"Then they tell you to report any unusual dreams," said Serge. "Dreams by definition are unusual. If you dream about sitting in a waiting room, then there's a problem. And 'avoid contact with application sites'? Hey, I don't know who's using what or where. I could bump into someone on the street and suddenly have an early onset of puberty. Next topic: How would you go about organizing an anarchist group? Maybe advertise on one of those public bulletin boards with hand-printed notices for babysitting, lost pets, algebra tutoring and ill-attended support meetings for memory loss—using a sheet of paper with a bunch of strips at the bottom where people can tear off phone numbers, except I'd leave all the strips blank. 'Upper Bay Anarchist Membership Drive: Stay Away!' And heaven help the person who's elected secretary. What would the official minutes look like? 'Meeting not called to order,' 'Minutes from the previous meeting shredded,'

'Agenda rejected,' 'All officers impeached,' 'Group disbanded,' 'After-meeting meal at Denny's.' "

"That's a good dilemma topic," said Matt. "We have those discussions all the time in philosophy class, like the liar's paradox, or *pseudómenos lógos* in the ancient Greek."

"What's that?" asked Serge.

"There are several variations," said Matt. "But it mainly boils down to a pair of statements like 'The following sentence is true. The previous sentence is false.' Great minds have pondered the ramifications."

Coleman giggled. "You've got to be kidding."

"It's no laughing matter," said Matt. "In the third century B.C., the philosopher Philitas of Cos reportedly became so consumed trying to resolve such paradoxes that he went without sleep and food until he died."

Coleman's eyes glazed a moment, then he shook his head. "What a load of crap. Over a stupid riddle?"

"It's more than possible," said Matt. "And it has nothing to do with the paradox. Just whether the person has a severe enough case of obsessive-compulsive disorder."

Serge finished snapping a hundred photos of rock-and-roll memorabilia. "I prefer the term 'focus-intensity gifted.'" He turned the camera the other way. *Click, click, click.* "And I can attest from personal experience that Matt's right. I once stayed awake in a tiny, windowless room for three days wondering what happened to Richie Cunningham's older brother."

"I forgot about that," said Matt. "In the first season of *Happy Days*, Ron Howard's character had an older sibling named Chuck, who disappeared from the series without any explanation."

"And all the other family members went on with the show as if nothing was out of place," said Serge. "But here's what I think really happened: You know how even the nicest families can have one 'off night' that results in an unspoken agreement never to mention it again? I can just see the Cunningham parents staring down in the living room. 'Good God, what have we done! Look at all the blood! Kids, go to your rooms.' They're still freaking out when Fonzie shows up and goes, 'Whoa! . . . Joanie, go get the shovel.' "

The waitress arrived with their oyster sandwiches. "Top off your coffee?"

"Yes!" said Serge.

"Anything else?"

"We're conducting a bonding ceremony," said Serge. "It's the perfect place: rock history, unusual dreams, the Cunninghams chopped up the older brother. Could I trouble you for a wedge of lemon? This statement is false."

MEANWHILE . . .

Another pleasant afternoon inside the First National Bank of Wobbly, Florida.

"Yup."

"Mmm-hmm."

The door opened.

Vernon tossed his newspaper aside and stood. "Martin, great to see you! And let me be the first to apologize for the little mix-up last night. We run a much tighter ship around here than that."

"It's already forgotten."

"In the daylight I can see the family resemblance," said Jabow. "You're definitely Steve's cousin."

Martin hoisted a heavy sack onto the magazine table. "Here's what Steve said would be coming."

"But how come he didn't bring it by himself as usual?" asked Otis.

"Stuck in Miami. Some disagreement with one of the car dealerships. Several vehicles got damaged."

"How?"

"Long story."

"This town runs on long stories."

"The dealership threw a big weekend bonanza, you know, with strings of colorful pennants and hamburgers and an obnoxious radio station van. They had this giveaway contest for new cell phones and put the winning tickets inside a few balloons, then filled them and a whole bunch more with helium, but not all the way so they'd fly off—just enough to hover over the crowd until people could eventually snatch them. Except they apparently were giving away one of those super-popular new smartphones that people have a hard time getting. A mob showed up with BB guns, fishing gaffs and crossbows."

"That's why we don't like Miami," said Vernon. "Would never happen here. At least not twice."

"You got a nice community," said Martin, looking around and nodding. "Steve told me how special it is. And what a beautiful drive up here." Another nod. "I could see myself dropping anchor in these parts."

"We'd love to have you."

"Except the cell reception is terrible," said Martin.

"And we like it that way," said Vernon.

Martin opened the top of the canvas sack, and the others looked inside.

"Junk cars must be in style," said Jabow.

"I won't need the bag back," said Martin. "The zipper's broken."

Vernon grabbed the sack—"Wait here"—and sauntered over to the teller window, where Glenda already had the cash counter out.

Large-denomination bills fluttered through the machine. Martin grabbed a chair and joined the gang. "So what do you guys do for fun around here?"

"This."

The counting finished, and Martin waved as he left. "Pleasure meeting you."

"Don't be a stranger."

The door closed.

"Nice enough fella."

"Real friendly."

"But not like Steve."

"No, Steve is great."

"Yup."

"Mmm-hmm."

"Been meaning to ask," said Jabow. "When did you learn how to launder money?"

Vernon grabbed the sports section. "I *don't* know how."

"Then why'd you tell him you did?"

A page crinkled as it turned. "Because I like the sound of an eight percent fee."

"But what if he wants his money?"

"We give it to him, minus our cut, and tell him it's clean."

"Will it be clean?"

"Not really."

"I don't know," said Jabow. "I mean, look what business he's in. Appears harmless enough, but do we actually have any idea what he and his cousin are capable of?"

"Who cares?" Vern turned another page and scanned the obituaries with a mixed sense of dread and hope. "There's no possible way he can ever find out the money isn't actually being laundered."

Outside, a Mercedes left a metered parking space. "Which way did I come from?" Martin glanced around as he rolled slowly along a side street. The car neared the edge of the bank, where Martin happened to notice an old '55 Ford pickup sitting in the alley by the back door. "Man, that thing still run?"

Three young men emerged from the rear of the bank and began cramming themselves in the truck's cab.

The Mercedes came to a stop. Martin chuckled. "Not those clowns who burned down that barn . . ." He stopped and stared.

The last of the trio carried a canvas bag. The same one Martin had just deposited with the town leaders. Judging by its ballast, the heft of the contents hadn't changed.

"What the hell?"

Chapter NINETEEN

THE NATURE COAST

A chopper thundered away from Neon Leon's.
Serge pulled out his camera as they passed a restored two-story cottage with an oversized veranda on the waterfront. "The old Homosassa Lodge, landmark sportsman's paradise," Serge said into his helmet mike. "My favorite painter, Winslow Homer, first visited this area in 1904, taking a steamer up from Key West. While here, he'd stay at the hotel, where some of his finest watercolors emerged, including the iconic *Red Shirt*, depicting a tiny man in a canoe wearing such apparel as he fishes along the tall palms guarding the banks of this river. Now housed at the National Gallery of Art. Watercolors are the best! I just realized I like some colors way more than the taste. Avocado."

"Can we stay at the lodge?" asked Matt.

"Negative," said Serge. "It's now a private residence, which is why I refuse to divulge the address because I'm all about privacy. The nearby state park is another matter. They're paid to be pestered, and I'm all about getting bang for my buck."

They circled back to Highway 98 and followed the signs before entering a parking lot filled with out-of-state plates.

"Look at all the tourists!" said Coleman.

"The ones with taste." Serge grabbed a clipboard from his knapsack and led them inside the welcome center for Homosassa Springs Wildlife State Park.

A young man in a smartly pressed uniform greeted them inside the door.

"What's your name?" asked Serge.

"Kevin."

Serge jotted on his clipboard. "Kevin, what's 'Homosassa' mean?"

"I'm not sure."

"Native American for 'place of many pepper plants,'" said Serge. "Where's the Winslow Homer display?"

"Who?"

"That was another test," said Serge. "I already know where it is. It's the small room at the end of that hall on the left with a barely noticeable sign because it's tragically become an afterthought. Please get that fixed. There's a framed photo depicting how the old fishing lodge looked in the early part of last century, along with a page from the guest register that indicated the famous artist paid eighteen dollars a week. He was from New England, but I'll give him an honorary Floridian waiver just for *Red Shirt* alone. You need to know this in case the tourists ask, and if they don't, tell them anyway because it's important. Are you getting all this?"

"Excuse me," said Kevin. "Are you with the state?"

"You have no idea how much." Another notation on the clipboard. "I'll check back with you in a month and expect a full report . . . Come on, guys . . ."

The three companions neared the end of the hall.

"Serge," said Coleman. "I think we have trouble."

"Why?"

"It looks like the kid back there is talking with his supervisor and pointing at us."

"Let him."

They went inside the room.

"You're right," said Matt, bending his neck close to the wall. "Here's his lodging receipt. Looks like he hired a boat for three dollars and bought lunch for his fishing guide."

"And here's a letter to his brother Arthur." More scribbling on the clipboard. "Bragging about the climate and catching trout."

Coleman tugged Serge's shirt. "Don't look now, but the supervisor's here."

An older man in another uniform approached the visitors. "I'm sorry if there was some miscommunication with one of our new hires." He tried to sneak a glance at the clipboard. "And we'll get a bigger Winslow Homer sign."

"There's nothing to worry about." Serge placed a hand on the man's shoulder. "We're all in this together."

"Glad you feel that way."

"There's no other way to feel . . . Where's Lucifer?"

"Lucifer?" The park supervisor took a reflexive step back, then remembered: "Oh, *Lu*." He pointed. "Outside by the water . . ."

The threesome took a twisting path down to a rippling lagoon of unnatural ice-blue clarity. "Here we are at one of Florida's most magnificent springs, bubbling thousands of gallons a minute up from the aquifer and forming the headwaters of the Homosassa River, flowing nine miles to the Gulf of Mexico. Did I mention it stays a constant and pleasurable seventy-two degrees?"

"I believe those are West Indian manatees," said Matt.

"You have a sharp eye."

"But what was the deal back there with Lucifer?" asked the student. "You kind of threw him off balance."

"The clipboard already did that," said Serge. "But to answer your question, they shortened Lucifer's name to 'Lu' for public digestion."

"I still don't know who Lu is."

"Follow me." Serge launched another short expedition guided by a map in his brainpan.

They waited at the back of a visitors' line before descending stairs into a small, dim room of emerald-green light. The walls of the chamber were lined with angled-out panes of thick glass, and everything had an unsteady sensation of equilibrium.

"Whoa." Coleman grabbed a railing for balance.

"I got a little more messed up last night than I thought."

"It's not you," said Serge. "This is a floating underwater observatory, nicknamed 'the fishbowl,' one of the funkiest remaining 1950s-era roadside attractions in all the state."

"Look at all the sea life!" Matt's hands pressed against the glass. "There are thousands schooling all around us."

Serge pressed his own palms. "Sheepshead, crevalle jack, channel bass . . ."

"And there's a manatee," said Matt. "He's turning and coming toward us. Now he's right up to the window looking at us."

"Hope your hair is combed."

"What a magnificent creature," said Matt. "I never knew until I viewed one in a setting like this."

Serge knocked on one of the observatory's steel beams. "It's the perfect way to see aquatic life. Other marine attractions capture stuff and put it in tanks and people look in from the outside. I don't know about fish, but I get the strong feeling that sea *mammals* understand the difference. Dolphins and killer whales keep swimming around wondering, 'What's the deal with this? I just keep going in bullshit circles. I had bigger plans.' But here, the humans are in the container and everything else gets to swim free in their natural environment, and if they choose to come look at us, they can. Then they go on their merry way, straight, serpentine, abrupt angles, all of them thinking: 'This is way better than circles.'"

"But what about Lu?"

"Next stop."

The gang climbed back up to ground level and marched a brief distance down a curving trail until Serge overlooked an enclosure. "There's Lu."

"A hippopotamus?" said Matt.

"Been here since 1964." *Click, click, click.* "An exotic-animal company used to winter down at the springs and lease their critters out to Hollywood for the big screen. Lu, here, starred in many notable jungle films and the smash-hit TV series *Daktari*, plus guest appearances on *The Art Linkletter Show* and Herb Alpert specials, becoming a sixties wild-life celebrity, though it's murky whether the Tijuana Brass was involved."

"I remember *Daktari*." Matt pulled out his note-book. "Not the hippo."

"The noble animal eventually ended up in the hands of the state, along with others from the traveling Ivan Tors Animal Actors troupe," said Serge. "Conservation officials—with the best of intentions—scheduled deportation because Lu didn't fit the indigenous habitat."

"But he's still here." Coleman convulsed with a beer belch. "I should lie down."

"Lu had stolen the locals' hearts and they took up the banner," said Serge. "In 1991, Governor Chiles granted the hippo state citizenship so he could remain. Lu is now well past normal life expectancy due to diligent care, and ever since he turned fifty in 2010, local newspapers royally report each birth-day complete with bio tidbits like Lu's best friend was another refugee from the animal company, a donkey named Susie, whom Lu would faithfully follow wherever she went. It was never a problem if officials needed to move such an immense African land mammal to another part of the park. They'd just get the donkey. Unfortunately Susie passed away, and I'm getting misty thinking about Lu's empty heart."

"I'm sincerely in awe," said Matt, writing fast and flipping pages. "How did you discover so much trivia? How do you *remember* it? . . . Mostly useless but still entertaining."

"Useless on the surface." Serge tapped his chin with the wisdom of experience. "But you never know . . ."

WOBBLY

Martin waited until the vintage pickup began moving out from behind the bank. Then he turned into the alley and followed. Based on the antics of the truck's occupants the previous night, he wasn't worried about being spotted.

A short, peaceful drive later, the Mercedes sat on a lonely road with a clear view of an even lonelier trailer and a '55 pickup parked outside.

Martin pressed buttons on his cell phone. "Damn, no reception."

Two strategies presented themselves. One: Frontal. Knock on the door with pointed questions. Which would result in lies and messiness. Or two: Be patient and find out what these idiots were really up to. Martin tossed the phone on the passenger seat and sat back and waited.

And waited.

Night fell. A TV lit up the mobile home.

After a while, the door opened. Empty Budweiser cans flew outside. The door closed.

More waiting.

The door opened again. Three young men came out and fired off bottle rockets for a period of mild amusement. They were down to their last firework and had a brain-drizzle. Slower dropped his pants and bent over as they inserted the bottle rocket's stick a couple inches into his rectum.

His brother aimed a cell-phone camera to capture the festivities for social media.

"This is going to be so great!"

They lit the fuse.

The opposite of rocket science. The force of the propellant fell short of dislodging the stick from Slower's derriere, and a shower of sparks singed his butt and chased him, jeans around ankles, waddling and screaming until the climactic explosion of the rocket that sent him headfirst into the side of the trailer, knocking himself unconscious.

The others poured beer on him as the antidote. He woozily came around and they high-fived and popped more beers and went inside to see how many Internet strangers approved.

Martin squinted through his windshield. "What is wrong with these people?"

Eventually, just before midnight, the trio stumbled out with the canvas bag from the bank.

Martin threw the Mercedes in gear. "Now we're talking."

The two vehicles wound through the night countryside, past horses and rusty windmills and abandoned tractors. The pickup finally turned down one of the nicer dirt roads in town and headed up a driveway until it reached a dark residence. Martin cut his lights and parked a hundred yards back. At first he thought they were going to the home for some kind of secret meeting. But then, "What on earth are they doing?"

The trio removed a loose piece of lattice from the side of the house and wiggled into the exposed crawl space, dragging the canvas bag from the bank.

Martin got out of his car. "Just when I thought it couldn't get weirder." He checked his cell phone. Crap, still no reception. He decided to send a text, which would automatically go through as soon he hit an area of better coverage. He stuck the phone in the console between the seats and weighed options again. He grabbed an automatic pistol from the glove compartment, racked the chamber, and walked toward the lattice. "Okay, let's see what kind of brainlessness we're dealing with . . ."

Underneath the house, Elroy continued leading the way with a collapsible camping shovel. "Where's Slower?"

"Back here. I think I got a splinter in my butt-hole."

"I ain't breaking out the tweezers, so deal with it."

The shovels snapped into open position, and a familiar routine of flinging dirt began.

"Elroy—"

"Don't even start again about why we're the guys who always have to crawl under houses."

Slow closed his mouth.

Another spade full of dirt flew. Elroy realized the hole was taking longer than usual. Because only two shovels were in play. He looked around with his flashlight, then barked the loudest whisper he dared without waking Jabow. "Slower! Where are you?"

An echo from a distant part of the crawl space: "Digging the hole. I was wondering where you guys were."

"You dolt! . . ."

Martin got down on his hands and knees—"Steve owes me big-time"—and shimmied under the house . . .

A shovel hit something. Elroy's hands swept dirt away from the previously buried cash. "Hand me that bag." New cash went on top of the old.

Martin continued crawling with stealth, led by the sound of curt whispers up ahead. Occasionally there was a flicker from a thin flashlight, then darkness again. He reached in his pocket for the pistol.

"Is that the last of it?" asked Elroy.

Slow turned the canvas bag inside out. "It's empty."

Elroy's arms began herding displaced soil back into the hole. "Let's fill this sucker up and get the heck out of here."

Slow felt something pressed against the back of his head.

"Nobody's going anywhere!"

A startled Elroy raised up and smacked his head on a floor beam. "Ow, shit! . . . Who's there? . . . Jabow, did we wake you?"

"It's Martin from the bank. I believe that's my money." He shoved Slow down in the dirt. "Somebody better start explaining fast."

"*Your* money?"

"Yes!"

"Look, man, we just do what we're told."

"Who gives your orders?"

"Anyone on the city council. Until we work our way up to the big table in Lead Belly's, they get to bust our balls and run us around everywhere, like the other night at that farm with the airplane and Christmas lights."

"A stellar piece of work that was." Martin stretched out his shooting arm. "Turn on your flashlight . . . Not in my eyes—at my hand . . . See this? Don't think I won't use it. Now start filling that bag back up. Then we're going someplace a little nicer and having a long talk."

"Whatever you say." Hands furiously clawed the ground.

Martin smiled maliciously. "That's better—"

Wham.

Thud.

"Martin?"

Silence.

Elroy clicked on his flashlight again. Martin lay motionless in the dirt. Behind him was Slower, smiling and wielding a shovel. "I found my way back."

"What made you hit him?"

"I saw him pointing that gun at you," said Slower. "Figured that wasn't good."

Elroy snatched the pistol from Martin's listless hand. "Slower, this just might be the smartest thing you've ever done."

"Really?"

Elroy tapped Martin on the cheek. "Tables are turned, city boy. Now we're going to have that talk—but on *my* terms."

"He's ignoring you," said Slower.

"He's just still unconscious," said Elroy. "Shake him."

Slower did. "Still not moving."

Elroy slapped his cheek harder. "Martin! Wake up!" He shined the flashlight. "Oh no."

"What is it?"

"Fuck me," said Elroy.

"What's going on?"

"Look at his face," said Elroy. "Blood's coming out his nose."

"So he has a nosebleed. No big deal."

"It's a huge deal. You hit him in the back of his head, not the face," said Elroy.

"And now blood's coming from his ears," said Slower.

"Exactly. His brain is bleeding." Elroy grabbed a wrist for a pulse. "No, no, no! Not this!"

"Is he going to be okay?"

"He's dead."

"What?" said Slower. "I just hit him once."

"This isn't like the movies where people in bars bash each other over the head with bottles and keep on fighting," said Elroy. "You hit a guy in the head even once with something hard like a shovel, you can easily kill him."

"Didn't mean to."

"This is definitely the stupidest thing you've ever done!"

"I don't understand."

"Do you have any idea who this is?"

"Yeah, Martin."

"Steve's cousin," said Elroy. "They're doing serious business with the city council. And they're dangerous characters. Landing planes secretly at night: What did you think that was? . . . Don't answer. The important thing is that nobody can ever find out about this. He just disappeared. Swear to me you'll never speak a word."

"I'm not saying anything," said Slower.

"Me neither," chimed his brother.

"Okay, let me think. We have to get rid of his body."

"Let's just throw him in the woods somewhere."

"No, they're always finding those. It has to be a place he won't ever, ever be found." Elroy looked straight down and nodded to himself. "Grab your shovels."

"Why?"

An hour later, they crawled out from under the house.

"I never want to do that again," said Slow.

"Shut up!" snapped Elroy, reaching in his pocket. "Here are the keys to the Mercedes. We need to ditch it. There's one kind of place to abandon cars where it will look like a million other suspicious things might have happened. People are always ditching cars there for the same reason. Follow me."

They replaced the lattice and drove away from the house.

Twenty miles east, Elroy's nerves finally began to uncoil. "Looks like we dodged a real bullet." They continued on through God's country. Slower drove the Mercedes past a hill with the flashing red beacon of a cellular tower on top. Inside the car's console, a phone glowed back to life.

Three hundred miles south, in a forty-eighth-floor Miami penthouse, a text alert jingled. A man in a bathrobe checked his phone's display and pinched his lip. "What the heck is *that* supposed to mean?"

Chapter TWENTY

HOMOSASSA

Just after nightfall, three traveling companions sat cross-legged on the ground.

"I love camping!" said Serge, arranging freshly gathered kindling wood into a small pyramid. "This is just like *Easy Rider*! My favorite parts were them bonding around their fires! And I'm going to make this the best campfire ever! Coleman, give me a light . . ."

"Serge?"

"What is it, Matt?"

"But we're in a motel room."

"Right, I love camping but need A/C, TV and Wi-Fi." Serge flicked the lighter. "To balance it out, I picked one of the worst-rated budget motels in the area so we could really rough it."

"No, I mean I don't think a campfire in the room is a good idea."

Serge held the flame in front of his face. "It just says 'No Smoking.'"

"I'm afraid I'm with Matt on this one," said Coleman. "Remember the fire I started in that one room?"

"You're right." Serge let the flame go dark. "That didn't go well at checkout."

He grabbed his laptop, hit a few keys, then set it on the floor between them. It began playing a You-Tube video of a campfire.

"Much better idea," said Matt.

"And now that we're living off the land, let's again resurrect the art of conversation that's been lost in the age of technology. I'll turn on the TV." A news report about a small tornado with great cell-phone video from a viewer.

"Television is roughing it?" said Matt.

"It's not a flat-screen," said Serge. "That's pretty uncivilized. I'll pick the first topic. The conspiracy of cable news. They're all in it together."

"I don't know," said Matt. "CNN may be neutral to the point of banal, but Fox and MSNBC couldn't be more philosophically different."

"And that's what they'd have you think, but here's when the secret mind control dawned on me: I'd be watching one station, and it would go to a commercial. I don't want to watch a commercial; I need more data on celebrity misbehavior, so I'd switch the channel, and there would be another ad, and another on the third station, sometimes the exact same commercial. First it was just frustrating. *No, I don't want to leave the Situation Room with Wolf Blitzer where five people are talking at once*, and then I'm stuck in a bunch of ads for airlines I didn't even know existed. How many CNN viewers can be flying to Korea? I never want to let accusations fly before I check my facts, so I monitored the trend for twenty-four straight hours, and the bombardment of commercials took its toll. *I don't want to know that since I had chicken pox, the shingles virus is already in me. I don't need to reverse my mortgage. I still don't want to fly to Korea.* In the end it became obvious that they were all colluding—despite the smoke screen of political differences—to synchronize commercials." Serge raised an index finger. "That's how it always starts."

Coleman grabbed the remote and clicked to another news station.

". . . *Post-menopausal intercourse doesn't need to be painful . . .*"

"Ahhhhhhhhhhhhhhhh!"

"Serge, are you okay?"

"Just a flashback. And now I'm oddly attracted to Asian flight attendants. Next topic: strange circumstantial emotions that defy explanation, like when you realize you're on the wrong street and have to turn around in someone's driveway, and for no reason at all you feel outrageously guilty, hurrying up to get the car in reverse like a thief, hoping they don't peek out the windows. And then, 'Oh my God, they're peeking out the windows! The shame is too great! I must get the hell out of here!' So you fishtail backward from their driveway and take out the mailbox. But you were already back on a public street and the mailbox was technically on city easement, so it's clearly not your fault: 'Those assholes in that house made me tense.'"

Matt raised his arms and yawned. "I'm getting tired."

"And I need to blog today's developments," said Serge. "Did I mention that this is the county where Tom Petty had his musical awakening in the sixties?"

"Every half hour."

Serge grabbed his laptop, and the others grabbed pillows . . .

Hours later, Coleman woke up and crawled out of the bathroom. "Is Matt awake?"

"No, still sleeping like the proverbial baby." Serge tapped furiously on his laptop. "That's what I hate about youth: the ability to immediately conk out. I probably close and open my eyes at least a hundred times before I drift off."

"I've noticed how you keep popping up and down," said Coleman.

"First, I jump up to check if my wallet's where I left it . . . Then I close my eyes again: Did I actually see where my wallet was when I got up just now, or became distracted and simply imagined that I looked? . . . I need to put my wallet someplace safer . . . Did I just fall asleep and only dream that I checked on my wallet? . . . I need to leave myself a note where I just hid my wallet in case I forget in the morning . . . But if a burglar breaks in and finds the note, it will lead him straight to my wallet . . .

Where should I put the note? I know: I'll hide it in my wallet." Serge stopped typing. "Where's my wallet?"

"Behind your laptop," said Coleman. "Have you been on the computer this whole time?"

Tap, tap, tap. "I'm surfing fetish websites."

"I didn't know you were a pervert."

"Here's an all-points bulletin," said Serge. "Everyone's a pervert. It's just a question of how in fashion your uncontrollable quirks are."

"What about prudes?"

"*Especially* prudes," said Serge. "That's why they're prudes. They secretly have a good idea what they'll find if they start rummaging around the dark closets in their subconscious."

Coleman staggered over. "Can I see what you're looking at?"

"Sure, but I'm afraid you'll be bored." *Tap, tap, tap.* "Although I freely admit I'm as perverted as the next guy or gal, my interest in these searches has nothing to do with sex."

"It doesn't?"

"When you mention fetish, people think of the obvious: bondage, bestiality, latex, feet, dudes with staggering collections of unlaundered and alphabetized panties that force them to knock out non-load-bearing walls for industrial shelving space." He refreshed the browser. "But what's most fascinating is the stuff that's so far afield from any normal sexual appetite that it's a jarring non sequitur."

"What am I looking at?" asked Coleman. "There's just a lot of steam."

"Psychrophilia," said Serge. "Arousal from extremely cold objects. This guy is packing all his most prized everyday possessions in dry ice."

"That's weird."

"It's only the start." *Tap, tap, tap.* "One of the most riveting aspects is the specificity of the subject matter, like an endowed college chair. There are separate websites for Girl Scout troop moms in high-top sneakers, tattooed chicks playing the cello, androgynous squirt-gun fights, encasing oneself in Bubble Wrap, sniffing subtropical fruit—seedless or regular, but not both."

"What's *that* guy doing?"

"Forniphilia. Sexual arousal from posing as a piece of furniture," said Serge. "He's a TV stand. See the Zenith on his back?"

"I had no idea all this was going on."

"Most people don't," said Serge. "It's an accident of unsynchronized human evolution. Our imaginations have outpaced our animal urges . . . A perfect analogy is cooking. Primal instinct programs us to eat for survival, but nature never intended green-bean casserole with those crunchy onion things that you'll never encounter outside of the holidays if everything's going right. Likewise, the sex chefs give us this . . ."

Coleman scooted closer to the screen. "A hot babe in work boots smashing lightbulbs?"

"That's a new one on me." Serge grabbed his notebook as the video progressed. "Now she's going for the niche markets, stomping energy-saving bulbs . . . fluorescent tubes . . . outdoor floodlights . . ."

"Can I try?" asked Coleman.

Serge relinquished his chair. "Be my guest."

Coleman moved the cursor to start another video. Two minutes in: "Oh my God! Look at this!"

"What is it?"

He covered his eyes. "I can't watch any more."

"What can possibly be that bad?" said Serge, turning toward the screen. "Jesus! That's one of the most unnerving things I've witnessed in my whole life! What kind of fucked-up potty training did these people have?"

"Turn it off!" said Coleman.

"Wish I could," said Serge. "But I can't let this go unaddressed. I'm all for live and let live—to a degree—but this is just wrong. And it's happening in Florida. I can tell from the palm trees out the window."

"I thought she was just going to step on lightbulbs, but then she went on to ants."

"And who hasn't stepped on ants?" said Serge. "But when she progressed to grasshoppers, I knew this wasn't trending well."

"Next came lizards," said Coleman.

"*Lizards!*" said Serge. "They're my friends. I'd catch them as a kid, but just to put in my pocket. And as an adult, I can't tell you how many times I've rescued them from buckets of water or swimming pools."

"I had a pet hamster."

Serge clutched himself and bowed his head with closed eyes. "I'm rarely this disturbed."

"So what are you going to do?"

"Research." *Tap, tap.* "Okay, here's an article out of Miami. A woman was arrested on animal cruelty charges in what's apparently called 'crushing videos.' Authorities uncovered a sex website run by a fishing-boat captain. One of the women killed a bunny, blew cigarette smoke and sprinkled pepper on the body—more sexual white-noise static. Then this other woman gave a guy a hand job while using the other hand to cut a chicken's head off with hedge clippers." Serge grabbed his stomach. "I may be sick."

"But they got arrested, right?" said Coleman. "Everything's okay now?"

"For the Miami website, but not this other one we just saw."

"But it's on the Internet. How can we find these people?"

Tap, tap, tap. "Here we go. A way to order DVDs through the mail. It's got a PO box near Ocala."

"That doesn't help."

"Ye of little faith." Serge stood up and grabbed a pen. "I'm going to leave a note for Matt. He doesn't need to see this . . . Where's my wallet?"

THE NEXT DAY

A bustling lunchtime crowd in lobster bibs filled the rib joint.

The city council sat around three pushed-together tables, topping each other with jokes.

"No," said Otis. "I don't have any naked photos of my wife."

"Want some?" asked Vernon.

The tables filled with hearty laughter.

"Hey, that's not funny!"

"Oh, lighten up."

The front door opened.

"Look," said Jabow. "It's Steve."

"Hey, Steve." Vernon waved him over. "Join us . . ." He stopped and appraised the newcomer's black Under Armour outfit. "Looks like you just got back from Miami. Better change those clothes before someone mistakes you for a city slicker."

More laughs from the table.

"Steve," said Jabow. "*Steve?* . . . Is something the matter?"

A worried look. "I can't reach my cousin."

"He was just here yesterday," said Vernon. "We saw him at the bank."

"And you don't have any idea where he might be?"

"No, why should we?" said Otis. "Told us he was heading back south."

"He always stays glued to his cell phone when out of town."

"You know the terrible reception around here," said Clem.

"I haven't heard from him in almost twenty-four," said Steve. "That breaks our ironclad rule. You sure nobody's seen or heard from him?"

"We'd definitely say something if we had," said Vernon. "But I'd be happy to put the word out for our patrolmen to keep their eyes open."

"His Mercedes had a GPS that we tracked," said

Steve. "Found it abandoned in the next county behind a strip club."

"Gee," said Vernon. "That could mean any number of things might have happened."

"It's also the first place where people ditch cars when they want you to *think* any number of things might have happened," said Steve. "Everyone knows that."

Blank looks from the tables.

"One more thing," said Steve. "Just after midnight I got a text message from him." He handed his phone to the mayor.

Vernon's eyes widened as he read.

"What's it say?" asked Jabow.

"Yes," said Steve. "Why don't you read it to everyone?"

"Uh, *'They're crawling under a house with the money.'* That's odd."

Steve took the phone back. "Yes, very odd. And I think it rings a bell."

"What? . . ." "Us? . . ." "We don't . . ." "Huh? . . ." "Strangest thing . . ."

"I think all of you know exactly what that message means," said Steve. "What have you done with my money?"

"Laundered it, like you asked."

"So where is it right now?" said Steve. "I want it back."

"Can't," said Vernon. "It's out being laundered."

"I'm paying you eight percent to wash that cash, and you're just burying it! What was I thinking?"

"Steve, calm down," said Jabow. "You know we really like you—"

"Knock off the country-fried horseshit!" A fist pounded the table, spilling iced tea. "I want my money."

"Okay," said Vernon. "We all understand you're upset about a missing relative and not thinking clearly, so we're going to let it pass this one time."

"Fuck you!"

Vernon stood and began opening his mouth. When he did, he saw something he hadn't noticed before in the crowded restaurant: two immense men in white suits standing silently by the door, hands clasped in front of them and weapons bulging under their jackets. "Who are they?"

"I'll be back!" said Steve. "I want my money! And my cousin!"

He stormed out of the rib joint, and the linen suits followed.

"What the hell was that about?" asked Jabow.

"Goddammit!" snapped Vernon. "I hate a pissing contest when the other guy knows more about my dick than I do."

"What now?"

"Get ahold of those three morons and bring them here as soon as possible so we can find out what really happened last night."

Chapter TWENTY-ONE

An eclectic line of humanity stood at a counter.
"*Next . . .*"

Everyone moved up a space. Envelopes, brown boxes. FBI Wanted list on the wall. Poster for new commemorative stamps featuring mallard ducks. Typical post office.

"*You can't use twine in the mail . . .*" "*It'll never make it to New Zealand taped like this . . .*" "*You forgot to address all of these . . .*" "*It has to be under seventy pounds even if it is a rock collection . . .*"

"Have any of these people ever mailed anything before?" asked Coleman.

"Unfortunately, many times."

"Serge, I agree it's a good idea to stake out the PO box, but we don't know when someone will show up," said Coleman. "We could be waiting here all day."

"Not when money's coming."

They finally reached the counter. "How may I help you?"

"What time do you deliver to the PO boxes?"

"Guaranteed by noon."

"Thank you," said Serge.

"Is that all?"

At the next window, someone placed a large ceramic unicorn on the counter. No box, nothing. *"Can you help me mail this?"*

Serge aimed a thumb sideways. "How often does that happen?"

"More than you'd ever imagine."

"My sympathies . . . Come on, Coleman."

They waited outside on a parked motorcycle, talking with radio helmets.

"It's hot," said Coleman. "I'm bored."

"Promise it won't be long." He checked his watch. "One minute past noon . . . Wait, see that guy through the window? He's going for the PO box."

"What's our move?" said Coleman.

A hand reached into a knapsack. "You're going to have to ride bitch behind me."

"But I like the sidecar . . ."

Serge hopped off the bike as a man exited the post office flipping through a stack of envelopes containing money orders and personal checks. His silk shirt unbuttoned halfway down his chest. Gold chains, dark monogrammed sunglasses, pointy Spanish boots.

"Excuse me," said Serge. "Lizards were my childhood companions."

He raised his face. "Huh?"

"I think you know what I'm talking about."

"Do I know you?"

"We might even get to be friends," said Serge. "As soon as you take down all your animal-crushing videos and promise never to do it again."

"Oh, I get it. A dissatisfied customer." The man nodded. "Did you pay for something and not receive it?"

"I'm not a customer, but I'm definitely dissatisfied," said Serge. "I totally understand there's no accounting for sexual fetishes. One person's Wiffle ball is another's butt whistle. But can't you use animation or special effects or something?"

"Shit," said the man. "Another animal-rights wingnut. How many of you assholes are out there?"

"Don't worry," said Serge. "I'm not like anyone you've ever met before."

"Just get the fuck out of my way!" *Shove.*

Serge stumbled backward, and the man took a step forward, misjudging his adversary's reflexes.

Serge was right back in his face. "You must have slipped. Because otherwise that would be no way to launch our summit talks."

"You're a fruitcake!" The man cocked his arms back for another hard push. But before he could deliver: "Ow! What the hell was that?"

Serge raised a syringe and flicked a clear drop off the end of the needle. "Just a little something for your nerves. Everyone's so uptight these days."

"I am talking to a dead man! You're going regret ever . . . *eeeeee-oooooooo.*"

"Easy, big boy," said Serge. "Take it slow. Let me give you a hand walking . . ."

Ten minutes later, Serge's chopper cruised west through relaxing miles.

"Coleman, ease up on your grip around my stomach. I can't breathe."

"But I'm scared to fall off the back."

"Can't you just chill out like our guest?"

Coleman glanced over at the sidecar. The passenger's head was in a helmet, slumped to his shoulder.

"How long will that tranquilizer last?"

"Long enough to get him out of sight," said Serge. "Why are you laughing?"

"*Easy Rider* has become *Weekend at Bernie's*."

THAT NIGHT

Another quiet evening in the charmingly restored two-story country home. No lights. A balmy breeze blew through lace curtains.

Peter Pugliese lay peacefully in a Queen Anne bed.

His eyelids flew open. "I can't sleep." He looked at the digital alarm clock. "A sandwich and milk would help me sleep."

Peter put on slippers and shuffled to the kitchen. He stood indecisively in front of the open refrigerator door for an extended duration of time that men only do when their wives are out of town. "Baloney."

He grabbed the Oscar Mayer and a jar of mayo, then put the jar back. "No, I want it fried, like in college," also because his wife wasn't home. He got out a skillet and made strategic slices in the meat so the middle wouldn't bubble up. While it began to sizzle, he opened the fridge again. "Ooo, didn't see the cottage cheese before. That goes great with corn chips."

Peter sat at the table with his fried baloney and milk and used a remote control to turn on a tiny kitchen TV that flipped down from under the cabinets. He felt mildly guilty about using a remote for such a close distance and decided to mow the lawn in the morning. The cable channel showed a controversial rancher holding a dead calf to somehow prove he was justified in not paying taxes because of Negroes . . . "I'm feeling sleepy."

He took the cottage cheese and corn chips back to bed and munched until his eyelids drooped. Peter dozed a second, then startled awake in terror at the messy snack on his chest, reflexively spinning his head to locate his wife. Then he remembered . . . He set it all aside on the nightstand and rolled over, burying a smiling face in the pillow.

Peter lay tranquil. He sprang up. "I can't sleep." He looked at the alarm clock. "It's still only ten o'clock in Sacramento."

He went back in the kitchen with his cell phone and dialed.

"Peter, what are you doing up?"

"I can't sleep. How's the trial?"

"The killer wore these Velcro shoes from the Payless chain called Cross-Trekkers, and I thought we'd caught a big break, but didn't realize how popular they were because the social stigma against Velcro shoes is lifting among certain youth subcultures. Then we lucked out because the killer kept going to this video store . . ."

Peter got a curious expression. His ears perked up at a faint, low-frequency sound that he wasn't sure he was actually hearing. Then it grew louder and he became sure. But what was it? Wide-open possibilities: plumbing pipes, joists adjusting to temperature, a stereo playing too loud on the other side of the hill. He decided to walk to the window.

". . . Peter? Are you there?"

"I'm here."

"Were you listening to me?"

"Absolutely."

"What was the last thing I said?"

"Velcro."

"That isn't the last thing I said. Video store."

"Who has those anymore?"

"Cold case, twenty years."

"Sorry, I just went to the window."

"Why?"

"Looking for pigs."

"Pigs?"

"They live in the woods, but that might just be rumor."

"Are you interested in what I'm saying? It's a really exciting trial. I'm in a Marriott. I've had a little wine. So the murderer wore these shoes a million other guys now wear—not ones that I personally would marry, but some women—except the shoes were like a fingerprint because the guy's video store had a parking lot experimenting with a new silica aggregate that was supposed to change everything but only bankrupted the company and convicted the defendant because of teensy-weensy jade granules—"

The vibrations became louder. Peter ruled out pigs and thought, *What else?*

"—which were distinct hexagons that stuck in his soles and will probably send him to death row. Isn't that wonderful?"

"What?"

"You said you were listening to me."

"I am. It's just . . . this noise in the house."

"What's it sound like?"

"Odd." He poked his head toward another window. "Do they have earthquakes here?"

"I don't know. But whatever it is, it must be getting loud," said Mary. "I can hear it over the phone. Sounds like a herd of buffalo outside."

Peter grabbed the kitchen counter for balance. "Now it's like the buffalo are *inside*."

"What's happening back there—"

Mary didn't hear an answer because her phone was filled with the sound of a bomb going off . . .

. . . Back in Florida, the phone had shattered. Peter found himself dazed on the floor. A thick cloud filled the room. Peter got his bearings and pulled himself up at the sink, splashing his eyes and rinsing dust from his hair. He was definitely convinced there'd been some kind of detonation. "Was that a gas explosion? Because there's no way someone would want to *bomb* me. I don't have any enemies . . ."

Peter wanted to call 911 but remembered the useless phone. So he grabbed a D-cell flashlight from the junk drawer and went investigating through the haze. Room after room, all clear. He reached the end of the hall and the master bedroom, where he had just been lying down.

The flashlight's beam swept the space, but he couldn't see anything because the cloud was impenetrable. This had to be ground zero of whatever craziness had happened. He took a cautious step forward but still wasn't able to make anything out. Then another step. He peered closely as the smoke and dust began to clear. His eyes must be playing tricks. The haze wasn't the only reason nothing was visible. Because nothing was there. No dresser, nightstand, not even the bed. "What the—"

Peter took another bewildered step forward. His front foot slipped, and he fell backward on the wooden floor. He moved forward again, this time crawling and feeling with his hands for what had made him trip. His fingers found something that didn't compute.

An edge.

He aimed the flashlight down. Not just any edge. The side of a cliff. More haze dispersed, exposing a twenty-foot-deep hole in the earth the size of the entire room. "A sinkhole?" The bright beam searched the bottom but found nothing. The cave-in had covered all the furniture and everything else with dirt and clay. He grabbed his pounding heart. "My God, if I hadn't gotten up to call my wife . . ."

Peter knew sinkholes, knew they could spread. Some dirt clods broke loose from under the floorboards beneath his hands and tumbled into the abyss. He prepared to crawl backward as gingerly as possible. Just before he did, the flashlight caught the only discernible feature at the very bottom of the collapse. "Is that what I think it is? . . . No, you've been having too many nightmares lately. That can't possibly be . . ." Peter and the flashlight patiently waited for more dust to settle. "Dear God!"

He abandoned composure and scrambled in dizzying panic out of the room, then the house, and threw up in the geraniums. "I have to get to a phone!"

Chapter TWENTY-TWO

Coleman stared at the yellow sign.

VENOMOUS SNAKES IN AREA.

"Will you come on!" yelled Serge, feeding coins into a coffee machine.

Coleman trotted up and pointed over his shoulder. "This rest stop has poison snakes?"

"Of course," said Serge. "Those signs are at dozens of our welcome areas."

"That's odd."

"Here's what's even stranger." Serge collected his cup of joe. "Check out that vending machine."

"The candy bars?"

"No, the other one with sundries that travelers forget: toothbrush, razor, aspirin."

Coleman stooped in front of the glass. "I didn't know you could buy snake-bite kits from vending machines."

"They're adapting to local needs, like how McDonald's in Paris sells Cabernet," said Serge. "Snake-bite kits in rest-stop vending machines bring up another daily hurdle only encountered in Florida: 'I'm starting to see spots *and* I don't have correct change.'"

Coleman looked back at their motorcycle's sidecar. "He's still out cold. Aren't you worried that everyone can see him?"

Serge shook his head. "The best place to hide something is in plain sight."

"But I think people are getting suspicious," said Coleman. "They're staring at him as they walk by."

"That's more out of disgust than suspicion, because his head is hanging over the side with drool coming out," said Serge. "They were staring at you the same way earlier in the trip, except you weren't around to see it."

The chopper roared away from the rest area and took an exit below Ocala. It pulled through the gates of a parking lot with rows of orange-striped vehicles.

"Why do we need a U-Haul?" asked Coleman.

"Because U-Hauls are the best! They have limitless possibilities!" said Serge. "I've been fascinated with U-Hauls since I was a kid. Back then, I desperately wanted one because it would be the perfect escape pod for when the adults disappeared."

He went inside the rental office and approached the desk. "I need a U-Haul for a sensitive experiment."

The manager had begun getting out the forms but hesitated. "What exactly are you going to do with it?"

"First, load my current favorite possession, that *Easy Rider* chopper sitting outside your window."

"Oh, I get your experiment now." The manager slapped paperwork on the counter. "We often get bikers who are concerned because they haven't transported their wheels before. But don't worry; the trucks that will fit your motorcycle have special tie-downs inside."

"For the record: Ever since I was a little kid, I've had the utmost respect for U-Haul, from concept to execution," said Serge. "During my wonder years, I'd see them going down the road and think: 'What are those people fleeing from?' I always begged my parents to rent one, but they kept telling me they didn't have any need. And I said, 'I do. Just park it in the backyard and I'll go about my business. You'll forget I even live here.'"

The manager handed over the keys. "You know we're not actually the U-Haul company."

"But . . ." Serge looked back out the window. "The trucks and trailers?"

"Bought some used inventory and opened an independent office."

"Good for you," said Serge. "Then the U-Haul people won't mind what I'm going to do."

"And I won't, either," said the manager. "Bikers are some of my best customers. Guess it's overall vehicle pride, because they always return them spotless. You should see some of the other stuff we get back. Once there must have been some kind of struggle inside because of all this blood."

"I'll try to watch that."

Serge took the keys and led Coleman out to one of the trucks. The manager stood at the window, observing them lower the back ramp and push the chopper up the incline with someone still in the sidecar.

A helmet began lolling back and forth.

"Serge, I think he's starting to come around."

"Then we have to hurry." Serge grabbed his knapsack off the rear of the bike, removing rope and duct tape. He saw the manager staring from the office. Serge grinned and waved and pulled the roll-down back door closed behind them.

"It's dark in here," said Coleman. "And hot."

Serge clicked on a flashlight. "Only take a minute to immobilize and silence him. I love U-Hauls! If only my parents had rented one, they wouldn't have had to repair the ceiling."

"Ceiling?"

"It can only hold so much weight. They were watching TV one night when suddenly: 'What the hell are all these coconuts falling out of the attic? . . . Where's little Serge?'"

"I think you tied him up pretty good," said Coleman.

"Let's rock."

Serge began raising the door but stopped a quarter way when he saw the manager standing outside.

"Is everything okay?"

The pair crawled out quickly, and Serge closed

the door. "Reminiscing about childhood. They also found coconuts under my bed."

The manager rubbed his eyes as Serge and Coleman climbed in the truck's cab and sped away.

It was another winding country drive back to the motel. This time, not even small towns. Just tracts of land and isolated buildings. Fire tower, church steeple, No Dumping, some kind of quarry, a soccer field for migrant workers, an overgrown cemetery where the latest date was 1933, a wedding dress in a ditch. The traffic was different, too. An open-bed semi brimming with fresh oranges, a pickup full of watermelons, an obese woman in a Cadillac with a row of stuffed animals in the back window.

"Serge, I think I hear the theme from *Miami Vice*."

"My cell phone . . . Hello?"

"*Where are you guys?*"

"Oh, it's you, Matt."

"*I found your note when I got up yesterday and I've been waiting and waiting, and you still weren't back this morning.*"

"Had a bunch of errands to run."

Thud, thud, thud.

Coleman tapped Serge's shoulder. "I think he's flopping around back there."

"He'll wear himself out."

"*Who will wear himself out?*"

"Nobody you know."

"*You guys aren't doing any cool stuff on the tour that I'm missing, are you?*"

Thud, thud, thud.

"Definitely not," said Serge. "You'd be completely bored."

"I'm completely bored here."

"We'll be back tonight," said Serge. "Meantime, just do what college kids do. Study for a test, occupy an administration building."

"That was the sixties."

Thud, thud, thud.

"Got to go." *Click.*

Coleman cracked a Pabst and looked out the window. "I just saw another mailbox shaped like a chicken. That makes five, including the rooster."

"It's the defining difference between inland and coastal Florida. Near the ocean, people with money have manatee and dolphin mailboxes," said Serge. "Out here, poultry is the class distinction."

"So what's the plan now?"

"Stop voter suppression," said Serge. "Another goiter on the American Dream. It's supremely immoral to use the false pretext of in-person voter fraud to disenfranchise hardworking citizens. You should have seen the line I had to stand in for the last election."

"But how can you vote if you're a fugitive?"

"With a fake ID," said Serge. "I'm not about to let them destroy the integrity of the process."

"That's just not right."

"Especially after they cut back early voting," said Serge. "I always cast my ballot before Election Day because I have flexible hours, so I drove to the local precinct at the library and went in one of the meeting rooms where I always vote. Can't tell you how heartened I was to see all these lines of fellow patriots itching to be democratic. I took my spot at the end of one of the lines with my sample ballot already filled out. Soon I realized the lines were barely moving, and I'm like, 'What the hell are they trying to pull now?' Then all the people got down on the floor and sat cross-legged, obviously because of the long wait, except they pulled their feet up uncomfortably over their thighs. I remember poll taxes and literacy tests from the sixties, so I yelled, 'We have every right to vote without this stress-position bullshit!' Then someone explained that early voting had been pushed back and I was in a yoga class."

"What happened?"

"I didn't get to vote, but I learned the lotus position."

Coleman nodded and drank beer. "So what's the plan?"

"I just told you."

"No, I mean right now." Coleman looked over his shoulder. "The guy in the back of this van."

"Oh, I thought you meant *the* plan: Stand up to China, fix immigration, get some new Supreme Court justices who will play ball . . ." Serge passed a chicken mailbox and watched a sign go by. He hit the brakes.

"What did you see?"

"That farmhouse."

The moving truck turned off the street and headed up a solitary dirt road.

Someone on the porch saw a cloud of orange dust

approach from the distance. He continued rocking in his chair.

The truck pulled up sideways, and Serge ran to a porch railing. "Saw your sign by the road."

"If you say so." The whiskered man in a straw hat took a leisurely sip of sweetened iced tea and bourbon.

"You selling horses?" asked Serge.

"That what the sign says?"

"Yes."

"Then I don't see why not. You want a horse?"

"No," said Serge.

"You here for conversation?"

Serge pointed at a much smaller animal. "I want that."

"You want to buy Betsy?"

Serge got out his wallet. "How much?"

"Wasn't plannin' on sellin' her."

"Name your price."

The farmer shook his head. "She's part of the family."

"Five hundred," said Serge.

"I'll go get her."

"Not necessary." Serge handed cash over the railing. "We'll just drive down and load her in the back. Here's another hundred for that wheelbarrow."

"Nice doin' business."

The truck headed away from the house. A chair resumed rocking.

A half hour later, Serge entered Citrus County. He flipped down his visor to shield the setting sun.

Thud, thud, thud.

Coleman took a hit and flicked a roach out the window. "I'm totally confused."

"You just nailed human existence."

"We got a hostage to take care of with a new science experiment you haven't explained." He pulled out a baggie to twist a fresh one. "But buying that thing back there is only going to slow us down."

Serge winked. "Unless Betsy is part of the plan."

MEANWHILE . . .

A "Closed" sign hung in the front window, and all the doors were locked just after dark. But Lead Belly's was definitely open for business. A private party.

The search had taken forever, but it finally yielded the three bug-eyed, stuttering young men sitting up as straight as they could in a row of chairs against the wall. Elroy, Slow and Slower.

"You got to be shitting me!" yelled Jabow. "You buried him under my house! I'm going to strangle all of you!"

He lunged, but the others got between them and wrestled him back.

"Jabow!" shouted Vernon. "The last thing you need to do now is lose your head. We have to close ranks on this."

"What are we going to do?" asked Otis.

"Give me some space to think," said the mayor. "Obviously the first thing is to get that body out of there. Then we'll worry about the cover story . . . Guys, get the pickup truck and some shovels."

Jabow pointed with menace. "Those assholes ain't going anywhere near my house!"

"Fair enough," said Vernon. "But we have to start moving because we've got a lot of work and the sun will be up before we know it." He turned to the petrified trio against the wall. "Elroy, exact location?"

"Uh, third piece of lattice from the end on the south side, then straight in twenty yards."

Vernon turned a different way. "Otis, stay here with them and don't let anyone leave until we get back. The rest of you, follow me . . ."

A small convoy raced through back roads at ninety.

"I still want to kill them!" said Jabow.

"Let's stay on task," said Vernon. "There's your house now."

They pulled up and piled out. A piece of lattice was pried away. Vernon peeked underneath with a flashlight, then stood up. "Okay, who's going with me and Jabow?"

The rest leaned on shovels, looking at each other and the sky and the ground.

"Come on!" said Vernon. "If I'm going, you can, too. Floyd? Clem? Harlan?"

"It's really dirty." "There could be insects." "My back."

"Jesus!" said the mayor. "Okay, I'll make this simple: Either we all go, or nobody goes. And then we all hang together and rot in jail."

Vernon got on his hands and knees with a flashlight, followed by Jabow and a yardstick, then the reluctant remainder of the gang joined them in the blackness of the crawl space.

Worms and ants and spiderwebs. "How much farther?"

"Just keep crawling."

"Eighteen," said Jabow, dragging the yardstick. "Nineteen . . . Twenty. Here we are. Shovels?"

The trailing members slid a couple forward. The first clump of dirt flew. Then another, and another. Jabow was motivated but tiring. "How deep did they say?"

"They didn't," said Vernon. "But with those three, I'm guessing not a lot of elbow grease was involved."

They kept digging until Jabow stood hip-deep in the ground. "This can't be right."

"Then we'll just have to widen the hole."

An hour later, everyone was panting with futility.

"Now I'm really going to kill them!" said Jabow.

A flashlight slowly panned boards and beams. "It's got to be here somewhere," said Vernon. "The only other answer is they were lying, and they're too stupid and scared for that."

"What do we do?"

"Fan out and dig a bunch of shallow test holes every few feet."

Another hour passed. People shouted from various corners beneath the house. "Nothing here." "Same here." "I've reached the end."

Vernon turned to his brother. "Jabow, I know how you feel about this, and with every right. But now we have no choice. We've got to bring 'em out and show us."

"Then I get to kill them?"

"Fair enough."

Everyone piled back in the vehicles. Just as they were pulling out, a police radio squawked. A hand grabbed the mike. "Vern here."

"This is Officer Phibbs."

"Phibbs, it better be damned important."

"It's leaning that way . . ." And the cop laid it out.

Vernon keyed the mike again. "And this happened *last* night? Why are you just telling me about it now?"

"I'd rather not say any more over the radio."

Vernon hung up the mike and yelled out the window at another car. "Jabow . . ."

"I heard on my own radio. What a crazy night."

"I've got to go out there," said the mayor. "You head back and gather the peckerheads."

They reached the road at the bottom of Jabow's drive. The pickup headed back to town, and Vernon went the other way, hitting lights and siren. "Of all the rotten times for another sinkhole!"

Chapter TWENTY-THREE

BACK TO NATURE

Unhurried citizens strolled through crosswalks. Optimistic notions of how the evening's dinner menus would come together. Some lugged plastic and earth-friendly sacks; others were followed by bagboys pushing shopping carts. One woman had second thoughts about her veal with peppercorn.

The grocery store's automatic doors opened again; an effervescent man in a tropical shirt sprinted out holding a pair of sacks high over his head. "I scored! I scored!"

The crosswalk traffic parted as Serge and Coleman raced back to their moving van. "Publix is a Florida treasure! Where shopping is a pleasure!"

"But we just bought fruits and vegetables," said Coleman. "I hate it when you only let us shop along the walls of the store with all the yucky stuff."

Serge checked his appearance in the rearview. "Jedi Master, the force of the beer aisle is strong with this one."

Later that night, the rental truck pulled into an empty parking lot at Homosassa Springs Wildlife State Park.

"Serge, duck your head down!"

"Why?"

"A security guard! And there's another!"

Two golf carts pulled alongside the driver's door. "The park's closed. Can we help you with something?"

Serge held up a road map. "Checking my route."

Thud, thud, thud.

"What was that?" asked a guard.

"Must not have stacked the boxes right." Serge folded the map. "Hope nothing's broken or I'm in trouble. You married?"

"So you're not parking here overnight or anything?" asked one of the guards.

"Leaving right now." Serge started up the engine and got back on the road.

"That was close," said Coleman. "I guess you'll have to call off your project."

"Just the opposite." Serge swung onto a small road below the park and cut his lights. "That was exactly what I expected. Simply needed to recon their security rounds before I put everything in motion."

Serge opened the back of the truck and rolled out the chopper, hiding it in the darkness of the side street. Then he resumed driving deeper into marsh country.

"Hey, there's Neon Leon's again," said Coleman. "Why are we back here?"

"Because the houses really start to spread out, and

there's a lot of vegetation for concealment." Serge slowed and checked each residence for a number of criteria. "No . . . No . . . No . . . No . . . Okay, this one looks promising."

The truck quietly drove across the lawn and pulled around behind the house.

"Why did you pick this place over all the others?"

"Four reasons." Serge rolled up the rear door of the truck and climbed in. "First, it's on the Homosassa River. Second, there's enough space between homes that it's out of view. Third, the lights are out at an early hour, which means the owners aren't home."

"What if they're just having dinner at Leon's?"

"We'll be long gone by then anyway." Serge dragged the wriggling captive by his ankles across the cargo bed, then pushed him over the bumper, where he fell to the ground with a groan.

"What's the fourth reason?" asked Coleman.

Serge glanced toward the water. "They have one of those."

"Cool."

"Give me a hand with Betsy . . ."

A few minutes later, Serge and Coleman moved slowly and quietly through the night, cool wind in their hair, oak branches overhead.

"*Mmmmmmmm!*"

"Serge, your prisoner is trying to scream again under the duct tape."

"Doesn't he know this is a nature area?" Serge looked down and delivered a swift kick to the ribs.

"You're disturbing the wildlife." Another kick. "There's more where that came from."

"Mmmmmmm!"

"Crap! Another challenged student!" Serge ripped the tape off his captive's mouth, producing a brief schoolgirl scream. "So you want to talk?" He pressed a .45 auto into the captive's right eye. "I'm all ears."

Nothing but frogs belching in the dark.

"That's what I thought." Serge tucked the gun away under his tropical shirt. "You're all cowards! When it comes to sexual quirks, I'm as weird as you are! No, weirder. There's not a chance you can keep up with me in that pantheon." He bent down and covered the prisoner's nose and mouth until he couldn't breathe. "When it comes to getting your freak on, my motto is the same as the oath physicians take: Do no harm."

"Mmmmmmmmmm!"

"You'll have to speak more clearly. I can't understand a word you're saying." *Kick, kick, stomp, kick.* "In all my years, I thought I'd been around every fetish block there is, but not this ghetto." Extrahard kick, this time to the throat. "Trouble breathing, eh? Think about those poor, small animals you tortured and mutilated just for sexual gratification and, worse, profit!" Another stomp that broke his nose.

"He shut up," said Coleman, looking skyward at the canopy of brilliant stars in the reacquired tranquillity. "This is actually kind of nice."

"Who says work needs to be stressful?" Serge stood confidently at a steering wheel. "That's why I love environmental experiments."

Coleman stared over the side into black water. "I've never ridden a pontoon boat before."

"Necessary for shallow drafting—and when you need a stable, flat deck." Serge turned the wheel, and the craft calmly followed a bend in the river. Along the banks: docks and davits and homes with flickering TVs.

"Serge," Coleman whispered. "I thought boat engines were noisy."

"Very much so." Serge turned the wheel the other way. "And that big ninety-horsepower Evinrude on the back of this baby would wake the whole neighborhood. That's why I'm using the auxiliary electric motor to run silently. Most riverboats have them because the owners generally like to fish, and on the final approach to their favorite spots, they switch to electric so it doesn't spook their prey."

"The motor's really tiny."

"With a pontoon boat this size, you can only go a couple miles an hour," said Serge. "Which is fine because we're in a wake-free manatee zone—another spiritual commandment with me—and I don't need to make waves that could bang around those boats anchored at the bank and draw attention."

"*Mmmmmmmmm!*"

Kick.

"You're right," said Coleman. "We couldn't be more quiet if we tried. And dark."

"I killed the running lights," said Serge. "That's a no-no, but the animals don't mind."

A barely audible movement of air came toward them as something took shape in the blackness. A large blue heron swooped over the boat and disappeared. An owl hooted from an overhanging branch.

"Nature's cool," said Coleman.

"Then take a gander off the port side."

"Which is port?"

"Left."

Coleman leaned over the edge.

"Your other left," said Serge.

"Oh." Coleman walked across the boat.

"Here's how you remember: Port has fewer letters than starboard, and left has fewer letters than right. I can't help you with the basic right and left."

"Better write it on my shoes again." Coleman suddenly leaped back and seized his heart.

"What's the matter?"

He pointed with a quivering arm. "There's something giant and alive in the water! Now I know what you're going to do to that guy."

"Chill out." Serge ran fingers through his hair. "That's one of the gentlest creatures on earth."

Coleman cautiously looked over the side again. "I recognize it now. It's one of the manatees we saw earlier."

"Grab one of our grocery bags and get out a head of lettuce. They like that."

Coleman dropped the leafy ball in the water. "You're right. He's nibbling. So that's why you made us stop at the store?"

"Not entirely."

They continued up the river, bend after bend. More birds and unseen things in the trees. Then it became eerily quiet. The boat approached a bridge.

Coleman stared up as they slipped under the span. "This reminds me of *Apocalypse Now*."

"Near the end of our mission, there will be certain parallels."

Serge cut the engine back until they were barely moving.

"There's that underwater tank where we looked at fish the other day," said Coleman. "We're inside the park now?"

"Keep your voice down." Serge pointed up the right bank. "And your head."

They watched the roof of a golf cart zip by.

"I think this is a bad idea," said Coleman. "Those guards are bound to see us."

"Not if we stay low," said Serge. "They're on vigil for trouble coming at them from the road. They never expect the river. And the moon won't be up for a while, so as long as we stay on schedule, we'll have cover of total darkness."

"But I just don't see how it's possible to break into an official place like this."

"Chaos is always possible in Florida," said Serge. "Sea World has far more security, but remember in 1999 when that guy snuck into a tank in the middle of the night to swim with the whales? They discovered his naked body the next morning. And he was just some loon who stupidly stumbled through all their precautions, so this place should be a cakewalk."

Serge steered toward the bank and turned the motor off, allowing the pontoons to drift harmlessly into the mud and reeds. Then he hopped ashore and secured the boat with a rope around the nearest tree.

Coleman followed Serge on hands and knees as they crept to the perimeter of a large enclosure. Serge taped an envelope to a fence post.

"What's that?" asked Coleman.

"Money for repairs because I have total respect for the sanctity of our state parks." He started snipping the fence with bolt cutters. Soon he had enough clearance to peel back a wide flap. "Now help me unload the boat . . ."

Moments later, they were crawling again. Coleman had a grocery sack and a leash. Serge pulled a pair of ankles.

"*Mmmmmmmm!*"

Serge grabbed the man's crotch. "I swear to God I'll pop your nuts if you don't shut up! . . . That's better."

They slithered through the opening in the fence.

"You were right," said Coleman. "We made it inside."

"Don't celebrate too soon." Serge removed his backpack. "We've got critical work to do. Hand me the leash . . ."

WOBBLY

Vernon's car skidded to a stop at the top of the driveway, and he cut the siren.

Officer Phibbs was still interviewing the person who had originally called 911 the day before.

The mayor ran up. "Peter, are you okay? Are you hurt?"

"I'm fine. Just freaked out."

Other official cars were already there. Several sheriff's cruisers and unmarked vehicles. Detectives taking photos.

"God, I hate those county bastards!" said Vernon. "This is all we need." He turned to his officer. "You were kind of vague when you called me on the radio. This happened last night?"

The officer nodded.

"And I'm only hearing about it now?"

"Peter ran to a neighbor's house down the road, which may or may not be over city limits," said the officer. "So the call went to the sheriff's office, and it fell through the cracks . . . Deputies finally got around to coming out, and when I saw all the commotion while driving by, I figured you'd want to know, because of that *other issue*."

"Excuse me," said Peter. "What other issue?"

"Your house is located in disputed border country."

"I don't know what that means."

"Has to do with that strip of land we annexed so we could catch speeders on the highway," said

Vernon. He glanced around to see if anyone was eavesdropping. "Surveyors cost a lot of money, so we just sort of eyeballed it."

More sheriff's cars came pouring up the drive. Deputies began unwinding yellow spools.

"Excuse me, Mayor," said Officer Phibbs. "I didn't exactly tell you everything before, because it was over the radio. Could we step aside for a moment?"

The officer gave him the lowdown.

"What!" Vernon jumped back. "You're completely serious?"

The officer nodded.

Vernon heard car doors slamming across the lawn.

"Who are those guys?" asked Peter.

"No time to explain," said Vernon. "Listen very carefully: Don't say a single word. I'm getting you a lawyer."

"But I didn't do anything."

"Doesn't matter," said Vernon. "This is one of those rural political feuds, and you've just become an innocent pawn in the border war. Forget fair. Anything—and I mean anything—can happen way out here in the country."

"You mean like that song 'The Night the Lights Went Out in Georgia'?"

"Just keep your yap shut!" Vernon turned and smiled and held out a hand. "Sheriff Highsmith, it's a pleasure. What brings you out to these parts?"

"Vern, are we going to have to do this the hard way again?"

"I don't know what you're talking about."

"Sure you don't." The sheriff pivoted. "You must be Peter Pugliese?"

"Peter," said Vernon. "Remember what I told you. You don't have to talk."

"Interfering with a witness?" asked Highsmith.

"I don't know about your jurisdiction, but in my town reminding someone of the Constitution is patriotic," said Vernon. "And speaking of jurisdiction, aren't you out of yours?"

More cars arrived. Men got out on the edge of the property, setting up tripods with highly calibrated telescopes.

"Surveyors?" said Vernon.

"We've been requesting your official annexation map for over a year," said Highsmith. "The preliminary one we got looked like someone had drawn the lines freehand after drinking."

"Someone needs to get their vision checked." Vernon turned. "Peter, don't say a damn thing."

The sheriff stepped up to the mayor nose-to-nose like a baseball argument. "I know exactly what kind of town you're running here. Speed traps, the subdivision, lost utility-bill records and all the other off-the-books corruption. It stinks to high heaven!"

"That's slander," said Vernon. "Phibbs, you heard that."

"I haven't been able to prove anything yet, but you're dirty and I'm going to take you down," said the sheriff. "In the meantime, I'm bringing the witness in for questioning. Peter, this way . . ."

Vernon's mind swirled at the ramifications: the

fake geology report, groundwater pumping, everything. Peter was a city boy who wouldn't take well to a twelve-hour interview in some outback shithole. He might crack and say anything.

"Sheriff!" yelled Vernon. "Mr. Pugliese is a hard-working, upstanding citizen of this community, and I strenuously object—"

"Save it," said the sheriff. "Let's go, Peter . . ."

Chapter TWENTY-FOUR

LEAD BELLY'S

Knock, knock, knock.

"We're closed."

"Otis, it's me. Jabow."

The door opened and he stormed inside.

Three young men sitting in a row saw him coming. They snapped their heads back, hitting the wall in succession.

"Don't hurt us."

"As much as I'd like to . . ." Jabow bore down on them. "Where'd you bury the money and the body?"

"Just where we told you," said Elroy.

"We dug up the whole place and then some," said Jabow. "Didn't find nothing."

"But it's there—"

"Get in the truck!"

They raced back across town and turned up the driveway to the house. Jabow jumped out of the cab and ran around to the pickup's bed. "Get out!"

It was like the trio was spring-loaded.

"Now you're coming with me!" said Jabow. "And you're going to show me exactly where you were digging!"

"Okay."

The three climbed back into the bed of the truck.

"Dammit!" said Jabow. "How simple are you?"

"What do you mean?"

"I told you to show me where you buried the stuff!"

"Right." They sat still.

Jabow's face turned blood red. "What the hell are you doing?"

"We're going to show you," said Elroy.

"So get the fuck out of the truck and get under my house!"

"But that isn't your house," said Slow.

"Of course it's my house."

"No, it's not."

"I think I would know my own home—" Jabow suddenly stopped and hung his head in exasperation. "Under exactly which house were you digging?"

"We'll take you there," said Elroy. "It's just up the road, next turn."

"You of all people should know where it is," said Slow.

"You live there, after all," said Slower.

The sheriff began walking Peter back to one of his cruisers.

Another car came up the drive. An expensive one.

A distinguished man in an oxford shirt climbed out of the black Lincoln.

"Senator Pratchett," the sheriff said respectfully. "What are you doing here?"

The senator placed a friendly hand on the sheriff's shoulder. "Heard there might be a tiny misunderstanding."

"To say the least."

"But this is the sort of thing that has a way of getting in the papers, and there's been a tad too much of that lately for my taste. Not good for anyone. I'd like to see if we can come to an amicable resolution."

The sheriff pointed accusingly. "It's him! He gives a bad name to the whole county!"

Pratchett manufactured a pained expression and nodded with sympathy. "I'm familiar with the history around here. Give me a second and let me see if I can't reason with him. In the meantime, I would consider it a great personal favor if you could put everything on pause."

"Anything to help you."

The senator walked over to the mayor.

"You're up late," said Vernon.

"Jabow called me."

"Jabow?"

A '55 Ford pickup raced toward them and skidded to a stop.

"Vernon!"

"Jabow, what's going on?"

Jabow whispered in his ear.

Vernon's eyes flew wide. "Jumping saints in heaven! Can this possibly get any worse?"

Pratchett gestured down the driveway, where Peter was about to be placed in the back of a cruiser. "Yes, it can."

"What do I do?"

The senator whispered in Vern's other ear.

"But won't that make everything worse?"

"Just do it," said Pratchett. "It'll stop the bleeding."

The pair walked down the driveway, and Vernon pulled out a pair of handcuffs. "Peter Pugliese, you're under arrest for murder."

"Hey!" shouted the sheriff. "You can't take my witness!"

"He may be *your* witness, but now he's *my* homicide suspect. That trumps."

"Like hell it does." The sheriff gestured across the driveway. "My coroner's van says otherwise. The medical examiner is a county office, which gives me the bigger bite of this pie."

"Take it up with the judge in the morning," said Vernon. "Which is me . . . Come on, Peter."

Sheriff Highsmith looked toward the senator for help.

"I did my best." Pratchett shrugged. "But you know how unreasonable he is."

At the top of the drive, Vernon pressed Peter's head down as he stuck him in the backseat of his car.

"But I didn't kill anyone!" Peter protested.

"I know that," said Vernon.

"Then why are you arresting me?"

"You're not really under arrest."

"What?"

"Just shut up and look guilty."

The car left the driveway, and Jabow followed in the pickup truck with three young men in the back bed.

"What happened to that house?" Slow asked Slower.

"They said a big sinkhole opened up under the bedroom."

"Wow, I sure hope Jabow's okay."

THE HOMOSASSA RIVER

A full moon rose on the horizon, gleaming through the trees.

Serge and Coleman were crawling again. This time leaving the park. Twenty more yards to their exit through the vandalized fence. Coleman glanced back at the captive's plight. "Can we stay and watch? It's going to be so excellent!"

"Wish we could." Serge looked up at the trees. "But we need to get back to the boat and out of here before the moon lights up the whole river."

They made it through the fence. Serge pulled the chain-link flaps closed, then secured the breach by sewing the broken links back together with heavy-gauge wire. "Coleman, go get on board."

"Aren't you coming?"

"One last task." Serge kept his head low, waiting

and checking his glow-in-the-dark wristwatch. The roof of a golf cart appeared right on schedule above some vegetation, and just as quickly it was gone. Serge pulled something from his backpack, stood up and attached it to the top of a fence post.

Coleman was waiting with a beer as Serge untied the mooring line from a tree and hopped back on the boat's deck, sending vibrations through the water.

"Shoot!"

"What?"

"Cut it too close." Serge pointed at sparkling ripples in the river. "Moon's already up. We're exposed."

"What do we do?"

Serge cranked the outboard engine with abandon and roared out of the park.

"There's another manatee," Coleman shouted above the noise.

"Manatees! Shit!" Serge cut the engine. "You're never supposed to go above wake speed around them. I almost did something immoral."

"Don't look now, but a golf cart is coming down the bank behind us."

"There's cover of darkness under those trees up ahead," said Serge. "If we can just get around this bend."

"He's shining a flashlight in the water," said Coleman. "I think he knows we're out here. The beam is coming this way."

Serge grabbed Coleman's shoulders. "Get down!"

The guard's searchlight swept through Spanish moss where Coleman's head had just been. The pontoon boat silently drifted out of sight.

The electric motor started, and the craft trolled to the nearest clearing on shore. Serge hopped out.

"Where are you going?"

"Just follow me."

They only had to jog a hundred yards before coming across the chopper that Serge had hidden in brush on the side of an empty street. He pulled a small box from his backpack and tossed it deeper into the bushes, then climbed on the bike. "What are you waiting for?"

Coleman stood in surprise. "What a coincidence our bike was here."

"Just get in the sidecar."

Matt was peeking out the window of the budget motel when the chopper pulled up.

The door flew open. "Where have you guys been?"

"Just some housekeeping." Serge pulled a canvas bag off one of the handlebars. "You like carrots?"

"What?"

"It's late," said Serge. "Let's all get inside and go to sleep."

"You're not telling me something," said Matt.

"What? Me?" said Serge.

"We didn't do anything wrong," said Coleman.

Matt eyed them warily as they turned down the covers.

"Since you're the guest," said Serge, "I'm going to make the supreme sacrifice and sleep with Coleman so you can have the other bed."

Matt stood by a nightstand. "Your arm. Is that blood?"

"Good night." Serge turned off the lamp.

Matt slipped under the sheets. "Is something going on I should know about?"

"Coleman!" yelled Serge. "Did you fart?"

"Me?"

"That's it," said Serge. "It's the Dutch oven for you!"

"No! Not the Dutch oven!"

Serge pulled the covers over Coleman's head.

"Let me out!" Coleman thrashed underneath. "It's like the gas chamber!"

Matt shook his head and rolled over on the mattress to face the other way.

Time passed.

Serge stood over Matt. He waved a hand in front of the young man's face. No response. He returned to the other bed and shook a shoulder. "Coleman, wake up."

"What?"

"We have to get going."

"Where?"

"Just don't make any noise."

The pair crept out of the room and mounted the chopper again . . .

. . . Ten minutes later, the motorcycle returned to the motel parking lot. The engine was off as it coasted the last fifty yards to their room.

"Remember not to wake Matt," Serge whispered.

Coleman climbed out of the sidecar with a small cardboard box they had just retrieved from the brush next to the state park. "What's in here anyway?"

"Remember the thing I attached to the top of the fence post just before we split on the pontoon boat?"

"I don't know what that was, either."

"A mini video transmitter powered by a nine-volt battery," said Serge. "They're all over the Internet for ninety-nine dollars. We couldn't stick around for obvious reasons, but there was no way I was going to miss the season finale."

"So we'll get to watch it after all?"

"As many times as you want." Serge took the package from Coleman. "The transmitter's great but has a limited broadcast strength. This box contains the accompanying portable receiver and digital recorder. I had to stash it within signal range. Now all we have to do is plug it into my laptop and watch our new nature documentary."

"Remember *Mutual of Omaha's Wild Kingdom* from the sixties?" asked Coleman. "How did their cameras always seem to be at the right place when shit went down?"

"It was uncanny," said Serge. "One minute into every show, you'd hear Marlin Perkins's solemnly reassuring voice: *We have been on our quest for days, but the jungles of Madagascar have withheld their secrets* . . . Then, just off camera: *Okay, boys, release the rhinoceros with the trained chimp riding on its back smoking a cigar.*"

"Nature's cool!"

Serge swiped his magnetic room key. "Be as quiet as possible."

They slunk inside and Serge configured the electronics to his computer. "Here we go . . ."

A finger pressed play.

A grainy picture in amber light.

Coleman touched the screen. "There's our guy lying on his back in the dirt, held in place with tent stakes."

"Move your hand." Serge swatted it. "I want to see Betsy make her entrance."

"There she is." Coleman's face glowed from the screen. "And she's eating your carrots. How'd you know?"

"Just a hunch, but they like almost anything."

"Now the dude's head is twisting every which way like he's super scared." Coleman leaned closer. "Uh-oh, I think he just crapped himself." Giggling.

"It's funny that he's defecating?"

"No, Betsy," said Coleman. "The guy's terrified for his life, and Betsy's wearing that funny straw hat the farmer put on her, with little holes cut out for the ears to poke through."

"Normally I'm against the anthropomorphic dressing of animals because house cats don't dig Brazilian beach thongs, but in this case it adds a detail that the reporters will be helpless to resist."

"How'd you get the whole idea to begin with?"

"I was looking for something like Betsy anyway, regardless of whether I had a student to instruct." He placed a hand over his chest. "When I heard that Lu had lost his soul mate, Susie, it broke my heart.

I said to myself, 'Whatever else I do before leaving town, I'm buying a donkey.'"

"She's eating more carrots."

"It's official now: love at first sight," said Serge. "Lu the hippopotamus is following her everywhere."

"That guy on the ground seems worried."

"Why? They're not bothering him, and the park rangers are sure to discover his plight in a few hours," said Serge. "This is probably the easiest bonus round any contestant has ever played."

Coleman bent even closer. "Did you deliberately place all the carrots in a circle around that dude?"

"Me?"

"Betsy is stepping over him to get to her next snack . . . and here comes Lu . . ." Coleman covered his face with a hand, peeking through fingers. "I can't watch . . . *Ouch!*"

"That was just an arm," said Serge. "He's got another. Imagine if that was his chest."

"I don't have to," said Coleman.

"Ooo." Serge winced. "That tickled."

"Humans are a lot like tomatoes," said Coleman.

"Looks like Betsy missed a carrot on the other side," said Serge. "She's coming back."

"So is Lu," said Coleman. "Make that ketchup."

"Damn." Serge tapped on the keyboard. "Thought it would last a little longer."

"What are you doing now?"

"My latest task in social engineering for a brighter tomorrow," said Serge.

"Which is?"

"A sentimental touch. I'm posting this on the Internet." Keys tapped. "The best part is that Lu re-discovered true romance . . ."

Footsteps and a yawn. "Can I see what you guys are watching?"

Serge slammed the laptop closed. "Criminy sakes! Matt, don't sneak up on us like that!"

"Sorry." He sat down on the edge of a bed with mussed hair, smacking his lips and tongue with cotton mouth. "So what was that on the screen anyway? Looked like someone in serious trouble."

Serge turned the laptop over and studied its underside. "There's something wrong with the power supply. It does that at the worst times."

Chapter TWENTY-FIVE

THE NEXT DAY

Late-morning traffic whizzed by on U.S. Highway 19. Out-of-state tourists in SUVs and rental cars slowed as they approached the parking-lot entrance, then continued on when they saw the barricades and police officers waving orange batons.

The roadside attraction didn't have any visitors this day, but its lot was still full. Police and other emergency vehicles. Detectives, state officials, satellite trucks.

A TV reporter stood on the side of the road in front of the crime tape.

"This is Jessica Meredith reporting live from Homosassa Springs state park, the site of an overnight tragedy reminiscent of the killer-whale death at Sea World. Police are releasing few details, but apparently an intruder cut through a fence under cover of night and found his way into the pen of the locally beloved celebrity hippo named Lu, where he was inadvertently stomped to death. Those

close to the case describe *a macabre scene too gruesome for words, as well as the presence of a mystery donkey seen in this photo wearing the cutest little hat . . .*"

Medics wheeled a zippered body bag to the coroner's van.

"*. . . Unnamed sources have identified the victim as Rudolph Blix, the operator of a controversial sex website that has been assailed by animal-rights activists such as those who can be seen here to my left . . .*"

A row of roadside people cheered and waved signs at traffic:

HONK IF YOU LOVE LU!

"*. . . In a final twist to the already bizarre chain of events, someone anonymously posted an Internet video supposedly showing the actual moment of death, and those knowledgeable in the field say it has become an instant viral favorite among the crushing-fetish community . . .*"

A high-handlebar motorcycle honked as it sped past the sign wavers.

ACROSS THE STATE

Another packed lunchtime crowd in Lead Belly's.

Baby backs, pulled pork, slaw. Three tables formed a long one. Everyone pushed empty plates forward. "Let's get started."

"Court is in session," said Jabow. "The Honorable Judge Vernon presiding."

He used a saltshaker as a gavel. "Bail is set at a hundred dollars."

"I don't have that on me," said Peter.

"What you got?"

He looked in his wallet. "Seventeen."

Saltshaker banged. "Bail reduced to seventeen dollars. Defendant is free to go."

"I am?"

"No, Jabow's taking you to a safe place until all this blows over."

"But—"

"Kid, you're not from around here," said Vern. "When things get ugly, it's butt-ugly."

Jabow looked up at a wall clock advertising defunct root beer. "We better get going before you-know-who shows up."

"Take the rear door," said Vernon. "Car's waiting."

"Do you *have* to put a coat over my head?" asked Peter.

"Yes."

They disappeared out the back, and Steve came in the front.

Vernon stood and waved with a smile. "Come on over!"

Steve walked purposefully with an air of deliberate action. Most who had seen it before didn't see it, or anything else, again. He stopped at the edge of the table. "Maybe I need glasses, but there doesn't seem to be any money or my cousin."

Otis pulled out a chair. "Please have a seat."

Steve just glared. So did his goons, who were much closer to the table this time, no longer caring if other customers noticed they were packing.

"First," said Vernon. "I'm sorry we had words

yesterday. But it caught us totally off guard because we had absolutely nothing to do with any of this."

Steve's stone face said he wasn't buying.

"It deeply concerned us," the mayor continued. "So we got right on the case. I put all my officers on it. From what we've learned, it was totally understandable how you reacted."

Otis nodded. "We all would have done the same."

Steve's head turned slowly from one face to another. "You have something to tell me, or are we just getting old here?"

Vernon slapped the empty wooden chair. "You really need to have a seat. Then we'll give you every last detail."

As they say, the silence was deafening. Nobody spoke in the high-stakes staring contest. Vernon thinking: *This could go either way.*

Finally, Steve looked over his shoulder with a brief tilt of his head, and the goons fell back to flanking positions on each side of the front door. He sat down. "Speak."

"This is kind of hard to say, so I'll just say it: Your cousin's dead."

If Steve's eyes were lasers, everyone at the table would have burst into flames. "What happened?"

"We haven't pinpointed the exact cause yet, but it was definitely murder. And definitely connected to your missing money," said Vernon. "I was horrified to think such a thing could happen in our lovely town—and to a relative of one of our finest citizens, I might add. So like I mentioned before, we threw every resource we had at this, and you'll be happy to know we've already made an arrest."

Another glare.

"Maybe 'happy' isn't the best word."

A single measured syllable: "Who?"

"Peter Pugliese. You've seen him in here, mid-forties, office type."

Steve inhaled hard through flared nostrils. "My patience has left the building. You just made the wrong enemy."

"What? Why?" Vernon held out innocent hands. "We gave your concerns our total attention and got immediate results."

"You think I'm so stupid I can't see through your bullshit?" said Steve. "Scapegoating some cubicle gnome?"

"He actually works in the field," said Vernon. "With a real hard hat."

"He's a dork who wouldn't last five minutes in Miami." Steve shook his head. "It was all of you. I know it as sure as I breathe. Martin uncovered what you were doing with the money, and you took him out before he could say anything."

"But it was Peter—"

"Then how do you explain the text Martin sent me? 'They're crawling under a house with the money'?"

"That puzzled us, too," said Vernon. "But if you notice, it doesn't specifically say who 'they' are. We have reason to believe Peter buried your money under *his* house."

"Why?"

"Because that's where he also buried your cousin's body."

Steve swallowed hard at the news. "Where's his body now?"

"Still under the house."

Another stare from Steve, but this time from his brain locking up. "This is the craziest fucking town."

"I know it's complicated, so just hear me out," said Vernon. "Turns out Peter was into all kinds of deep shit that we never imagined. Remember you said he was a dork, but consider this: People would have thought the same thing about you, sitting in here in that dry-cleaned shirt eating ribs with a knife and fork. Because that was the false image you were creating. So was Peter . . ."

Steve's expression said: *You just bought yourself another minute.*

". . . I don't want to go into specific details here for obvious reasons, but we also had some money of our own that needed a little rinse cycle. Somehow Peter got wind and approached us. Said it was one of his specialties, so we gave him a shot."

"Then he just buried the money?"

"Apparently that was just a waypoint before he could get the funds offshore," said Vernon. "But he really came through. We've actually seen our accounts in the Caymans and Panama. So when you needed the same service, we told you we could handle it through our bank but instead gave the money to Peter and split the commission."

"So you lied to me?"

"Steve, we didn't lie. We just didn't tell you about Peter—just like you wouldn't want us giving *your* name to *him*," said Vern. "We were insulating you. I'm sure that's how you'd want us to handle business."

That part did make sense, but: "I'm still not convinced."

"I wouldn't be, either," said Vernon, reaching into his pocket and unfolding paper. "Check these out."

Steve scanned the pages. "What am I looking at?"

"Peter heard we had an issue with an insurance underwriter pulling out of our subdivision project," said Vernon. "So he came to us again and said he could fix our problem, but it would cost much more than his usual testing fee. Those are his geology reports."

Steve held the pages side by side. "Why two reports? And why are they completely different?"

"He filed the false one with the underwriters," said the mayor. "To give the project the go-ahead."

"What about the other report?"

"He just gave it to us," said Vernon. "We asked him about it, and all he said was that it was *his* insurance. But the insinuation was clear: If we ever double-crossed him, he'd claim it was the real report and we had switched them. Got to admit that's pretty sharp. We're also looking at some irregularities at the water plant due to another report he provided without us even asking."

"This really is on the level?"

"He blindsided us. And on our own turf," said Vernon. "Don't underestimate him."

"Okay." Steve stood. "I'm going to have some people look into it further, and if all this bears out, it might get a little messy around here. Can I count on your police not to be vigilant?"

"It's the slow season. I need to schedule a lot of vacation time," said Vernon. "Sorry about your loss."

Steve and the goons departed without pleasantry.

The guys at the table watched until the door closed.

"Now Phase Two," said Vernon. "Follow me."

They went outside and piled into the mayor's car. Vernon broke open a package containing a prepaid, untraceable cell phone. Then he dialed a familiar number and wrapped the phone in a handkerchief.

"Sheriff Highsmith here."

"Sheriff, I understand you're investigating a homicide out at the Pugliese residence."

"Who is this?"

"That's not important. You need to take a look at what business the victim was in. His cousin recently bought a home here, and they've both been making frequent trips to Miami."

"I'm listening," said the sheriff, getting out a notepad and clicking a pen.

"A little bird also told me some airplanes without flight plans have been landing at night in certain fields around here."

"Wait, this voice sounds familiar," said the sheriff. *"Do I know you?"*

Vernon smashed the phone apart on the dashboard.

"What just happened?" asked Jabow.

"You've heard of vicious circles?" said Vern. "This is a vicious triangle."

"Huh?"

"Peter knows too much. We don't need him remaining the prime suspect and risk getting interrogated by the sheriff. So we just diverted the sheriff's suspicion to Steve. And we didn't want Steve suspecting us, so back in the rib joint we diverted his suspicion to Peter."

"And Peter's now walking around free so Steve can make sure he never talks?"

"And after Peter's out of the way, the sheriff takes *Steve* down."

"You mean you actually had this whole thing all planned from when you first arrested Peter?"

"Love to take credit, but it was Senator Pratchett's idea."

"So all we have to do is sit back and enjoy the show?"

"Almost," said Vernon. "There's one more loose end."

"What is it?"

"We want that money."

"But it's thirty feet down a sinkhole at a crime scene . . ."

"It's also a public hazard, and we wouldn't be responsible if we didn't keep this town safe."

"I see the light." Jabow smiled. "Now who around here could possibly be qualified to deal with sinkholes?"

Chapter TWENTY-SIX

DISPUTED BORDER COUNTRY

The rural road was normally a relaxing drive, but not today with all the news trucks. A row of reporters jockeyed for space on the grassy shoulder.

"*This is* Live Eye Five *coming to you live at five from Wobbly, Florida, and the site of the latest fatal sinkhole that swallowed an entire bedroom . . .*"

"*. . . Authorities are still attempting to recover the body, but cite difficulties due to unstable ground conditions . . .*"

"*. . . The victim's name is being withheld pending notification of next of kin; however, property records shows the home belongs to a Peter Pugliese of Saratoga Springs . . .*"

A gray Buick Skylark came up the road. The driver reached an arm across the front seat. "Get your head down."

"Why?" asked Peter, looking up from under the dash.

"Vultures." The Buick rolled to the police checkpoint. The cops had recognized the vehicle from a distance and already removed the cones.

The mayor gave a half salute as he passed. "Thanks, Reemus." And continued up the drive.

The outside of the house was ringed with activity. Deputies and county investigators eating sandwiches, drinking coffee, laughing.

"Sheriff," said Vernon, approaching the crime tape. "You still here?"

"I'm not leaving until we retrieve the body." He glanced back at the coroner's van.

"I know, I know, jurisdiction," said Vernon. "Then why are all your boys just standing around chatting so festively, or is that the latest crime-fighting technique in the big fancy departments?"

"You're the one who's delaying everything," Highsmith checked his watch. "The sinkhole could widen. We have to wait for your certified expert to arrive and declare the site safe."

"He just got here . . . Peter, come on over and say hi to the sheriff."

"Him?"

"One of the best. Done some excellent work for us in the past, so we contracted his company with a personal request. And as you know from the statutes, decisions over structural safety fall to municipalities."

"But . . . he's your suspect."

"Not anymore," said Vernon. "New shit has come to light."

The sheriff was about to say something, but stopped when he heard that last comment. He was hot on the trail of an anonymous tip . . . Had the same person also called Vernon? He'd sat at this card table before with the mayor, time after time, and didn't want to push his chips forward until he had a better idea what kind of hand his nemesis was holding. "So, uh, what is this new information?"

"Confidential because of our ongoing investigation," said Vernon. "But since I like you, a little professional courtesy wouldn't hurt. Peter agreed to take a polygraph and passed with flying colors."

"I did?"

Vern elbowed him.

The sheriff smiled. Gotcha. Vernon had just given him a straight flush. He knew Peter wasn't guilty. And also knew he could provide valuable information. "Well, since he's no longer under arrest, I'd like to bring him in for questioning."

"Peter doesn't want to."

Highsmith smiled again, ready to collect Vernon's chips. He reached behind his back for a pair of cuffs. "Then I'm afraid you leave me no choice but to arrest him. He's still the only suspect . . . Peter, turn around."

"That's your call," said Vernon. "But if, at this very moment, you're already looking at another suspect, and arrest Peter anyway, you open the county to a massive lawsuit. And if that other suspect ever goes on trial, Peter's arrest today will torpedo that case with reasonable doubt because the second you snap those cuffs, you've created an alternate theory of the crime. But what do I know? I'm just a country poke."

Damn, thought the sheriff, *Vernon definitely must have gotten the same call.* His straight flush had just turned into a hand of nothing. He stowed the cuffs. "Changed my mind. It's a higher priority for him to help us get at the body before the whole place falls in."

The radio in the Skylark squawked. *"Vernon? . . ."*

The mayor reached through the window for the mike. "Go ahead."

"There's someone down here who says he knows you . . ."

Vernon looked toward the foot of the driveway, where a late-model Mercedes was detained behind the cones. "Yeah, he's good. Send him through."

The sedan rolled up the hill and parked next to the Skylark. Steve got out. He froze at the sight of Peter. The sheriff froze at the sight of Steve. Vernon grinned inside at the sight of his triangle.

"Steve," said the mayor, putting an arm around his shoulders. "Can we talk for a second?" He walked him out of earshot.

Steve could barely contain his rage. "What's *he* doing here?"

"Take it easy," said Vernon. "The sheriff's watching."

"Someone called me with an anonymous tip that I'd find something of great interest out here."

Good, thought Vernon, *he didn't recognize the voice*

of the puppet master, which is me. "We're walking him through the crime scene."

"Why?"

"To build our case against him. He thinks we hired him for geology work with the sinkhole, but we're actually hoping he'll let something inadvertently slip."

"I thought you were going to let me handle this my way," said Steve. "For family honor."

"We are," said Vernon. "But if I don't stall by pretending to build a case, the sheriff will immediately grab him and you'll never get the chance."

A large industrial truck from Peter's company arrived. Men raised the roll-up back panel and unloaded scientific instruments and robot probes.

"Okay, then, just act normal," Vernon told Steve. The pair walked back around the cars. "Sheriff Highsmith, I'd like you to meet Steve DeVinsenzi, one of our other fine new citizens. Auto brokerage, I believe? Well, I'll let you two talk . . . Peter, we need to get started inside."

The mayor and the geologist ducked under crime tape.

Back in the yard, it was like the first dance in junior high.

"Sheriff? . . ."

"Uh, it was Steve, right? . . ."

Vernon led the way into the living room and turned to Peter. "You're in charge."

"Nobody step any farther." Peter raised his chin, checking the usual spots for plaster cracks, then held up earlier police photos for comparison to see if additional settling had occurred.

"How's it look?" asked the mayor.

"So far, so good." Peter headed back to the door. "Now I need to get the equipment under the house. Radar should tell whether it was a confined breach in the limestone bedrock or if it's wider, and the tertiary layer of clay is only temporarily supporting the overburden."

"Whatever you just said." Vernon followed him outside, and Peter waved his crew toward the crawl space on the side of the house.

A '55 Ford pickup arrived and three young men got out. They saw a pair of loafers disappear under the building.

"Vernon," said Elroy. "What's going on?"

"He's not wearing the right shoes . . ."

Two hours later, Peter wiggled out from under the house.

"What's the verdict?" asked Vernon.

"I'm somewhat surprised, but we're good to go." Peter looked down at his shirt and thought of the new drip-free caps on laundry detergent.

"That means we do what?"

"My guys will erect a scaffolding with floodlights, which will be anchored through doorways in other rooms, because we want to distribute the weight away from the hole, and they'll be standing on wide base plates with large, load-bearing footprints, like snowshoes."

"That doesn't sound like we're good."

"Nothing's a hundred percent, but I'm confident." Peter walked to the back of the company truck. "Then I'll strap on a harness and they'll lower me with a safety pulley. And we always use the buddy system, so one of the other guys will go down with me."

And maybe spot the money, thought Vernon. *That's one too many pair of eyes.* "No! . . . I mean, I didn't mean to shout, but I want one of our people to be your backup."

"Don't worry." Peter grabbed a handful of thick orange straps with mountain-climber D-rings. "They're experienced."

"That's not it," said Vernon. "It's for your own protection. This is still a crime scene, and you've only just been cleared. Relations aren't the best with the sheriff right now, and if a representative of the city is present down there, it'll protect you from any future accusations of tampering with evidence."

"Fine with me." Peter pulled straps up between his legs and snapped them in place. "You know this area better than I do. But he'll have to sign a company release."

"We can do that."

"I'll grab a second harness. Who's the lucky volunteer?"

Vernon approached the young trio and grabbed Slower by the arm. "Do not fuck this up."

"What?"

"You're going down in that hole with him."

"I don't know anything about sinkholes."

"You don't need to know squat," said Vernon. "Just keep an eye out for the money. And keep an eye on Peter, in case he happens to spot it while retrieving the body."

"Money?"

"What you buried, you moron."

"But we buried it shallow."

"Shut up and put on the harness."

A fire engine arrived, complete with firemen who got out and leaned against it. EMTs readied the precautionary first-aid station.

The pair of adventurers went inside, where other people from Peter's firm attached them to the pulleys hanging from an iron I-beam. No way that was going anywhere. Someone else fitted them with tool belts.

"Ready," said Peter.

"Hard hats."

"Right."

And down they went.

Chapter TWENTY-SEVEN

THE HOLE

They reached the bottom twenty feet below.

The support crew waiting above in the house didn't venture near the edge for fear of causing a secondary cave-in. It was all over-the-horizon communication.

"How's it going?"

"We're fine," said Peter. He had a six-foot-long metal pole, thin but heavy, like a rebar. The topsoil of the hole's floor was soft, like plowed dirt. The only compacted areas were under their feet.

"Stand perfectly still and don't take a step," Peter told Slower. Then he began poking the pole down into the dirt in a precise matrix of half-foot intervals—only moving forward once he had cleared the area ahead. He turned around at the hole's southern wall and headed northwest. The pole thrust down again but didn't penetrate as far. Two more nearby thrusts with the same result. He extended the testing radius and the pole descended to its usual depth.

A shout echoed upward. "Think I've got something."

"What is it?" asked an unseen voice.

"Tell you in a minute." Peter unclipped an entrenching tool from his belt, got down and began digging. Soon the tiny shovel was back on his belt and Peter used his gloved hands to carefully whisk away the last bits of dirt like an umpire at home plate. He was used to the anxiety of sinkholes. Not dead bodies. He jackknifed and dry-heaved. A moment to compose.

Another upward shout. "Found him."

Peter unhooked his harness and told Slower to do the same. The ropes went back up, and investigators from the coroner's office attached the two clasps to opposite ends of a human-length mesh-metal basket used in helicopter rescues. Now it was recovery.

Peter grabbed the pulley lines until the stretcher rested on the bottom. "Slower, come help me."

Unpleasantness began.

They dug a moat of sorts around the body and fit the bag over it upside down. Then they rolled Martin into the stretcher. Peter gave two tugs on the rope. "Good to go."

He stared straight up as the litter slightly rotated on its ascent, rising into the floodlights hanging from the I-beam.

Slower was looking the other way. He approached one of the sinkhole walls that they hadn't explored yet. To himself: "What's this?"

A corner of a clear plastic bag. Slower glanced back at Peter, still looking up with focus. The younger man grabbed the plastic and tugged. It began emerging. Green-and-white paper. "The money." He pulled some more.

From behind: "What the hell are you doing?"

Slower spun around to hide the discovery. "Nothing."

Peter looked up again. "Uh-oh."

Faint vibrations became a rumble.

"Get away from there!" Peter yelled as he lunged. Too late.

Above: *"Everyone out! Now!"*

The hole's western wall came down with fury.

It had been supporting three more of the home's foundation piers, which gave way, taking out sixty square feet of floor. A bedroom wall collapsed, along with half of the adjacent kitchen.

Everyone who had evacuated onto the lawn watched high-velocity plumes of dust shoot out sideways from the crawl space and front door. The middle of the roof began to creak, then fell in half-way and lurched to a stop. Everyone held their breath. The roof stayed put, for now.

Sheriff Highsmith urgently swung his right arm toward the house. "Back inside!"

The firefighters grabbed searchlights and breathing masks and axes. They were first to the expanded hole. The dust still too thick for even the highest candlepower beam. "Can anyone hear me down there?"

Cough, cough. "Yeah." *Cough, back.*

"You okay?"

"Just hard to breathe," Peter said with the front of his shirt over his mouth.

"I'm tossing down a mask," yelled the firefighter. "Say something else."

"Like what?"

"That's good enough." He pitched the mask in the direction of the voice. "Got it?"

"Hit my leg." He put it on.

"Okay," shouted the rescuer. "Did the litter with the body fall back down there?"

"It's here."

"Detach the clasp and hook it to your harness."

"All right." *Click.*

"Hang on. We're pulling you out."

"Wait! You can't!"

"Why not?"

"The other guy's still here." Peter fell to his knees and began digging. "I have to find him."

"No time," said the firefighter. "Everything's unstable and could go at any second."

"But I have to."

"It's not your call." The rescue team began pulling the rope.

After a few seconds of tugging, the line gave out, zipping up through the pulley, and they all fell on their backs.

"Did it break?" asked one of the rescuers.

Another reeled in the rope until he came to the end. "No, here's the clasp. He unhooked it."

They threw the line back down over the edge.

"Hook yourself up!"

Silence.

"Peter! Can you hear me? Answer!"

Peter just continued digging blindly in a widening circle. He cleared enough weight in dirt that the ground beneath him shifted with life. He plunged his hands and found Slower. Was it an arm? Leg?

"Peter! Answer us! . . ."

He clawed frantically in swirling directions, trying to find the head. "Here it is." One hand burrowed under the shoulders, and the other reached the back of the skull. He pulled with everything he had. Dirt flew and Slower sprang up in a spastic fit of coughing and spitting dirt.

The young man broke down crying like a child, and Peter cradled his head in his arms. "You're okay now. I'm getting you out of here."

"Peter! . . ."

"I got him. I'm grabbing the rope." *Snap.* Then he got belly to belly with Slower and snapped the clasp to the second harness. "Just hang on to me and you'll be safe in no time." The traumatized young man wrapped his arms tightly around Peter's neck.

"Peter, you ready?"

He looked upward into the ghostly, search-beam-lit haze. "You're going to have two on the line!" He gave the rope a pair of quick yanks, and rescuers began pulling. Except they didn't have the greased ease of the pulley. Just extra weight and heavy friction against the sinkhole's wall.

It became a tug-of-war. Firefighters and deputies on their rears, scrambling backward as their feet fought for purchase on the hardwood floor.

It was three feet up and two feet down, with jolts each time, dirt falling in, rescuers sliding toward the hole. Peter dug the toes of his shoes into the wall of clay and soil, trying to climb and aid their retrieval.

At first it was helping, but then after each of Peter's footholds, stuff began caving beneath them, sending up more of the enemy dust. Another jolt as the pair fell back a few feet and rescuers thudded to the floor above.

Word spread out on the lawn. Others ran inside without masks and grabbed the line.

"I think I see them!"

The tops of their heads rose even with the edge of the floor.

"Hold that line fast!"

Three of the team got down on their stomachs, reaching over the lip and grabbing the pair under their arms. They pulled them back out of the hole, then everyone hustled from the house as the floor where they had just been disappeared.

Peter sat on the grass as an EMT came over. "I'm fine."

"Still have to check you out."

Slower required a bit more. They irrigated his nose, mouth and eyes; gave him oxygen.

Vernon came up and crouched beside the young man. "How you feeling, son?"

Slower nodded.

Vernon leaned to his ear. "See the money?"

Another nod.

"Did Peter?"

He shook his head.

Vernon patted his arm. "You did great."

The mayor went back to huddle with the city council.

"Well?"

"He saw the money."

"What do we do?"

Vernon looked back at the house of cards. "Find a way to get in there when nobody's around."

MIAMI

Balloons and strings of pennants. The aroma of grilling hot dogs. The salesman had a clip-on tie and short-sleeve dress shirt. He grinned with force and slapped the hood of a Fiesta. "Low miles, easy credit, better life."

A prospective customer dabbed mustard from his mouth. "I don't know. We've had good luck with GM products. Something in a full-size, like a Caprice or Impala."

The salesman winced for effect. "Just sold the last one."

A roar boomed behind them with heavy reverb effect. A DJ stood with a microphone outside the WPPT-FM Party Parrot broadcast truck. ". . . *I'm here with the Mobile Mayhem Van at a weekend blowout tent-sale extravaganza you won't want to miss! With live music, free munchies, the Party Parrot's Bouncing Jugs Dancers, and prices so low you'll swear the owner went insannnnnnnnnnnnnnnnnne! . . .*"

Another roar, this one up the road. The salesman

spotted a car-transport truck. "Wait," he told the customer. "I think we might have something you want coming in on that trailer."

He ran to the side of the lot and slid open the giant chain-link delivery gate. The truck pulled in. Straps and chains released. New used cars began backing off the skids.

"There's a Caprice now," said the salesman. "Let's take a test drive—"

Suddenly, sirens and lights.

Nondescript sedans with tinted windows had been parked along the street. They now came to life and poured into the dealership. Drug Enforcement agents jumped out with bulletproof vests and hands on holsters.

"Nobody move!"

A man in a parrot costume stopped spinning a sign.

The team brought in the drug-sniffing dogs and trotted them alongside the transporter. They all stopped and barked at the Caprice. An agent opened a door and a German shepherd hopped onto the passenger seat, staring at the headrest. He received a bacon-flavored treat as they sliced upholstery.

An agent shook a clear test tube that turned blue. Positive for heroin.

The drugs went in an evidence bag, and handcuffs went on the truck driver and car salesman. The Caprice went back up on skids, but this time a government impound truck.

Someone began walking away.

"Stop!" yelled an agent. "Who are you?"

"I was just shopping for a car when everything went crazy," said the customer. "Are these men dangerous criminals?"

"Show me some identification and you can go."

"Sure thing."

LATER THAT NIGHT . . .

The regular gang gathered at their regular table in Lead Belly's. It was not a regular meal.

Steve was also there, back to wearing his plaid country-boy shirt. "He actually saw the money?"

"Sure as day," said Vernon. "We just have to come up with a plan to get it back."

Jabow noshed a rib. "But given that we'll be doing most of the heavy lifting, a salvage fee would be in order, say a third."

"The money's lost to me as it is," said Steve. "Why not? As long as it still includes our side deal for my arrangements concerning a certain person."

"Then it's settled."

"So what's your plan?"

"We all drive out after dark tonight," said Vernon. "The I-beam is still up in the house. We just go down and collect our paycheck."

"But none of us knows anything about sinkholes," said Steve.

"What's to know? Anyone can work a pulley."

"Smells risky to me," said Steve.

"Have faith," said Vernon. "Besides, it's my lucky night. There's a blue moon."

"What's a blue moon?" asked Jabow.

Vernon shrugged.

"It's the second full moon of a month," said Steve. "Lunar cycles are twenty-nine-and-a-half days, so it happens once every couple years or so."

"Check out the IQ on Steve," said Vernon.

The cell phone in the newcomer's pocket sounded a text alert. He checked the message from a Miami car lot. "Shit, I'll have to catch you later."

He reached the restaurant's front door just as Sheriff Highsmith opened it. Accompanying DEA agents swiftly cuffed him. "Stephan DeVinsenzi, you are under arrest for importation and distribution of a controlled substance."

The door closed.

"Right on schedule," said Vernon, pulling apart barbecue.

"I thought we needed him to take care of Peter."

"We do." A big messy bite. "His lawyers will get him out by arraignment tomorrow."

"Then why have him arrested in the first place?" asked Otis.

"So he won't be around tonight. We'll tell him we ran into some kind of trouble at the sinkhole," said the mayor. "Then we won't have to split all that cash."

"You planned this, didn't you?"

Chapter TWENTY-EIGHT

SOMEWHERE ALONG U.S. HIGHWAY 44

Radio check," said Coleman. "My tummy's talking to me."

"I'm hungry, too," said Matt.

"Food it is."

Serge exited the highway and scrutinized a dozen idling cars circling a building. "I'll blow my brains out if I have to wait in that drive-through lane. We're going inside."

The trio entered a glass side door and stepped up to the back of a shorter line. Parents herded laughing children. Teens tried to be popular. Other teens in restaurant uniforms hustled backstage, filling orders displayed on flat-screen monitors that flashed red if they went past three minutes.

"Kids don't know how good they have it today," said Serge. "In the sixties, we didn't get to run out to fast-food joints on any whim. Relatives back then actually remembered who was in the family by seeing each other around the dinner table every night. The downside was the menu."

"I had to eat liver," said Coleman. "And gizzards."

"Kids who got liver and gizzards didn't know how good they had it." Serge craned his neck to see how their line was progressing. "Families in the Kennedy years experienced firsthand the struggle of clawing their way into the middle class, so they learned to economize. It wasn't half bad if your parents were ethnic and knew how to cook—or had imagination at the grocery store. I rolled snake eyes on both counts. We ate roots."

"Roots?" asked Matt.

"Every single night, the same thing, a totally root-based diet," said Serge. "Only the colors changed: potatoes, beets, and turnips that came in huge mesh bags from Publix. The worst part is they'd just skin them and throw 'em in a big pot of boiling water, then stick these steaming bulbs on my plate, and I had to finish the job crushing it all down with a fork. I think about it every time I watch a depressing documentary on nineteenth-century Ireland. And the beet juice would run and make the potatoes pink."

"No meat?"

"Hamburger, which kids normally love," said Serge. "But they boiled that, too!"

"Boiled hamburger?" said Coleman.

Serge nodded. "Started out promising enough with a frying pan, except then they poured in a bunch of water and put a lid on it, and what ended up on my plate was an indestructible gray shoe sole. Don't get me wrong: I'm totally grateful."

"Doesn't sound like you are."

"It's just that every time I see a bunch of young people using credit cards to buy french fries, I want to grab them by the necks and say, 'You need to wake up from this dream in a fucking hurry! After graduation, you're flying straight into a force-five economic hurricane! Do you want to eat pink fork-track potatoes and shoe-sole hamburgers the rest of your life?'"

"When you put it that way," said Matt.

"Totally cherished childhood memories of appreciation." Serge glanced around the line again. "And you know what my main sixties memory of eating was? *Not* eating."

"You didn't eat?"

"It's like my folks forgot they were kids once, too. They constantly thought I was lying about the gag reflex."

"They thought I was lying, too!" said Coleman.

"But we really were gagging." Serge stuck a finger in his mouth for emphasis. "It's how nature programs kids to survive into adulthood: an extra-sensitive throat reflex carried over from caveman days so we wouldn't eat the poison berries. I kept trying to tell my parents this, but it was always the same answer: 'This isn't a cave, and that's not poison. Now eat your parsnips.'"

"So you didn't eat?"

"In hindsight, I believe these were the first signs that I had gifts of extraordinary behavioral stamina. I remember an entire childhood of sit-in protests at my plate, frozen like a statue staring at uneaten meals, hour after hour, long after everyone else had left the table because back then you weren't allowed to get up until you cleaned your plate. Then I'd stay sitting into the night while the grown-ups went in the other room and watched a prime-time lineup of intriguing TV that I could only hear. *I Spy*, *Ironside*, *The Courtship of Eddie's Father*. Finally came bedtime, and they sent me to my room hungry."

"That sounds like abuse."

"You can only judge through the context of the times," said Serge. "What's an expression of love in one generation brings social workers to the house today. Besides, nature also programs children to adapt to harsh environments, and I developed a highly ordered survival skill set. At every supper my family would also place a glass pitcher of milk in the middle of the table, along with a bag of Wonder Bread. Knowing that I'd inevitably be thrown back into the *Deer Hunter* bamboo cage they called my bedroom, I loaded up like Gunga Din on that bread and milk, but I had to be coy, using my fork to move mashed roots around my plate, station to station, creating the illusion of cooperation. Naturally everyone else in my family has completely different recollections of all this."

A kid with a bag of food bumped into Serge while texting on his phone. "Oh, excuse me."

"Excuse me!" said Serge. "Did you buy that with a credit card?"

"Yeah, why?"

"You need to wake up from this dream in a big f—!"

One minute later. "Serge, everyone's staring at us again."

"Because they can't handle the truth." Serge checked his watch. "Maybe we should have tried the drive-through after all. Anyway, every time I'm in a fast-food restaurant, you know what I think about?"

"No."

"The space race."

Matt scribbled in a notepad. "Elaborate."

"Nobody cares now, but back when McDonald's hamburgers were nineteen cents, everyone was shitting their pants over the Russians dropping atomic bombs from Sputnik. So our space program became a national obsession. And you know how the Golden Arches always likes to beat the latest craze to death like ninja turtles or *Toy Story*? When I was a kid it was genuinely educational. They gave me a folded road map, except it was a map of the solar system with Ronald McDonald floating around in an astronaut helmet. I got home and built this hellacious cardboard space capsule in the center of the living room and taped up the McDonald's planetary chart, pretending it was my view out the window. Then I'd sit crouched over in my spaceship, training for long-duration flight that was required to land on the moon. Again, focus."

"What about your parents?" asked Matt. "Didn't they mind that big mess in the living room?"

"Normally it would have gone right in the trash," said Serge. "Except I had reached an age of intellectual curiosity and begun exploring how all the contraptions around our house operated inside. The way I figured, I was just a kid, and if I could take it apart, they surely could put it back together. Then my mom would walk in the kitchen and see me standing on a chair at the counter, holding a screwdriver with disassembled components all over the place. 'What the heck's going on?' 'I'm intrigued how the blender works.' So I'm hunched down in my capsule watching another Gemini launch on TV that all three networks covered nonstop from rollout to splashdown. And I can hear my parents whispering: 'How long has he been in there?' 'Going on five hours.' 'Has he moved?' 'No.' 'What do you think he's doing? . . .'" Serge shrugged at Matt. "I wanted to tell them about the training program, but the vacuum of space doesn't carry sound."

"What happened?"

"My mom said something like 'I don't want that piece of junk in the house,' and my dad said, 'He's staying still. Let's leave well enough alone.'"

Coleman looked around the restaurant's interior, dominated by lime green and banana yellow. Then his eyes went up to a lighted menu board with an overwhelming volume of nutritional data. "I've never been in a fast-food place like this before."

"It's one of the nuevo healthy bistros where you pay more not to have heart attacks," said Serge. "The gimmick here is they air-fry everything."

"How do you air-fry?"

"You don't." Serge bobbed anxiously on the balls of his feet. "They're secretly baking stuff in superheated air tunnels."

Coleman looked back up at the menu board. "What are New Age Cookies?"

"Gluten-free," said Serge. "Baked by prisoners of conscience."

"Only two more people ahead of us," said Coleman. "Hey look: The girl at the cash register has a tip cup. I've also never seen that in a fast-food place."

"Another offspring of these trendy new spots," said Serge. "And I'm all for it. That kid could be out with her friends eating designer yogurt like it's an entitlement, but instead she's in here learning a work ethic for crappy pay. And the people don't really tip; they just occasionally toss loose change."

"One more person ahead of us," said Matt. "Have you checked this guy out?"

"He's been on my radar ever since we got in line," said Serge.

"On his cell the whole time," said Matt. "Talking really loud."

"That's the point," said Serge. "He needs everyone to hear."

"*. . . Then send in the lawyers. He's not the first competitor I've crushed. Don't these amateurs ever learn? . . .*"

"He's got one of those expensive European shirts like soccer fans wear," said Coleman.

"Except I caught the logo on the front when he turned around. It's a Ferrari shirt."

"*. . . Remember to forward my calls to Saint Kitts this weekend. And phone the resort. They stuck me with a dump of an eight-hundred-dollar room last time . . .*"

"Plus those fancy sunglasses on top of his head," said Coleman.

"Ferrari sunglasses."

"You think he likes Ferraris?" asked Coleman.

"He *owns* one." Serge pointed out the restaurant window. "And it's not good enough that he has the car. He's got to wear all the Ferrari shit so people know about it when he's forced to be on foot."

"It's parked in the handicapped space," said Matt. "That's breaking the law."

Serge bent over and pointed again. "Worse. He's got a handicapped tag on his mirror."

"But he doesn't look handicapped," said Coleman. "In fact, he looks in great shape."

"He is."

"... *Another interview request? Unless it's* Time, *tell them I'm at the house in Marseilles. Once you've been on enough magazine covers* ..."

"But how can he have a handicapped tag?"

"Easier than you'd think," said Serge. "You just need a doctor's note. And if all those celebrities can score exotic pharmaceuticals in Malibu by saying they've been on edge lately, a handicapped car tag is child's play."

"That's not right," said Matt.

"... *So change distributors. Doesn't he know everyone wants my business? He'll be in a bread line before I'm finished with him* ..."

"I hate to stereotype, but I've seen the type," said Serge. "Nobody else matters. If he wants extra space so his precious car doesn't get scratched, then the wheelchair people will just have to pick up the slack."

"He's up to the register now," said Coleman. "She's ready to take his order, but he's still on the phone."

"*. . . Yeah, a supermodel again. But you get tired of that . . . No, I'm not going to tell you what she's into . . . Okay, I'll let you guess . . .*"

Serge tapped him on the shoulder.

"*. . . Hold on.*" The man turned around. "Can't you see I'm on the phone?"

"That's what I wanted to talk to you about." Serge gestured behind them. "There's a pretty long line, and that girl's waiting to take your order. But she's just a kid and too polite to say anything."

"So?"

"So the proper thing to do is get off the phone," said Serge. "Please, come join us in the merriment of polite society."

"Unlike you losers, I have important business." Then back into his cell: "*No, just some jack-off . . . Tell that other idiot I can have him fired with one phone call . . .*"

"Serge," said Coleman. "You know how you asked me to remind you to count to ten when your face gets that color? . . ."

Chapter TWENTY-NINE

The Florida state capital appears detached from the rest of the state. It might as well belong in any of its bordering Bible Belt neighbors, from the syrup accents to biscuit-and-gravy world view.

Kudzu.

The capitol building itself was the twin of the one in Alabama. In both states sat the ancient, original structures from the 1800s, now museums preserving an antebellum musk and spittoons. Behind each of those stood the new capitols: tall, narrow skyscrapers accompanied on each side by domes for respective chambers of the legislature. The overall resulting shape was the source of discussion.

Today, it was hot. Inland hot. Trapped air and humidity. Condensers worked overtime pumping coolness into the senate committee room. A long curved table rose above those who were summoned. A tall burgundy leather chair sat in the middle of the curve, behind the engraved nameplate of the committee's chairman, Bolley "Bo" Bodine. Always wore suspenders *and* a belt, so he could unbuckle in buffet restaurants.

"This hearing is called to order." The chairman gaveled. "Our committee is in session today to discuss an extremely unsettling matter. As a practice, we normally respect local governance, but irregularities have come to light that make it incumbent upon us to consider revoking the articles of incorporation for the city of Wobbly."

"Mr. Chairman?"

"The chairman recognizes our esteemed colleague from Calusa County, Senator Ryan Pratchett."

"Thank you, Mr. Chairman," said Ryan. "Since my district represents the good people of Wobbly, I would like the record to reflect that I have found no finer group of citizens in the entire state who will give you the shirts off their backs. The senator yields."

"That's it?"

Pratchett reclined in his own massive chair and nodded.

"Now then, a current state investigation into corruption in Wobbly has turned up some serious questions—"

"Mr. Chairman?"

"The senator from Calusa County?"

"Is it not accurate that thus far no corruption has been proven?" said Pratchett. "I would then respectfully request that the terms 'law-abiding and devout' be added to the official record."

"Would that make you happy?"

A nod.

"So ordered," said Bodine. "If we may finally proceed, I would like to begin taking testimony from our first witness, state auditor Franklin James . . . Mr. James, please raise your right hand . . ."

A storm of camera flashes filled the chamber as a lithe man with wire-rimmed glasses took the oath.

"Mr. James, we have a copy of your preliminary report right here, which I deem highly disturbing. Would you begin by substantiating your first finding?"

An awkward clearing of a throat, and he started speaking . . .

"Excuse me," said the chairman. "Could you move closer to the microphone? We can't hear anything you're saying."

The auditor scooted his chair and reviewed notes. "The city of Wobbly has, um, issued as many traffic tickets as some of the largest cities in the state, yet has a population of less than a thousand. Almost all of the citations issued in the last year came along a hundred-yard stretch of State Road 92 that the city annexed with a long, narrow corridor of land. There can be no other conclusion than Wobbly's police are issuing the citations almost solely as a revenue generator."

"Mr. Chairman?"

A sigh. "The senator from Calusa County?"

"I would like to say that I fully support the good men and women of this fair state who put on the proud uniforms of law enforcement and risk their lives each day to protect us from speeders." Pratchett sat back.

The chairman stared a moment, then turned to the witness. "Continue."

"When we visited the town with our requests for documentation, we could find no accounting for the fines. In addition, there was a similar lack of paper trail for water bills and pet registration fees."

"How did they explain this?"

The auditor looked down at his notes. "There was a fire, a flood, it was lost in a tourist attraction."

"Attraction?"

"A sinkhole."

"Anything else unusual?"

"They were holding traffic court in a barbecue restaurant."

"Mr. Chairman?" said Pratchett. "I have a couple of questions for this witness."

"Go ahead."

The senator smiled behind his microphone. "Were they nice?"

"What?"

"When you were in Wobbly asking for this documentation, were they nice to you?"

"I guess, but—"

"Would it be accurate to say they're the salt of the earth?"

"I don't see—"

"Did you try the ribs?"

A gavel banged. "Senator Pratchett!" said the chairman. "Please! I've given you significant latitude, but we're getting off track!"

"Really?" said Pratchett. "In a land that so many of our military heroes fought and died for, listening to all sides is getting off track?"

"Senator!"

"Fine, if you don't want the complete picture. It's your committee."

"Are you finished?" asked the chairman.

Pratchett shrugged.

"Thank you . . ."

Two hours later, they called the next witness.

The chairman looked over the top of his reading glasses. "Sheriff Highsmith, the committee would like to express its appreciation for taking the time to travel all the way to Tallahassee."

"No problem."

"When state investigators visited your county, you described some troubling trends that I would like repeated for this panel."

"Well, one by-product of the speed trap is a large number of arrests for reckless driving and other more serious traffic infractions. Since the only jail is the county's, they bring the suspects to us, but we have to turn them away."

"And why is that?"

"They're issuing so many tickets that it's far more than the town's three officers can handle. So they started deputizing citizens for traffic duty, except there's no protocol. It's almost as if they're just handing out badges. The people bringing the prisoners to us are driving personal cars, wearing street clothes and often have alcohol on their breath—half the time we don't know which one is under arrest.

We've also had to respond to a number of clashes between rival neighborhood watch groups."

"Rival?"

"Disputed border territory," said Highsmith. "Both groups are standing their ground. We have surveyors working on it."

"Anything else?"

"People are starting to go missing."

"Missing?"

"We found the body of a Miami man in a sinkhole," said the sheriff. "And an insurance underwriter still hasn't turned up."

"Mr. Chairman?" said Pratchett. "May I?"

"Go ahead."

"Sheriff," said Pratchett. "Would you say that you and I have a good working relationship?"

"Absolutely."

"And that you and some of the officials in Wobbly do not?"

"To say the least."

"Could your testimony be subconsciously tainted by last year's pig races?"

"What?"

"No further questions . . ."

The last witness of the day took the stand shortly after four.

"Mr. Abernathy," said the chairman. "We've heard previous testimony about an unusual configuration of land that was annexed. As an investigator with the attorney general's office, do you have an opinion on this?"

"We've never seen anything like it," said the witness. "It's beyond unusual: this thin, long append-age so out of place that the only logical answer is it was designed to take advantage of unsuspecting motorists."

"I see," said the chairman. "And do you have any knowledge how this configuration came to be?"

"As a matter of fact, I do. The city was incorpo-rated in 2012 with the guidance of a then–Calusa County attorney, who subsequently helped the city annex the land in question for the previous-mentioned scheme. This appears to be part of a quid pro quo arrangement for votes."

"Votes?"

"That fall, the attorney in question was elected to his first term in the state senate: Ryan Pratchett."

Gasps.

Cameras furiously flashed.

"Mr. Chairman!" yelled Pratchett. "So now we're into character assassination?"

The gavel banged. "You're out of line!"

"You've got to be kidding me!" said Pratchett. "Your evidence is that a city has a weird shape?"

Bang, bang, bang. "Order."

"Have you looked at your own gerrymandered voting district?" said Pratchett. "It's shaped like copulating giraffes . . ."

Laughter, gavel bangs.

"Order!"

Pratchett stood and dramatically waved a piece of paper over his head. "I have in my hand proof of the real corruption that this committee is trying to cover up from the citizens of this great state!"

The pool of news photographers stood and rushed forward with another blinding wave of flashes.

Bang, bang. "Order!"

"I hold a copy of a traffic citation that the chairman of this committee received last year in Wobbly. This entire sham of a proceeding is nothing more than an attempt to fix a speeding ticket!"

"Order!"

"My conscience refuses to allow me to stand idly by and listen as an entire community of patriotic, God-fearing people is unfairly maligned just because the chairman wants to drive faster."

"Order!"

"Mr. Chairman, at long last, have you no shame?" yelled Pratchett. "Attack me all you want, but I will not let you slander the name of our Lord, Jesus Christ!"

"What?"

The senator stormed out of the room, and the press corps followed.

"Order!"

Chapter THIRTY

U.S. HIGHWAY 44

Vehicles stacked up in the drive-through lane. So did people at the counter inside.

"Eight, nine, ten," said Serge.

"Your face color is getting better," said Coleman.

Serge looked at the ceiling and performed breathing exercises. "Is he off the phone yet?"

"Yes," said Coleman. "But he's still not ordering. He's waving down a manager."

"*. . . Excuse me, how much is the escrow to reserve a new franchise location? Is there a regional price break for six or more? . . .*"

"I, uh, don't know."

"*. . . What's next quarter's earnings projection? . . .*"

"Look, I just watch the kids."

"*. . . No problem. I'll have my people call* corporate . . ."

"Serge," said Coleman. "You're vibrating."

"I know this guy."

"You've met before?" asked Matt.

"Not specifically," said Serge. "But yes, we've crossed paths dozens of times. Some people are unable to simply walk among us and conduct simple business. Everywhere they go, they're compelled to bullhorn that they're a player. They can never just buy something *from* a store without letting you know they can buy *the* store."

"He's starting to order now," said Coleman.

"Oh God, not that!"

"I thought you wanted him to order," said Matt.

"No, look," said Serge. "He took the Ferrari sunglasses off his head, and now they're dangling from the corner of his mouth by one of the ear things. I *hate* the guys who do that."

"The girl behind the register looks confused," said Coleman. "He's having to repeat his order . . . She's still confused."

Serge tapped the shoulder.

The man spun. ". . . *Mbgkeheygrblat!* . . ."

"She might be able to understand you if you took the sunglasses out of your mouth."

". . . *Fgjhdkjuusthezaz!* . . ."

Serge grabbed the sunglasses. "I'm sorry. I couldn't make out what you were saying."

The man shuddered in shock. "You touched my sunglasses!"

Serge handed them back. "There's still plenty of leg room left in the brotherhood of mankind."

"That's assault! If you weren't so unimportant, I'd press charges and have my attorneys ruin your entire family for the next century."

"Or you could just order food and be happy like everyone else."

The man pursed his lips with bulging eyes, then spun to the register . . .

Ten minutes later, Serge and Coleman and Matt sat at a table by the window, mustard on their mouths.

". . . Another thing kids today don't appreciate," said Serge. "They all have music libraries in their pockets that they listen to with earbuds. You know what we had in the sixties? A bud. *Singular.* You plugged it into a transistor radio and listened to the audio fidelity of a string and Dixie cup. We used phone *books,* and if we needed to set a clock, we called 'time of day' and listened to bank ads. But most essential of all, nobody even *considered* throwing out a television. They were sacred family possessions, like an automobile in Havana they keep fixing for decades. TV repairmen were always visiting our house with suitcases of vacuum tubes, and my whole family sat around the living room watching him in teeth-gnashing terror like we were holed up in a Yukon blizzard praying he could start a fire with wet matches. Except for me, because I was still stuck at the kitchen table glaring at a plate of un-eaten roots until I could slip outside and crack coconuts. We lived like savages."

"All the long lines are gone at the registers," said Coleman. "Is something going on?"

"It was just our luck to hit the end of the lunch-hour crunch." Serge grabbed a napkin to dab his face. "These places become tombs in the mid-afternoon."

"The Ferrari dude is getting up and going back to the counter."

"I was seriously trying to forget about him."

"He's pointing at the dessert menu," said Coleman. "I think he wants a New Age Cookie. . . . Yeah, that young girl is getting him a chocolate chip."

"Okay, I know I'll regret this." Serge turned around and eased back in his chair. "But I have to watch, even though I can't imagine how he could possibly lower the bar of social behavior any farther."

"Serge, did he just do what I thought?" asked Matt. "He must have, because of that girl's expression."

"We have a new limbo champion." Serge got out his keys and slid them across the table. "Matt, there's been a change of plans. I need you to take the motorcycle up the road and check in at the Primrose Motel."

"How are you and Coleman going to get there?"

"We've got some temporary wheels," said Serge. "But you need to hurry because that motel fills up pretty fast."

Matt stood and gathered his trash. "You're not going to ditch me again like last time, are you?"

"Oh, no, no, no, no."

The Princeton student took a deep breath. "Whatever you say."

Serge watched as Matt pulled away on the chopper, then turned his head toward another table.

The sports car owner finished his cookie and left the crumbs and everything for someone else to clean up. He headed outside and was about to get in his restored '84 Berlinetta.

"Yo!" yelled Serge. "Joe Ferrari."

The driver looked back. "Don't you ever give up?"

Serge grinned and held out a palm. "Give me a dollar and six cents."

"So now you're a beggar, too?" He stuck a key in the car door. "Fuck off and get a job!"

"I'm not begging and I'm asking nicely." Serge closed the distance. "A cookie is ninety-nine cents, and sales tax brings it to a dollar-six."

"What?"

"You're such a player, yet you paid for your cookie out of that girl's tip cup at the register." Serge extended his hand again. "I'm sure it was a mistake, and since you're so busy, you can just place the money in my hand and I'll return it to her. While you're at it, I'll also take the handicapped parking tag."

"Do you have any idea who you're fucking with?"

"No," said Serge. "Because you're not special."

"You're about to find out!" He opened the driver's door.

"I'm still being polite," said Serge. "This is as good as it gets. From here it goes down rather steeply."

The man stuck his head in the car and came back out. "*This* is who you're screwing with!"

"Nice pistol," said Serge. "Ruger nine-millimeter semi-auto. So now you're contributing to the gun violence epidemic?"

"I feel threatened."

"You're just saying that to lay the legal pretext for brandishing a deadly weapon," said Serge. "You don't really feel threatened . . . Although you should."

The man snickered and aimed the gun between Serge's eyes. "How does it feel now, loser?"

Serge turned to Coleman. "Do I look like a loser?"

Burp.

"Well put."

"Shut up!" yelled the man. "Now apologize and maybe I'll let you leave."

"Coleman, I've always wanted to drive a Ferrari."

"I've always wanted to ride in one."

"Shut up! Shut up! Shut up!" The man stiffened his shooting arm. "I'm the one with the gun! And the bullets!"

"Is a bullet in the chamber?"

"What?"

"That's an automatic pistol, and you can't fire until you've chambered a round by racking the slide," said Serge. "So have you?"

"I said shut up!"

"That means you haven't," said Serge. "Which is good. Most people who have a gun in their cars don't chamber a round until ready to fire. Those are the safety rules. Thank you for complying."

"What's your point?"

"Unfortunately for you, I'm not safe." Serge pulled his own pistol from under his tropical shirt. "I hear these cars drive like dreams, but the trunk space is terrible."

THAT EVENING

A Buick Skylark pulled up the winding drive of a tastefully restored country farmhouse that was now a two-and-a-half-star bed-and-breakfast. The newest guests were sinkhole refugees.

Honk, honk.

Peter Pugliese opened the front door. "Be right there."

Mary walked up behind her husband, carrying a brown paper bag that had been prepared with affection. "Don't forget your lunch." She rethought timeframe as she looked out at the night sky. "Or dinner."

"Thanks." Peter gave her a quick kiss and trotted down the steps. He jumped into the car. "All set."

Vernon threw the vehicle in gear and took off. "Peter, I'm so glad you accepted our invitation to join us tonight. I feel absolutely sick about everything your family has gone through lately, and this will give you a chance to get your mind elsewhere. It also shows your commitment to becoming part of the fabric of this town."

"How could I not accept?" Peter stared into his paper bag. "This kind of thing is very important to me and Mary."

The drive was over before Peter knew it. Vernon pulled into the parking lot of a darkened corner gas station. Four other cars and a pickup were already waiting.

"May I have your attention?" the mayor called

out. "I'd like you to meet the latest member of our neighborhood watch group . . ."

Peter already knew most of them by sight. He began shaking hands. "You know, I used to be on a neighborhood watch up north. It was a great way to meet other families and show appreciation for the role of local law enforcement."

"That's how we feel down here," said Jabow.

Peter assessed the identical appearance of the others. "Was I supposed to dress all in black?"

"Next time," said Vernon. "Everybody, let's get moving . . . Peter, what are you doing?"

Peter stood holding the open passenger door of the Skylark. "Getting ready to go."

Vernon shook his head. "The vehicles stay here."

"We're patrolling on foot?" asked Peter. "But I thought neighborhood watches observed in cars and phoned in tips to the police if anything seemed out of place."

"Times have changed. And we're the police." Vernon walked around to his trunk; the rest of the gang gathered behind him. The lid popped open.

"Good God," said Peter. "What's with all the guns?"

"You're in Florida now." He began handing out revolvers and automatic pistols and shotguns. "Here's your weapon."

"I'm not taking that thing."

The others stopped and turned with misgivings. Vernon raised a paternalistic eyebrow.

"I guess I could. Is this what they call an assault rifle?"

"And here's your cap."

Peter grabbed the black knitted piece of apparel. "Good thinking. It could get cold tonight." He placed it on his head and rolled it down to his hairline. He realized there was a lot more to the cap and continued rolling until it completely covered his face. "A ski mask?"

"Probably won't come to that," said Jabow. "You can keep it rolled up for now."

Vernon twirled an arm in the air. "Move out!"

The gang briskly strolled a few blocks. They reached the end of a sleepy residential street and, without communication, silently fanned out in rehearsed formation. People in the houses peeked out curtains and closed their blinds.

"Peter," said Vernon. "Since this is your first time, stick with me."

"I thought this town didn't have much crime."

"We don't."

"Then what's all this about?"

Vernon pointed at the end of the road, where street lights caught a group of dark silhouettes scattering with precision.

"More of our guys?" asked Peter.

"No, the rival neighborhood watch."

"A rival watch?"

"This is disputed border territory."

"Like India and Pakistan?"

"Except hairier," said Vernon. "Started when our

town annexed this land, but we didn't anticipate an insurgency movement."

The rival groups advanced toward the middle of the block, where they began to enmesh and follow one another in man-to-man coverage. Some proceeded in straight lines. Others paired off and pursued each other in circles.

"Why are you following me?"

"Why are *you* following *me*?"

Peter looked at Vernon in befuddlement. "This is about city limits?"

"Much more than that," said the mayor. "In Florida, a lot of people need to be mad to be happy. They're just looking for a reason, any reason. Luckily we have a new state law to help them."

Peter paused again to take in the action. Here and there, pairs of competing watchmen had ceased moving and faced each other.

"I'm standing my ground."

"I'm standing *my* ground."

Peter continued observing in disbelief. "How long does this go on?"

Vernon checked his wristwatch. "Until now." He pulled out a referee's whistle, and a shrill warble filled the neighborhood. The groups dispersed in opposite directions.

Peter followed Vernon back to the cars. "That's it?"

"Just dinner break."

A bunch of the guys piled in the Skylark, and Vernon handed out beers from his cooler. "Peter?"

He waved off a Pabst Blue Ribbon. "We're carrying guns."

The men passed around a cardboard bucket of cold KFC. Peter unfolded a paper napkin on his lap and opened his brown bag. Each item individually wrapped. Dill pickle spear, hard-boiled egg, dietetic portion of potato chips in a clear baggie, an orange. He unwrapped wax paper around a sandwich and lifted the top piece of white bread. "Baloney, excellent." Then he read the note Mary had inserted. "Have fun with your friends tonight. Love, Me." The *i*'s were dotted with hearts. Peter smiled and stuck the note back in the bag. He realized the car was silent. He looked up. Everyone staring with open mouths.

"What?" said Peter.

The others fought to contain giggles.

"Hey," snapped Vernon. "Peter's got a loving wife. I know what some of you are going home to tonight."

"He's right," said Jabow. "Peter's a lucky man."

"Mary's a wonderful woman."

"You're a good husband."

"Give me a drumstick. Crispy, not original."

They resumed dinner and popped a second round of beers.

"I have a question," said Peter. "What's this Stand Your Ground law?"

"Levels the playing field," Otis said with his mouth full. "They enacted it because there was too much burden on a crime victim to fully retreat. You had to be completely cornered before fighting back."

"I totally agree with that," said Peter. "If you're busy retreating and end up with your back to the wall, you decrease your odds."

"But the law also had some unintended benefits," said Jabow.

"Such as?"

"Well, before, if you picked a fight on the street with a complete stranger and started to lose and had to shoot him, you couldn't claim self-defense. What's up with that?"

"Plus these new neighborhood watch groups are insanely dangerous," said Otis.

"But *you're* in a watch group," said Peter.

"Not us," answered Jabow. "That other watch group. They scare the shit out of me, running around at night with guns, confronting people. It's just reckless."

Vernon checked his watch again and closed the cooler. "Time's a-wastin'."

They piled out of the car and Jabow called Vernon aside. "Why'd you bring Peter along? I mean, with everything else that's been going on and all."

"That's the whole point," said Vernon. "I want to keep an eye on him. Who knows if he'll crack up and start blabbing before Steve gets out of jail."

They headed back toward the street where the other gang was already waiting with bellies full of Arby's and Schlitz. But before the group could get there, one of them spotted something of greater concern and sounded the alarm.

"Hoodie!"

Vernon's team sprinted up the road, pulling down

ski masks before surrounding the unknown pedestrian and aiming guns in a circular firing squad.

"Freeze!" shouted Jabow. "What the hell are you doing in this neighborhood?"

The person reached up and pulled the hood off his head.

"Oh, Senator Pratchett," said Otis. "We thought you were someone else."

"What is wrong with you guys?"

"But you were wearing a hoodie," said Jabow.

"Because it's cold! It's just a hoodie!"

"Sorry," said Vernon. "But what *are* you doing here?"

"Telling you to knock off this idiocy." He pointed over his shoulder at a woman peeking out a bedroom window. "I just got back from the committee hearing in Tallahassee and there's too much heat right now, so stop these ridiculous patrols before someone gets hurt—"

Bang.

Jabow went down. "Ow, he shot me!"

The senator rolled his eyes at the sky.

Vernon snatched the gun away from Slow. "Why did you shoot him?"

"He looked scary to me."

"But it's Jabow!"

Slow shrugged. "He was wearing a ski mask."

"This is exactly what I'm talking about!" Pratchett bent down next to Jabow. "Let me see that arm . . . Good, just a flesh wound."

"Except hospitals are required by law to report all gunshot injuries no matter how minor, and Slow is on probation," said Vernon. "We need someone who has a clean record . . . Okay, everyone listen up. This is the plan. Peter here was the shooter . . ."

"What!" said the geologist.

"You'll be a hero. Just follow along." Vernon faced the others. "Peter grazed Jabow while protecting us from an assailant who took the bullet and got away. Then we put out an alert for all area hospitals to be on the lookout for a bloody sleeper-cell foreigner in a hoodie." Vernon handed Peter the gun he had confiscated from Slow. "Point that in the air and fire."

"Why?"

"We need gunshot residue on your hand."

"Peter," the senator said calmly. "Give me the gun. I'm taking Jabow to a doctor I know who will discreetly give him antibiotics and stitches. Or is that too complex?"

They all decided to call it a night and began walking at a more leisurely pace back toward the cars.

"So, Peter," said Vernon. "How have you been holding up?"

From behind:

Bang.

"*Ow, shit!*"

Peter started turning around. "What was that?"

"Probably nothing."

Chapter THIRTY-ONE

A NEW DAY

Birds chirped. A rainbow. Young boys with base-ball cards in their bicycle spokes pedaled past the First National Bank of Wobbly.

The front door opened. Otis rushed in lugging a stack of newspapers bundled with twine. "Had to drive halfway to Orlando!"

Jabow adjusted the sling on his wounded arm. "We really made the *New York Times*?"

"I know!" Otis said ecstatically as he sliced the string with a pocketknife. "Most of our names are in it. I bought extra copies that we could mail to relatives."

They all got busy reading.

"It mentions Lead Belly's . . ."

"And the neighborhood watch . . ."

"Our world-famous sinkhole . . ."

The door opened again.

The gang looked up. "Hey, Senator! Have you seen today's *New York Times*?"

"Yes," snapped Pratchett.

Otis quickly turned a page. "We're like celebrities!"

Jabow held up his own paper. "Senator, your name's in here, too. A lot more times than anyone else's."

"You morons!"

"Why so crabby?" asked Otis. "The article makes you look great. Says the city of Wobbly cast more votes for you in the last election than there are people in the town."

"Everyone, close your traps!"

"What's the matter?" asked Vernon. "We loved what you said on TV, sticking up for us in the committee hearing."

"Stop calling attention to yourselves!" said Pratchett. "It doesn't take much digging around here."

"So what do you want us to do?"

"Shut it all down!"

"What's that mean?"

"The speed trap, the neighborhood watch, and I know you're still overpumping at the water plant," said the senator. "Most important of all, make sure nothing happens to Peter Pugliese. Not even a splinter."

"What do you mean?" said Vernon.

"I got a pretty good idea what you've been doing on the side with your Miami friends," said Ryan.

"And normally that's your business. But right now, if anything suspicious happens to him, it'll bring in the FBI and put this whole place under martial law."

"Would they still let us have Founders' Day?"

"Shut up."

CLEWISTON

A fit young man in a Ferrari shirt sat tied to an uncomfortable motel room chair. He looked toward the dresser, where his captor had his back to him, working on something unseen.

"I already gave the cookie money back! Please let me go!"

"Put a sock in it!" said Serge. "You think that just because you have tons of money, you can poop on everyone else?"

The man continued watching Serge with confused dread. "W-w-what are you going to do to me?"

"This is what!" Serge spun and ran toward the chair, seizing the hostage by the hair on the back of his head. "Eat the fucking Dorito taco!"

"No! Not that!"

"Eat it!"

"I won't!" He clenched his lips tight.

A cell phone rang. Serge answered with his free hand.

"*You ditched me again! I waited all night at the motel!*"

"Matt, something unforeseeable came up—"

"I won't eat the taco!"

Slap.

"*Taco? What's going on?*"

"I'm losing reception . . ." Serge threw the phone in the corner, then pinched the hostage's nose shut until he had to come up for air. "In goes the taco!"

"Mgrmmghphmmm . . ."

Serge stepped back as the man spit out what he could.

Coleman stumbled over with a joint and giggled. "He's got guacamole all over his face."

"For the rich, this is worse than water-boarding."

"That's it?" said Coleman. "You're only going to make him eat a taco?"

"Just batting practice," said Serge. "I've been planning this one for so long, but never had an ass-hole in the right tax bracket. All the logistics are already in place."

Serge duct-taped the man's mouth, then gave him a booster shot of tranquilizer. The prisoner's chin fell to his chest.

"What now?" asked Coleman.

"Back to the Ferrari," said Serge. "I like how it handles."

A half hour later, the sports car pulled out of another rental business with a small moving trailer in tow. It skirted the underside of Lake Okeechobee and turned into a parking lot surrounded by a fence topped with spools of barbed wire. Row after row of garage-type doors.

Coleman accidentally inhaled a tiny roach, and washed it down with Southern Comfort. "You're going to rent a storage unit?"

"Already have one." Serge pulled the Ferrari up to unit 127. "Told you the logistics were in place."

He twisted a combination lock and raised the door.

"Look at all these bags," said Coleman. "They're like giant sacks of fertilizer."

"Fifty pounds each." Serge hoisted the first one onto his shoulder.

"How many are there?"

"Fifty." Serge walked to the back of the trailer and tossed the bag inside.

"But what's in them?" asked Coleman.

"Let me give you an impenetrable hint: Read the labels."

Coleman crouched and slowly moved his lips. "Where on earth did you get this stuff?"

"Only takes money and the Internet," said Serge. "And it's far easier to procure than fertilizer, because that contains nitrates that can be converted into explosives. But this stuff is totally harmless. It's just that average citizens never have the imagination to ask for it. You simply find a big distributor that supplies the kind of massive factories you see all the time on cable shows about how things are made."

"You're going to make things?"

"I won't be able to do anything if you don't stop yapping and give me a hand."

Coleman strained to raise a bag and decided to just drag it on the ground. "Serge, help me get it over the bumper."

"Here you go."

Thud.

Coleman paused and stared back at the Ferrari's trunk.

Bang, bang, bang . . .

"Serge, I think your new friend has a question."

"Soon he'll have more answers than he'll know what to do with."

Thud . . .

Eventually the last sack landed in the trailer, and Serge wiped his hands on his pants. "That about does it. Forty-seven bags for me, three for you."

They closed up the storage unit and headed south again. The Ferrari left Lake Okeechobee behind and dove down into the vast low-horizon wasteland of sugarcane country. No traffic, just a raised berm of a road that let them see thirty miles in all directions across the top of the fields. The road ran alongside a drainage canal of deceptive depth and reached a place called Okeelanta, a town so small that it's literally only a name on a map. Just a crossroads in the middle of nowhere with four empty corners and nothing else in sight but more endless miles of cane waving in the wind.

Even farther south, they turned off the pavement and onto a dirt road running through one of the anonymous cane fields. About a mile in, Serge stopped and pulled a GPS from his backpack, setting coordinates. Then he pulled the hostage from the trunk.

A groan as a rib cage slammed the ground.

Serge crouched like a baseball catcher. "Here's the deal: That tranquilizer's pretty much worn off.

You're still tied up good, but don't penalize me for a savant gift with knots. And I think by now you've learned a valuable lesson about courtesy that you'll never forget. Did I guess correctly?"

The man nodded emphatically.

"It's amazing how often I get that one right. It's like thirty in a row. Anyway, here's the bonus round and your chance to escape. I've tied your hands *in front* of you, which means you can crawl the mile back to the main road. I'm afraid it'll seriously suck to slither that far, but consider it the price of personal growth. No need to thank me. And just because I'm a people person, I'll leave a knife on the side of the road so you can cut off your bindings when you get out of this field. Then it's a long walk to the nearest town, but a migrant truck or something will probably come along first."

Serge and Coleman climbed back in the sports car and sped off, kicking up a billowing contrail of dust and pesticide. Crawling commenced . . .

"Don't take this the wrong way," said Coleman. "But what you did to that guy back there didn't seem up to . . ." He snapped his finger. "What's the word I'm looking for?"

"Par?"

"No, that's not it."

Serge grinned. "You're forgetting the fifty-pound sacks o' fun."

"Yeah, I did forget," said Coleman. "When do I find out what they're for?"

"It's the next item on today's zany schedule," said Serge. "Another piece of logistics already in motion."

The northbound Ferrari reached the lake again and turned west. Off a spur into the countryside sat a large metal shed and a small house. Grassy acres lay flat and sprawling.

A man came out of the cottage when he heard visitors. The mailbox said BABCOCK. First name was Dylan. Sixty-eight and still going strong from a regimen of strenuous chores around the property. Full head of white hair, faded jeans and a large Western belt buckle with crossed rifles. He'd done the same thing for a living his entire life, marking years with the seasonal cycle of the burning of the sugarcane. He strolled up to the driver's door. "Got the rest of my money?"

"Right here." Serge climbed out and handed Dylan a thick envelope.

They both went around the back of the trailer and unloaded sacks.

"Done the same thing my whole life," said Dylan. "And I ain't never done this."

"It's the movie business," said Serge. "Our lawyers want us to use something that's absolutely harmless to humans, animals and plants. Plus, white is so bland. This stuff will add a bit of color to our filming."

"That it'll accomplish," said Dylan. "How realistic do you want me to make this?"

"We've taken every safety precaution with our actor," said Serge. "So cut it as true to life as possible."

Once the truck was empty, they opened wide doors on the metal shed and wheeled out an unusual-looking aircraft with a small bubble cockpit. "You realize there's only room for two."

"Coleman needs to stay and watch the car anyway."

Soon the glazed-red airplane picked up speed as it bounded across the field and lifted off. Serge handed Dylan a scrap of paper with the GPS coordinates.

"What kind of movie did you say you fellas were doing?"

"Another remake," said Serge. "It's an homage to Hitchcock."

"Think I saw the original when it first came out in the fifties," said Dylan. "The one where Cary Grant gets stuck at the crossroads?"

"An all-time classic," said Serge. "How can anyone not love that flick?"

"Except for what happened to the pilot."

"Don't worry," said Serge. "We took care of that in rewrites."

Travel by air was much quicker than even a limited-edition Ferrari.

"We're almost over your site," said Dylan. "Where are the movie cameras?"

"Hidden," said Serge. "Since this is the big scene, we're filming from multiple angles and can't have other cameras show up in the footage. Made that expensive mistake the last time."

"Think I see your actor now." Dylan looked down from the side of the cockpit. "He's coming out the cane field and heading up that road."

Dylan pushed his stick forward, putting the plane into a shallow dive.

"Can I pull the release lever?" asked Serge.

"Be my guest."

The crop duster swooped low over the road, spraying a thick orange cloud that settled broadly over a hundred-yard swath.

Joe Ferrari began coughing and rubbing his eyes. He was barely able to see when he heard the plane returning for another pass. He looked around. Only one place to hide. He dove back into the rows of sugarcane. Another orange cloud wafted gently over the crops.

More coughing and spitting on his hands and knees. He stood up as the plane banked in the eastern sky for a third run. He took off deeper into the sugarcane.

"How many times do you want to do this?" asked Dylan.

"Until we're empty," said Serge. "He's got a gas mask, so there's no such thing as overkill."

"Where'd your actor go?"

"Just follow the ripple through the cane field."

"He's really thrashing around," said the pilot.

"One of the best actors working today," said Serge. "Take her down."

"You're the boss," said Dylan, putting the plane into another dive. "I can cross this off my bucket list."

"So can he."

Chapter THIRTY-TWO

Open-bed trucks of migrant workers waited behind police lines. The only people getting through on the lonely road south of Clewiston were detectives and a coroner's van. Onlookers gathered as the satellite trucks set up shop.

"*This is Roberta Blanco reporting live from sugarcane country just south of Lake Okeechobee, where authorities have discovered the body of a hedge-fund trader who was first thought to be the victim of a freak accident. But police are now interviewing a local crop duster who appears to have been the unwitting accomplice in a bizarre murder plot. Also cooperating is the sales department of a regional food processing distributor. The preliminary coroner's report identifies the cause of death as asphyxiation from a severe lung coating of dust that was an equal mixture of Doritos cool ranch, mesquite barbecue, and sour cream and onion . . .*"

A Ferrari Berlinetta raced by the TV cameras. Serge opened her up along the deserted eastern shore of the lake and made it back to the Primrose Motel in record time. The sports car skidded to a stop next to a chopper as Matt burst out of a room.

"There you are! I've been calling and calling!"

"My bad," said Serge. "I'm sure you can understand that in my line of work, a lot of people unexpectedly make demands on my time."

"But I wasted another whole day in a motel room," said Matt. "The only reason I didn't head back north is I felt responsible for your chopper."

"And I'm going to make all that up to you," said Serge. "Get your stuff. We're heading to another inspirational event where the spirit of the sixties still thrives in a most unlikely location. If you thought the Suwannee River fest was great . . ."

Matt was staring next to the motorcycle. "Where'd you get the Ferrari?"

"I have friends who just give me things. It's weird."

"That's the same car from outside the restaurant the other day."

"Don't be ridiculous."

"Coleman's got bruises, and it looks like you have spots of blood on your shirt, just like the last time you disappeared." Matt carefully looked them over. "Something's going on. You're keeping secrets from me! I'm not leaving here until you come clean and tell me what you're really up to!"

Serge slowly lowered his head. "Okay, when you're right, you're right." He looked up and placed a trusting hand on the young man's shoulder. "Matt, you're one of the good guys, and we've been traveling together long enough to establish bonds of trust. If you're going to continue on with us, it's only fair to reveal something important that you don't know about me. And after I tell you, you're free to go your own way if you so choose, no strings attached . . . Ready?"

Matt took a deep breath and braced himself. "What is it?"

"I'm able to create thousand-island dressing from the condiment section of any convenience store," said Serge. "Packets of ketchup, mayo and relish. Comes in handy on the road."

"*That's* your secret?"

"I haven't told anyone but Coleman because there are millions of dollars at stake. It's the perfect business model: Condiment packets are free, and I can bottle and sell the dressing endlessly with no ingredient cost. Plus, my recipe is a close molecular cousin of sandwich spread, and if you subtract the ketchup, you've also got tartar sauce. A whole product line is ready to explode . . ."

"Serge . . ."

"Except the grand plan hit a kink. Sure, they *say* the condiments are free, but try walking out of a convenience store with a bulging backpack. So now I'm forced to hit a million places and get only a few at each, like the meth guys running around town all day buying Sudafed. The meth dudes are called smurfs, and we've started crossing paths, nodding at each other out of professional courtesy . . ."

"Serge . . ."

"Except the condiment crackdown is much more severe." He reached into his pants to show Matt some packets, then put them back. "I've been banned from every convenience store where I live. That's why I can only make my collection rounds on the road and sometimes, when funds are low, I'm forced to go missing for otherwise inexplicable periods of time. I did it all for you, Matt, to continue financing your thesis journey."

"All right, all right," said the student. "Let's just go."

"I was ready to leave a while ago, but you're the one who's acting all suspicious."

WOBBLY

The front door opened at the First National Bank.

Men in overalls looked up from newspapers.

"Steve!"

"You made bail?"

"Even better. All charges dropped."

"But how?"

He took a seat. "Good lawyer. The transport driver and car dealer were clean and passed voluntary polygraphs. And the vehicle with the dope was bought by one of the guys I hired to hit the auctions, who turned out to be clean as well. It never came within miles of me, so they had nothing."

"Then how'd the drugs get in there?" Vernon asked with a wink.

A sly grin. "The only possible explanation is that

they were already in the vehicle when we bought it just a week ago, and, as my attorney pointed out, it had numerous previous owners, including one with substance issues."

"If I ever need a lawyer . . ." said Jabow.

"I'll give you his card," said Steve. "Now my turn: How'd that blue moon work out for you the other night?"

Vernon sighed. "Terrible."

"Trouble getting down in the hole?"

"Worse. Right after we entered the house, the sheriff showed up," said the mayor. "Out of no-where. We had to abort."

"But you're going to try again?"

"Not right now."

"Why not?"

"Because deputies have increased patrols ever since," said Vernon. "And I believe we have a more immediate problem. Don't you think it was a little too coincidental that you got pulled in by the sher-iff? A few hours before he *happens* to come by that house when we were about to recover the money?"

"I was already wondering about that," said Steve. "Who do you think the informant is?"

"Follow the motive," said Vernon. "Who stands to gain the most by neutralizing both of us?"

"That son of a bitch! I knew I should have taken care of Pugliese when I first had the chance."

Steve stormed out of the bank, and men in over-alls picked up newspapers.

"Yup."

"Mmm-hmm."

MEANWHILE, TWENTY MILES AWAY

Night fell. Coleman waddled through the darkness with a crooked smile and a beer in each hand. It was a giant wooded expanse way out in the sticks, which meant DeLand, Florida.

Coleman was properly roasted to dig the weirdness of the place. Here and there in the moss-draped trees, strands of twinkling little lights. And all around, faint, competing music of unseen origins: rock, zydeco, mystical twangs from India.

Ahead of him, a form took shape in the forest. The person approached Coleman, also grinning with two beers. They silently exchanged looks of kinship as they passed. Coleman continued deeper into the woods, scraping his legs on brush. He began hearing drums, then noticed flames flickering through branches. By the time he reached the clearing, his beers were empty. He saw some people lying on blankets outside a cluster of tents. A man in a fringed leather vest played a homemade flute. A peace flag flapped from an old-growth oak. Coleman adjusted his course.

He reached the group and tripped, ending up on his back like a turtle. "Hi, I'm Coleman . . ." He rolled onto his stomach and pointed at their cooler. ". . . Can I buy a beer for a dollar?"

The man stopped playing the flute. "No, but you can have one. There are no possessions here. We are all connected; the separateness of our beings is but an illusion."

A young girl with daisies in her hair gave Coleman a Budweiser; another handed him a tambourine.

Coleman began chugging and banging the percussion instrument on his hip. "Far out."

Then it was time to be moseying along. He entered the woods again, shaking the tambourine along the way, until he emerged in another clearing.

Serge and Matt were sitting outside their own tent when a jingling sound came toward them from the tree line.

"Where'd you get the tambourine?"

"It came with the beer." Coleman lit a joint under the stars. "This place rules! There are people all through the woods getting righteously fucked up. You never know what excellence you're going to stumble across!"

"It's one of the best." Serge stared toward the largest fire of all, glowing through distant trees. "An annual event that's Florida's biggest haven for preserving the essence of the individual."

Coleman exhaled toward the sky. "The flute dude said we're all connected."

Matt leaned over a notebook. "You were explaining before Coleman came back? . . ."

"It's DeLand's Burning Man music festival, held way, way out in the countryside at a secret location each year that's only revealed word of mouth."

Coleman blazed a fatty. "Because they want to make sure everyone's cool!"

"Word of mouth?" Matt looked around. "And still *all* these people came?"

"Like I said, Burning Man is special. Or rather that's what it used to be named. Now it's called 'the event formerly known as Burning Man.'"

"How did it start?"

"They got the idea from the original Burning Man out in Nevada's Black Rock Desert, which was created to reject the plastic greed of the material world's war machine and embody the hippie idealism of free communal love, higher conscience and ultimate harmony."

"Why did DeLand change the name of its event?" asked Matt.

"They received a threatening legal letter over infringement."

Coleman pointed at a luminous blue beam sweeping through the woods. "I want to check out the stage shows."

Serge stood up. "Let's rock."

The forest was bathed in a surreal soup of smoke and strange light. Serge, Coleman and Matt wandered through shadows and lasers. Swirling rhythmic sounds moved in and out of the space all around them. They passed a row of bongo players who played feverishly for a few moments, then stopped and were answered faintly by other far-away bongos. The woods opened into another modest clearing. Along the edge were small makeshift platforms for musicians. In the middle, beach blankets and lawn chairs. More colored lights spun over a band performing a techno-synthesized version of Santana's "Soul Sacrifice."

"This whole scene is giving me an eerie feeling," said Matt. "Like a kind of preternatural vibe that something really big is about to happen."

"Something big *is* about to happen." Serge led them to the largest clearing of all, brightly lit by flames lapping high into the night. Hundreds of people several rows deep surrounded the giant moon crater of a fire pit, rubbing their arms to stay warm in the uncommonly chilly night. Over their heads, long poles suspended a gigantic X-shaped human form that had been lashed together from straw and sticks. It was raised over the pit and quickly engulfed in a spectacular display that seemed dislodged from some ancient Mayan ritual.

The crowd: "*Oooooooooo.*" "*Ahhhhhhhhhh.*"

Serge turned around. "Matt, what do you think?"

"That creepy feeling I had is just getting stronger." The student held cold hands toward the fire. "And I'm not the superstitious type. It just seems like this is some final quiet evening before all chaos breaks loose."

"Nonsense," said Serge. "It's simply your brain's unfamiliar reaction to all the unusual sensory bombardment."

"I don't know," said Matt, taking a step back. "I've never felt this way before. I'm getting kind of scared."

"Matt, you're an educated person," said Serge. "You know how stupid that sounds?"

"I don't care if I do sound stupid—"

Coleman shook a jingling round piece of wood

over his head. "Hey guys! I never knew I could play the tambourine! And I never even took a lesson!"

Serge looked back at the student. "You were saying?"

"Forget everything I just mentioned." He began walking. "So where are we heading tomorrow?"

"Thought I'd let you pick," said Serge. "To compensate for all the time you were stuck in the motel room."

"Hey, I know what would be a hoot," said Matt. "How about that wacky small town that's been in the news lately? I think it's nearby. Wobbly."

"Then Wobbly it is."

Chapter THIRTY-THREE

WOBBLY

A man peeked out the second-floor window of a red-brick building. The old Railroad Hotel was built in 1922 when people still came to Florida by rail. Then they didn't. The hotel sat boarded up for fifty years until the tourists and antique hunters discovered the town. So it was restored, including the elevator where you had to pull the accordion door shut. The front desk still had the original wooden mail slots and brass room keys. They bought a new chandelier that looked old.

The upstairs view from room 201 began with Shorty's Garage down below, then Lead Belly's and the rest of Main Street, fluttering with hopeful Founders' Day banners. A pair of eyes moved over the unhurried routine of a small town. Longtime residents emerged from the barbershop and pharmacy with crew cuts and ointment. On the sidewalk, small children played jacks and paddleball and hopscotch, except they played them on smart-phones. Peter Pugliese pulled the curtains tight and took a seat on one of the beds.

"I don't understand why I can't go shopping," said Mary. "We're supposed to just *stay* in the room?"

"It's only temporary."

"What was wrong with that nice bed-and-break-fast in DeLand where we were at?" asked his wife. "And what's all this new drama about keeping out of sight?"

"It's nothing," said Peter. "I don't want to worry you."

"Well, you are. So I want to know everything."

"Remember that body they found under our house?" asked Peter.

"You don't forget something like that," said Mary. "And then they arrested you!"

"I already explained," said Peter. "It was a turf war with the sheriff, and they were protecting me from being used as a pawn. The case was immedi-ately dismissed."

"They have a strange way of doing business around here. And you still haven't told me why we're prisoners in this room."

"We're not prisoners," said Peter. "The mayor and the others are just taking extra precautions. Some of the dead guy's relatives came to town and were upset about the charges being dropped."

"Didn't they explain that you're innocent?"

"Over and over," said Peter. "Vernon told me the family seems harmless, but to be on the safe side we need to let them cool down. They're still in the stages of grief. Frankly, I think the mayor's over-reacting."

"How are we supposed to eat?"

A knock at the door.

Peter sprang off the bed and froze. Then he crept forward and checked the peephole. He opened up.

"Here's your barbecue."

"Thanks, Otis."

Peter returned with a pair of hot sacks. "Mayor said he'd take care of the meals."

"You're a little on the jumpy side," said Mary.

"From hunger." He unwrapped corn bread and set out the plastic utensils.

Mary got up and went to the window herself.

"Don't open the curtains that wide!"

She turned and stared at Peter. "Okay, first your startled reaction to the knock at the door, and now this. What aren't you telling me? I want to know right now!"

"It's just a rumor, but there's a farfetched story floating around—I think it's just because they're from Miami—that the dead guy and his cousin might sort of be, like, in the . . . drug business." He quickly took a bite of ribs.

"Drugs!" yelled his wife. "We need to go to the police!"

"The mayor and his buddies *are* the police," said Peter.

"Not this Barney Fife crap. The real police. In a city."

"And what will they do?" said Peter. "The thing

about small towns is they're all-powerful. They don't mind cutting corners when it comes to fending off outsiders to protect locals. I think we're much safer here."

"I don't."

DELAND

A late-morning fog began to lift from the forest floor as campers stirred in their tents. Someone scrambled eggs over a propane burner. Others rolled up sleeping bags.

Serge finished lashing all his gear to the chopper. "That was one heck of a night."

Coleman crawled out of the bushes with pine needles and sap in his hair. He stood and smacked a tambourine. "Burning Man rules!"

"Off to Wobbly! . . ."

Serge had the perfect sound track for the rolling hills leading south into Calusa County. Joplin, Steppenwolf, the Byrds.

". . . *Eight miles high* . . ."

"Radio check," said Coleman. "Love bugs keep getting in my mouth."

"You know how to fix that?"

"Not really."

"Wait a second," said Serge. "What's that noise?"

The siren grew louder. Serge turned around and saw the flashing blue light. "Shit!"

"It's a speed trap," said Matt. "Like they reported in the papers."

"I know." Serge angled the motorcycle onto the shoulder. "That's why I was deliberately going under the limit . . . Let me do the talking."

Serge removed his helmet as a man in jeans and mirror sunglasses walked up. "Good morning, Officer. I'm sure I wasn't going that fast. I was watching the gauge very carefully because I'm committed to your mission."

"License and registration."

"Can't help you there," said Serge.

"No license? Other ID?"

Serge shook his head. "I hid my wallet too good last night with the reminder note inside."

"What about your friend?"

Serge glanced at Coleman in the sidecar. "That's an even longer shot. Since I wasn't speeding, are we done now?"

The auxiliary officer retreated a step and placed a hand on his hip holster. "Don't move." Then he waved ahead at another squad car. The signal for assistance.

Moments later, Serge heard handcuffs snap behind his back. "This isn't good."

Then Coleman got the bracelets. "What's your plan?"

"Don't have one."

They twisted Matt's arms. "I have ID if that helps." *Snap.*

"Which pocket?"

Matt craned his neck. "Right side."

The first officer pulled out the billfold and removed a New Jersey license. He showed it to the other cop, who walked ahead and leaned in the passenger side of his patrol car.

"What's going on?" whispered Coleman.

Serge shrugged.

Up at the squad car, a whiskered man in overalls stuck his head out the passenger window and looked back at the chopper . . .

The officer soon returned and called to his colleague. "Uncuff 'em."

Matt rubbed his wrists.

"Here's your license, Mr. Pugliese. We're very sorry for the misunderstanding. We didn't know who you were."

The officers left.

Serge and Coleman glanced at each other, then slowly turned toward the college student. "What happened?"

"I haven't the faintest."

They rode on.

"Turn up here," said Matt.

"You know this place?" asked Serge.

"Never been."

The chopper cruised deep into the countryside.

Matt tapped Serge's shoulder. "Pull over."

All three got off the bike and stared.

"Man, it looks like a bomb hit the place," said Coleman.

"More like a sinkhole," said Serge. "Matt, why'd you bring us here?"

"That's my parents' house."

"Your parents?"

"It's the whole reason I suggested we visit

Wobbly," said Matt. "But I wanted it to be a surprise, both for you guys and my folks. Except I didn't realize there was this much damage. I thought they were still living here while repairs were going on."

"Do your parents know you're in town?"

"Not yet."

"Then I think you ought to call them."

Matt nodded and walked over to the other side of the road.

"What a trip." Coleman puffed a one-hitter. "That traffic stop and now this."

"Why do I get the feeling that the surprises have just begun?"

Matt came back and stuck the phone in his pocket.

"Did you find out where your parents are?"

A glance at the ground. "Yeah."

"What's the matter?" asked Serge. "You look concerned about something."

"Not sure." Matt furrowed his brow. "My dad didn't sound right. Matter of fact he sounded terrible, almost as if he was . . . afraid."

"Have any idea what it could be?" asked Serge. "Anything unusual happen lately?"

"Nothing, except he got arrested."

"For what?"

"He told me it was just for show. Part of a local feud between the mayor and the sheriff." Matt pointed across the field. "Right after they found the body under the house—"

"Whoa! Stop, back up, slow down," said Serge.

"We've just entered a surprise theme park. Take your time and start at the beginning and tell me everything."

"Okay, my dad's a geologist and he moved down here because of all the new work . . ."

Chapter THIRTY-FOUR

DOWNTOWN

A bell dinged in the restaurant's kitchen window. A rack of ribs was up. A waitress carried a tray of sweetened iced tea. Children with crayons colored paper place mats. A stegosaurus.

The front door of Lead Belly's flew open. Steve marched straight for the table in back. "You were out at Peter's house *twice* the other night! Someone saw you go back again after the sheriff left! I want my money!"

"Will you keep it down?" snapped Vernon. "And pull up a chair. We've been looking all over for you."

"Bullshit."

"Please, there are families," said Jabow. "Have a seat and hear us out. We need to work on this together."

"Things have gotten out of hand," said Vernon.

"Gee, you think?" said Steve.

"We *did* go back out to the house the night of the

blue moon," said Jabow. "We couldn't do anything the first time with the sheriff there."

Vernon leaned over potato salad. "Peter's got the money."

Steve reclined and folded his arms. "I don't believe you."

"We went down the hole under the house and there was a big cavity where someone had been digging. We found a few loose bills. *Only* a few loose bills." Vernon reached in his pocket and handed them across the table. "These look familiar? . . . Otis saw Peter's car out at the place earlier in the evening. He took the money. Why else would he disappear?"

"He's gone?"

"Vanished," said Vernon. "You do the math: He's got a company job, regular hours and movements, a wife, then poof! Nowhere to be found."

Steve glared.

"Still need convincing?" said Jabow. "Here's a photo of his burned-out car that we found this morning in a ravine behind the Clancy farm. Probably already has new ID and everything."

"That son of a bitch!" Steve started getting up.

"Sit back down," said Vernon. "And here's where we need to keep our voices really low. Where's the best place to hide when everyone thinks you're a thousand miles away?"

Steve began to smile. "He vanished . . . but you found him? He's still in town?"

"We each have our own roles to play," said Vernon. "This falls into your area of expertise. We can't get involved in what we're guessing you'll have to do, but we won't interfere, either."

"Where is he?"

Vernon tilted his head up the street. "Room 201." He pushed a brass key across the table.

Steve grabbed it and left without further words.

Everyone around the table watched silently until the restaurant's front door closed behind him.

"Think it'll work?" asked Otis.

"We'll use the sheriff so there's no tracing it back to us," said Jabow. "They'll pick him up tonight after the deed is done."

THE RAILROAD HOTEL

Knock, knock, knock.

"*Barbecue . . .*"

No answer.

Knock, knock, knock.

"Anyone in there? . . . I got your food."

Still nothing.

A brass key quietly slipped into a knob that was turned with excruciating slowness. Steve stuck his head inside. All clear. And luggage still in the room. Perfect. Then he saw the bathroom door closed and heard the sound of a shower running.

Plan A was to jump Peter if he answered the door. Steve enjoyed the theatrics of Plan B better. He would take a seat and wait with a gun for him to return. He'd done it before. The look on the faces was priceless.

And the room was perfectly configured. There

was a short, narrow hall next to the bathroom door, which created a blind spot in the bedroom for him to sit concealed in the corner for maximum shock value when the person walked farther into the room.

Steve walked farther into the room.

He stopped. The seat in the corner was already taken. A man in a tropical shirt pointed a gun.

"Who are you?"

"Serge Storms. You must be Steve."

"Do I know you?"

"You will." Serge waved the barrel. "Take a seat."

Steve eased himself down on the edge of the bed, buying time until he could reach for his own gun. "You have any idea what you're doing?"

"Do you like getting taken for a ride?"

"What?"

"Because that's what those guys in the barbecue joint are doing to you."

"What are you talking about?" said Steve.

"You laundered a lot of money with them and now it's missing," said Serge. "Don't act surprised. I know because I also laundered with them and now mine's missing, too."

"You must be thinking of someone else."

"I'll bet they told you it was Peter Pugliese, the geologist," said Serge.

Steve was suddenly off balance. "How'd you know?"

"Because I just had the same meeting with them at Lead Belly's." Serge held up a brass key. "And they gave me this. Look familiar?"

"But how? Why?"

"Peter's dead."

"You killed him?"

"Hell no," said Serge. "Use your brain. I wish I had. I'm up here pacing around wondering why Peter isn't in the room, because it makes no sense that he'd risk being out and showing his face right now. So I'm standing at the window scratching my head when I see you marching up the sidewalk from the restaurant. And I say to myself, 'Isn't that Steve from the bank?'"

"How do you know who I am?"

"You were on your way out once when I was coming in with my own money. Vernon told me . . . So when I saw you walking toward this hotel a minute ago, I could have kicked myself. *How could I have been so stupid?*"

"What?"

"Don't you see?" said Serge. "Peter's body is probably lying right now in an easily discovered location."

"They showed me a photo of a burned-out car, but said it was empty."

"And you believed them? Probably wasn't even his vehicle," said Serge. "Then what did they persuade both of us to do next? Walk past the security cameras in the lobby, break into the room of a murder victim and get our fingerprints all over the place." He stomped a foot on the ground. "What an obvious frame job! And I fell for it!"

"But—"

"There's more," said Serge. "They sent us here one after the other, knowing you'd probably bump into me. If they got lucky, maybe one of us would shoot the other, maybe both . . . And they would only be doing all this if they'd already gotten the money. They're playing the country hicks."

Steve clenched his eyes shut. He finally opened them with a sigh. "Dammit, I should have listened to my gut. Something just wasn't right about their whole story, but everything you just said fits perfectly . . . So what now?"

"Looks like we're a team of necessity," said Serge. "We should start by wiping down anything we've touched. Can I stop aiming this gun at you?"

"Please."

They both grabbed hand towels from the bathroom and went to work.

"What do we do next?" asked Steve.

"'Revenge and money' has a nice ring to it."

Chapter THIRTY-FIVE

THE NEXT DAY

DeLand is a town much like Wobbly, except no speed traps, incest, corruption or murder. But other than that, a postcard-perfect main street of restored brick buildings. Antiques, wine tastings, art strolls.

Across the road from a fish house, in a motel room numbered 113, a mother hugged her son. "I'm so glad you're safe."

Matt wriggled. "Mom, stop squeezing so hard. You're hurting me."

"Everything is going to be just fine from now on," said a man in a tropical shirt loading a semi-automatic pistol. "We've got it all under control."

The plump guy standing next to him nodded and chugged a Coors and burped.

"Son," said Peter Pugliese, "where exactly do you know these people from?"

"It's okay, Dad. I completely trust them." Matt pulled a notebook from his knapsack. "Met them working on my thesis. If you've gotten yourself in any kind of jam here in Florida, you couldn't be in better hands."

Peter turned as Coleman crumpled a beer can against the side of his head. He looked back at his son. "How long have you known them?"

"Your skepticism is understandable," said Serge, slamming the clip home in his pistol. "That's because we barely spoke at our initial meeting. I was forced to react fast due to a dizzying series of events that prevented proper social graces. It happens a lot in my line of work. But after freaking people out, I grow on them."

Peter looked toward his son again.

"I'll vouch for that," said Matt.

The father released a deep breath. "It's just that I'm not used to this. It's been a crazy twenty-four hours . . ."

. . . Twenty-four hours earlier, a gleaming chopper with a coconut gas tank rolled down a country road and passed a sign announcing the city limits of Wobbly, population 947. Serge turned the corner at a barbecue joint and parked down an alley. "We'll enter through the back, just in case."

They sprinted a short distance past an old red caboose and opened the rear door of the Railroad Hotel. Ancient hardwood floor with faded area rugs that gave the lobby the whiff of an estate sale.

"This way!"

They ran up the staircase and approached the door of room 201.

"Matt," Serge whispered. "You knock. Me and Coleman are going to stay out of sight so we don't alarm him when he looks out the peephole."

"Okay."

Knock, knock, knock.

An eye went to the peephole. "Oh, it's you, son." Peter opened the door. "Sorry I seemed a little anxious on the phone, but some things have made me nervous lately—"

Serge burst into the room with a gun at the ready. "Nobody be alarmed."

The couple screamed.

"Didn't you hear me?" Serge aimed his gun through a side doorway at a toilet and tub. "Bathroom's clear!"

The couple clutched each other and huddled in the corner.

"Dad," said Matt. "Everything's okay."

"Actually it's not," said Serge, getting down on the floor and aiming the pistol again. "Bed's clear!"

"W-w-what's going on?" asked Peter.

Serge stowed the pistol under his tropical shirt. "No time to talk. Matt told me everything. Then I instructed him to call the sheriff, ostensibly to report you missing. They requested he immediately come in for questioning. Matt played his part perfectly, acting distraught, and he was able to milk them for details. They asked him about money laundering, a body, drugs, Steve and Vernon, the whole nine yards. Jesus, I said no time to talk, and listen to me babble! Bottom line is you're in great danger. We need to evacuate you immediately."

"Dad," said Matt, "I'll explain later, but you need to do as he says as fast as possible."

"If you say so." Peter took a rigid step toward a suitcase.

"No time for luggage," said Serge. "And I'll need it for props anyway."

Matt took his mom by the hand. "We really have to go."

"But where?" asked his father.

"I already got the address."

Serge glanced out the curtains. Someone left Lead Belly's and turned purposefully toward the hotel. "Shit! . . . Go! Now! Out past the caboose!" He ran into the bathroom and turned on the shower. "It's going to be close!"

Matt raced them down the stairs and out toward the alley. The door closed behind them as the front door of the hotel opened . . .

. . . Back to the present.

"I haven't moved that fast down a flight of stairs in years," said Peter.

Serge checked out the window of the DeLand

motel room. "Good thing you did, or Steve would have seen you for sure."

"So can you finally tell me what all this craziness is about?"

"In due time." Serge took a seat on a bed. "But right now I need to ask you some questions."

"What could I possibly tell you?"

"Your geology business and every last detail about the sinkhole in your house." Serge opened a door next to the dresser that connected to the adjoining room that he also had rented. "We should probably talk in private. Some of my questions might upset your wife and son."

"Too late," said Mary.

"We won't be long." Serge led Peter into the other unit and shut the door.

Mary and her son took seats. Nobody talked for the longest time. She got a disgusted look on her face. Coleman was analyzing a booger. He looked up. "Sorry." He pulled a fat one from over his ear.

"You're smoking marijuana?" said Mary.

"I was going to give you some."

"What's wrong with you?"

"But your son and I—"

Matt made a slashing gesture across his throat.

Coleman closed his mouth and put the joint away. He fished in his pocket for an airline miniature of whiskey and sucked it dry.

Mary glared.

Coleman grinned.

Silence resumed.

The door to the next room opened.

"Coleman, we're all set." Then to everyone else: "In a few hours, this will be nothing but a bad memory. Just don't leave this motel under any circumstances until I come back and give the all clear."

"Why do you suddenly look so happy?" asked Matt.

Serge smiled radiantly. "Do you realize what day it is? . . ."

Chapter THIRTY-SIX

FOUNDERS' DAY

Balloons, pennants, laughter, amplified bluegrass music. Kids bounced in the inflatable bouncing castle. Adults in wide-brimmed hats filled the sunny street, holding corn dogs, cotton candy and fried elephant ears. A low-grade Ferris wheel rotated slowly above the treetops behind Lead Belly's.

Men in overalls gathered outside the barbershop with steely eyes aimed up the street.

"What do you mean we can't make them leave?" asked Vernon.

"It's First Amendment," said Senator Pratchett.

The gang snarled again in the direction of countless satellite trucks parked on the edge of the historic district.

"Why are they picking on us?" asked Jabow.

"Because you served it up camera-ready for television: a colorful country fair against the backdrop of legislative hearings to disband a scandalous town," said Pratchett. "I kept warning you about the speed traps and water pumping, but did anyone listen?"

"Well, we'll see about their First Amendment," said Jabow.

"What are you going to do?"

"A couple broken cameras will get the point across toot sweet."

"And give the other cameras better video than they could ever hope for?" said Pratchett. "Have you all lost your minds?"

"Got a better idea?"

"*Any* idea is better. But yes, I have one in particular: Be nice."

"What's that supposed to mean?"

"Romance the press," said Pratchett. "They're going on the air with a story anyway, and it's one of the first axioms of politics: Half the viewership is already prepared to side with you if you're simply polite."

"That actually works?"

"Wouldn't hurt to throw in some of the remarks I made during the senate hearing. Doesn't need to be word for word. Just keep changing the subject and people will forget the original question."

"Anything else?"

"Feed them."

"Feed them what? Information?"

"No, literally. Reporters are notoriously cheap." Ryan pointed over his shoulder. "I'm due at the dunking booth . . ."

Back up the street, a smartly dressed woman checked her hair in a compact mirror before grabbing a microphone.

"Good afternoon, this is Natalie Valdez reporting live from Wobbly, Florida, during the town's annual Founders' Day celebration. But despite the pleasant weather forecast, a dark cloud hangs over this year's festivities as hearings at the state capitol are probing allegations of rampant corruption. Meanwhile, the search continues for a missing insurance underwriter while authorities investigate a suspicious overnight fire that burned down a Triple-A speed-trap billboard— . . . Wait, I think I see the mayor . . . Mayor! Can we have a word with you?"

"Absolutely!" Vernon strolled over with the city council in tow. "And I can't thank you enough for taking the time to drive out here on our proudest day and showcase what a wonderful little community we have."

"Actually we came because a senate panel is looking into questionable—"

"Where are my manners?" said Vernon, addressing the entire press corps. "Everyone here must be absolutely famished!"

The city council stepped forward with Styrofoam bowls.

"Who wants some of our *deeeeelicious* strawberry shortcake?" said Vernon, turning toward a camera lens. "Available for only two tickets in our Down Home Vittles Tent."

"Mr. Mayor," said Natalie. "As journalists, we're not allowed to accept any gifts, no matter how small . . ."

Several of the guys wearing battery belts raised their hands. Various camera shots became momentarily unsteady as the bowls were distributed and consumed.

"Now then." Vernon returned to the TV reporter. "You were saying about our wonderful jubilee here today?"

"No, I was asking about the allegations of fraud and public misappropriation . . ."

"And I understand the lame-stream media bosses are forcing you to ask such questions even though you're so sweet and would never want to taint this joyous occasion for our children and grandparents."

"Do you have any response to the charges?"

"All the great folks in Wobbly want to get along with everyone. But no matter what we do, some people in big government just don't like small towns."

"Why is that?"

"Because we base our lives on the teachings of the Bible," said Vernon. "Last year they wouldn't let us put the Ten Commandments on top of the city hall dome . . ."

Otis glanced at Jabow. "We never tried to do that."

"Shhhh!"

". . . But even though this is a special day," said Vernon, "my faith won't permit me to stand silent while big-city politicians continue saying such horrible things about our Father in heaven . . ."

As the interview continued, a red banner crawled across the bottom of the screen for the benefit of viewers watching from treadmills in health spas. MAYOR: DON'T BAD-MOUTH GOD.

Half the TV audience took his side.

Vernon walked away and the reporter turned toward a blurry white lens. "You just heard it straight from the mayor's mouth. This is Natalie Valdez reporting from Wobbly, Florida." The correspondent continued smiling a few extra seconds. "Are we off the air? . . ." She threw down her microphone. "You got fucking whipped cream on the camera."

Back up the street, children waved colorful pinwheels as they passed a hotel courtyard and a red caboose. In one of the caboose's windows, two pairs of eyes rose to the bottom edge and glanced back and forth.

Nearby, a prom queen stood in a booth with her tiara, accepting pecks on the cheek for a dollar. A softball hit the bull's-eye and a local senator splashed into the dunking tank. Judges placed a blue ribbon on a big yam.

"Got to hand it to the senator," Jabow told Vernon. "That TV stuff back there was a thing of beauty."

"Excuse me, Mr. Mayor!"

"Not another reporter." He turned around to see a man in a tropical shirt munching a corn dog. "Can I help you with something?"

"Yes," said Serge. "I just moved here and wanted to say how much I admire everything you've done for the townfolk."

"That's mighty kind of you," Vernon said impatiently.

"They always say never buy real estate in a small town, because of all the bullshit they can pull on you." Serge reached in his back pocket. "But that's just selfish people who move in and don't put their best foot forward to show they're on the team. So I'd like to make a campaign contribution." He produced a giant wad. "How about a thousand? . . . Ah, make it two. You get what you pay for, after all."

"Jesus, put that down!" Vernon glanced over at the cameras, then surreptitiously slid up next to Serge and tucked the money away. "Sorry about that, but the press has been harassing us . . . Now then, I think you're going to get along very well here in Wobbly . . ." He stopped and noticed a pudgy man behind Serge with cotton candy in his hair. "And I want you to know we're tolerant of all lifestyles."

Serge looked at Coleman, then back at Vernon. "Oh, we're not gay."

"Not that there's anything wrong with that," said Coleman.

"Of course not," said Serge. "But we do have alternate lifestyles. More on that later. What I wanted to talk about is a problem of mutual concern."

"How can we help?"

"It involves a person who's caused me a great deal of trouble, a local resident I think you know quite well named Peter Pugliese—"

"Stop." Vernon studied Serge's face. "Who *are* you?"

"Someone who got ripped off laundering money through Peter. I've been keeping this whole fiasco under surveillance for some time."

"Mister," said Jabow, stepping up chest to chest, "just who do you think you're messing with?"

"Hear me out," said Serge. "I know you got the money the other night."

"We have no idea what you're talking about," said Otis.

"The night of the blue moon when you ran into the sheriff out at Peter's place," said Serge. "And what happened is fine by me. Because there's more money. A lot more."

That got their attention. "This is still all nonsense," said Vernon. "But go on."

"Peter didn't keep all the money in one spot. I know where he stashed the rest of it," said Serge. "I can take you there right now."

"You're piling it up pretty deep," said Vernon. "If you know where this so-called money is, why didn't you just get it yourself? Why come to us?"

"The money is at Peter's house, which is still a crime scene, and there will be a lot of exposure getting to it. A lot could go wrong. But since you're the law around here, everything's kosher if we go together."

They appraised him with skepticism.

"Look," said Serge. "All I want is what Peter stole from me. Everything else is total profit for you. It's a win-win."

Vernon raised a finger. "Give us a moment."

Serge took a bite of his corn dog. "I've got all the time in the world."

The gang gathered off to the side.

"What do you think?" asked Jabow. "Should we trust him?"

"Hell no," said Vernon. "He's definitely up to something. Have you forgotten that Peter was an innocent dupe we used as a fall guy? He never laundered any money in the first place, so this guy's already lying about that."

Otis looked over at Serge. "Then what should we do?"

"Play along for now," said Vernon. "He says he knows where there's a lot of money, and there's no harm taking a peek. Meanwhile, we'll find out what his game really is and deal with him in our own way."

The huddle broke and the gang returned to the line of scrimmage. "We still have no idea what you're talking about," said the mayor. "But since you've reported a possible crime, it's our obligation to check it out."

"I understand the need to maintain deniability." Serge popped the last bite in his mouth. "Meet you out there."

The chopper was already parked and waiting by the house when a pair of pickups came barreling up the dirt road.

Coleman slapped a love bug on his arm. Serge typed on his cell phone and hit send: *WE'RE ON.*

The trucks disgorged their bucolic contents. "All right," said Vernon. "Time to show your cards."

"Right this way." Serge led them through the front door. "Cold, cold, warm, warmer, hot, hotter, you're burning up!"

Vernon and his kin stopped at the edge of the master bedroom and glanced down in the sinkhole. "So where is it?"

"When everything went sideways and all the cops and deputies were swarming this place, Peter had to move the money," said Serge. "And what's the one spot nobody would ever think of looking?"

They shook their heads.

"Right down there."

They took another gander into the earth.

"Bullshit." Jabow pulled a .44 on Serge. "Time to start telling us the truth. And you don't have much time."

Serge raised his hands. "Yikes! What's going on? I thought we had an agreement."

"We don't know what it is you do know, but clearly it's too much," said Vernon. "Otis, grab that rope in the corner." He seized Coleman and marched him to the side of the room.

"Wait, wait, wait!" said Serge. "I got a flashlight in my pocket. Just let me show you before you blow a fortune."

"Don't move a muscle! . . . Jabow, keep him covered." Vernon reached out and dug into Serge's pocket, expecting a weapon. "It *is* a flashlight."

"Can I have it?" asked Serge.

"You got exactly thirty seconds."

"No problem." Serge shined the beam down the southern wall of the sinkhole. "See that right there?

The shiny spot? If you look close, it's bundles of hundred-dollar bills wrapped in plastic."

"Well, I'll be," said Vernon. "It is."

Jabow kept the gun on Serge. "Are you shitting me? He was telling the truth?"

"Not by a mile," said Vernon. "But money's money." He looked around the room. The scaffolding, ropes and pulleys were all still there. Even the harnesses. Vernon took the gun from Jabow. "I'll keep him covered. You guys go retrieve it."

"Why do you get to stay up here?"

"Because I'm the mayor!" said Vernon. "You go first, Jabow, then Otis and Slow . . . Where's Slower?"

"Living up to his name," said Jabow, strapping on the harness.

"And you!" Vernon briefly swung the gun toward Coleman. "Stay seated against that wall!"

"I'm happy."

It was clumsy and laughable, and crisis was averted only because Vernon pressed Serge into service manning the pulley ropes. The last of the gang reached bottom.

Vernon called down into the hole. "Dig slowly around the package. We don't want more of this falling in."

As soon as fingers began clawing into the dirt, something fluttered down.

"Son of a bitch!" yelled Jabow.

"What is it?" asked Vernon.

"Only a small piece of plastic and some Monopoly money. There is no package. He tricked us!"

Just then, Vernon felt a cold metal barrel in his spine.

"Don't move," said Steve, reaching around for the .44 in the mayor's hand. "And I'll take that."

"You have no concept what you're doing."

"I have every concept." Steve gave a quick shove, and Vernon fell into the pit with a shriek.

Yelling of questionable negotiating strategy came up from below: *"You bastard!" "You're a dead man!" "Get us out of here!"*

Serge turned to Steve. "I see you got my text."

"I don't know how you pulled this off, but it's a thing of beauty. We should work together again."

"Something tells me this is a one-off." Another quick push, this time from Serge, and into the hole went Steve.

Serge shined his flashlight, illuminating a stand-off: Steve's back against one of the walls, aiming his pistol, and Jabow with his recovered .44, aiming from the other side.

"How's it going down there?" yelled Serge. "Looks like you're in a bit of a pickle."

"Fucker!"

"Hold that thought," said Serge. "Coleman, you know what to do."

Serge waited patiently until hearing several gas engines behind the house start up in succession. He went to the kitchen and found a thick outdoor extension cord snaking through the window. It had a switch in the middle. Serge walked backward, unrolling the wire until he returned to the pit.

"What's that noise?" yelled Vernon.

"The generators," said Serge.

"Why do you need generators?"

"Because geology is a fascinating science," said Serge, sitting on the floor with his feet hanging over the edge of the hole. "I got to talking with Peter this morning and he taught me so much, like how they do inspections to determine if the ground is stable enough to lay a foundation. Have you noticed those new metal rods stuck all around the perimeter of the hole near your feet?"

"What are they?"

"I came in this morning and installed them," said Serge. "I know, trespassing. Guilty as charged. But science can't wait for the law to catch up. Anyway, one of the inspection tests is soil resistivity. Here's the fun part: Dirt is highly resistant to voltage, so you need a whole bunch of electricity just to get a half-decent reading. But electricity also is quite lazy and constantly looking for alternate paths of least resistance. Did you know a human body contains so much water and salt and other electrolytes that it's a rather good conductor?"

Serge grabbed the cord and flicked the switch. Electricity did what it does best.

Screams of agony echoed out of the pit. Then:

Bang, bang, bang, bang, bang . . .

Steve and Jabow were vibrating like robots gone haywire, involuntarily emptying their guns with spasming arms. The pistols wildly missed their marks and sprayed unstable dirt walls that began to give way.

"Yowza!" Serge quickly yanked his legs up. "Didn't see that coming."

He took off running as an aggressive dust cloud chased him out the front door.

Coleman came trotting around the corner from the backyard. "What happened?"

"Another cave-in," said Serge. "Glad I tested to see if it was safe."

Chapter THIRTY-SEVEN

MAIN STREET

Clowns twisted balloon animals. Contestants sat with hands behind their backs, facedown in blueberry pies. Raffle tickets were sold to win a year of oil changes. Tubas sparkled in the sun as a high school band marched past Lead Belly's. Followed by a chopper.

"Parading without a permit!" exclaimed Serge. Then a boyish smile. "I've always wanted to say that."

The motorcycle pulled over to the sidewalk, where the Pugliese family was waiting after getting the all-clear phone call back at the motel. "Didn't I tell you everything would turn out fine?"

"What happened?" asked Mary.

"You don't want to know." Serge dismounted and locked up his helmet. "But you're totally safe now."

"Are you sure?" said Peter. "I mean, is it wise for us to be out in public like this so soon?"

"Absolutely," said Serge. "It would be a crying shame to miss the rest of Founders' Day. I *love* small-town jamborees. It's the perfect thing to get your minds off what you've gone through."

"We're just relieved our son's safe." Mary gave him another too-tight squeeze, and Matt had the expression of a small dog tolerating overaffection.

"Yes," said Peter. "Thanks for looking after Matt."

Coleman pointed. "Beer tent."

"Well . . ." Serge waved as he headed off behind his friend. "Got to keep an eye on this one. Enjoy yourselves."

They did.

Candy apples, guess your weight, throwing Ping-Pong balls into goldfish bowls. Overhead, an aerobatic plane performed somersaults to the delight of the crowd. Workers began loading a platform of fifty vertical tubes for the evening's fireworks display.

The afternoon wore on. A clown chased Coleman out from behind a face-painting booth, but his big shoes wouldn't let him keep up. *"If I catch you smoking dope again . . . !"*

Volunteers loaded pigs into starting gates. Serge leaned against the railing near the finish line.

"And they're off! . . ."

Coleman arrived out of breath and collapsed against the fence.

"What just happened to you?" asked Serge.

Coleman grabbed his heart and panted. "There are good clowns and scary clowns."

A herd of pigs ran by.

"*Serge . . .*"

He turned around. "Mary. Is everyone having a great time?"

"Have you seen Matt?"

"No, why?"

"He's been gone since lunch."

"It's a fair, and he's a kid," said Serge. "The whole object is to avoid your parents."

"I'm just worried because it's so soon after . . . you know."

Serge nodded. "You're a good mother. I'll find him for you. I'm guessing his phone is GPS enabled?"

She nodded.

"Do you know his password?"

"I think he uses *mpugliese* for just about everything. Lowercase, no spaces."

Serge tapped it into his own cell and hit Find My Phone. "It worked. I'll be right back."

He followed the tracking program up the street like a divining rod. The blue dot on his small screen brought him to the sidewalk in front of Lead Belly's. He went inside. A roomful of happy diners in bibs. No Matt. He went through the employees-only swinging doors to the kitchen.

"You can't come in here!"

"Orders from the mayor," said Serge. "I'm looking for a missing child."

"Haven't seen one."

Serge checked his phone again. "Is this the whole restaurant?"

"Yeah, I mean there's a storeroom, but nobody's been in there today."

"Thanks." Serge wandered out behind the kitchen and down a hallway. He checked the men's and women's rooms. Nothing. By process of elimination, he arrived at a final door. Locked. But flimsy. He put his shoulder into it, and the wood easily popped open.

"Matt, what are you doing back here?"

"Serge . . ."

"You've got your mother worried sick!"

"Serge . . ."

The door closed behind them, and Serge turned around.

A man in a button-down oxford shirt pointed a gun.

Serge rubbed his chin. "Did I forget someone again? Why do all my adventures end like this?"

"It's Senator Pratchett to you."

Serge smacked himself in the forehead. "Of course!"

"I got a call from the mayor on his way to Peter's house, and when I didn't hear back, I drove out there myself." Pratchett stepped closer and stiffened his arm. "You've ruined everything!"

"We can talk this out," said Serge.

"Too late for that!"

M ore balloons hung atop a sign on the north side of town.

WELCOME TO WORLD-FAMOUS WOBBLY SPRINGS.

Children shrieked and laughed as families splashed in the town's highly touted attraction. The cave divers not so much.

Ripples filled the water as small arms flailed. The ripples got bigger. Then a shaking sensation. Parents looked up and saw small rocks crumble from the walls of the grotto.

"Everyone out of the water!"

The last child was pulled to land as larger rocks crashed into the spring. Then a massive shudder.

Underneath the sinkhole, a huge slab of limestone collapsed all the way to the aquifer, and joyous cave divers were sucked deep into the earth.

The tremor was felt all the way to Main Street, but it was mixed in with so much else that nobody gave a thought. Soon it couldn't be ignored. The festivities ceased as revelers stopped where they stood, mumbling to each other.

A heavy lurch silenced everything.

They all waited and wondered.

Then a tremendous jolt.

"Look! The barbershop!"

It sank in slow motion, red-striped pole and all, until there was nothing left. Followed in equally slow cadence by the pharmacy, hardware store and Shorty's Garage.

The crowd was no longer quiet or still. They ran screaming past Lead Belly's, where boxes fell off shelves in the storeroom.

"What the hell's going on?" yelled Pratchett.

"It's a sinkhole," shouted Serge. "We're going down! . . . Matt, come on!"

"Don't move another inch!" said the senator.

"You can shoot me outside," said Serge. "But we're all dead if we stay here!"

"Wait up!"

The senator chased them into the pandemonium of the street, fighting against the oncoming human tide. "I'll shoot!"

"Matt, this way!"

Pratchett quickly gained ground because he didn't mind shoving children and pregnant women. A clear shot was about to open up . . .

Lead Belly's crumbled next, then the old Railroad Hotel. A fireworks mortar accidentally fired sideways, freaking out livestock that burst through a gate.

The stampeding crowd screeched to a halt and reversed direction. *"Pigs!"*

The senator's finger began pulling the trigger just as he was overrun, first by people, then swine. He got up. "Where'd they go?"

Another fireworks shell went off. All the explosives technicians leaped off the platform and ran for cover. The remaining forty-eight cannons fired in unison at random angles, blanketing the sky with brightly colored explosions.

Up in the wild blue yonder: "What on earth?" An aerobatic pilot flew into an unexplained storm of chromatic flak.

The earth swallowed a red caboose. A parachute popped open as a smoking aircraft did loop-de-loops on the horizon. Pigs circled the block, from their race training, chasing people back the other way.

Pratchett spotted Serge and Matt again, hiding behind a row of newspaper boxes on the corner. A sadistic grin as he headed across the street. "I can *seeeeeeeee youuuuuuuu*!"

He stood in the middle of the street with a wide-open shot behind the boxes. Serge arose with his hands in the air.

"Can you find it in your heart? For Founders' Day?"

Pratchett aimed the pistol again as a deafening buzz fell over the street.

The senator looked up—"*Ahhhhhhhh!*"—straight into the propeller end of a nose-diving stunt plane.

It finally became still as Serge surveyed the dusty, flaming post-apocalyptic wasteland.

"Just like I planned."

Epilogue

A quaint two-story bungalow with ample acreage sat on the outskirts of a non-scandalous small town. A woman in the kitchen set a rhubarb pie on the window sill and thought of Norman Rockwell. The home had recently been purchased with an insurance settlement over a sinkhole. She heard someone coming up the driveway.

The front door opened.

"Honey, I'm home."

Mary Pugliese trotted out of the kitchen wiping her hands on a towel.

She gave her husband a quick kiss. "I see you have a guest."

"I'd like you to meet Billy," said Peter. "And this is my wife, Mary."

Billy gave a respectful nod. "Ma'am."

"I know I'm dropping this on you," said Peter. "But if it's okay, I'd like Billy to stay with us for a while. Since Matt is away at college, the house is kind of empty."

"I'm sure that will be fine." Mary smiled at the young man. "Peter, can I talk to you for a second?"

"Sure thing." He looked back at Billy. "Be right back."

Another polite nod.

The couple met privately in the hallway. "You're bringing home strays now?" She wasn't angry, but, well, it was just unexpected.

"He needs to get his GED, then hoping to attend trade school."

"What's the connection with this kid?" she asked. "You old war buddies or something?"

"Something like that."

"I'm guessing there's quite a story behind this."

"Oh, there's a story all right," said Peter.

"Then why don't you tell me over dinner?"

Peter sniffed the air. "Is that what I think it is?"

"Your new favorite." Mary called down the hall: "Billy, why don't you join us for dinner."

The kitchen table was the kind of distressed wood now known as shabby chic. The two men took seats, and Mary opened the oven. Soon it was all bibs and ribs.

"Ma'am, this dinner is delicious."

"Why thank you, Billy. More iced tea?"

He nodded with a mouthful of black-eyed peas.

"Okay, then, Peter. I'm ready to be knocked out." Mary refilled her own glass of tea and squeezed a lemon wedge. "What's this big story of yours?"

Peter finished swallowing and wiped his face with a napkin. "It all started a month ago during the last full moon. That was the evening, the investigators later told us, that Vernon and his gang went out to our house in the middle of the night. Remember?"

"Quite vividly."

"They said that particular full moon was a blue moon. Everyone's heard the term a million times, but I never knew what it meant until I checked it out on the Internet. Whoever came up with the cliché 'once in a blue moon' could have simply said 'every two or three years' . . ."

"The story?" said his wife.

"Oh, right. So just after dark . . ."

THE NIGHT OF THE BLUE MOON

Two shadows crept across the lawn behind an isolated farmhouse, and ducked under crime tape. Peter unlocked the back door with his own key. It was safe to turn on the flashlights. "This way."

The pair reached the edge of a sinkhole where the bedroom had been. Two heavy canvas duffel bags hit the floor with a clang of metal.

Peter unzipped one and removed coils of recently purchased mountain-climbing rope. Then he pulled out a contraption that was some odd configuration of steel wheels.

"I don't know if I'm strong enough to handle the line," said the second man. "Wouldn't want to be responsible for hurting you."

"Won't be a problem," Peter said as he strapped himself into his harness. "That's not like the old pulley. It's a *compound* pulley."

A facial reaction of non-understanding.

"Billy, that means it uses physics to divide the weight," said Peter. "You'll have to pull four times as much rope, but it'll only be a quarter of the normal weight."

Peter snapped a clasp to his harness and smiled at his new partner. "All right, Billy, now the easy part. Grab hold of that line."

"Can I ask you a question?"

"Sure thing."

"Why are you so nice to me?"

"What do you mean?"

"You call me Billy."

"That's your name."

"Nobody else calls me that. It's always been 'Slower.' And you never say I'm stupid and stuff."

"Because you're not stupid."

He looked askance. "I know what I am."

"Hey, Billy, look at me," said Peter. "You can't be what other people say you are, especially if they're unkind. I know you. You're a really good guy."

Billy looked down.

"Don't go tearing up on me. We've got work to do."

Billy wiped his eyes. "Sorry."

"And don't apologize."

"I never thanked you for saving my life. I don't think the others would have."

"We'll talk more about this later. Just don't let go of that line."

Peter stepped off the edge and swung gently over the center of the hole. He slowly descended as his helmet light split the darkness.

Billy kept letting out rope until it went slack. "You okay?"

"Just reached bottom." The shovel came off his belt and dirt began to fly.

Nothing for the longest time as Billy concentrated on that line. He thought he heard a noise. Yes, he definitely did. Whatever it was kept growing louder until it echoed down the hole. Peter stopped digging. "Billy, what's that sound?"

Before he got an answer, the room above lit up. "Are those headlights?"

Billy set the line down and ran to the front windows. "Oh no." He raced back to the hole. "They're here."

"Who is?"

"All of them. Vernon, Jabow, the rest."

"Shoot." Adrenaline ran options through Peter's brain in microseconds. He pulled his cell phone from his pocket. "Darn, no reception down here . . . Billy, this is very important. You have to catch this and make sure you don't fall."

"Okay."

Peter wound up and pitched the phone hard. It fumbled off Billy's fingers.

"Sorry, it fell back in the hole."

Peter's helmet lantern searched the bottom. "Where is it? . . ."

Outside, a small platoon with shovels marched toward the house.

"What if something goes wrong like last time?" said Jabow.

"Nothing will go wrong," said Vernon, ducking under the crime tape.

"Then why don't *you* go down the hole?"

"Because I'm the supervisor . . ."

Inside, Peter reached back again and hurled. The phone flew over Billy's head.

Crash.

"Did it break?" yelled Peter.

"Hold on, the battery just popped out." *Snap.* "Still works."

"Listen carefully," said Peter. "You need to run out the back door and hide. And after you do, I need you to dial . . ."

A crowbar cracked the frame of the front door.

"The bolt's still in," said Jabow.

"Try again."

This time the wood splintered but good. Vernon led the way with a Rayovac flashlight until they all stood at the edge of the hole. "Luckily the rope's still here. Pull the line back up."

Otis gave a tug. Then harder. "It's stuck on something."

Vernon shook his head in disgust, then tilted it. "Jabow?"

Jabow spit in his palms and rubbed them together, then grabbed the line. Several grunts. "He's right. It won't budge."

"I'll see what it is." Vernon crawled to the edge of the hole and reached his hand down with the flashlight. The beam hit the far wall and began sweeping toward Peter, who cringed as he delicately eased the clasp off his harness. The beam reached his feet.

"Vernon, the line's free."

The flashlight turned off. "You're up to bat."

Jabow climbed in a harness. "Where do I snap the clasp to the rope? . . . Dang, it's on backwards." Another fitting of the harness. "Now my legs are in the wrong holes." Another attempt. "That's no good either . . ."

"What's taking so damn long?" said Vernon. "Slower could do it faster."

"You want to try?"

"Every extra second is more risk of being spotted!"

"Good news." He fastened the clamp to his properly arranged harness and swung out over the hole.

Otis began lowering him. Ten feet, fifteen feet . . .

A voice echoed up out of the depression. "You better not drop me."

Otis dropped him.

"Ow, damn!"

Jabow stood and arched his back.

"What's going on down there?" called Vernon.

Jabow's head swiveled in darkness. "I lost my flashlight."

"So find it— . . . Uh-oh."

"What is it?" yelled Jabow, staring up as the room above grew brighter.

"Headlights," said Vernon. "Somebody's outside."

They all ran to the windows. "Shit, it's the sheriff," said Otis. "What's he doing here?"

"Quick, get Jabow out of the hole!"

Three people grabbed the line and reeled hard. Jabow's feet leaped off the ground.

Dirt flew as Peter sat up quickly from his self-burial spot.

Sheriff Highsmith and three deputies came through the door. "I'd ask who's in here, but judging by the cars in the yard, I'd be wasting my breath. Are you messing with a crime scene that's still under dispute with the circuit judge?"

"Sheriff, no, we heard there might be a break-in, so we came out to investigate," said Vernon.

"Yeah, I heard the same thing," said Highsmith.

"You did?"

The sheriff looked at the still-swinging rope and the harness around Jabow's waist. He laughed inside. "Looks like someone busted up that front door pretty good with a crowbar. Wonder who it could be."

Vernon itched his neck. "Us, too. So we're just going to take a look around."

"No objection from me."

"Okay, then . . ." Vernon smiled.

"Okay . . ." The sheriff smiled back.

They continued standing in place, silently grinning.

"So we'll take it from here," said Vernon.

"Go right ahead."

"You're staying?"

"Thought I'd stick around and learn from the best," said the sheriff. "There isn't any particular reason you want me to leave, is there?"

"Of course not."

Vernon headed toward another bedroom, followed by a whispering Jabow. "There's no way we can do anything with the sheriff snooping around."

"Don't you think I know that?" Vernon checked a bathroom. "Let's act like we're clearing the house, then come back later."

The mayor returned to the living room. "Looks like everything's in order. Whoever was here ain't no more, so we'll just skedaddle."

Highsmith tipped his Smokey the Bear hat. "Give my best to the missus."

The brooding gang slunk out the door, followed by the deputies, and the sheriff was left alone.

In the crawl space under the house, Billy lay on his back with a cell phone that had recently dialed 911 about a burglary in progress. He stared up through slits in the floorboards as the sheriff's shoes slowly creaked toward the I-beam.

Highsmith's eyes moved from the pulley down into the hole. "What the heck is so important down there?"

BACK TO THE PRESENT

Mary Pugliese leaned over the kitchen table on her elbows. "So what happened?"

"Let's take a walk."

All three of them went outside to the driveway and circled around behind Peter's car. He popped the trunk.

"Holy cow!" said Mary. "How much money is that?"

"Four million, give or take. Our share is two." Peter patted Billy on the shoulder. "You're a rich man."

"I still want to get my GED and go to trade school."

"Good for you."

Mary was phasing in and out of shock. "This can't be legal . . . We'll be arrested! . . . Where did it come from?"

"The hole. Before that, it's just unsubstantiated speculation according to the law." Peter slammed the trunk. "We hired an attorney, who said the issue is rampant in Florida because people are always ditching money and other contraband, and innocent people are constantly finding it in the cushions of a love seat from a yard sale. We just follow his instructions to report it with the proper authorities, and if nobody comes forward within a specified period of time—which my lawyer says never happens in these circumstances—it's ours."

"I need to go inside and sit down," said Mary.

"I need to get this to a bank."

Matt Pugliese returned to New Jersey.

His thesis wasn't officially rejected. But the ethics committee strongly suggested he withdraw it under grave overtones of making up shit.

"But it's all true."

"Many of the details, especially some of the more arcane history and culture, don't show up anywhere, even on the Internet."

"I thought you told us not to use the Internet for research."

"It would be better if you remained quiet."

"But it all came from this academic in Florida doing firsthand research," said Matt. "That's why I flew down there. My extra effort must count for something."

"Son, we contacted Florida authorities, and your source's website is connected to a suspect in multiple homicides."

"What?"

But even before returning to Princeton, Matt had already decided to change majors. He withdrew the thesis without regret and walked across campus.

A week later he was back in another imposing university office.

A professor reclined in his chair and flipped pages. "Are you sure you have the correct department?"

"Creative writing, right?" said Matt.

"But you submitted a thesis."

"Exactly," said Matt. "It's a novella in the structure of a college paper. I don't think it's been done before."

The professor handed the paper back. "Too over-the-top. Even as fiction, nobody would ever believe Florida is this weird."

Matt sighed and tried to imagine what Serge and Coleman were up to . . .

A chopper with a sidecar rumbled south down U.S. Highway 1 from Miami to Homestead.

Sign-spinner alley. Batman, Spider-Man, purple dinosaur, Gumby. CASH FOR GOLD, WE BUY HOMES . . . Female mannequins featuring breasts were beginning to replace some of the regular spinners because they attracted more attention and required no hourly wage.

"Radio check," said Coleman. "Look at that next spinning sign. It's for another one of those healthy fast-food places like we were at a few days ago."

"I'm way ahead of you," said Serge, angling the motorcycle into the drive-through lane.

Moments later, the chopper with a coconut gas tank pulled back onto the highway. Up at the corner, two gorillas shoved a blond mannequin into traffic in front of a city bus. Serge swerved around a plastic head rolling through the intersection as he and Coleman happily munched corn dogs.

". . . *Born to be wild!* . . ."

"Radio check," said Coleman, mustard streaking

back across his cheeks in the wind. "These things are pretty delicious for being healthy. I guess there's no possible way to get a bad corn dog."

"You're absolutely right," Serge said as they thundered off into the sunset. "Corn dogs are like blow jobs. If you complain about one, *you're* the problem."

Comic tales of Florida murder and mayhem

by **TIM DORSEY**

ATOMIC LOBSTER
978-0-06-082970-4

Serge and Coleman crank up
the fevered action as the pot boils over on
a street called Lobster Lane.

HURRICANE PUNCH
978-0-06-082968-1

When Serge and his buddy
Coleman go storm-chasing, bodies begin
turning up at a disturbing rate.

THE BIG BAMBOO
978-0-06-058563-1

Serge A. Storms
is on a new mission: to convince
the West Coast movie industry
bigwigs to do their business in his beloved
Sunshine State.

TORPEDO JUICE
978-0-06-058561-7

Serge A. Storms is motoring
down to the Florida Keys in search of Ms.
Right and finding his doped-up bud
Coleman along the way.

CADILLAC BEACH
978-0-06-055694-5

Serge A. Storms
has busted out of the state mental
hospital. It's all good for Serge. Not so much
for anyone else.

TD 0916

by **TIM DORSEY**

THE STINGRAY SHUFFLE
978-0-06-055693-8

When serial-killing local Florida historian Serge A. Storms is off his meds, no one is safe — especially when $5 million in cash is involved.

TRIGGERFISH TWIST
978-0-06-103155-7

Ensconced in a lovely tropical villa, Jim Davenport anticipates the good life to come — but the neighborhood is not quite what it seems.

ORANGE CRUSH
978-0-06-103154-0

Unthreatening Florida governor-by-default Marlon Conrad is a shoo-in for re-election, until he undergoes a radical personality shift during military action in the Balkans.

HAMMERHEAD RANCH MOTEL
978-0-380-73234-0

Visitors come well armed to the Hammerhead Ranch Motel, because there's a different schemer or slimeball lurking behind every door.

FLORIDA ROADKILL
978-0-380-73233-3

A handful of people are about to cross paths with a suitcase filled with five million dollars in stolen insurance money, and all of them want it.

TD1 0916